Victoria Clayton published two children's books when in her early twenties. She then read English at Cambridge as a mature undergraduate, married and had two children before returning to writing fiction. *Running Wild* is her fourth novel. Her previous three novels shortlisted for the 1999 Romantic Novel of the Year Award.

RUNNING WILD

Elfrida Swann, 'Freddie', a struggling portrait painter, is about to marry Alex Moncrieff, a successful barrister. Preparations for the great day, arranged with magnificent extravagance by her smart stepmother in the hope of inciting bitterest envy among her acquaintances, are on schedule. Then, two days before the wedding, Freddie decides that she cannot go through with the marriage. She runs away to Drop Cottage in Dorset, lent to her by a friend. At first sight, its state of dilapidation is so extreme that Freddie feels she cannot possibly stay. But rapidly she falls under the spell of its idiosyncratic charms — and events conspire to detain her . . .

Books by Victoria Clayton
Published by The House of Ulverscroft:

PAST MISCHIEF

VICTORIA CLAYTON

RUNNING WILD

Complete and Unabridged

CHARNWOOD
Leicester

First published in Great Britain in 2000 by
Orion Publishing Group Limited
London

First Charnwood Edition
published 2002
by arrangement with
The Orion Publishing Group Limited
London

'Haymaking' by John Clare from *The Rural Muse*,
2nd edition 1835 ed. R. K. R. Thornton
from the original manuscript.

British Library CIP Data

Clayton, Victoria
    Running wild.—Large print ed.—
Charnwood library series
    1. Dorset (England)—Fiction
    2. Love stories
    3. Large type books
    I. Title
823.9'14 [F]

ISBN 0–7089–9312–5

Published by
F. A. Thorpe (Publishing)
Anstey, Leicestershire

Set by Words & Graphics Ltd.
Anstey, Leicestershire
Printed and bound in Great Britain by
T. J. International Ltd., Padstow, Cornwall

This book is printed on acid-free paper

For my daughter Cassie

Tis haytime and the red complexioned sun
Was scarcely up ere blackbirds had begun
Along the meadow hedges here and there
To sing loud songs to the sweet smelling air
Where breath of flowers and grass and happy cow
Fling oer ones senses streams of fragrance now
While in some pleasant nook the swain and maid
Lean oer their rakes and loiter in the shade
Or bend a minute oer the bridge and throw
Crumbs in their leisure to the fish below
— Hark at that happy shout — and song between
Tis pleasures birthday in her meadow scene
What joy seems half so rich from pleasure won
As the loud laugh of maidens in the sun

'Haymaking' John Clare

1

Darling Freddie [said the note], *What has happened* [underlined twice] *???!!! My aunt says that Fay telephoned yesterday and told her the whole thing's off! I can't believe it! What can you be feeling, you poor darling! And you were so certain! It isn't a joke, is it? I feel as though the sky has fallen in. I mean it's so unlike you to be rash. For years we've all worshipped you as the embodiment of wisdom and common sense. Not that I've stopped worshipping, Freddie, don't think that. Apparently Fay was practically screaming with temper and kept saying, 'It's the ingratitude I find so unforgivable,' until my aunt said, 'What exactly is it you've done for Freddie that she's supposed to be grateful for?' My aunt can be very squashing in her cool way. Well, that shut Fay up for half a sec before she began to moan about the hideous cost of everything and the embarrassment of explaining to people. Anyway, I've been ringing your flat at least every hour in the intervals between people ringing me — I'm petrified every time I answer it in case it's Alex but so far not — asking where you are and they do sound just the teeniest bit het up and white-lipped. A mixture of fury — all the people who were looking forward to a good bash — and hope — all those who are in love with either of you — and umbrage — all those who like to be the first to know. It's just occurred to me that you've probably gone to earth and, frankly, darling, I don't blame you. I'm ready to do anything* [underlined five times] *to help* [a drip of something that looked like red wine obscured the next part] *so then it came to me! I can modestly claim a flash of inspiration for once. My godmother died a few months ago and left me three*

1

hundred pounds and her cottage in the country. Naturally I've already spent the three hundred pounds but you can borrow the cottage if it's any use to you. She was in a nursing-home hopelessly gaga for ages, poor old thing, so I don't suppose it's in the most wonderful state. But it would be a roof over your head and no one would know where you were. You could lie low for a few days and enjoy a period of calm reflection, as they say. Darling, I don't like to make conditions but could you just send me a PC with something cryptic on it like 'sound in wind and limb' or even just 'OK'? I really am so worried about you. The address of the cottage is 9 Plashy Lane, Pudwell, near Tarchester, Dorset. I'll keep ringing the flat until I hear. Here's the key just in case. Best love, Viola.

* * *

I put down my cases on the platform at Porsley Heath, which was the nearest station for Pudwell. I was the only passenger to alight. I took the key from my pocket, turning it over and over in my fingers, as though it were an amulet from which I might gain courage. Throughout the journey I had stared with incomprehension at the countryside as it slipped past, too tired and unhappy to focus my thoughts, aware only of a sharp pain under my rib-cage and a sick feeling that the world was out of joint. Now, as a sharp March wind snatched at my scarf and blew up the tails of my unbuttoned coat I wondered what on earth I was doing there, so far from home and in a place where I knew no one.

'Arternoon, Miss,' the porter shouted in my ear as an express train rushed through the station — a roaring leviathan carrying sensible people who knew where they were going and why. 'Ye'll be arter the bus I don't doubt. It'll be an hour and a bit yet, being as it's market day. Clym always has a drink or two afore setting off. A taxi? Well, now, there is and there isn't in a manner o' speaking. Will Dewy's at market, too, and I dare say in the Rose and Thorn wi' Clym. Pudwell, ye say?' He pronounced it to rhyme with muddle. 'Why, ye can walk it easy and save th' expense.'

I had only myself to blame for my predicament. I fastened my coat, put on my gloves, picked up my cases and accompanied the porter to the station exit. 'Straight as the crow flies, Miss. Through that liddle biddy copse. Over the bridge, 'cause the ford's too deep just at present, what wi' all this rain we've been havin'. Cross the meadow, up the hill and down into the valley. You can't miss Puddle.'

'You don't think it might be better to wait for the bus?' I asked. The terrain looked wild, almost savage, to one accustomed to the discreet vegetation of Belgravia.

'That I don't. When he's had a drop Clym's more'n like to be tardy. Last market day he had to put up for a while at the crossroads and sleep it off, he were that giddy with the drink he couldn't tell which way was forwards.' I turned reluctantly in the direction of the porter's helpful finger. 'Take no notice o' the bull in Borlock's field,' he shouted after me. ''Tis gentle as a lamb. Just pick up a stick and shake it and show him 'ee mean business.'

If it had not been for the knowledge that a cordon of furious friends and relations was staking out my flat I would have turned and gone back to London then. The possibility of a mild-natured bull was less frightening than the absolute certainty of human wrath. I braced my shoulders and for the sake of my friendly guide tried to put a spring in my step.

All went reasonably well at first. The liddle biddy copse was pretty and provided shelter from the wind. I admired the graceful shapes of the trees against the reddening sky, inhaled the bosky scents of damp

Nature, paused to listen to the whirring wings of pheasants in search of a good branch for the night, and pretended that I was enjoying it. As a child I had been passionately fond of the country, and though I had not seen so much as a corn stook or a staddle stone for fifteen years, I cherished the idea of it. This was the country of Thomas Hardy, whose novels I had always loved. In these very groves the fickle Fitzpiers had courted the gentle Grace and the bewitching Eustacia Vye had fascinated Wildeve. Apart from a line of telegraph poles and a chewing gum wrapper there was nothing to say that this was the spring of 1977 and not a century earlier.

As I emerged from the wood a deluge broke over me, turning the ground to a greasy slide in seconds. The top of my head became numb with cold, and my hair fell out of its ribbon and flew into my eyes. The river was a churning flux of brown water several inches higher than the planks of the footbridge. I debated whether to turn back for the bus. The station was out of sight now behind the wood. It seemed wiser to continue. The flood filled my beautiful crocodile shoes with an icy suddenness that made me shout. I tried to hold my cases above the tide, terrified of losing my footing.

The rain stopped as quickly as it had begun. I was puffing up the hill from the river, thinking sadly about my shoes, when Borlock's bull came bustling out from behind a bush, taking me entirely by surprise. I stifled a scream in order not to provoke it for it had an unfriendly look in its rolling eyes. Its tail lashed angrily against its muddy hips. A reconnoitre of the area revealed the meadow to be virtually stick-less, nothing larger than a twig. Lamb-like nature or not, I was alarmed by the way the animal was swinging its head from side to side and snorting. I broke into a brisk walk that became a run as I heard the pounding of hoofs on turf behind me. Cresting the hill I saw a gate and a man

4

on a horse the other side of it. He made no attempt to come to my rescue, but waited until I had reached the gate before opening it with his whip.

'She won't hurt you, you know,' he said mildly, as I hurled myself through. 'Cows are curious creatures. She only wanted to know what you were doing. If you'd said, 'Shoo,' she would have gone away.'

'I thought it was a bull.' I was almost sobbing with shortness of breath. I put down my suitcases and rubbed my wrenched arm muscles.

The man began to laugh. 'You need a few lessons in anatomy.' He pointed with his whip at the cow as she trotted off, udders swinging.

'I don't know what's so funny.' I gave him a cold look. He had a high forehead, good cheekbones and a mouth that was elegantly curved. These are the kind of things I notice because I am a painter of portraits by trade. It was an interesting face, I had to admit, though I disliked him immediately. He continued to laugh, though I could not see what was so amusing about a simple mistake. I picked up my luggage.

'Where are you going to, my pretty maid?'

'Puddle.' I thought I'd show him that I was not without local knowledge.

'It's a mile from here, if you mean Pud-well. You'll be shattered. I'll carry your cases for you if you'll lead my horse.'

'Thank you.' I eyed the great leggy brute. It wrinkled a lip to expose big, canary-coloured teeth. 'I can manage.'

'All right. Don't sulk. You're much too beautiful to be shrewish,' he called, to my retreating back.

This was insufferable. I continued to stroll along with my suitcases with an air of one enjoying the sharp breezes of malevolent Nature as he ambled behind me. I knew I looked ridiculous. A stile was welcome in that inevitably it ended our acquaintance but it is hard to be

5

dignified clambering over one with heavy luggage and a tightish skirt.

'Farewell, my lovely,' he shouted after me as I strode down the lane. A signpost said half a mile to Pudwell. I allowed my shoulders to droop and slowed to a dawdle. It was nearly half past four and the light was beginning to fade. The lane was sunken and so shaded by trees that in places it was almost dark. The hedgerows rustled constantly, no doubt with creatures seeking a bed but now and then I thought I heard a snapping branch or a footfall. I stared hard into the undergrowth on either side but could make out nothing. Then the whistling began.

At first I put it down to a celebration of the day's good things from a jovial blackbird but the initial random twitterings became longer refrains that were almost tuneful. Then I detected a bar and a half of 'La Donna è mobile' and I knew that I was being followed.

'Why don't you come out and show yourself?' I shouted into the webbing of tree roots and brambles that made up the walls of what was effectively a tunnel. The whistling broke off abruptly. 'Come on, don't be childish.' Absolute silence. I gave an invisible shrug in the darkness and set off again at a quicker pace. But my heart was beating fast and the back of my neck felt vulnerable. I concentrated on maintaining a steady speed, though I longed to stop and rest my arms. After twenty yards the whistling began again but this time the phrases were sweeter and sadder, almost cajoling.

I was thankful to see the trees growing thinner ahead. Quite suddenly the lane rolled over a humpback bridge beneath which the river splashed silver in the fading beams of day. On the other side stood a handsome timbered building with a jutting top storey, a mill even to my untutored eye. In the open doorway stood a man, pale as a corpse with little blinking eyes and a wide slavering mouth. His body listed to one side like a crooked tree blasted by the prevailing wind. As I watched he lifted his hand to wipe his forehead and was enveloped in a cloud of dust.

'Lookin' for someone, are ye?' he asked, with scant friendliness in his tone. ''Tis late to be wandering alone.'

'I'm going to Pudwell,' I said, as brightly as I could, which wasn't very.

'This be Puddle.'

'Could you tell me the way to Plashy Lane, please?'

Ignoring me, the man lifted a huge tankard to his lips. I could see his throat working as he drained the contents in a single draught. He smeared his arm across lips that appeared startlingly dark against the whiteness of his face. 'That's the first o' five. George!' He had turned his head to yell into the interior of the dwelling. 'Where *is* the booger? George!' A boy with dark curly hair and a strikingly handsome face came to the door. He had a brooding look, with heavy-lidded eyes and a beautifully shaped mouth. There seemed to be an abundance of good-looking people in this part of the world. The man aimed a blow with the back of his hand, which the boy dodged. 'Ye're never where ye're wanted! Get me a drink now and fetch yer coat. Ye can show this young leddy to Plashy Lane.'

'I don't want to put you to any trouble — ' I began.

'Ye won't be. He's nothing better to do. Lazy, that's what he is.' George had returned with the tankard, which the man snatched from him. We stood in silence while he drained it for the second time. Slowly he lowered it and made a belching sound, while stroking his chest amid puffs of dust, as though easing the passage of the liquid.

'Milling's the thirstiest work there is,' he muttered, not without pride in his tone.

'Aye! And the hardest and the dullest and the stupidest,' cried George. He put up his elbow to defend

7

his ear from a second cuff.

'Tarnation! Be off wi' 'ee, ye little booger! And mind ye're back afore six or there won't be no tea!'

'I don't care. I hate bully beef! You can give mine to the rats.'

The miller turned his back on us both and went inside without another word. George doubled his hand into a fist, bit his thumb and shook it in the direction of the parting back. He set off up the lane ahead of me, and I saw how he dragged one foot behind him. The leg was withered and the toe turned inwards. He worked hard with his arms to get his body along quickly as though he were rowing through the air. I had to hurry to keep pace with him.

Could this be my phantom whistler? I doubted it. George's stance was one of out-and-out defiance. I could not imagine him capable of those plaintive airs. He continued to scull up the lane without once looking back to see if I followed him.

'Wait!' I panted, as we came to the top of a small rise. 'I must — have — a rest.'

George turned and came back to me. 'You're nesh for a grown girl. I suppose you townfolk are always starving yourselves.' His expression was scornful.

'Nesh? What does that mean?'

'It means weak, I suppose.'

'If I wasn't before I am now. I've lugged these cases over hill and dale, through flood and thicket, and I'm sick of it.'

I saw something almost like a smile on George's lips. 'Is that how folk in Bournemouth talk? Like people in books?'

'I don't know. I come from London.'

'Never!' George was evidently much struck by this.

'The population of London is a good seven million or so. I don't know why I shouldn't be one of them.'

'At the last census it were six million, four hundred

thousand, Miss Clever Dick!'

'Well, now it's six million, three hundred and ninety-nine thousand, nine hundred and ninety-nine, Master Smarty Pants.'

George frowned then began to laugh. 'You can give me that bag. I don't mind carrying it.' He looked too delicate for such a burden but I did not dare to refuse. After we had walked side by side for another few hundred yards we came to a fork in the lane. 'That way leads up Gildry Hill.' George indicated the right-hand fork with a jerk of his head. I had an impression of trees crammed oppressively together rising steeply towards the crimson-streaked sky. 'This left 'un goes to Plashy Lane. How come if you's from London you ent staying at Gildry Hall? They goes to London a lot theirselves.'

'I don't know them. I don't know anyone here.'

'You don't?' George stopped to consider me. 'I don't know what you're here for, then.'

Nor did I.

'What's the name of the people who live at Gildry Hall?' I asked, to change the subject.

'Gildry, o' course. They've lived there hundreds o' years. Very bad, they are. See, there's two roads goes up the hill, one clockwise that goes to the church and the Rectory, and the other widdershins that goes to the Hall. They crosses twice but you mustn't take the wrong one or you'll meet the devil afore midnight.'

He was grinning at me now and I knew he hoped to frighten me.

'You look rather old to believe in such stories. I'd have thought you were ten at least.'

George scowled. 'I'm twelve and I don't believe it. 'Tis only the women as get theirselves into frights over it. They say it's the two ways to riches — the riches of heaven and the riches of the here and now.' He gave a snort of derision. 'I know which I'd rather have.'

'Are the Gildrys very rich, then?'

9

George gave a hoot of laughter. 'You don't know nothing, do you? They own all these parts. The whole valley!'

'Goodness! Lucky them!'

'As to luck now, that's something else. I wouldn't say they was lucky. There was two sons and there's only one now — Mr Guy. And Mrs Gildry — she weren't lucky. They say he hated her. He cursed her and she died of a terrible fever.'

Though I was certain it was just gossip, I was intrigued. 'Do you like him? Mr Gildry, I mean.' George pulled a face of disgust and spat close to the toe of my shoe. 'You could just say no.' I frowned at him though I was beginning to like this fierce boy.

'All men spits. You're just a girl. You don't know about these things. My granfer can spit from here to that tree.' He pointed to a stump some ten yards away. 'And no wouldn't be saying it strong enough. I hate Mr Gildry. They do say God cursed him for blocking up the gate in the wall betwixt church and Hall. He fell down in a fit and he has to walk on sticks.'

'How interesting.' I stared up at the densely wooded slope. 'Widdershins to the devil.'

I was talking to myself, but George said at once, 'That's right. I read that in a book. Witches always go counter to the sun to see Old Nick.'

'You like reading, then?' George seemed to be master of an unusual quantity of facts for a boy of his age.

'Knowledge is power, ent it? I read that somewhere. I like that.'

'What do you want power for?'

'So as I can tell Dusty to stuff his bloomin' old mill.'

'Dusty?' I was being ridiculously slow. I hadn't slept properly for days.

'Granfer. Millers are always called Dusty, ent they? You don't know much, do you?' He raised his fine black brows and looked at me pityingly. 'He wants for me to take it on when he's gone. I don't want to end my days farting into me bedstraw, a great pudding of sweat and flour. I hate flour, I hate beer, I hate the sound of stones grinding. I'd like never to go near water again.'

'What have you got against water?'

'Ask a lot of questions, don't you?'

'I'm sorry.' I sighed. 'Let's go on, I can't think properly any more.'

'You'll be all right with me. I can think better'n anyone. Whereabouts is it exackerly you're going?'

'Number nine.'

He thought for a moment. 'I don't remember a number nine. Sure you got the right place? There's a grand hotel for London folk at Bournemouth. P'raps you'd rather go there.'

'I don't particularly like grand hotels. I just want a few days on my own, away from . . . things.'

'Things?' George looked canny. 'You running away from something? The police maybe? You robbed a bank? Nah! You haven't the strength to lift a sack of grain, even, let alone a sack of gold. Here, give me that!'

He seized my other case and, tacking from side to side with the weight of his burden, set a fast pace along the left hand fork. The road dipped down towards a pretty cottage, thatched and whitewashed, whose garden was filled with pale splashes of primroses. I felt quite hopeful when I saw how invitingly the lights glowed behind drawn curtains and smelt the wood-smoke in the air.

'This is Plashy Lane.' George took a torch from his pocket and shone it on the gate. 'This here's number five. I mind there's a cottage down the lane a bit, all deserted. No one's been livin' there a good long time though.'

The road grew much narrower and was made gloomy by a long, high hedge on one side and thickly growing trees on the other. We walked in silence for some time.

11

Suddenly I was alone in the blowing darkness.

'George! Where are you?' I was unable to keep the anxiety out of my voice.

'Here! I found 'un.' George emerged from the hedge. I couldn't see an opening. 'Here 'tis. We calls it Drop Cottage.'

He flashed the torch into the middle of the hedge and I caught a glimpse of a gatepost, a little crooked and quite overgrown. On it was the figure nine. There was no sign of a gate, just a slight thinning of the twigs to mark the entrance. Drop Cottage, Plashy Lane. A drip of rain landed on my cheek in conformity with the wateriness of the address. I wanted to avoid another soaking.

'Can I borrow your torch?'

'It ent mine. Dusty's fearful mean with the batt'ries.'

'I'll buy you a new battery. Come on, do lend it to me.'

'It'll be a hiding if I do.'

'Oh.' I felt in that case it would be unethical to press the point.

'Tell you what. If you can guess this riddle I'll take the hiding. As long as I live I eat. But when I drink I die. What's the answer?'

'I don't know. What *is* the answer?'

'You really are daft. Don't you know the rules? You can't be told. You have to guess.'

'I can't!' Suddenly I wanted to stamp my foot and scream. I was standing in the middle of nowhere on a filthy night, cold, wet, tired and being required to guess riddles. The knowledge that I had brought it all upon myself only made it worse.

'I'll be going now, then. I want my supper.'

'I thought you hated — what was it? Bully beef?'

'I like it fine. I didn't want him to think he could grind me, that's all.'

'Wait. Let me give you something.'

George examined the coin. 'Fifty p! What's this for?'

'Well, you found the cottage and you carried my luggage.'

'I'll carry your bags anytime. It's nothing to me. I'm strong, I am.' He hesitated. 'I'll let you have the torch for that.'

'No. I don't want to get you into trouble.'

George looked at me, considering. Then he thrust the torch into my hand. He flipped the coin into the air and it glinted in the half-darkness like a leaping fish before he caught it. He swung himself away without looking back and was lost from sight long before I ceased to hear the sound of his dragging foot.

2

Thorns scratched my face and a shower of stingingly cold raindrops trickled down my neck as I pushed through the hedge. I shuddered to think of the damage to my beautiful black alpaca coat, which had been a present from Alex. The torch showed something that might once have been a path. It was bordered by brambles that snatched at my hem and clawed at my tights. As I looked down to avoid the brambles, the branch of a tree stretching across the path dealt my skull a stunning blow.

Tears of pain and tiredness filled my eyes. I heartily wished myself back in my studio with the last two days' work undone. What had persuaded me to run away to this wilderness of spiteful verdure and hostile weather? And why, when my life had been so satisfactorily ordered had I thrown it into confusion? Had I gone mad? I put down my cases and paused to catch my breath.

The trouble was I was no longer capable of thinking clearly. The emotional torment of the last few weeks, interlaced with sleepless nights, had made me wretchedly overstrung. The lease on my flat had expired this morning. I was supposed to be spending my last night of spinsterhood with my father and Fay, my stepmother. It was a nod to convention that I thought slightly ridiculous but Fay had thought it suitable and she and Alex were so hand in glove that it had not occurred to them to consult me. When I thought of Alex I was aware of an undertow of feeling that was almost terror. Now that I had begun to run from him he had become a monster.

I picked up my suitcases and followed the narrow

tunnel through the trees. Viola's godmother must have been senile for some time, poor thing, to judge from the state of the garden. A tiger and a python or two would not have seemed out of place. I stepped into a deeper shadow and the next second I was falling downwards like Alice inside the rabbit hole but, even had there been interesting things on shelves, there would have been no time to look at them for I hit the ground almost immediately with such a smack that the breath was knocked out of me. For a moment everything was dark. Gradually a pinprick of light appeared within a frame of branches. I was lying on my back staring up at the evening star.

I have no idea how long I lay gasping, my thoughts in disarray. Eventually I turned my head and saw, a few feet away, a trail of light. I shifted on to my hands and knees and crawled towards the torch. I had difficulty breathing but nothing seemed to be broken, apart from the locks on one of my suitcases. I saw it upside down and open not far off. Behind me was a wall of grassy mud. I had fallen down a practically vertical slope of ten or twelve feet.

A few tears of shock and despair rolled down my nose as I gathered my clothes from the mire. Suppose the cottage had fallen down? How was I to get back up to the lane, carrying two suitcases? Perhaps this had never been a path at all. Probably I was wandering miles from the beaten track and years later my body would be discovered as a collection of clean-picked bones. It might be easier to lie down and let nature take its course. What had Napoleon said? Something like, oh well whatever happens, there's always death. But in French, naturally. I was verging on delirium. I must pull myself together. I stood irresolute. Should I go on or back?

An owl hooted, startling me. Then, from above my head, came a gentle whistle. Just three notes, twice over.

15

Was it a bird breaking curfew or was I alone on a hillside with a madman? I found I didn't want to die, after all. Not yet, anyway. And certainly not here. The clouds rolled briefly from the face of the moon and through a descending avenue of trees the beam of my torch flashed on a pane of glass.

The prospect of civilisation gave me an injection of courage and energy. I had the key. I could lock myself in, bar the door, defend myself somehow. I set off towards the window, staggering now from lacerations and drenchings and the effects of my fall. The wind was gusting noisily through the branches. The undergrowth was so dense here that I had to kick my way through it. Was that rushing noise only the wind? Just in time I stopped and shone the torch directly downwards into a chasm.

It was a channel six feet wide and possibly as deep, through which coursed a torrent of water. A plank spanned it. I looked at it with deep aversion but the fear of what might be behind me was stronger. I edged on to it. It began to wobble in rhythm with my trembling knees and the cases seemed to double in weight. I took tiny steps and did some controlled breathing — in, two, three, hold, two, three, out, two, three — that I have found invaluable all my life for testing moments. Half-way across the plank sagged abruptly and in my struggle to keep my balance I threw up my arms, or would have done if I had not been holding two heavy cases. The torch flew out of my grasp and I saw its friendly light bobbing away on the flood. Perhaps I would be carried after it, down to the greater surge of a river and from thence to the sea where my drowned corpse would be washed up at high tide to lie among the jellyfish and bladderwrack. It hardly seemed to matter now. I threw self-preservation to the winds and ran the rest of the plank. Viola's godmother must have been eccentric to the point of lunacy. I hobbled with bowed shoulders as quickly as I could down towards the cottage.

Fitfully the moon revealed a low building with bulging walls like a cheese pressed under a weight. The broken windows and untidy thatch gave it a forlorn, apologetic air. A wooden arch round the door had broken beneath a tangle of thorns and sagged across the door. At my approach a bird shot through one of the windows, screeching, into my face. I was too crushed to screech back. I put my hand between the branches and felt the door give a little. It opened a few inches in response to a shove from my knee. I bent down and crawled inside.

It was perfectly dark and smelt of compost, as though ancient vegetables had been left to turn brown and seep. When packing my things in London it had occurred to me that the electricity supply might have been turned off when Viola's godmother was taken off to the home for the deranged — where I would soon be joining her — so I had thrown some candles and matches into my luggage. I patted the walls on either side of the door to make certain. I couldn't find a light switch. I fumbled in the suitcases until I heard the rattle of a matchbox.

The match flared into brilliance and I saw chairs and a table. My view was partial and objects swam waveringly in and out of my ken as though I were exploring a wreck at the bottom of the sea. On the table were bottles and plates and, oh, joy! a three-branched candelabra. Eagerly I fitted candles into the cups and lit them. Then, holding the candlestick high, I walked around the room.

It was long and low with a large fireplace in the middle of its length and windows at each end. A sofa and a chair stood on either side of the brick chimney-piece. The grate had not been swept and there were half-burnt logs among the heaps of ashes. Beside them was a pile of kindling. I had bought a copy of

17

Vogue to read on the train, not the best sort of paper for burning. I pumped away with the bellows like mad before a closer examination revealed a hole in the leather. Of course, on this darkest of all dark days nothing was going to be that easy. I knelt down to blow and after getting ash in my eyes and up my nose the fire began to burn. I peeled off my sodden coat and hung it over the back of the chair. I found my ribbon in one of the pockets and tied back my bedraggled hair. The sofa looked uninviting, damp and probably full of crawling things but the minute I sat on it I was convinced I would never be able to get up again. I took off my shoes and tights and held my bare feet towards the blaze. As sensation returned to my limbs I was overwhelmed by lassitude. I leaned back, pillowing my head on my scarf to prevent the sofa's inhabitants climbing into my hair.

Gradually the sounds of the house enfolded me. The crackling of the dry wood burning and hissing as spots of rain came down the chimney. The pattering sound of something, a mouse, I hoped, running about overhead. A shower of rain like dried peas against what remained of the glass. The fire glowed brighter, the candle flames fluttered in the eddies of woodsmoke. I was quite alone. Only three people in the world knew where I was and two of those cared nothing at all about me. I cherished this unaccustomed solitude.

I closed my eyes. Alex's white face loomed in my imagination and I pushed it away. My life in London had lost something of its reality. It seemed to my oppressed fancy more like a spectacle, perhaps a tragicomedy. It required some suspension of disbelief to see my own part in it as anything that could be called real. Scenes revolved in my mind, snatches of speech, moments of high drama and low farce. I sat in the dress circle, watching the cast act their lines. How lucky that the pain in my arms and the throbbing of my scratched legs would prevent me falling asleep, I thought, as the characters performing in my brain tore up the script and broke into burlesque.

★ ★ ★

I woke abruptly, bewildered to find myself in a strange place in semi-darkness. The fire was hot and crimson, the candles had burned down a couple of inches. I peered at the face of my watch. Half past seven! Something had woken me. I listened. The scratching of fingernails on wood, repeated at intervals. I thought at once of the phantom whistler.

'George?'

The scraping resumed with a new vigour. I found my shoes, still cold and sopping. Taking the candlestick, which was heavy enough to be a useful weapon, I went to the door. The blast of freezing air that rushed into the room doused the flames at once. I felt something brush past my knees. A shadow moved between me and the fire. It dropped to the floor and let out a low whine.

My hands were unsteady again, this time with relief, as I relit the candles. 'Hello.' I bent down to stroke the damp head of my visitor. 'Are you an orphan of the storm, too?' It looked up at me, tiny flames reflected in its eyes and I felt the draught of a tail waving. 'Good boy.'

The dog gave a polite grunt in response. It was quite large, about the size of a Labrador but hairier. It seemed friendly. I knew virtually nothing about dogs. When I was small we had a grey cat called Lulu. I was very fond of her. That was before my mother died. My father married Fay soon after and our house became a shrine to good taste where animals would have been, at best, irrelevant. Lulu had found a new home with our housekeeper.

'Would you like something to eat?' I asked. The dog wagged its tail more energetically. I had brought with

19

me a carrier bag of bread, cheese, pâté, fruit and a bottle of wine. I unpacked it on the sofa. It would be cleaner to eat it straight from the greaseproof wrappers. The dog ate a piece of bread slowly. The pâté went down much faster. We shared the cheese, a piece of very good Roquefort.

The dog licked its jowls and paws then lowered its head to the floor and lay blinking at the fire. Gradually it moved its chin to rest it, delicately, on one of my feet. The presence of this gentle, well-intentioned creature was an immense comfort.

After a while I became aware of a pressing need for a lavatory. 'I hate to disturb you when we're so comfortable,' I said. The dog lifted its chin and whined. I got up and held the candlestick high. Opposite the fireplace was a pointed doorway, like an arch in a rood screen. Apart from the front door this was the only egress. I wondered how former inhabitants had got upstairs. I knew there must be one as I had seen a dormer in the thatch. I stepped through the archway only to make an abrupt and unexpected descent for the second time that day. This time it was only a step but it jarred my bones and made me bite my tongue. I straightened up with a groan and cracked my skull smartly on the ceiling.

Holding the candlestick aloft I saw that a broad beam stretched across the entrance to the room. A particularly silly place to have it, I thought angrily. I saw a long narrow room, half the size of the sitting room with a large, shallow sink beneath a window. Beside it was a door. I hoped this might lead to the bathroom. It was bolted at the top. I hit it several times with a saucepan that lay on the draining-board. The bolt gave way and the door swung open, extinguishing the flames with a blast of cold night air. While I crouched beside a bush — I assumed it was a bush from its extreme prickliness and wetness — the dog licked my nose affectionately.

I wondered what sort of mazed, whimsical creature could have chosen to live in this extraordinary cliff-side residence, a cross between an eagle's eyrie, an Anglo-Saxon hut and an Eskimo *tupik*. It was a relief to get back to the fire. The dog leaned against my leg while I stroked its ears.

I tried to imagine the house in Cheyne Walk, where I had grown up, with a dog in it. I had begged to be allowed to have a kitten and Lulu had appeared on my fifth birthday. My mother had thought it cruel to keep animals in London. She was certain they must pine for fields and trees and good smells. Now I realised that it was she who pined for those things. She hated the noise and stink of traffic, the hardness of brick and concrete, the dirt and the litter, the confinement of people's lives into small spaces.

My parents had bought the house in Chelsea cheaply at the end of the war. It was to be a temporary lodging. 'As soon as Daddy's rich, darling,' my mother used to say, 'we'll buy a lovely old house in the country. We'll have lawns and flowers, an orchard with hens and a wood with foxes.' She added more things as time went on and my father was never quite rich enough for the move. I couldn't understand why it was taking him so long. He often talked about the market and complained of its unpredictability. I imagined him standing behind a colourful stall piled with fruit and vegetables like the ones in my picture books. It was a great disappointment when I realised that it was to do with something called stocks and shares that were dull bits of paper.

By the time I was seven the house in the country had a sundial, a dovecote, stables, a boating lake, and a trick fountain with which you could soak unsuspecting guests and still Daddy wasn't anything like rich. It was about then that Daddy started to be away more and Mummy started to eat less. The change was gradual. I only really noticed it because of something Uncle Sid said. He was my mother's brother and he still lived in the jolly red-brick and flint farmhouse by the sea in Norfolk where they had both grown up.

I loved Uncle Sid devotedly. He had fat shiny cheeks and wonderfully crooked teeth, which I enjoyed drawing much more than my father's white even ones. He spoke with a lovely rich accent, like my mother's but much more pronounced. When she was with him, my mother sometimes used to drop her Hs. When he came to see us he brought fish with sharp silvery scales, little brown shrimps and bits of seaweed and shells for me. We'd have a fish-and-chip supper in our basement kitchen and Uncle Sid used to tell us stories about the sea, which was his great love. He had been prevented from going to sea because he was the only boy and had to take over the farm. It was really only a few acres of marshy ground on which he kept some sheep, geese, goats and a cow for the house. Money was always short. Sometimes I was allowed to stay with him on my own. We used to get up early and walk over the marsh to collect samphire to sell in the local town. In the evenings I'd help Uncle Sid make boxes and frames and ornaments out of shells we'd picked up on the beach. Mummy used to laugh when I said that the farm was my idea of the perfect place to live. 'It's got no electricity and the chimney smokes and there's mud around the back door from September till May,' she used to say. 'Wait till you see *my* house. It'll be the most beautiful place in the world!'

'Sylvie,' said Uncle Sid, on one of our fish-and-chip evenings when my mother had repeated something on these lines. ''Ow's Charlie these days?' Charlie was my father. 'If 'e ain't rich yet it can't be for want of trying. Bless me if I can remember when I last saw 'im.'

I remember watching with interest and mystification as a dark tide rose up my mother's neck all the way to her eyebrows. 'Don't call him Charlie, darling. You know he hates it.'

'Aye. But I like a little friendliness. You'll always be Sylvie to me and I ain't going to call my little Freddie Elfrida for love nor money. Whatever possessed you to call her such an outlandish thing?'

'It means *elf peace*. I found it in a book. I thought it was pretty. It made me think of fairies dancing in a ring in a wood.' My mother was a true romantic.

'Maybe. But you ain't answered my question. Where does Mr Charles Swann — if 'e's got to 'ave 'is true title — lay 'is 'ead at night? 'E does keep awful late hours for a family man.'

I think she laughed and said something about Sid being an old stick-in-the-mud with his country ways. I can't remember the rest of the conversation. But it came back to me often in the months that followed because it was true. My father hardly ever *was* at home. The only photograph I have of my mother, which Uncle Sid gave me after she died, shows a slender girl in a wedding dress, a wreath of roses in her hair, her eyes looking straight into the camera and laughing. The photograph is black and white but I remember that her hair was red like mine and her eyes were green like peridots. But the strongest memory I have of her is sitting on the window-seat in our first-floor drawing room, staring out at the traffic and the boats on the river when her eyes were dark with a secret sorrow.

It wasn't long after that when I started finding bottles about the place, in drawers and hidden at the back of cupboards and behind the curtains. There were a lot under her bed. They smelt absolutely horrible, like the stuff my father filled his cigarette lighter with. She used to sleep a great deal and her movements got very slow. When my father did come home they had rows. Once when Uncle Sid called in to see us my mother was asleep on the kitchen floor.

23

'Oh, Sylvie. My dear little Sylvie,' he said, in a way that made me want to cry, it was so sad. He had picked her up — very easily for she was now so thin that in the bath her ribs and shoulder-blades stuck out, like those poor donkeys in Egypt the woman down the road was always collecting for — and put her in a chair. Then he muttered under his breath, 'My God, what I wouldn't do to 'im if I could, that mean, low-down devil.' My mother had opened her eyes and said in her sleepy voice with all the words running together, 'Don't be angry with him, Sid. It was my fault. I've pulled him down in the world. Marrying out of your kind doesn't make for happiness. Oh, Sid, I'm so — ' Then she saw me and shut her eyes and wouldn't say any more.

After that she started to spend a long time in the bathroom being sick and her face was sweaty much of the time and very pale. My father used to shout at her to pull herself together and eat, for God's sake, but she only looked at him with her green eyes filled up like pools. Then he called the doctor and there was a long, low-voiced conversation in the drawing room. I had my ear pressed to the door. I didn't understand very much about it. Words like 'strain' — 'liver' — 'complete rest'. She was sent to bed and a smiley nurse put in charge. She smiled all the time even when it was raining and Mummy was being sick and there was absolutely nothing to smile about. I wondered if she smiled in her sleep. She always called me her lamb, which I rather resented but I didn't say anything.

Anyway, this seemed to work for a time. Mummy stopped being sick and her eyes were much brighter and all the bottles were taken out of the house. We had long talks as in the old days about all the pictures and poems we both liked and I used to tell her about the teachers and the other girls at school and make her laugh. I drew her a lot and I was always careful to make her cheeks pinker than they were and her lips redder. But still she could not eat.

Sometimes I would give her spoonfuls of things like ground rice and beef soup that the nurse had made and we'd pretend I was the mother bird with a worm. I would scold her for being a naughty little chick. Then she'd to ask me to finish her supper so that the Nurse would not be angry with her. 'Honestly, darling, I ate all my lunch while you were at school and I'm getting really fat. Look!' She would pinch the white flesh of her arms and we'd make believe that there was more of it than before. When she pleaded with me I had to give in. I could not have refused her anything. I loved her so much.

'Oh, Freddie,' she said once, 'I am trying, my darling. I want to get well so that you and I can go away. We'll go to stay with Uncle Sid and you can run about on the beach and I can finish Evangeline.'

Evangeline was the doll she was making for me. My mother could sew beautifully. Evangeline was made from pale pink velvet and had embroidered blue eyes and a tiny cushiony rosebud mouth and two little red French knots for nostrils. Her hair was fair and curly, made from strands of silk, and she had a cherry red coat and a blue dress and one brown leather shoe. Though the leather was glacé kid it was still too tough for my mother to push the needle through with her hands, which were as frail as sparrows' feet, so she was waiting to get her strength back before making the other one.

Every afternoon after school I'd go upstairs and read to her. Evangeline used to lie on the pillow beside my mother, her soft pink arms over the sheets next to Mummy's white ones, her blue eyes wide, listening hard. Then I'd look up and Mummy would be asleep. I'd put away the book, pull down the blind, kiss them both and go away very quietly.

One day when I looked up from the book I saw that

25

Mummy had gone to sleep with her mouth a little open. I could see her bottom row of teeth. And when I got closer I saw that her eyes were open as well. I pulled down the blind but it jerked itself out of my hand and rolled up with a dreadful clatter. Luckily Mummy stayed sleeping. I kissed her face and this time I gave her an extra kiss on her nose because I was so pleased that she was having such a good rest.

'Mummy's having a really long sleep,' I told the nurse, when I got down to the kitchen. 'Even though her eyes are a bit open.'

'I'll just nip up and see her.' I wondered what had upset the nurse. She wasn't smiley at all.

I went upstairs behind her, three flights, which usually made the nurse pause on each landing and clutch her heart and say, 'Mother of God, these stairs'll be the death of me.' But this time she went all the way up without stopping. She stood panting in the doorway of my mother's room then went over to the bed.

'Will her eyes be sore when she wakes up?' I asked in a whisper. The nurse put down her hand and closed them.

'No, my lamb. They'll never be sore any more. Your mummy's gone to be with Jesus and He makes all things better.'

Though I had not begun to comprehend the awful truth I started to have a very horrible feeling that crept up from my feet and ran like fire all round my body. I knew at once, intuitively, that He had not made things better for me.

3

I was sitting in the stalls at Covent Garden. The orchestra played the overture to *Swan Lake*. The manager came before the curtain to ask if anyone in the audience knew the role of Odette/Odile as the *prima assoluta* had broken her leg. I sprang from my seat, pirouetted down the aisle and up on to the stage. The conductor was my father. He waved his baton and in a drift of snowflakes I was clothed in white feathers with pink satin shoes. He began the music for my entrance. With a thrill of horror I realised that I had absolutely no idea of the steps. I pranced, I hopped, I waved my arms. The audience rocked with laughter. Rothbart, the evil sorcerer, appeared on stage in a plume of red smoke. He pointed to the lake that lapped at my feet. The audience began to boo. Rothbart took off his mask — it was Alex — and raised his arms. The flood rose up to engulf me.

I woke with a racing heart. I was extremely cold and unable to move my legs. I lifted my arm and saw, to my surprise, the sleeve of my jersey. Then I remembered. A wavering greenish light, like reeds in a current, made the objects in the room emerge and recede. I heard the smacking of lips. The dog was lying on my feet at the end of the sofa. Only the warmth of its body had enabled me to sleep at all.

I looked at my watch. It was half past seven in the morning. It had been a terrible night. Between fearful dreams I had floated in a state of semi-wakefulness in which I was aware that I was lying on a dirty sofa in a ruined cottage in wettest Dorset, far away from everyone I knew. Threading through these phases of half-consciousness were odd sounds, mostly unidentifiable but sometimes something like tuneful whistling. At one point I surfaced from sleep and recognised the dawn chorus. Comforted, I had begun to drowse again only to wake with a start. Birds do not sing 'Soave sia il vento', of which I identified several bars. Or thought I had.

Now, in the light of day, the night terrors seemed ridiculous. I was acutely aware of physical discomfort. My mouth was dry and tasted horrible. I had not brushed my teeth for twenty-four hours. There was hardly a part of my body that did not ache and, except for my feet, I was very cold. The fire was a heap of ashes sparkling with vermilion pinpricks. I tried to get up. The dog groaned and rolled away, freeing my feet.

'Hello.' I felt I ought to respond to those expressive eyes fixed so enquiringly on mine. 'Won't your master wonder where you are?' The dog was yellowish-brown with darker shading to its ears and along its spine. It had a handsome leonine face. Judging from its grey muzzle, it was quite old. Its coat was long and in good condition. It did not look like a stray. 'Are you thirsty, too? We'll try the kitchen.'

The dog clambered stiffly from the sofa and followed me. I remembered the deep step down and the low beam. By the light of day the kitchen looked more friendly. A dresser elaborately draped with cobwebs like a prop for *Great Expectations* held some pieces of china. There was a small black range and a table. I wondered what the brick-shaped greenish thing on the table could be, that fell into crumbs when I touched it. The bread knife, which lay nearby, gave me the clue. A single tap was suspended above the shallow sink from a pipe that had become unscrewed from the wall. A few cups and plates stood among the leaves that had blown in through the broken window. Viola's godmother must have been taken away very suddenly.

The draught from the shattered pane stirred the leaves. A branch grated against the glass and the dog's claws rattled on the flags as she had a good scratch. Homely sounds, but the dereliction of the place made them melancholy. I tried to imagine the woman who must have stood so often before the sink as I was standing now, gazing out through trickling rain into the garden, musing about her life, running through its satisfactions, identifying causes of discontent, coming to terms with disappointment, planning to mow the lawn in the next dry spell, perhaps, or deciding what to cook for a friend coming to stay.

Most of the little I knew about country life came from novels. A seasonal cycle of fêtes, cricket matches on the green, tea parties, bridge or whist in the long winter evenings. There would be parish council meetings, talks about local history in the village hall, neighbours calling in for a glass of sherry at Christmas. Perhaps she had rushed through the washing-up to get to the vicarage for a meeting to discuss embroidering new hassocks for the church.

Hanging on the wall to the left of the sink was a mirror. I looked at myself in the brindled glass. I saw a white face, with dark thumbprints beneath the eyes. My hair, pale red and slightly wavy, gave me a pre-Raphaelite Burne-Jones look. It was not how I liked to think of myself. I enjoyed fey romanticism in others but for myself, I wanted to see things as clearly and comprehensively as possible. After the elemental rigours of the previous day, my hair stood out round my forehead in tendrils, like a corona of flames in a child's drawing of the sun. I put up my hand to smooth it.

Had Viola's godmother also looked anxiously at her reflection, seeking signs of change? She must have been aware at the onset of her illness that something was wrong. An increase in forgetfulness, perhaps, or clumsiness in speech. I tried to imagine the slow dispersion of self, the panic of disorientation, the relief when things seemed to fall back into their old places, the gradual displacement of one's familiar image by a timorous stranger. Usually decisive, during these last weeks I had found myself uncertain and irresolute. I was deeply disturbed by the feeling of being out of control. Dementia must be terrifying. The realisation that one was forgetting how to do ordinary things, like making tea or dialling a telephone number. The inability to carry out the ordinary tasks that give a shape to the day. Finding oneself walking the dog in one's nightdress.

I had a flash of intuition. The dog was sitting at my feet, its patient eyes trained on my face. '*That*'s why you came last night. You thought she'd come home. You're *her* dog, aren't you? Oh, how sad!'

The dog pushed its head against my hand and I bent down to stroke its ears. I imagined strangers coming to take away its mistress, arranging, perhaps, for a neighbour to take the dog. They had carried her off to some unfamiliar place to begin the lonely process of dying . . . I stopped this particular train of thought. Anxiety and lack of sleep were making me morbid. The tap resisted my efforts but gave way at last with a shriek. A stream of rusty water splashed down into the sink, swirling the leaves and collecting a scum of dust. After a minute or so it began to run more or less clear. I washed my face and hands and felt better. I rinsed a dish and filled it for the dog. It lapped politely for a few seconds then turned away.

I picked up the dish and looked at it more carefully. It was painted with figures in a landscape in red, green and black with a creamy-white smooth glaze. It looked to me like eighteenth-century creamware. The rest of the china in the sink matched it. At first glance it seemed at odds with the extreme rusticity of the cottage. I examined the curtains. Beneath the cobwebs and dead flies was a pretty chintz of flowers and birds, not only lined but interlined. They were clumsily hemmed and had evidently been cut down from a larger, grander pair. There was a glass on the draining-board, hand-blown with an air-twist stem, obviously old and, I thought, quite valuable. I brushed a dangling web as big as a handkerchief from a painting that hung opposite the sink. It was a charming mezzotint of Jupiter seducing Venus in the guise of Diana, in a *verre églomisé* frame.

Presumably the contents of the cottage belonged to Viola. I wondered if she had a sentimental attachment to her godmother. She had never spoken about her but there had always been something a little mysterious about Viola's life. She had been brought up by her aunt, and as she had never mentioned her parents I had not liked to ask about them.

I had known Viola since she was a small, shy child with short dark curls. Her aunt and my stepmother were friends, though I suspected it was an unequal intimacy with the balance of keenness being on Fay's side. She had done some interior decorating of the rather grand house in Richmond where Viola's aunt lived and had made much of the connection. Because of the six-year gap between us, Viola and I had not actually become friends until a year ago when we had met at a series of evening classes on Watteau and French painting. By then the difference in our ages was unimportant and we had liked each other immediately. Before leaving for Paddington the day before, I had sent her a postcard as requested, saying only, 'Gone to earth. F.'

I walked back into the sitting room. The windows were smothered with creepers, dappling the light that had crept day after day, year after year, into this deserted place, revivifying the dead leaves that draughts had blown into trails across the floor and making bright the worn Persian rug before the fire. The accumulated value of the furnishings of the cottage could not be enormous but everything had been chosen carefully and

31

with an eye for beauty. My mind wandered again to the previous owner, imagining her searching local antique shops, bearing home in triumph something new to add to her collection.

On a table by the window was a wind-up gramophone with a horn and a stack of seventy-eights in brown paper slips. I opened the lid and took the record from the turntable, blowing away the coating of dust. The last movement of Elgar's violin concerto. I was surprised by such full-blooded romanticism and adjusted my idea of Viola's godmother accordingly. I wound the handle, blew the fluff from the needle and started the motor. The sound was scratchy and distorted as though coming up from the bottom of a well but the swelling, expressive music corresponded with my mood. A window-seat ran the width of the room and for several minutes I sat there, listening to the rapid and brilliant passages of the *cadenza* and wondering what she had been thinking as she heard it for what had been, as it had turned out, the last time.

Between the fireplace and the window was a bookcase that covered the whole wall. On the top three shelves were Shakespeare, Dickens, Hardy and Anthony Trollope. On the lower shelves were volumes of Blake, Keats and Donne. There was a handful of writers in translation, Tolstoy, Balzac and Goethe. All these one could expect to find on any bookshelf, possibly unread. But there were also novels by Mary Webb, Compton Mackenzie, Elizabeth von Arnim, Constance Holme and E.F. Benson that suggested a real enthusiasm for fiction.

A book lay open, face down, on the window seat. It was *The Nebuly Coat* by J. Meade Faulkner, a novel I had always loved. It seemed almost more than a coincidence. I closed my eyes, desiring to conjure up an image of Viola's godmother by some vague, super-sensual means but my tired eyes stung and I saw only the tremulous patterns of the window panes.

There was a gap between Katherine Mansfield's *Bliss* and Meredith's *The Egoist*. I closed the book and put it back into its place. She had kept her faculty of reading and understanding, then, to the last. Or had it been a reflex action to hold a book in her hand as she sat gazing out on to the garden?

As I looked round the neglected room I decided to do what little I could to preserve this collection of objects that amounted to perhaps a lifetime's selection and discrimination. I knew that I must go back to London at once. Running away had been childish, irresponsible and selfish. The least I could do was to let Fay and my father — and anyone else who had been affected by my defection — heap reproaches on my head. And I must humbly submit myself to Alex's wrath. As I thought of it I felt physically sick. But I would delay my departure for a few hours to make an inventory of the contents of the cottage so that Viola could decided whether to keep or sell them.

The dog began to bark. Seconds later I heard a shrill whistle and George put his head round the door. 'Mrs Creech sent me. She wants to know if you needs anything. Well, hello, old girl, what are you doing here?' The dog, recognising a friend, stopped barking and lay down before the still warm cinders of the fire.

'How very kind. Who is Mrs Creech?'

'She's postmistress and has the shop. 'Tisn't kindness. She heard from Granfer that you'd come and she wants to let other folk know all about you when they come for their goods.'

'Oh. Well, I'm afraid there won't be much to tell. I'm catching the next train back to London.'

'Never!' George looked amazed. 'You come all dressed up in fancy clothes for a sight of Drop Cottage, which ent no better'n a wreck, and then you turns round and hops it back. What's to do, then? Are you homesick?'

'Not at all.'

'I could go three times around the world and not be homesick. I could go and live on the moon and be glad of it.'

'I don't doubt it. It wasn't you, was it, whistling in the garden last night?'

''Twas Old Nick, most like.' He pointed to the dog. 'What's Clowy doing with you?' He pronounced it to rhyme with 'cloudy'.

'Clowy? What an unusual name.' Clowy lifted her head from her paws in polite acknowledgement. 'I thought perhaps she used to live here.'

'Whatever made you think that? She comes from the Hall.'

'Oh.' I was dashed to find my intuitive powers mistaken. 'Would you get me some things from the shop? I think I'll feel better if I have breakfast before I go. A small loaf of bread. Some unsalted butter. And a packet of china tea. And you'd better get something for the dog. What do you think she'd like? Sausages, perhaps?'

George seemed to find this extraordinarily funny. He hooted until he was red in the face and slapped his thighs and hugged himself until I began to grow impatient.

'You don't know much, do you! Sausages for a dog! I suppose you've got a cheque book and a bank account and all to pay for this. Chiny tea and what sort of butter was it?'

'Unsalted. Of course I've got a cheque book and . . . ' I paused, remembering that my bank account was now as useful to me as a heap of cowrie shells or a string of wampum. Alex had insisted that I transfer my modest savings into a joint account so that he could 'keep an eye on it'. I had protested but you couldn't win an

34

argument with Alex. The minute I drew any money from our joint account Alex would know and be at my side faster than you could say 'deferential bank manager'. 'Here's a pound note. See what you can do. Buy yourself some sweets.'

'All right. But I don't reckon sausages for Clowy. Likely they'd make her sick.' He whistled. 'Here, girl, you can come with me.'

Clowy followed him as he went out, leaving the door wide open behind him. I could hear him laughing all the way to the plank bridge. The temperature of the cottage, already low, became glacial. I set to with the remains of *Vogue* to put new heart into the fire. The next thing was to boil a kettle. There was a gas stove in the kitchen but, unsurprisingly, when I turned on the taps not the faintest hiss came from the rings. A black kettle swung on a pivot over the fire basket of the range. I had to use the paper my supper had been wrapped in to light the kindling. In order to keep the remains of the fruit out of the dust I stood it on my bag, the only remotely clean thing in the cottage. I could not include myself as I was now filthy from lighting two fires, besides the havoc wrought on my appearance by the walk from the station and a night spent on the sofa.

I let the tap run to get rid of the first outpourings of rust, unhooked the kettle and began to fill it. Immediately water flowed over my shoes from a hole in the base. I was standing by the sink, muttering imprecations on the beastly thing when I saw a face — not my own — in the mirror.

'Goodness me, you can scream and you can swear! I'm sorry I startled you. I called out but you didn't answer.'

Without his horse and close to, the man I had met the day before looked younger, probably somewhere around thirty. As he bent to rescue the kettle lid which had rolled beneath the dresser, his smooth light brown

35

hair flopped across his high bony brow. He was wearing riding clothes and boots, that give a dash to the plainest man. And one could not truthfully call him plain. I was conscious of my crumpled clothes and wild appearance.

'Do you usually stroll into people's houses in this lordly way?'

'Of course.'

'Oh.'

'People round here are pretty informal. I came to see if I could do anything for you.'

'That was good of you.' I felt I was being ungracious. 'How did you know I was here?'

'I met George coming up the lane clutching a pound note and looking very important. He was keen to tell me of your aberrant shopping habits. I suppose you always shop at Fortnum's.'

'Doesn't everyone?' I smiled coolly. 'If you want to be helpful you could get this fire going. It's being very obstinate.'

'Probably there's a jackdaw's nest in the chimney. Are you staying long? I could arrange for a sweep to call.'

'That's very kind but I'm leaving today.'

'What you might call a flying visit.'

He looked at me speculatively and really I could not blame him. My behaviour must seem erratic if not actually crazy. His eyes were light brown, golden when the light was on them, and the upper lids were heavy. His top lip was almost effeminate, well-shaped with a pronounced central V.

'Well, the thing is, I wanted to get away for a few days and a friend, the girl who owns this cottage, suggested I stay here. She had no idea how bad a state it was in. Viola's godmother was taken away when she fell ill, you see, and it was evidently longer ago than we thought.'

'Viola's godmother?'

'The owner.' He really was rather slow, though he did

36

not look stupid. 'I don't know what her name was. Perhaps you do.'

'Afraid not.' He continued to smile. 'You know, despite the black streaks, you really are as lovely as I first thought.'

I did not allow my eyes to stray in the direction of the mirror. I could behave with dignity even if appearances were against me. 'Don't you think nine o'clock in the morning is a little early for flirtation?'

'Perhaps it is.' The suggestion of cynicism in his expression vanished. He looked affable, almost apologetic. 'Now let's find a pan for the water and I'll make the toast. Then, after you've eaten you can tell me at what hour you consider it proper to begin. Here's the toasting-fork'. He unhooked it from the wall above the range. 'Where might the bread knife be? Aha!' He took it from the table and presented it to me. 'Breadboard here — in need of a wash. Now we need a teapot and two cups.'

'Two?'

'You don't think I'm going to allow you to spend a miserable breakfast all on your own, pining for the Albert Memorial? By the way I added milk and marmalade to George's list.'

'How did you know I live in London?'

'I asked Rolliver. He's the porter at the railway station. My curiosity was piqued by the sight of an elegant and beautiful creature staggering through the mire with suitcases, obviously a stranger to these parts. Rolliver confirmed my suspicion that you'd been delivered by the London train. Now, I shall try to breathe life into the other fire — you're not much of a Girl Guide, are you? — and then, as a master stroke of seduction, I shall lay the table.'

I watched him walk into the sitting room, then took a surreptitious look at myself in the mirror. A smudge of soot, probably from the kettle, marked my forehead like a badge of penitence. As I scrubbed it off with freezing water I wondered whether I ought to allow him to take control in this way. The truth was that I was not altogether sorry to have a companion. I was lonely.

It was a rare feeling with me. A portrait painter almost always establishes a peculiarly intimate relationship with his or her subject. For most people the process of being painted, being alone with and closely observed by one person for hours on end, breaks the seal on conventional reticence. I usually enjoyed this privilege. The dullest high court judge was a Don Juan, in intention anyway, the most fashionable hostess a maelstrom of complexes and inadequacies. I was called upon to be both psychiatrist and priest and was hardly ever bored.

'Got your things.' George came into the kitchen followed by Clowy who scraped enthusiastically at my knee with a muddy paw as though she had felt the quarter of an hour's separation badly. I was flattered. 'Mrs Creech said there ent no call for unsalted butter. I better not tell you what she said when I asked her for Chiny tea.' George grinned as he stuffed a collection of paper bags into my hands. 'She likened you to the Queen of Sheba and it weren't a compliment.'

'Mrs Creech can — well, never mind.' I reminded myself that George's ears were young. 'Is this ham for Clowy?' I opened the packet of watery, purple slices. 'It hardly looks like meat at all. I don't think it can be good for her.' Clowy gave a convincing demonstration of an indifference to processing methods, disposing of the entire quarter of a pound in three chews. 'Mm. New Zealand butter. And PG Tips. And what's this? A pot of anaemic jelly with three slivers of peel. Evaporated milk! Well, thank you, anyway. Did you get yourself something?'

George opened his mouth, displaying a fiercely crimson gobstopper. 'I got two. All right?'

'Certainly. Do you want to stay for breakfast?'

'Okay, George. You can cut along now,' said a voice from the sitting room. 'Go and tell Deacon he's to get on with the hedges in the bottom fields and not wait for me. Here's five p if you go now.' George looked inclined to disobey. I gave him a fifty-pence coin and he looked even less like going. My breakfast companion appeared round the kitchen door. 'Hop it! Or there'll be trouble.'

George hopped it. The despot pronged a slice of bread and held it before the kitchen fire. The country air, though confined so far to bitter, moisture-laden winds subtly tainted by rank vegetation, had done marvellous things for my appetite. The smell of toasting bread was so delicious that I could have eaten it butter and marmalade-less on the spot. Clowy came to sit on my foot and together we watched him turn the slice and begin to cook the other side. He glanced down at the dog. 'Hello, hound. This isn't for you, you greedy girl.' Then, to me, 'I see you can charm dogs, too.'

'Clowy came last night while I was asleep.'

'Actually it rhymes with snowy. Greek, you know.' He was laughing at me. 'Do you know Meredith's *Tale of Chloë*? Her mistress is intending to run off with a wicked philanderer, so to save her employer's virtue Chloë generously hangs herself from the hook on the back of a door. I call that an over-reaction. I mean, she might just have locked her in and thrown away the key. But this Chloë would allow anyone to be ravished in return for a biscuit.'

'I haven't read it but I noticed it in the bookshelves here. That's a coincidence, isn't it?'

'There must be a few from time to time or there wouldn't be a word for it.'

I stroked Chloë's head. 'Actually, I was convinced that she'd lived here at one time but George says not. I wonder if the people at Gildry Hall are worried about her?'

'You're quite a student of dialect, aren't you? It's actually pronounced Gilderoy. And no, we aren't.'

'Then you're — '

'Guy Gilderoy.' He transferred the toasting-fork to his left hand and held out his right. We shook hands. 'The pleasure's all mine.'

I thought there was a little irony in his voice of which I took note.

'I'm Elfrida Swann. Everyone calls me Freddie.'

'I had made up my mind your name was something ethereal. Rosamunda, perhaps. Or Letitia. But I like Freddie. It's sexily androgynous like a Shakespearean heroine. Come, Miss Elfrida Swann, your breakfast awaits you.'

He had dusted the tables and chairs and found a jug for the milk. 'Funny tea, isn't it? The sort of stuff that ought to be drunk from a billy-can.'

'On the steps of a gypsy caravan.'

'I'll have some milk sent down from the farm later.'

'That's very kind. But I'm going home today — that is — ' It was disheartening to remember that I had no home to return to. 'I shall go back to London just as soon as I've made a list of what's here for Viola. These things are too good to be left to fall to bits. Or someone might come in and take them. The door wasn't locked.'

'Good idea. I'll help you. Now, have some toast and marmalade.'

'Thank you.' I began to spread a little butter, feeling ravenous. 'But I'm sure you've got things to do. I mustn't take up any more of your time.'

'It's Saturday. Even farmers have a rest sometimes. What's the matter?'

Saturday. I looked at my watch. Half past nine. At this moment I should have been having my hair arranged and my nails polished. I didn't mind at all that I would never wear the dress of ivory duchesse satin, embroidered with pearls on the bodice and sleeves. Nor the diamond tiara that Fay had borrowed from Viola's aunt to hold in place the train of antique Brussels lace. With every fitting they had seemed to grow heavier and more restricting. The clothes were beautiful, but wearing them I felt like a heifer garlanded for sacrifice.

I certainly did not regret the ceremony and the reception. Every embellishment added by Fay had increased my dread of them. But I was acutely aware that my escape from an expensive and ostentatious ritual could hardly weigh against the fact that in five minutes I had radically altered the entire course of my life and made myself homeless, futureless and loveless. The inconvenience, in fact the raging discomfort, of Drop Cottage had worked wonderfully as a distraction from misery but now I was overwhelmed by feelings of anxiety and loneliness. To my dismay I felt my mouth tremble and I put my hands over my face to hide it.

'I'm a bloody fool,' I said. 'If only I knew what the hell I ought to do! I honestly wonder if it wouldn't have been better instead of getting on the train to throw myself under it.'

The pathetic melodrama of this last speech made me feel even worse.

'Now, look here, things can't be as bad as that.' Guy Gilderoy's voice was sympathetic, the bantering tone gone. He put his hand on my arm. 'Why not tell Uncle Guy all about it? I promise not to flirt or to try to take advantage of you in any way. And for goodness sake, eat before the toast gets cold.'

The kindness in his voice was my undoing. I began to cry. He made no attempt to stop me, but squeezed my arm comfortingly from time to time. In my current state of guilty wretchedness there was relief in the shedding of tears. As soon as I could, I stopped crying and sat sniffing over my toast crumbs. 'I don't think I've ever made such an idiot of myself before. It's just as well

41

we're complete strangers. I don't think I could stand it otherwise.'

'How beautifully you weep. Your eyes have gone several shades lighter, like river water with the sun on it. I really enjoy seeing girls cry. It fills me with noble sentiment and tender impulses. What you need is another cup of Tinker's Ruin. I do hope whatever you've done it's been really wicked. You've murdered your dear old sainted granny for her diamonds? Or you've sold a house full of dry rot and built over a mine shaft to an orphanage? I know. You once had a torrid affair with your best friend's husband and now you're threatening to tell her everything if he doesn't give you all his money. Do you really not want that?'

I looked sadly at the toast, briefly so tempting and shook my head. 'It's very nearly as bad.'

'Now, now. You've done the tears bit. I'll have it, then.' He took my plate. 'You'll feel much better when you've told me.'

'I was supposed to be getting married this morning.'

'You don't mean to say the poor devil's going to be standing there like a prize pumpkin, in full view of all his friends and relations, and you're not going to show? Phew! That *is* mean, I must say.'

'No! It isn't quite as dreadful as that! I told him yesterday — or was it the day before? I feel so confused — that I couldn't go through with it. But the humiliation will be terrible. By now everyone will have been telephoned and all the arrangements will be cancelled. Six bridesmaids and two pageboys disappointed, to say nothing of their mothers. The reception, musicians, food, champagne — the palazzo in Umbria we borrowed from Alex's friends for our honeymoon. Poor Alex! I know I've behaved unforgivably.'

'Big wedding, eh?'

'More than six hundred guests. I didn't want it like that. I'd have preferred a register office and a few close friends. But Alex and Fay got together and — '

'Just a sec. You must keep me abreast of the *dramatis personæ*. Alex is obviously the hapless groom. Fay is . . . ?'

'My stepmother. Of course she and my father are as mad as blazes and I can't blame them. I expect much of what she insisted on ordering will have to be paid for. The flowers alone cost five hundred pounds. Of course I'm terribly sorry about the expense. But when I remember Alex's face, when I told him I couldn't go ahead with it — '

Another small sob escaped me. Remembering his eyes, their expression of acute pain in which there was something akin to fear, made my stomach turn over with pity. He had attempted to light a cigarette but his hands were shaking too much and the lighter refused to work. He had given it up and thrown the cigarette into the fireplace. It struck me then that I had never, in the eighteen months I had known him, seen Alex at a loss.

4

The first time I saw Alex was in the crush bar at Covent Garden. It was the second interval of *Don Giovanni*. Giles Fordyce, a brilliant art historian who was going to marry Viola, was at the bar trying to catch the eye of the barman. Viola and I were standing by an open window, cooling ourselves. It was the last of the warm September evenings of that year and you could have baked a soufflé in the heat of the auditorium. Henry, who was supposed to have come with us, was at home with a bad cold.

'Who's that man staring at you?' Viola had said.

I turned my head and then, rather quickly, looked away. He was standing a little apart from the group he was with, holding a glass of something in one hand. When my eyes met his, he held my gaze without smiling.

'I've no idea. I'm certain I don't know him. You'd hardly forget that face.'

'He looks as though he'd like to add you to his total, like the wicked Don.'

'Who does?' asked Giles, coming over with the champagne.

'That man over there who keeps staring at Freddie. Perhaps he's a mind reader and is going to reel off a list of the contents of your bag.'

Giles looked over my shoulder. 'Oh, that's Alex Moncrieff. I've met him once or twice. He collects Gainsborough drawings. He's a QC. Nothing particularly sinister about him as far as I know.'

'Is he still looking at Freddie as though he wants to carry her away with him down to hell?'

'No. He's talking to someone. I think it's you who's getting carried away, Viola.' Giles looked down at her and smiled, unaware that his expression revealed just how much in love with her he was.

I thought of this later when the lights went down for the last act. The man who had stared at me so persistently in the crush bar had turned round in his seat in the stalls and was looking at our box. I suppose my attention was caught because everyone else was staring at the stage. Though his face was something of a blur, I felt it bore an expression far removed from tenderness. I forgot all about it in the excitement of Don Giovanni's dramatic exit to perdition and I did not see him as we left the theatre.

The following day I was alone in the studio, working on the hands of the girl I was painting at the time. It was dull stuff. They were smooth and pink, like the sitter's face, without so much as a freckle or an interesting vein. I was dissatisfied with the result. I was tired of hands. I painted so many that I feared they were beginning to merge into a general style that was almost a cliché. I had to remind myself that the electricity bill needed to be paid, to keep myself working. The telephone rang.

'Hello?'

'This is Alex Moncrieff. Will you have dinner with me this evening?'

I remembered the face I had seen for possibly three seconds as though it were etched on the inside of my eyelids. The contrast of pale skin, dark eyes and dark hair, like a woodcut.

'You've got the wrong number. I don't know anyone called Alex Moncrieff.'

'Don't be silly, Elfrida. You know perfectly well who I am. You were talking about me with the Otway girl. Fordyce will have told you who I was. That was my intention.'

'Oh.' I had been so taken aback by the coolness of this that I could not immediately gather my thoughts.

'Well, what about dinner?'

'Thank you — no. I don't go out to dinner with strangers.'

'Make an exception for me.'

'No. Really, I don't want to. Goodbye.'

I put down the telephone. I went back to those silly pink hands, like raw chicken breasts, and tried to give them a suggestion of musculature. But all the time I was thinking about the telephone call. How had he known who I was? I was sure Giles would not have given him my name without asking me first. How had he got my number? And what did he want?

An hour later the doorbell rang. A courier handed me a large, stiffened envelope marked Do Not Bend. I was expecting photographs of my sitter's dress, which would be a relief from the hands. I tore it open. Inside was a pencil drawing of a landscape with a church and two people in the foreground. It was peerless, unmistakably by the hand of a master. In the right-hand corner was a signature. Thos. Gainsborough. A piece of paper floated to the floor. I picked it up. 'For Elfrida. From Alex Moncrieff.'

When the telephone rang again later that afternoon I knew before I picked up the receiver that it was Alex Moncrieff.

'Hello?'

'Do you like it?'

'It's wonderful — exquisite — but of course I can't accept it.'

'Don't disappoint me. You don't look like a fool.'

'Thank you. But if it's foolish to refuse a very valuable drawing from a man I've never met then I'm afraid appearances are misleading. Please ask the courier to come for it.'

'Do you like it?'

'Of course. It's absolutely beautiful. But that has nothing to do with it.'

'On the contrary. It was intended to give you pleasure. It has. And I hope will continue to do so for a very long time.'

'But I've told you, I can't accept it.'

'Where is it now? Are you looking at it?'

'It's in the envelope, waiting for you to collect it.'

He laughed. 'What a bad liar you are.' I glanced guiltily across at the little easel where I had put it, so as to enjoy it during my brief period of ownership. 'You're looking at it now, aren't you?' I wondered if Viola's joke, that he had some mind-reading ability, could have any truth in it. 'You're afraid to accept it because it will place you under an obligation to me.'

This annoyed me because he was right. 'I'm not afraid of anything. But it would seem — dishonest to take such a thing from someone I don't know. As though I had it under false pretences. It's much too valuable.'

'So you'd accept a cheap bauble?'

'No! All right, it isn't just the cost of the thing. I don't choose to have an acquaintance with you forced on me.'

'Good. Now you're thinking clearly. You have just one chance to give it back. Have dinner with me tonight.'

'Certainly not. I shall take it to the nearest police station and explain that it was sent to me by mistake.'

'Even the police will recognise its value. They'll call in some art expert, who will inevitably get in touch with me. Every drawing in my collection is invisibly marked. I shall send it back to you.'

'This is persecution!' I was angry now.

'No. It's homage. When I saw you last night I thought — that girl is everything I want.'

'What rubbish! You don't know anything about me.'

'Oh, Elfrida! That's unworthy of you. I'm not talking about whether you like to eat fish rather than meat, or whether you prefer sea-bathing to yachting. I saw what you were in essence the minute I looked at you. Have dinner with me. I promise you have nothing to be afraid of. You can meet me at the restaurant — we'll go somewhere bright and noisy if you feel safer. Let's say the St James Hotel at eight o'clock. I shan't lay a finger on you without your permission. If you wish you can give me back the drawing and I promise I shall make no further effort to persuade you to accept it.'

'This is absurd — '

'Please!'

'Oh! All right!' I regretted the words the moment I said them but he had rung off.

That was how the affair began. I was determined it was never going to be that, but of course this was before I had felt the force of Alex's inflexible will.

All this I remembered in the sitting room of Drop Cottage. I groaned and put my head in my hands. 'I don't know if this is something that can ever be got over by either of us,' was all I said. Guy Gilderoy continued to stroke my arm and look at me with solemn eyes. For a fraction of a second I thought I saw a flash of amusement. But the light was too inconstant to be sure.

'Well, it's obvious you're still fond of the poor devil,' said Guy. 'What on earth did he do to make you ditch him at the last minute? It must have been pretty bad. A riotous stag night when he made love to the girl in the cake, naked but for a tarboosh? No, it must be something far worse than that.'

'He hasn't done anything. Most people would say his behaviour has been exemplary.'

'Then he's bad-tempered and miserly.'

'He never loses his temper and he's been more than generous.'

'He looks like Quasimodo and is a terrible yawn?'

'He's generally considered to be handsome and fascinating.'

'Then you, my dear Freddie, are beautifully and completely mad.'

'I was afraid that was it.'

I found my bag and searched the contents. 'What it had to do with, if anything other than my insanity, is this.' I put on the table a small brass pixie, the kind sold cheaply in gift shops across the length and breadth of Cornwall. Guy picked it up. Its shining cheeks bulged with a fatuous grin and its eyes were screwed up in a deranged squint.

'My God, it's perfectly hideous!'

'Yes. But, for what it represents, it's probably the most precious thing I own.'

5

'This seems a long way for a short cut.' I looked through the mud-smeared windows of the Land Rover as we bumped over ruts on a single-track path through dense forest. 'I thought it was only fifteen miles from Pudwell to Tarchester. And calling that a passing place is optimistic to the point of fatuity. Possibly two slim cyclists might be able to squeeze by.'

As though to prove my point an ancient tractor, brown with rust, loomed up from between the trees and forced the Land Rover up on to the bank at a steep angle. I slid down the front seat to rest hip to hip with Guy. Chloë removed her chin from my shoulder where it had lain lovingly since the start of the journey, and thrust her head through the window.

'All right, Chloë! That's enough! Be quiet now!' Chloë continued to growl, displaying black gums and enormous yellow teeth. 'Hello, Plumrose. Haven't seen you in an age. How are you?' In order to make himself heard above the combined roar of the engines Guy turned off the ignition. My spirits, already low, sank further.

''Morning, Maister Guy.' Plumrose tugged at something checked and greasy on his head. 'Well now, as it happens I've bin under the doctor again with me chest.' He tapped his sternum proudly. 'Ain't bin right since Michaelmas. I was laid up then, good and proper, and couldn't do the winter sowing. Cough! I couldn't keep me teeth in!'

There was more of this with much detail as to colour and quantity of sputum. I lost interest pretty quickly but I had to hand it to Guy: he showed a tender absorption that would not have disgraced a thoracic surgeon, and

50

when every scrap of information had been gleaned as to Plumrose's sucking in and blowing out he passed rapidly on to Mrs Plumrose's 'trouble' and Master Billy's glue ear. Plumrose seemed to have a sickly family, all teetering on the brink of invalidity. I sat as upright as I could and assumed an expression of polite concern but really I wanted to clutch my head and groan.

It had taken us the best part of two hours to make an inventory of the contents of the cottage. This was mostly my fault because so many of the things had been worth examination, particularly the books and china. There was a little French clock I had lost my heart to. The base was marble surmounted by ormolu figures of entwined lovers on one side of the face and Cupid on the other. Guy wound it up. As it struck the hour Cupid moved his arm and beat time with a gilded arrow. Above it hung a painting of sheep on a hillside which I was almost certain was by Thomas Sidney Cooper. When Guy had opened what seemed to be an unpromising cupboard to reveal a narrow flight of stairs I felt ridiculously excited. At the top was a room with sloping walls and three dormer windows. A painted iron bedstead stood in the middle of the floor beneath a white muslin canopy, infested with spider's nests. One pillow bore the dent of a head and the sheets and blankets were thrust back on one side as though someone had risen in haste. The pretty little walnut chest of drawers and the wardrobe were empty. On the back of the door was a nightdress of the most captivating rose-coloured silk with broad bands of lace at the bust and hem, presumably overlooked by whoever had packed Viola's godmother's clothes for her. A hollow-stemmed champagne glass with brown sediment inside stood on the bedside table beside an open copy of Dante Gabriel Rossetti's poems. To the last, it seemed, she had kept her spirit of enlightened

51

discrimination, even if she had not been able to remember what day of the week it was.

Guy had been helpful beyond the bounds of duty in the making of the list, sorting through the cooking implements in the kitchen drawers, investigating a dark lean-to shed filled with garden tools and trying to identify painter's signatures and porcelain marks. When we had finished I repacked my toothbrush and comb which was all I had felt it absolutely essential to make use of, and asked Guy if he would be kind enough to take me to Porsley Heath station.

'I will, of course, if that's what you want, but I think you'll find it an uncomfortable place to wait until nine thirty tomorrow morning.' His face was grave but this time it was obvious he was laughing at me.

'What? You can't mean that there isn't another train until then. I don't believe it!'

'There are plenty of trains but only if you want to go to Bournemouth or Exeter. If you want to go to London,' he looked at his watch, 'the train's just gone. It's a scandal, I know. We're always writing to our MP to get him to do something about it, but so far, no luck.'

'Oh, but that's ridiculous! Why didn't you tell me?'

'Sorry. Forgot the time. I was rather enjoying myself, as a matter of fact. Your expression when you're concentrating is fascinating. Two little lines here,' he pointed to my forehead, 'crossing and uncrossing as you frown. And your lips pout so deliciously that it was all I could do not to kiss them.'

I sighed. 'Do you mean to say I've got to catch the bus to Tarchester? I suppose there is a bus?'

'I'll drive you to Tarchester myself, if you're so set on going.'

'Would you? I'd be so grateful.'

'That was what I was hoping.'

'Isn't that the way to Tarchester?' I said a few minutes later, as the Land Rover swung abruptly left on to the

52

forest track, just as I saw a clearly marked signpost indicating straight ahead.

'That's the dull way for unimaginative, timid motorists. Also, this is much quicker. Now do look. Isn't this quite wonderful?'

It was. Although I had been longing for hot baths, hard dry pavements and a landscape unrelieved by anything remotely green, the dark swathes of trees, mostly coniferous, were magnificent. The massive trunks formed a natural undercroft of arches and still shadows, while high above them the topmost branches swayed and tossed like water lashed by a storm. Something small and lithe and bright brown slipped through the half-light beneath the trees.

'Look!' I said, delighted. 'That was a fox, wasn't it?'

When had I last seen a fox? Not since I was a child certainly. I must have been about ten. Uncle Sid and I had been up early, heading for the salt marshes to collect samphire for breakfast, when we saw a fox streaking over the field between two copses. 'That's the old vixen, that is. I'm glad she made it through the winter.' I had asked him how he could be sure which fox it was. Uncle Sid had rubbed his thick fingers over the top of his head which was bristly as he always shaved his head once a week — it saved him the trouble of going to the barber's. 'I don't know 'ow I know. It's the shape of 'er, I suppose. I've seen 'er, it must be five springs now, with 'er babies in that copse. Shall you and I go there later when the cubs are out the ground?'

I would have accepted any proposal that gave me the chance to be with Uncle Sid. I used to think it was a shame that there was a law forbidding uncles and nieces to marry. I knew there was because I had asked my father. Fay had overheard me. When she was angry her eyes narrowed and stretched almost to her ears, and her eyebrows, which were drawn on every morning after breakfast, appeared to disintegrate into a row of black dots. 'What did I tell you, Charles? He's a thoroughly bad influence on the child.'

He isn't, he isn't, he isn't, I had repeated under my breath but I hadn't dared to stand up for Uncle Sid. I knew I was no match for Fay. I remembered Evangeline.

'Do you hunt?' Guy looked sideways at me with the expression I was beginning to realise was usual with him. His tawny eyes were solemn but there was a twist to his mouth that was ironical.

'No. I can't even ride.'

'I'll teach you.'

'Have you forgotten? I'm going back to London.'

'So you are.' He smiled.

It was then that we met the tractor. The discussion of ailments went on so long that I shut my eyes and tried to think calming thoughts. This was difficult because every direction my ideas took led on to something painful. I must have dozed a little for I opened my eyes to discover that the tractor had gone and I was alone in the Land Rover. The bonnet was up and soon Guy's head appeared round it.

'It's the roller, I think. It does conk out sometimes. I shouldn't have turned the engine off.'

'Can you mend it?'

'Afraid not. It needs to be taken apart and cleaned. I haven't got a screwdriver.'

'What are we going to do?'

'I'll walk back to the road. I'll be able to hitch a lift from there to the garage. You can have Chloë for company. She'll protect you.'

'What from?' I looked around, a little alarmed. There was nothing to be seen but tree trunks and darkness. I heard a bird screech far off. 'I'll come with you.'

'I'll be much quicker on my own. Really, I won't be long. I'll lock you in if you like.'

I pulled my coat around my knees for it was cold with

the engine off. I was glad when Chloë clambered into the front seat and pressed herself against me. I closed my eyes again. In a few hours I would be back in London. Where should I go that Alex would not think of looking for me? The second after I thought this I was horrified. Had I become such a sneaking coward that I was afraid of him? And the answer came directly. Yes, I was. I told myself not to be stupid. He had hit me once under the most extreme provocation. As far as I knew he did not make a practice of it. It was not violence of the physical kind I feared but something more insidious. And for me, much more destructive.

6

The first time I had dinner with Alex, the day he sent me the Gainsborough drawing, I arrived at the St James Hotel feeling uneasy and resentful. I had found his number in the directory and several times that afternoon I had let the telephone ring more than a dozen times before replacing the receiver. Well, I need not go. His behaviour was bullying of the most arrogant kind. It would do him good to be humiliated. But whenever I looked at the drawing, which I did at least every five minutes, my resolve to disappoint its owner faltered. Its perfect beauty made pride seem petty. He had wanted to give me pleasure and he had certainly done so. Perhaps I owed him something for that.

I spent some time deciding what to wear. Nothing too low-cut or revealing. He was probably a sexual psychopath, firing off several Gainsborough drawings a week at girls who happened to catch his eye. In the end I chose a straight, low-waisted dress of grey silk shot with silver threads, which was elegant and suitable for the uncertain temperatures of late September. With it I wore emerald earrings inherited from a great-aunt. Such is the power of vanity that, knowing myself to be admired, I was unable to resist making efforts to look my best. Feeling ashamed made me angrier. But each time I admired the drawing, which was becoming dearer to me at every moment, I knew I must return it without delay.

He was standing in the foyer when I came through the revolving doors.

'Hello. The table's ready. Do you mind going in straight away?'

I felt unreasonably annoyed that he didn't seem either

surprised or particularly pleased to see me. The dining room was pretty and there was a sustained hum of conversation. Candlelight and chafing dishes added a sparkle to diamond necklaces and expensive scent mingled with the odours of beef and salmon. The establishment at play were convivial and expansive. I walked among the diners, following the waiter to our table, and wondered what I had been fussing about. We sat down at a table by the window. I put the envelope on the table between us. A waiter hovered.

'Champagne?' Alex didn't look at me.

'Yes. Thank you.'

He gave the order and continued to look about the room, at the other guests, at the contents of the trolley being wheeled past us, at the door to see who had just come in, even at the ceiling, presumably to admire the plasterwork. Then he turned his attention to the menu. 'What will you have?' he asked, still directing his eyes at the entrées.

I had been so distracted by conflicting emotions of curiosity and pique that I had not looked at the menu. 'I'll have *gnocchi à la Romana* and *côte de porc aux pruneaux*.' I chose the first item of each section.

Alex gave my order to the waiter and chose soup and turbot for himself. Then he inspected the wine list. He was older than most of the men I knew, perhaps forty or forty-five. I noticed that his nose turned down a little and that his eyebrows were finely arched like a woman's. His lashes were long and there were two vertical lines beside his mouth, which gave him a look of arrogance or perhaps even malice. His hair was glossy and grew a long way down his neck. His upper lip and chin, though close-shaven, were dark with impending growth. There was just the suggestion of the double chin to come. His clothes were impossible to fault, a well-cut suit, striped shirt and silk tie, no jewellery but discreet gold cufflinks. He gave his order to the wine waiter.

'What do you think?' he said, suddenly turning his eyes to my face. They were the dominant feature, the colour of expensive chocolate, the iris and pupil melting into one another. The skin around them was a shade darker than the rest of his face, which gave him a look that was not quite English. He told me, weeks later, that one of his ancestors had been a mulatto. In her youth she had been sentenced to deportation for witchcraft — specifically obeah — by Alex's great-great-great-grandfather, a magistrate and plantation-owner in St Lucia. But before the punishment could be carried out her black eyes had cast a spell over him. Her genes popped up with wild unpredictability. Most of Alex's relations were gingery with pale blue eyes. But one of his uncles had been as black as tar.

'Think about what?'

Alex smiled. 'You've been looking at me ever since we came in. I thought I'd better give you the opportunity for a thorough examination.'

'It isn't surprising that I'm curious about a man who wants to have dinner with someone he's never met.' I attempted to carry it off with a laugh.

'No, I'm not surprised. But you haven't answered my question. What do you think of me?'

'I don't know what I'm expected to divine from a quick look at your face.'

'Don't be disingenuous. It's your business to decipher people's natures from their faces, isn't it?'

I was disconcerted by this evidence of inside knowledge.

'How do you know so much about me?'

'I only know what anyone might know if they chose to be diligent. I followed you home after the opera last night.'

'I didn't see you.'

'Of course not. I waited in the taxi until you'd gone in.'

'Was that quite . . . honourable? I don't particularly like the feeling of being spied on.'

'It certainly wasn't dishonourable. And how else was I to find out who you were?'

'Well, how did you?

'There are three bells by your front door. I thought it unlikely you were Prof. A. J. Halliwell or Mr and Mrs Snip-Montague. Miss Elfrida Swann seemed most probable. Elfrida Swann. Yes, it becomes you. The windows of each floor were lit, obviously as a deterrent to burglars. I wanted to know which was yours. I went down to look into the basement. The camel dressing-gown thrown over a chair, the meerschaum on the table, the papers cluttering every surface convinced me that this could not be the abode of Miss Elfrida Swann. I forgot to mention that there were the remains of a processed meat pie and an empty tin of peas on the draining-board next to the window. All the evidence suggested that the owner of the basement flat was a typical academic with the usual indifference to comfort and beauty, by name Professor A. J. Halliwell.'

'Quite right.' I was amused by the light of triumph in his eyes.

The arrival of the champagne gave me another chance for a covert examination of my host. His ears were small and fine, and his hands, slender and pale, were well manicured. His lips were full and his teeth good.

Alex held his glass of champagne towards the light to examine the colour. 'I still had to decide whether you lived on the ground floor or the first floor. While I was standing in the basement area, wondering how to continue in my role of sleuth, I had a stroke of luck. A man ran up the steps to the front door above and let himself in with a key. I came up to pavement level and

59

crossed the road. Whoever had drawn the curtains had been in a hurry and there was a gap, allowing me a good view of the man who stood before a table in the window, pouring himself a drink. A few minutes later a car drove up. The street lamp revealed a girl with a red dress and black hair. She also let herself in with a key. Then she appeared in the window next to the man and I saw them kiss passionately. He unzipped her dress. I could not imagine this taking place in your drawing room in front of you. I felt a little like a voyeur but it was interesting. There was something about the intensity of that kiss which disposed of the idea that this was Mrs Snip-Montague. The conclusion I drew was that Mr Snip-Montague was making hay in the absence of his wife.'

'Actually the Snip-Montagues have been in Kenya for the last three months. I expect it was Gina, the au pair, and her latest boyfriend.'

The annoyance on Alex Moncrieff's face at making a wrong guess made me want to giggle. I had eaten nothing since a small salad at lunchtime and I was drinking too fast.

'Ah, well, I admit that didn't occur to me. By this time I was convinced that you lived on the first floor. I decided to wait for the chance of a glimpse of you. I stood in a doorway where a cat befriended me and played with my shoelaces. I felt like Harry Lime. Despite an inconvenient shower of rain I was rather enjoying myself. Then my patience was rewarded. You came to the window, the one with the balcony. I was struck by a sudden thought. Such a large window, perhaps a studio? Could it be that Elfrida Swann is an artist? You disappeared for a moment and then returned with a paintbrush in your hand. *Probatum est.*'

'I remember. I decided to work a little more on the hands before going to bed. I keep my paintbrushes on a table by the window.' I was entertained despite myself.

'But how did you discover that I paint portraits?'

'While I was drying out at home I telephoned an art-dealer friend. He rang this morning with the information that there was an Elfrida Swann in the Society of Portrait Painters' yearbook. He had a list of some of your former clients. It was easy from then on. I telephoned one whom I happened to know. The picture emerged of a girl who was very much in control of herself and her life, independent, accomplished and successful. It was exactly what I guessed, seeing you last night.'

I sipped at my glass reflectively. My gnocchi arrived at that moment, a large plateful of fat, creamy crescents baked beneath a layer of cheese. It looked delicious but the quantity was daunting.

'Mm. I see. I suppose that's how it might appear to an outsider.'

'Ah. So you're not quite contented?'

'Well, is anybody, ever?'

'Probably not, if they're honest with themselves. I'm not sure it would even be desirable. But what's the poison in your cup?'

'It's the perennial problem with commissioned portraits. You have to make them acceptable to the sitter.' I shrugged. Alex leaned back in his chair, waiting for me to go on. It's a technique I always fall for. Years of social training compel me to fill the conversational gap. 'Most people have an entirely mistaken idea of how they look. I didn't mind at first. I was so keen to get started, to make a living for myself. I happily prettified large noses and straightened crooked mouths. But much more difficult is the beautifying of people's natures. I'm starting to feel that I've forgotten how to look beneath the surface, that I'm painting to a formula.'

'This compulsion to be financially independent interests me. I know your father slightly. The last time we met was at a party for the outgoing French

61

ambassador. Fay was there. She asked me to dinner. Of course I had not seen you then or I should certainly have accepted.'

'Flattering of you but in fact I rarely go there.'

'That I discovered from a friend who knows Fay well. She's not an ideal stepmother — I thought her predatory.'

There was always the temptation when people were rude about Fay to relieve the frustrations of so many years by joining in the denunciation. But I knew from experience that the relief was short-lived and afterwards I felt ashamed.

'What sort of painting do you really want to do?' Alex asked, passing over my silence without comment.

'I honestly don't know. I haven't had the chance to find out. I'd like to paint something immense and remote instead of a person and a chair in a dull room. I try to persuade sitters to let me put in a landscape background but they hardly ever want to pay for anything not directly related to themselves. Ordering a portrait is akin to ordering a suit these days.'

'Perhaps they'd prefer the sort of symbolism that explores the spiritual nature of the subject. The sort of things the early painters went in for — dogs for marital fidelity, pearls and parrots for chastity, and so forth. It's a pity that the iconography of classical and religious themes has become meaningless to everyone except art historians. You know that self-portrait by Poussin in the Louvre?'

'With the woman on the left wearing a diadem with a single eye in it? Oh, yes, I have my own theory about the significance of that.'

I talked on, forgetting about being discouraging and distant. Alex was extremely knowledgeable but a good listener as well and tenacious in pursuit of meanings and definitions. He returned to the subject of my own dissatisfaction with my work. 'Really my clients want

62

something to blend with the curtains and carpets. Honestly I feel I've come pretty close to being a decorator,' I said, gloomily. 'Not that there's anything wrong with that if it's what you intend to be. But I had such ambitions to say something in paint about the way I saw things. Probably that's just vanity. I don't suppose it matters tuppence whether I do or not.'

'Not to the world. But it will matter very much to you. You must not join the multitude of the disappointed. Why not ask your father to support you for a year in order to give yourself time to think?'

'I'd rather set to with a roller and emulsion than ask him for money. Besides I'm twenty-eight. That's much too old to return to the nest.'

'I suppose Fay is the impossibility.'

Alex was right, of course. She bitterly resented anything that my father gave me and, though he had long ago abandoned any idea of standing up for me, I hated to see him the victim of her sulks and rages. Most of the time when I thought of my father it was with an exasperation that was not very far from contempt but there were moments when a fleeting expression of sorrow on his still handsome face penetrated the armour of indifference that I had carefully constructed during my adolescence. Then the old love that I had felt for him as a child flared up so powerfully that I was desolated.

'What's the matter?' Alex asked.

'Nothing.' I was aware that I had been drinking and not eating. The gnocchi, delicious though they were, seemed to have multiplied on my plate. I couldn't possibly eat them. I felt a rush of the familiar panic and nausea, a churning of my stomach, a swimming sensation in my brain. Alex summoned the waiter.

'Take this away and bring the menu.' He turned to me. 'You'd better change your order. The pork will be very rich and you don't seem hungry.'

63

Gratitude overcame any annoyance I might have felt at being treated like a child. 'Thank you. It was so silly of me — you're quite right. I wasn't thinking — '

'No. You were looking at me, trying to decide if I was going to bite.'

'I feel like a schoolgirl taken to a grown-up restaurant for the first time.' I laughed.

'What were you like as a schoolgirl, I wonder? Were you captain of games and did all the little girls have a crush on you? Or did you get expelled for smoking and leading the others astray?'

'I was rather fat, with spectacles. And covered with freckles.'

'I like the idea of that. Not the fatness perhaps, but the freckles. I see a few now.' Alex looked at my arms which were bare from the elbow. Instinctively I hid them beneath the tablecloth. I always took great care to avoid strong sunlight but the faintest pencil beam brought them out. I hated them. That first terrible year at school the other girls had called me Speckly Swann.

'I can assure you I looked a figure of fun. Also I was sick a lot from nerves.'

Alex smiled. 'If you're trying to put me off, I can assure you, you won't succeed.' He stopped smiling suddenly and looked at me so intently that my former unease returned. 'It wasn't a happy childhood, was it?' I pitied his victims in the dock. He missed nothing. 'Tell me what was so awful about this school.'

'You can't really be interested. It was exactly like everyone else's experience of boarding-school. Miserable to begin with but gradually improving as I went up the school. Horrible food, chilblains in winter, boring lessons, just the same torments you went through, I'm sure.'

'You're quite wrong. I was a day boy at St Paul's. I went home every night to the tender care of my mama. At the age of seventeen I spent all my free time in a flat in Albemarle Street, that belonged to my first mistress. Belinda was a woman of twenty-eight, just the same age as you are now. A fashion model. Utterly unlike you. Not very bright, nor very kind. I had six glorious months with her. She broke my heart by throwing me over for a handsome photographer.'

'Were you dreadfully sad?'

'Only for a few weeks, until I began an affair with a lovely girl who trimmed poodles for a living. Not intelligent but sweet and with the face of a madonna. This time *I* did the chucking. I'd learned a valuable lesson. I met Belinda again not long ago. Thrice divorced. And much knocked about by her travails. She wants me to defend her in a suit for obtaining money under false pretences — gratis naturally, for the sake of the good old days.'

'And will you?'

'That would be telling.' Alex smiled.

'I don't see why I should unbosom myself if you're going to be secretive.'

'You aren't particularly interested in me. Yet. That's why.'

I could not think of an answer. I would rather have had my tongue cut out and tossed in butter in a chafing dish than admit that I was more interested in him than I could have dreamed possible. Alex's turbot and my grilled sole were brought and we drank a good white Burgundy and shared braised chicory and a green salad between us. Alex was persistent in asking me about my childhood. His questions stirred memories that I had left buried a long time.

I was twelve years old, standing in the hall, waiting for the taxi that was to take me to the station to join the school train for my first term at St Catherine's. My heart was banging with fright as I went through the clothing list to make sure that everything down to my Mason Pearson hairbrush was marked clearly with my name and the initials of my house. My trunk had been sent on ahead but I had a red suitcase with me for overnight things. In this, hidden in the elastic pocket on the lid was Evangeline's leg. My father had come home unexpectedly, before his usual hour.

'Ah, good. I was hoping I'd catch you. Everything all right, old thing?' He only called me old thing when Fay was not in earshot.

'Yes. All right,' I had tried to look as though it was, though I was praying hard to be killed in a traffic accident before we reached Victoria.

'That's my girl. I'll miss you, you know.'

I knew it wasn't true, and he had the grace to look ashamed as he said it. For weeks Fay had been telling all her friends that I was to go in September and each time she said it she widened her eyes and inhaled deeply as though she could scarcely endure the wait. On the day of my departure Mrs Pope, the housekeeper, had been told to lay the table for two in the library with champagne and *foie gras* and veal cutlets, all Fay's favourite things.

'That'll be to cheer your dad up,' Mrs Pope had said kindly, when I saw her arranging the flowers for the intimate little supper. We both knew it wasn't.

'Don't forget to write,' my father had said. 'Let me see' — he got out his diary — 'when's the first visiting day?'

'It's October the third. But you and Fay are going to the Chattertons' for the weekend.'

'That's rather mismanaged, isn't it? Perhaps there's been a muddle as to dates.'

'I heard her change it to then on the telephone.' I looked at him, begging with my eyes that he should put his foot down and refuse to go away for my first exeat. I wanted it so badly that I tasted again the chicken sandwiches I had been made to eat at lunchtime. I swallowed so as not to be sick. My father patted me on

66

the shoulder. 'Well, we can't always have what we want.' I felt tears as well as the sandwiches begin to rise. 'Now, now. Where's my brave girl?' He looked around hurriedly. 'I popped into Underwood's on my way home.' Underwood's was Fay's jeweller. 'I got this for you.' It was a wristwatch, very pretty with an oval face and a strap of blue snakeskin. 'Let's see how it looks.' He fastened it to my wrist. It was my first piece of grown-up jewellery. As I saw it encircling my chubby freckled arm my heart lifted and I felt for a moment that I might just be capable of this awful thing that was required of me — to leave my father and Mrs Pope and next door's cat and go away to live among hundreds of strangers. I had been once before to the school to be shown round. It was dark and bare and ugly and smelt everywhere of disinfectant and rubberised gym mats, even in the dormitories.

Fay came out of the drawing room. She look annoyed when she saw my father. 'You didn't tell me you'd be home early. Where's that taxi? What's that on your arm, Elfrida?' I had pulled down the sleeve of my grey school coat but not quite quickly enough. 'Show me!' I looked beseechingly at my father.

'It's a trinket I picked up for her. Nothing of value.'

Fay took hold of my hand and pulled back my sleeve. 'Really, Charles, what a fool you are! It'll get broken at once. I wouldn't be surprised if they didn't confiscate it. It's much too good for school. Give it to me. You can have it in the holidays.'

Fay held out her hand. I bit it. As I watched the drops of blood ooze on her knuckles my spirits soared. Fay screamed and slapped my face so hard that my spectacles flew across the room and one of the lenses smashed. I didn't care. The future was so frightful with gloom and misery that I had nothing to lose. I was going away for six weeks and Fay would be powerless to take revenge. Mrs Pope came running to see what was

67

the matter and the doorbell rang at the same time. My father was incoherent with shock and disgust. Mrs Pope bundled me out to the cab. 'Goodbye, Freddie. I know you didn't mean to do it. Bless you, my lamb!'

'I did, Mrs Pope.' I stuck my head out of the window. 'I wish I'd bitten her harder. But I've got the watch. See?'

'Very nice, dear. Off you go and be a good girl. Oh dear. There'll be trouble for sure about this. I wouldn't be in the master's shoes.' Then she giggled. 'She had it coming to her.' Her eyes grew wet. 'Give old Pope a kiss now, will you?'

I threw my arm about her neck and kissed her heartily on the cheek. Then I was driven away. At the station I wandered about forlornly with my case, perspiring beneath the weight of my Harris tweed coat as the day was exceptionally warm. Then I saw a group of girls dressed like me but without coats. They carried wooden poles with little nets on. I found out later that they were lacrosse sticks. They were talking to each other and screaming with laughter, linking arms and pretending to push each other over. They looked utterly terrifying. I stood on the periphery of the group until a frowning woman with a whistle round her neck came and asked my name. The other girls addressed her as Miss Teal.

'Be quiet, girls! Hilary, put your hat on properly. Keep your voice *down*, Jeanette. Remember, you are the school's ambassadors!'

I was put into the charge of a tall girl with long brown plaits called Lydia Warrington-Smith. She looked at me with undisguised disdain. I expect I was a ridiculous sight, with a lens missing from my spectacles and my face red and running with sweat from heat and fright. Also I was wearing my grey felt hat with the brim turned up all round, like a bowler hat, instead of smartly turned down at the front.

'You'd better sit there,' said Lydia, when we got on the train, pointing to a corner seat. 'You can put your coat on the rack. You ought to have sent it in your trunk. Everyone else does.' She said not another word to me until we reached Reigate. I rested my right hand on my watch and stroked it whenever I thought I was going to be sick. The girls shouted at the tops of their voices, vying with each other about the outrageous things they had done during the summer holidays. I listened in bafflement, unable to grasp the point of most of the stories.

I was nearly left behind in the screaming rush for the school bus. The door was already shut by the time I got there and Miss Teal seemed to think that I had been deliberately slow to irritate her. As we drove in through the school gates there was a universal chorus of groans that changed to cries of repugnance as I was sick all over my skirt and shoes.

'Bad luck, Lydia,' I heard one girl say, as I was led out of the bus in ignominy to have the vomit scraped off me with a piece of paper by a grimly silent Miss Teal.

'I would have to get the piggy-looking sicky one, wouldn't I?' Lydia replied.

I went through the next hour in a haze of sour-smelling misery, putting my clothes on my bed for inventory check, making my bed then having to remake it because I had not known about hospital corners. Miss Teal appeared in the dormitory.

'Elfrida Swann to see Miss Bessamy at once.'

Lydia took me to the door of the headmistress's study. 'Probably she's going to blow you up for something,' were her last words of comfort.

Miss Bessamy was so tall that I had to crane my neck to look at her. Beneath an improbably wooden-looking crest of dyed blue waves her face was broad and flat with a mannish jaw.

'Your mother has telephoned me, Elfrida. She is very

69

angry and I must say I am shocked. Shocked! Never let it be said that the staff at St Catherine's cannot rise to any eventuality. But biting! Never in the history of the school has there been such an abomination.' I wondered what an abomination was exactly. Nothing to do with bombs, I was nearly sure. 'Give it to me.' She held out her hand. For a wild moment I thought she meant that I was to bite it but in the next second common sense reasserted itself and I undid the watch with shaking fingers. 'Hm! Thoroughly unsuitable for a young girl!' A flash of pain on my father's behalf made me long to protest but Miss Bessamy swept up a finger and pointed to the door. I slunk out and stood alone, sweating and trembling in the dark corridor. Luckily there was a large brass vase nearby in which I got rid of the last remains of the chicken sandwiches.

I described this episode briefly to Alex as he seemed so extraordinarily interested in these dull schoolroom tales.

'Don't you see? The things you remember are important to you.'

'They're just boring little anecdotes.'

'Then why have those memories persisted? Because those experiences bit deep. They tell me about you.' He laughed and then his expression grew softer. 'Poor little girl that you once were. If only you had known then how well things were going to turn out.'

I smiled in a disclaiming sort of way. But the combination of a great deal of champagne and the pleasurable indulgence of talking about oneself to an interested audience seized me and swept me away with a rush of optimism. I had a sudden conviction that he was right.

7

'Wake up, Freddie!' Someone was shaking me gently by the shoulder. I was surprised to find myself lying across the front seat of the Land Rover. Chloë sat up in the foot-well and pressed a friendly snout to my nose. 'What a pair of babes in the wood.' Guy was looking in through the open door. 'Lucky the birds haven't covered you both with leaves.'

'I would have been very grateful,' I dragged myself upright. My muscles felt stiff and intractable. 'I've never been so cold in my life. What time is it?'

'Lunchtime.' He climbed in beside me. 'I'm famished. We mustn't keep Mrs Deacon waiting.'

'Mrs Deacon?'

An unfamiliar, moon-shaped, beetroot-coloured face with exuberant side whiskers appeared at the window. 'That's the missus,' said its owner, in a strong accent, presumably Dorset. 'How do, Miss Swann? She'll be tickled pink to have a female to crack on with. She's allus complaining about having too much o' the menfolk. The rope's good and tight, Maister Guy. Ready when you are.' He got into the cab of the lorry that was parked in front of us.

I looked beseechingly at Guy. 'What about my train?'

'Ned — that's Deacon's boy — is going to try and get the Land Rover started after lunch.'

Guy signalled to Mr Deacon that he was ready. A noxious cloud of exhaust came in through the open window followed by fragments of mud thrown up by spinning wheels. With a jerk that practically dislocated my neck we were moving. It seemed a long way to the Deacon establishment and most of it was across unmade roads. I felt as though the contents of my stomach had been whipped to a fine froth.

The sight of the farmhouse temporarily restored me. It was a low building, as picturesque as a painting on a toffee tin, with tall chimneys and a sagging, stone-tiled roof. The red-brick walls were ivy-clad, obscuring small leaded windows. A few chickens and a large pig strolled up and down before the front door. Inside, it was dark with beams and a flagged floor, on which stood a stack of muddy gum-boots and jackets.

Mr Deacon instructed us to throw our coats on to the pile. I took off my beautiful alpaca reluctantly for the flags were glistening with damp. As soon as I arranged it carefully on the driest corner of the heap, a white cat leaped on to it and began to knead it enthusiastically with paws that were far from clean. Mrs Deacon turned from the kitchen sink to greet us, drying her hands on an apron that looked decidedly grubby. She had the same ample build and florid complexion as her husband but without the side whiskers. She wore a flowered overall that crossed over in the front and her hair was tied up in a duster. Her smile was kind and I liked her at once.

'Come in, Miss Swann, and welcome. Ye must be starved near to death, waiting in the cold all that time.' She ignored my protestations that I wasn't hungry. Five men were sitting round a large table. They stared at me and sniggered, scratching their armpits and beneath their caps, throughout Mrs Deacon's introduction. Their names were Bill, Bob, Ned, Ted and Jed. I thought I might remember which one was Jed as his left eye rolled in towards his nose, exposing a disconcerting amount of bloodshot white. The one who had a cold and no handkerchief, possibly Ted, coughed fruitfully and went over to the sink to spit out the result. 'I've got the very thing as'll put 'ee to rights, Miss Swann.' Mrs Deacon brought a large black bottle to the table. 'Ye'll have some of me best champagne, now?'

'Thank you. And please call me Freddie.' I cheered up a little. Farming must be a prosperous business in Dorset. I looked in wonder at the smoke-blackened ceiling and dingy walls, that were hung with ancient calendars, vicious-looking traps and tools, hub-caps from a car and a framed photograph of Doris Day, whose red lipstick was the only bright colour in the room. A gloomy fire blew choking smoke over the table. There were several large muddy dogs. One drew back and growled as I tried to pat its head.

''Tis last year's. There never were such a summer for elder-blossom. This'll be a first tasting, like.' She filled a large pewter tankard to the brim. 'Drink up!'

I took a cautious sip and sneezed as the bubbles surged through my sinuses. Though nothing like the stuff made from grapes, the elderflower champagne had a fresh sweetness that was enjoyable. 'Drink up and have another,' urged Mrs Deacon, when I praised it.

'Is it very alcoholic?'

'It's the milk of the hedgerows,' said Guy encouragingly. 'Won't do you a bit of harm, will it, Mrs Deacon?'

'Harm? Tchah! Round here they gives it to babies when they've trouble teething. Sit 'ee down now, and have some soup.' I sat where I was told, to the left of Mr Deacon. I was given a bowl of something that looked like brown gravy, on which floated golden coins of grease.

'It looks — delicious. What is it?'

'Lamb's tail soup. Yer in luck. We only gets it once a year. John docks their tails when they're five weeks.'

'You should hear them holler!' Mr Deacon whipped out a wicked-looking knife and held it to my throat. 'Hand the bread.'

I gave him the breadboard. He sawed a slice from the loaf and stabbed at it savagely, as though it were alive and might get away. I took a mouthful of soup, not breathing through my nose and taking large gulps of elderflower champagne. I began to feel sick.

I tried to distract myself by pretending an interest in the conversation but it was not one to which I could make any useful contribution. Bill thought they should castrate one of the rams and let him fatten a bit whereas Ted was of the opinion that the hapless creature should be sent for slaughter at once.

'We'll castrate 'un. 'S arternoon.' Mr Deacon made a swipe through the air with his knife.

'I'm so sorry, Mrs Deacon.' I put down my spoon.

'I'll have that.' Mr Deacon snatched away my bowl and finished my soup, smacking his lips after each mouthful.

'Now, you'll fancy this I'm sure.' Mrs Deacon put before me a pyramid of something grey and watery. I knew better, now, than to ask what it was. The texture was odd, a combination of stringy and gelatinous, and it had a strong, unpleasant smell.

'What is this?' Guy stared with suspicion at the contents of his plate. 'I just ate something that tasted like Cleopatra's suspender belt. Elastic that's lost some of its zing over the years.'

Mr Deacon thought this very funny and laughed at length, displaying a mouthful of blackened teeth and half-chewed food.

'Ye've got a way wi' words, Maister Guy.' Mrs Deacon laughed, too, but not quite so heartily. I saw that Guy was as a prince among his people, and that he was accustomed to behaving and speaking just as it occurred to him. ''Tis a sheep's head. 'Tis a delicacy wi' us. I hope 'tis to yer liking, Miss Swann?'

As I looked at her kind, anxious face I could not bring myself to disappoint her. 'Delicious,' I murmured.

'That's good. I'll have to let 'ee have the receipt. It's quite easy though it takes time. Ye hev to soak the head overnight in salt water to get the mucus out o' mouth

74

and nostrils. I takes out the eyes but I leaves on the ears. Then ye boils it for six hours. Deacon has the brains for his supper, floured and fried until they're good and brown.'

'And what the hell's this?' asked Guy, holding up something on the prongs of his fork.

'Dang me if it ent a ram's pizzle,' said Bob and everyone screeched with laughter.

I thought wistfully of trains. I felt terribly tired and still rather cold. The fire had died to a sullen glow. I was surprised to see inside the inglenook, amid the puffs of reeking smoke, a hand holding a pipe. As the smoke eddied I perceived the silhouette of a bearded figure raising the pipe to its lips.

'That's Gran,' said Mrs Deacon, seeing the direction of my glance. 'Don't 'ee take no notice of her. She can't see nor hear nothing.'

'I hope 'ee baint a picky eater,' said Mr Deacon gesturing in my direction with his knife. 'Ye've no more flesh on ye than a skinny hen. Fit for nobbut the stock-pot. A thin woman makes a hard bed to lie on, ha, ha, ha!'

Bill and co. became convulsed with mirth. Guy, who was sitting opposite me, caught my eye and smiled.

'Aye, we all know what Maister Guy's thinking, don't we, lads.' Mr Deacon was warming to his role as jester. 'It's one he'd like to try for size, ha, ha ha!'

'Now, John, yer embarrassing the young lady,' protested Mrs Deacon. 'She won't be used to our country ways.'

'Ye baint shy now a bit, are ye?' Mr Deacon paused in the motion of shoving a tablespoon loaded with food into his mouth to look at me. I shook my head mendaciously. The spoon went in but Mr Deacon continued to talk. 'Ye baint eating! Ye'll not get better meat 'n this.' A dribble of gravy ran down his chin. ''Tis all our own stock. See that ham?' I raised my eyes to a solitary leg that hung from the ceiling and spun slowly in the draught among the cobwebs. 'She were a most intelligent pig, brighter than most folk I reckon. Whenever I give her her tea she always give me a little grunt o' thanks before tucking in. And she'd come running to greet me when I come home at the end of the day as though she'd missed me, like. A right tidy pig, was Bessie. When I took the knife to her she had such a look in her eye at the last. Like amazement, it were.'

I put down my knife and fork, my heart swollen on behalf of poor betrayed Bessie.

'Like to come and watch me muck out the cows arter lunch?' Jed said suddenly. It was the first time he had spoken. All the time he had been eating, one eye had been fixed on my face.

'Thank you, that would have been lovely but I'm afraid I really must catch my train. I have to get back to London today.'

I could not understand why this remark was greeted with another burst of laughter. Ted and Jed nudged each other with their elbows and winked and guffawed until their eyes ran.

'Eat up, Missy,' A lump of potato rolled from Mr Deacon's mouth on to the table and from there to the floor. A snapping and growling broke out among the dogs. 'Ye be advised by me. Men like a nice bit o' something to get hold of.'

Bill and co. went off into paroxysms. By this stage I could not manage even a grin.

Mrs Deacon smiled complacently. 'Don't bully the girl, John,' she said, getting up and taking away my plate. I could have fallen on my knees in gratitude. 'Happen ye've got a sweet tooth. See how ye go wi' this.' She placed before me a piece of treacle pudding, the size of a brick, veiled with unctuous golden syrup. I felt perspiration break out on my forehead.

After Mr Deacon had eaten my pudding as well as his, Mrs Deacon and I withdrew to the relative comfort of the inglenook while the men went out to join Ned who was mending the Land Rover. Suddenly I felt extremely drunk. I was disconcerted to find that Gran's gaze was locked on my face. She wore a homogeneous collection of grey woollen garments, with hair and downy chin of the same colour. Her eyes were filmy and her jaws were clamped to the stem of her briar pipe. Mrs Deacon tapped her shoulder. 'Tea, Gran,' she bellowed into the old woman's ear. Granny's fist, as grey as the rest of her, opened suddenly like a grappling hook and closed tightly round the mug. I wondered what it could be like to be cut off from the world, alone with the workings of one's brain. My own brain was of little use to me. The room was inclined to swim, the only fixed point being Gran's staring eyes. I felt very sick.

'I know what ye'd like to look at,' said Mrs Deacon. 'Our holiday snaps've just come back from the shop. We had a lovely week in the caravan at Penzance. Rain! It never stopped the entire week. But I got our Ned's jumper knitted. Arran, it were — real fiddly. Do 'ee knit, Miss Swann?'

'Freddie, please. I'm afraid not.' I took the packet of photographs and tried to focus my eyes. Instead of a caravan site beneath a pall of rain the first snapshot was of Mrs Deacon caught in mid-air in a Isadora Duncan leap, carrying a bunch of leaves in each hand, and without a stitch on. I glanced at her round poppy-coloured face beneath the acid yellow of the duster but she was busy casting on something in maroon wool, still talking. For a few seconds her plump body wavered and broke into two like a bubble of mercury. I rubbed my eyes. The next photograph was of Mr Deacon. The room shifted and I felt oddly light-headed. His head, neck and forearms were a dark red and the rest of his body, hanging in gigantic folds, was gleaming white. All except — His pose was uncompromising, facing the camera, and he appeared to be in a state of arousal that Priapus would have envied.

'O' course, the estate ent nothing like it used to be. There was money a-plenty when I married John. I mind when Maister Vere were born and folks came from Lunnon and danced till daylight. Mrs Gildry, poor soul, she did like a party. Maister Guy'll be the last o' them to hold the land, mark my words.' Mrs Deacon swapped needles and began a new row. 'What I say is, Miss Swann, ye don't want to lose yer heart too quick, if I may make so bold.' She nodded sagely at me. 'Handsome is as handsome does. Ye can't defy the laws o' nature. What evil ye send forth will come back to 'ee tenfold.'

What was she talking about? My head had a troublesome tendency to flop forward. I looked at the rest of the photographs. They were all of Mr and Mrs Deacon by a bonfire in a wood, wearing nothing but the occasional twig or feather. I had always imagined that naturists were of a certain kind: scrawny middle-aged intellectuals with beards, the men, that is, and strong views on diet and pacifism.

'Yer looking a mite queer, Miss Swann. Everything all right?' Some of the photographs slipped from my knee as the room began to spin. Mrs Deacon gave a scream. 'Well! If I didn't give 'ee the wrong photos to look at! Whatever must 'ee think of us? Did you ever see such a pair of boobies?' I tried to think of something tactful to say, on the lines that the naked human body in all its variety was a thing of beauty but I really wasn't up to it. 'Give 'em to me, dear. I shouldn't like Maister Guy to see me in the altogether. Now, these are what I meant to show 'ee.' She handed me another packet. I stared at a photograph of Mr Deacon sleeping open-mouthed beneath a knotted handkerchief in the shade of a caravan and my eyelids began irresistibly to droop. I closed them for a second, listening to the faint clack of knitting needles above the hiss of the fire. 'Of course, boys brought up without a mother are bound to go astray, stands to reason,' I heard Mrs Deacon say, through the mists of descending sleep. I tried to fathom her meaning but my thoughts scattered like birds taking wing.

8

'I do think you might have woken me up!'

The headlights of the Land Rover lit the undergrowth with gleams of silver as we lurched down the rutted drive away from the farm.

'You must blame Mrs Deacon. She's taken quite a motherly interest in you. She thinks you're peaky and sickly from too much faddy food and city fumes. She was determined you were to have your sleep out. I tried to explain that you fall asleep all the time. I suppose you're not narcoleptic?' added Guy, with an innocent air of concern.

'I just haven't slept properly for the last three nights. What am I going to do? Can there really be no more trains from Dorset to London after five o'clock?'

'You townfolk have no idea of the vegetative life we unpolished churls live. Up with the lark and to bed with the dark.'

'But what am I going to do?'

'Come and stay with us. My father will be delighted. He still has an eye for beautiful women.'

'Thank you. But I'd feel very uncomfortable. I hardly know you.'

'What? When we've spent practically the whole day, from breakfast onwards, together? Those parts of it when you've been awake, anyway. You look so sweet when you're asleep. Your lashes flutter like tiny winged creatures and your lips open just the smallest bit. You don't snore, luckily.'

'That's why I can't stay with you. You don't need any encouragement. What do the local girls think of your line in gallantry?'

'I never boast of my conquests.'

'How pleased with yourself you sound! What, never?'

''Hardly ever. And I'm never, never sick at sea,'' Guy sang tunefully.

Uncle Sid adored the Savoy operas and when I used to stay with him we listened to his old scratched recordings repeatedly so I did not immediately conclude that Guy was mad. Not mad, certainly, but was he bad and dangerous to know? He was certainly very attractive. This had less to do with superficialities such as good teeth and prominent cheekbones than with his resilient good temper and disposition to find everything amusing. It was difficult to be depressed when you were with him. I tried to imagine Alex dealing with a broken-down vehicle, mud, rain, the Deacons, and a woman who was exhausted, dishevelled and uncooperative. He would not have thought it funny. I remembered Alex's stricken face and my mood plummeted.

'I'm sorry to spoil your unbroken record of conquests,' I said, a little coldly.

'I haven't asked you to go to bed with me yet. It doesn't count until I do.'

'Oh! Well! This is a ridiculous conversation! Much more to the point, what am I going to do?'

'I thought you might object to taking shelter beneath my roof so when I was trying to track down a mechanic this morning I also telephoned Cissy — that's our housekeeper — and asked her to nip down to Drop Cottage and put clean sheets on the bed. Just in case. So if I really can't persuade you . . . '

I looked at him in surprise. I wouldn't have credited him with so much forethought. 'That was extremely good of you — oh dear, perhaps it would be the best thing.' I considered for a moment. 'I do hope . . . '

'What?' asked Guy when I paused.

'It's silly, I know, but last night I woke several times and I heard someone standing outside in the garden, in the darkness, whistling. It was . . . perhaps frightening is

81

too strong a word — disturbing, anyway.'

'That would be a nightingale. They don't only sing in Berkeley Square, you know.'

'Well, as it happens, that was what I thought at first. It sounded exactly like a nightingale to begin with.'

'As a girl who can't tell a cow from a bull I'm not perfectly convinced you'd know a nightingale from a hat shop.'

'I admit I'm no ornithologist. But when I was a child I used to love that recording of the nightingale singing a duet with the lady cellist. You remember, they used to play it a lot on the Third Programme.'

'A bit intellectual for our family. My father likes Wagner but only because it was favoured by the Führer. My father is devoted to the ideals of the Third Reich, racial purity and all that. When we were children he made us exercise until our poor little muscles squeaked, so that we were healthy minds in healthy bodies. *Mein Kampf* was our book at bedtime.'

'Honestly, I begin to wonder if you're not a dangerous fantasist. Some deep neurosis has turned you into a compulsive liar. It's very sad.'

'Oh, what a black little pot you are! A girl who can neither eat nor sleep — unless in conditions of acute discomfort — and who suspects innocent garden birds of villainous intentions is not at the peak of mental condition, I should say. Neurotic is an understatement.'

I sighed. 'You're right. It's very humiliating. But I'm sure of one thing. It wasn't a bird I heard.'

'What makes you so sure?'

'Nightingales don't sing highlights from *Così Fan Tutte* as far as I'm aware.'

'You're kidding.'

'No, really. Several recognisable bars.'

'Perhaps it was a mynah bird.'

'Now you're the one who's kidding. I tell you, someone was standing outside in the garden at one o'clock in the morning, whistling tunes from Mozart operas.'

'Well, that sounds lunatic but harmless.'

'I feel utterly reassured.'

'You wouldn't like me to doss down on the sofa tonight?'

'No, thanks. I wouldn't be able to sleep a wink for fear that you'd get it into your head to exchange the role of protector for seducer.'

'So you think you're irresistible, Miss Elfrida Swann?'

'If I do you've only yourself to blame.'

'Quite right, my darling.' Guy seized my hand and pressed it to his lips while negotiating a sharp bend in the road and we skidded to the edge of something that looked dark and precipitous. 'Nearly in the river that time. Sorry,' said Guy calmly, pulling the wheel round. 'I think Mrs Deacon's moonshine is still having its lethal effect. I feel as tight as a pair of sailor's trousers.'

'That's another bone I have to pick with you. You told me that stuff was harmless! Mrs Deacon said it was given to children.'

'No doubt it is, by some very bad mothers.'

'Didn't your mother ever teach you not to tell lies?'

'No. She ran off with the neighbouring landowner before I was old enough to understand abstract concepts like truth.'

'Oh. Oh dear, how sad. I'm so sorry.'

'Don't remember even a 'Goodnight, my little angel,' or 'Who's Mummy's blue-eyed boy, then?''

'You're teasing again.'

'It's God's truth. My mother ran off with Colonel le Maistre, of Spokebender Abbey, when I was still in leading strings. They escaped to Anacapri for a few blissful months before the Colonel's eye alighted on a donkey-driver's daughter and my mother hurled herself off the cliff.'

'Now I know you're making it up.'

'Cut my throat if I tell a lie.' Guy made the gesture and we did another small skid. 'I promise you it's true. For years my father regaled anyone who'd listen with the story of my mother's adventures. He's bored with the whole thing now, thank heaven. I haven't heard him mention her for several years.'

'I find that rather shocking if it's true. Your poor mother! What a sad and terrible end to her life.'

'Oh, she didn't die. It was quite a low cliff. She was picked out of the water by a handsome young fisherman who took her home to his mother. And as soon as she'd dried out they were married and lived as contented as two nuts in a nutshell for at least a year.'

'Honestly? All right, I believe you without you trying to put us in the ditch. Anyway, you only get one nut per shell, surely.'

'You've forgotten peanuts, my dear, sweet expert on botany.'

'So I have.' I smiled and then remembered that we were talking about his mother. 'What happened after that?'

'She tired, after the year was up, of staring seaward into the sunset with one hand shading her eyes. Besides, though the fisherman was handsome in a chunky sort of way, his conversation was limited to net-mending and gutting and other such unexciting subjects. She allowed herself to be picked up by a very, very wicked *principe*. He had a large estate and lots of lovely dosh but unfortunately, quite apart from being pretty ancient and frighteningly wrinkly, he had an unpleasant habit of nipping down to the family vault after dark and making love to the deceased members of his family.'

'You don't expect me to believe that!'

'It's true. You can ask my father. He sent out a private detective to see what had become of her. My mother left the *principe* on the grounds that he stank of putrefaction — '

'Not another word! I'm sorry I began this conversation.'

'All right, no details. Not unnaturally sick of men by this time, my mother went on to found a home for toothless old pussycats in Naples.'

'And now?'

'Died of cat-scratch fever five years ago.'

'Oh.' I was silent for a moment, considering this. 'It does sound very sad, although you make it seem funny. She must have been rather unhappy much of the time. And it must have had a profound effect on you.'

'How so?'

'Not ever knowing her.'

'If you mean do I feel sad on her behalf, the answer is no. I expect she had as much fun as most people.' We were approaching the humpbacked bridge which I recognised as the beginning of Pudwell. 'At least my mother did what she wanted most of the time and she wasn't bored for some of it. I don't feel sorry for myself, either. We might have disliked each other intensely. And if I'd loved her I'd probably have got an Oedipal complex. As it is, my father has done his absolute best to make up for any shortfall in maternal damage.'

When I heard the bitterness at the end of this carefree delivery I was sure that Guy had been profoundly hurt by his mother's defection.

'Here we are. *Chez nous.*' Guy pulled up beside the hole in the hedge that led to Drop Cottage.

'I think you mean *chez vous.*' Chloë jumped out across my knees and disappeared into the darkness. I hoped she was not far away. An owl hooted overhead and there were mysterious rustlings all around. I had a sudden intense longing for paving-stones lit by street-lamps. 'Goodnight. Thank you so much for everything.'

'I'm coming with you.'

I didn't argue. I was thinking of the path down to the

cottage. I had no torch this time and the moon was not yet up. I had managed it in broad daylight that morning with difficulty, holding tightly to Guy's hand.

'I'll go first.' Guy disappeared into the undergrowth. The wet bushes sprung back in my face like slingshots armed with water bombs. 'What are you bleating about? A little dampness never hurt anyone. I can see you need breaking in. A brisk walk over the hills tomorrow will do you the world of good!'

'Thank you. I must say if this is life in the country — to have ice-cold showers and abuse heaped on one's head — I'm heartily thankful to be going back to London in the morning.'

'I'm afraid not. Tomorrow's Sunday. No trains.'

'What? Oh, no! Oh, for heaven's sake! This is like living in the Middle Ages! I'm surprised you have the internal combustion engine! Oh dear!' We had come to the steep decline.

'Try turning round and going down backwards as though it were a ladder. I'll catch you if you fall.'

It was easier that way but there were still some frightening moments when I felt myself about to lose my grip.

'I hate heights!' I said crossly when I was standing at the bottom.

Guy laughed. 'It's all of eight feet! You could jump down and not hurt yourself.'

'I did jump yesterday, by mistake. And I did hurt myself. At least I was winded.'

'Did you, you poor darling?' I saw his eyes gleam in the darkness as he patted my arm. 'I shall look after you. Now, soon we'll be at the bridge. Careful. Hold my hand.'

I probably gripped it quite hard. The plank wobbled horribly as I set my foot on it.

'There! That wasn't so bad, was it?' asked Guy when we were on the other side.

'So bad as what? Less awful than walking the tightrope across Niagara Falls, perhaps.'

Whatever else I was about to say was forgotten as we rounded a bend in the path and I saw the cottage lit softly from within. Four windows glowed like eyes cut in a pumpkin beneath a ragged thatch of hair.

Guy shoved open the front door and we went in. 'Here we are, Cissy.' He looked around the sitting room. 'Well! I'd call this a transformation.'

The room was lit by a soft yellow light that came from several gas brackets with glass shades. The leaves had been swept up, the table laid with a cloth, candles and flowers. There was a stack of logs by the fire, which burned high, reflected in the shining brass tongs and poker. The sofa cushions were plumped, the rugs were brushed.

A woman came out of the kitchen. She was tall with angular shoulders. Her face was a cubist's dream. Square forehead, straight brows, a nose broad at the bridge and descending almost vertically to the nostrils. Her eyes were deep cuts and her mouth a large groove, set above an underhung jaw. I suppose she must have been in her early thirties. Guy introduced us. 'Miss Glim. Miss Swann.'

'How do you do? This looks wonderful!' I held out my hand, which she touched briefly before letting it fall. 'How did you do it in the time?'

'Anyone, even you I expect, Miss, could straighten three small rooms in five hours.' Her voice was cold and rough. I decided to ignore the rudeness and win her round if I could. I went over to the table.

'The flowers are so pretty. These are anemones, aren't they?' I touched the creamy blossoms with my finger. 'And these little ones, with the whiskery faces, are wild pansies. I've forgotten the country name.'

'Heartsease. They're just weeds I picked from the garden.'

'How thoughtful of you.'

'I was only carrying out orders from Mr Guy.'

I tried again. 'What's that marvellous smell coming from the kitchen?'

'It's the chicken pie left from lunch. There's some celery soup and treacle tart. And there's something for Chloë.'

'That sounds wonderful. Thank you so much.' I smiled at her.

'It's only leftovers.' She did not return my smile but looked at Guy. 'Will that be all, Mr Guy?'

'Yes, thanks. And you needn't tell my father where I am.'

Miss Glim buttoned her gabardine mac, her mouth turned down. 'I don't know as you or anyone in the family has ever had reason to doubt my discretion.'

Guy laughed. 'Come on, Cissy,' he said, in a kinder tone, going over to her and putting a hand on her shoulder. 'Don't give us such a frost. You're a good girl and I appreciate it no end.' He lowered his voice but I couldn't help hearing. 'I'll make it up to you. But be nice now. As only you can be.'

Miss Glim twisted her head to look into his face. Her expression had something in it of reproof and possibly anger. And also, I thought, of love. 'I'll be going, then.' She moved away so that he was forced to let his hand drop. 'Goodnight, Mr Guy.' She threw me a look of cold dislike. 'Miss.' Taking a torch from her pocket, she opened the door and was gone into the night.

'Shouldn't you have taken her home? It's a long way to walk in the dark. That treacherous bridge. And it's starting to rain again.'

'Rain's good for the complexion. Cissy's a country girl. The walk's nothing to her. Let's have that soup.'

The kitchen had been tidied of cobwebs and the sink had been scrubbed. Red embers glowed in the range. A bottle of wine, two glasses and a corkscrew stood on the table. A saucepan of soup stood on the stove, which was cleaned of grease and grime.

'How on earth did she manage to get a gas supply?'

'I expect she turned on a tap somewhere outside. Quite a few of these inaccessible places don't have electricity. They have gas cylinders instead. Here's to us.' Guy raised his glass.

'Here's to you and me.'

'That's a subtle distinction that's supposed to tell me something, is it?'

'I didn't like Miss Glim's assumption that you were going to spend the night here.'

'You needn't worry about her. She doesn't like women, that's all.'

'You mean she doesn't like women that you like.'

Guy smiled enigmatically. 'What a girl you are for leaping to conclusions.'

We carried the food into the sitting room and sat at the table. Chloë sank on to the rug before the fire with a groan of pleasure. The pale green soup looked inviting. I took a spoonful. 'Is she in love with you?'

'How should I know?'

'Oh, come on. One generally has a pretty good idea if people are in love with one or not.'

'Not at all. They can swear they're in love until their tongues are blistered but that doesn't mean anything. They might be deceiving themselves or they might be lying. What on earth does being in love mean? Usually that they don't want you to fuck anybody else. However much you might enjoy it. I don't call that love. That's just selfishness.'

'How delicately you put it. Supposing someone made a great sacrifice for you — giving up something they really wanted, for example. Or supposing they killed themselves for love of you. Would you believe it then?'

'Certainly not. They'd be hoping it would make you

guilty as hell for the rest of your life. Hardly a loving thing to do.'

'Don't you believe human beings are capable of loving others, if not better than, then at least as well as themselves?'

'I think love's all about possessiveness and putting obligations on other people to make sure of getting what you want.' I thought of Alex then. He had told me so often that I was the only woman he had ever loved. I was desperate for deliverance from the burden of his devotion. 'Every rich man,' Guy waved his spoon at me accusingly, 'must know in his heart of hearts that his wife puts up with his lovemaking simply for the cash. That would be fine by me, though, if you were thinking of it.'

'Have you got any money?' I couldn't help smiling at Guy's earnest expression.

'I've got a very handsome overdraft. But please don't let that stop you. Have some pie.'

'What about men who aren't rich? What do their women want, if it isn't love?'

'Lust, gratification of vanity, entertainment, companionship, security, children. Of course this applies to men, too. I don't mean to suggest that men are more altruistic.'

'I should think not.' As I contemplated Guy's idea of a selfish, rapacious world I heard a deep roll of thunder. 'Listen. There's going to be a storm.' The fire began to hiss as huge drops of rain gusted down the chimney.

'I like storms,' said Guy. 'Do you?'

'Not much. I know it's silly.'

'This squall will keep the whistler away, though. Have some more pie. I didn't know you could eat like an ordinary mortal. I thought you lived on air.'

I looked with surprise at my empty plate. 'I hope so — that it'll keep him away, I mean.'

'Why not let me stay?' Guy put down his fork and

picked up my hand in his warm one. But I did not want a lover. At that moment I doubted whether I would ever again risk finding myself in charge of someone else's happiness. He must have seen refusal in my eyes for instead of letting me answer he went on, 'What's the food problem?'

'It's the most tiresome thing. Something to do with nerves. The minute I even think about it I'm done for. But everyone has some kind of neurosis, I suppose.'

'When I'm anxious I find the remedy is to make love,' said Guy promptly.

'It isn't generally very convenient in the middle of lunch.'

'We could try a little therapy now — ' He broke off as a loud knocking at the door coincided with a violent crack of thunder overhead. Chloë left the fireside to press herself against my leg. Guy got up to answer it but Miss Glim, wrapped in glistening oilskins and a sou'wester and carrying a hurricane lamp, came in without waiting.

'The seven bullocks in the bottom field have been struck,' she said, evidently out of breath. 'Dusty came up to the house to tell me.'

'Oh, bloody hell! Are they dead?'

'Four are. The others are in a bad way, he says.'

'Have you sent for the vet?'

'The telephone's not working. Dusty says there's a post down.'

'Can't he go and fetch him?'

'All that way on a bike in this weather? Do you want to be the death of an old man with your carryings-on?'

She looked at me with triumph in her eyes. A rivulet of water ran down the brim of her sou'wester, plopped on to the end of her large nose and hung there, sparkling like a diamond pendant.

'Damn and blast! All right. Get in the Land Rover.'

'You'll have to hurry.' She stood resolutely in the

91

middle of the room, hurricane lamp held aloft like some allegorical figure of Virtue.

'Yes, go, go!' I said, anxious for the bullocks.

'Best bolt your door, Miss, when we've gone,' said Miss Glim. 'You never know who's about on a night like this.'

'Don't be absurd, Cissy. Only a lunatic would be wandering about in this deluge.'

Miss Glim threw back her head and the drip of rainwater from her nose went flying. No doubt she felt she had made her point.

9

'This is Geoffrey Searle, one of our hardworking churchwardens to whom we are so much indebted.' Mr Winnacott, Rector of Pudwell, sketched abstract shapes in the air with long double-jointed fingers as he made the introduction. His large chin butted several times in the direction of the churchwarden, who paused in his conversation to look at me. 'Miss Swann,' continued Mr Winnacott, 'is a temporary resident in our lovely village unfortunately — I mean that the shortness of Miss Swann's projected stay is unfortunate, of course, would that such lovely young ladies were more frequently to be found . . . ' Mr Winnacott became flustered and his teeth, which were large and splayed, made sucking sounds on his lower lip as he struggled for the right words.

'How d'ye do, Miss Swann?' Geoffrey Searle took command. He grasped my hand firmly and shook it vigorously several times as a dog might shake a rat. 'Pleasure to see a new face. Particularly such a charming one.' He folded back his wet red lips in a wide smile that on a dark night would have been frightening. 'This is Roger Windebank,' he waved at the man standing next to him, 'our local solicitor. I'm an accountant — lowest form of life — as well as being churchwarden and a country councillor.'

I wondered whether I should present my own credentials. Portrait painter, part-time student and heartless jilt. But Geoffrey went on talking about his role as secretary of the Tarchester and District Golf Club so I took it that my only claims to masculine attention were already on view. Roger's handshake was warm and limp.

'Visiting someone in the village, Miss Swann?' As Geoffrey paused to draw breath, Roger slipped in his question with an appearance of polite interest, belied by darting little eyes behind their lenses that ran over my face, down my neck and stopped at my breasts. Both men wore grizzled tweeds and held glasses of dark brown sherry. Mr Winnacott put a glass into my hand. I looked at it doubtfully. I don't much like sherry, even when it is properly dry. This was suitable only for a Christmas pudding.

'I'm staying in a friend's cottage. Back to London tomorrow morning, I'm afraid. I was out walking when I heard the church bells.'

The storm had died away during the night. I had heard nothing from the phantom whistler. Miss Glim had made up my bed with linen sheets, blankets and an eiderdown. What a difference those linen sheets made! Though they were old and had several small darns, the luxury of them restored my spirits. I had enjoyed lying in bed at midnight watching the shimmer of lightning behind the trees and listening to the rainwater dripping into the saucepan that Miss Glim had thoughtfully placed beneath the hole in the thatch. Even the thunderclaps that followed had no power to frighten me. In my absolute seclusion, withdrawn from all that was familiar to me, solitary as an anchorite, I felt a relaxation of tension. For the first time in weeks, I stopped reviewing the arguments for and against going through with the marriage. I found it possible to allow my mind to drift, to forget about Alex. I could not remember my dreams when I woke.

A bar of light lay across the boards that the years of fluctuating damp and drought had distorted until they swelled and bowed like a calm sea. I pulled the eiderdown around me and went to the window to look out. I had to crouch down, for the sill of the dormer window was on a level with the floor. The garden declined dramatically towards the bottom of the valley. The other side rose steeply, almost cliff-like. At the ridge there was a crescent-shaped dip as though a bite had been taken out of the top of the hill and through this came the beam of sunlight. When the sun moved on, the valley would be cast in shadow for some time until the sun reached its head. The brilliant light threw into dramatic relief a row of scratches on the window, crossing several panes of glass. The letters were crooked and difficult to read, the first cut more deeply than the last as though the writer had tired of his or her task. ANNA THOU LADY KILLEST ME.

The words were vaguely familiar. I picked up the book of Rossetti poems still lying open on the table beside the bed. Yes, there it was, a translation of an early Italian poet.

> *Thou, lady, killest me*
> *Yet keepest me in pain*
> *For thou must surely see*
> *How fearing, I am fain.*

When making the inventory I had seen a little box and a cup initialled with the letter A. Perhaps Anna was Viola's godmother's name. She might have had a stormy love affair. I very much hoped she had. The vision of parish council meetings and tombola stalls receded to be replaced by a dimly imagined tale of troubled passion. The sun had slid behind the hill at that point, pitching the room as abruptly into shadow as though a shutter had been closed, and cutting short my speculations.

I had dressed and gone downstairs. Chloë's affectionate, undemanding companionship suited my mood. Her eyes followed me about the room, and when I spoke to her she came at once to sit beside me, her head on my knee, slowly beating the floor with her tail.

We shared a piece of toast. I washed up quickly, seized with an unfamiliar desire to be out of doors.

Chloë pushed ahead of me into the garden. The bare stems of roses had grown together into a low arch, forcing me to bend as I followed her down steep steps cut into the slope. A cold wind rustled the grass that grew as high as my knees. A little way from the top was a small brick outhouse. There was no door but a most beautiful cobweb hung like a curtain across the top half of the opening. I ducked under and looked in. A wooden seat with two circular holes cut in it proclaimed this to be the bathroom for which I had searched in vain. I backed out, forgetful of the web, which now draped my head like a mantilla. Chloë watched me in amazement as I exclaimed and shuddered and flapped at my hair, imagining something enormous and leggy crawling down my neck.

I looked back at the cottage. Birds hopped about on the roof with pieces of straw in their beaks. I wondered how many more years of nesting it would take before the cottage was stripped bare. Part of the thatch sloped from the chimney to the ground. From the reservoir of useless knowledge stored in my brain a name for this floated up. It was called a cat-slide roof, generally housing a larder or dairy that needed to be cool.

Further down, the path snaked to left and right as the decline became steeper. The volume of birdsong was increased by the high, softly greening walls of unpruned shrubs and trees. By degrees I became aware of another sound. I pushed through undergrowth to find myself standing on a high bank at the brink of a fast-flowing river. Boulders stood in its path, which the water leaped or circumvented in a gush of foam. Some of the spray was flung up towards me, melting into iridescence as it flew into the path of the sun.

'What did you think of the sermon?' Geoffrey Searle lifted himself on to his toes then rocked back on his heels, throwing out his chest while staring hard at my mouth. He leaned towards me and said, in a voice that was not quite low enough, 'Rector's a terrible ass, I'm afraid. Bit of a cream puff. Know what I mean? The Church seems to attract them.'

I looked at Geoffrey, as he winked a small, calculating eye, with his fleshy jowls and corky nose as masculine as a rack of pipes, and marvelled at his complacency. Though I had not particularly enjoyed the sermon on the text 'In the morning sow thy seed, and in the evening withhold not thy hand', which, predictably, provoked prurient sniggering among the choirboys, I had been impressed by the patent sincerity of the Rector.

I had first met Mr Winnacott in the churchyard. I had taken the clockwise path up to the top of the hill to look at the church. The other path, I remembered, led to Gilderoy Hall. Though I was curious to see the house, I did not want to give the impression that I was looking for Guy. The church was a fine building with a handsome tower. I had been admiring the great pedimented and pillared portico of the house that could be glimpsed through the trees beyond the wall when someone hailed me from the porch of the church. The wind on the hilltop was savage and most of what he said was snatched away.

'Sorry. What did you say?'

He had galloped across the turf. Over his cassock he wore a blue plastic mac and on his head a deerstalker, knitted in brown wool with long bouncing earflaps. Chloë had growled and I had had to look away in order not to smile. Beneath the peak of his hat his eyes were protuberant and eager. 'I'm Swithin Winnacott. I was just about to ring the bell for Matins. We've had a little trouble in the parish — it's perfectly *maddening* — and now I've got to do the sexton's job as well. Are you staying in the village?'

'I'm leaving tomorrow.' The wind took my words and tossed them carelessly away.

'Tomorrow, did you say? What a pity. But you'll come to our service this morning?'

'Well, I hadn't intended — '

'Oh, *do* say you will! If you'd be so kind as to ring the bell I can get myself ready in the vestry. One of my churchwardens telephoned to say he'd be late and the other's gone to visit his sister at Brighton.'

'But I don't know how.'

'There's nothing to it. Mr Shaftoe, that's the sexton, used to read the newspaper while he rang it. Not that I quite approved but one mustn't be narrow-minded. I'm afraid there's going to be a lot of talk about him. Well, to tell you the truth, though one ought not to gossip — he's run away with a young lady. His wife is very upset.' Mr Winnacott looked sorrowfully at me and gnawed his lower lip. 'Poor Shaftoe, a very good fellow but the temptations of the flesh were too much for him — let he who is without sin and so forth — I do like to begin on time. Unfortunately Mary Filkins, the young lady who left with Shaftoe, was our strongest soprano.'

'I'm sorry to hear that but I really don't think I can — '

'Oh, *please* do say yes!' Mr Winnacott clutched my elbow and bent his knees, swaying a little in supplication. 'Bell-ringing does terrible things to my fibrositis.'

Ringing the bell was not quite as easy as Mr Winnacott had implied. For one thing you had to pull the rope quite hard to make it ring and for another there was a disconcerting delay between the tug and the peal. I never seemed to catch up with it. The congregation, dawdling in singly or in groups, gave me inquisitive stares. By the time I sat down in a pew at the back of the church I was breathing hard and felt hot. Chloë, unable to understand why she was excluded, barked and scraped on the porch door at intervals throughout the service. It was impossible to dwell on spiritual things.

Mr Winnacott was accident-prone and the service was 'high' which seemed to offer more opportunities for misadventure. During Communion he tripped on his way up to the altar and dropped the wafers on the floor. There was an unresolved struggle to synchronise the Elevation of the Host with the ringing of the bell. The altar boy swung the thurible in Mr Winnacott's face when he was opening his mouth to recite the creed and he was rendered nearly insensible by the smoke. As Mr Winnacott mounted the pulpit steps to preach he caught his chasuble on a nail and had to spend some time unhitching himself. The choirboys were beside themselves with laughter when Chloë began to howl during the blessing. Afterwards Mr Winnacott, still pale from breathing in the incense, insisted that I join the rest of the congregation at the Rectory for 'a pre-prandial sherry'.

'He seems exceptionally kind,' I murmured in reply to Geoffrey. I watched Mr Winnacott circling his guests, bearing a plate of vol-au-vents. Even without the deerstalker there was something a little absurd in his appearance. His face was the shape of a violin, narrow about the level of the ears and wider at the brow and jaw. He had an odd manner of walking, as though his bones were flexible. I noticed no one was eating anything and at every refusal he looked more disappointed.

'Swithin's well-meaning, of course, no one more so,' said Roger in a superior way. 'And he goes to a great deal of trouble for his parishioners. Pity they aren't more grateful. But he's such a silly ass.' I wondered what Mr Winnacott had done to deserve this collective contempt. I much preferred him to either Roger or Geoffrey. For one thing the vicar was not insufferably conceited. 'Did you say you're going back to London tomorrow?' Roger adjusted the knot of his tie, the equivalent, I suppose, of raising his tail feathers or expanding a coloured pouch. 'I'm driving up myself. Why don't I give you a lift?'

'Good morning, Geoffrey, Roger.' A young woman broke into our little group, forcing Roger to remove his eyes from my breasts. 'I'm Primrose Yardley. Everyone calls me Prim. And you're Miss Swann, I know,' she went on, before I could speak. 'Mrs Creech told me. You mustn't think you can buy half a pound of wet fish in this village without setting the tom-toms beating.'

'Do call me Freddie.'

Primrose Yardley, I guessed, was in her early thirties, tall with a large bust and generous hips. The length of her face was exaggerated by a shoulder-length bob of straight brown hair. Her nose was beaky and her chin small. She was saved from absolute plainness by her eyes which were beautiful, the colour of polished bronze, and her complexion that was clear and warm with soft pink cheeks. Her jersey was holey and her suit, an expensive tweed, was crumpled and not very clean. Her hands and fingernails were ingrained with dirt but a lovely diamond and pearl brooch was pinned to her lapel. She was smoking a small cigar.

'Don't, whatever you do, accept Roger's offer of a lift. He's the biggest tart in South Dorset. Sex is never out of his mind and no girl is safe alone with him.'

Geoffrey chortled until he turned crimson while Roger simpered and snuffled, and looked pleased.

'Jolly good, jolly good.' Mr Winnacott was at my elbow. 'The Sabbath should be a day of fellowship as well as worship. May I share the joke? Do eat something, Miss Swann. My wife makes these specially for our little Sunday morning get-togethers. The vol-au-vents are prawn.' I took one, though the pastry was grey and I hate that sort of thing. I had a poignant

100

vision of Mrs Winnacott toiling loyally in the kitchen to support her husband in his ministry, only to have the results of her labour despised.

'I think you've got it wrong, Prim.' Roger burnished his long nose with his handkerchief. 'Tarts are always female.'

'Times are changing,' said Prim. 'These days the charge of sexual incontinence can be levelled at anyone. Gender no longer excuses promiscuity.'

'What a *very* interesting conversation.' Mr Winnacott looked alarmed. 'I'm all for equality of the sexes. There is even talk of women priests in the Church of England — though one wonders whether they have *quite* the authority — '

'The church is full of old women already.' Geoffrey sipped his sherry, winced and put his glass down on a small table nearby, slopping some of it on to the polished surface.

Mr Winnacott attempted to balance the sherry decanter on the plate of vol-au-vents so he could wipe the table with his cassock. 'No one knows better than I, who am the least among them, the shortcomings of the cloth, Geoffrey, but — ah, hum — let us not censure without just cause the many hardworking and sincere — ahow!' He clutched the base of his spine. 'My sciatica!'

'Let me do that.' Prim took out her handkerchief and rubbed at the table. 'Geoffrey doesn't mean anything. It's just bombast. Take no notice.'

I bit bravely into my vol-au-vent which at once cracked into several pieces, more than half of which fell to the floor in a shower of greasy flakes. A black-and-white cat shot out from under the sofa. After a few eager sniffs it turned away. Our brows struck painfully as Mr Winnacott and I bent simultaneously to remove the mess from the carpet. There was nothing resembling a prawn among the remains. I was still chewing the original mouthful which had taken on the consistency of gum.

'Come here, Macavity,' said Prim, bending down towards the cat and making kissing noises. Macavity allowed his ear to be fondled. 'I don't think you're giving him quite enough to eat, Swithin. He's a bit thin.'

'Oh do you think so? Beryl always feeds him. She doesn't like me to interfere with domestic things. Perhaps you might like to mention it to her . . . ' There was something like fear in Mr Winnacott's gentle eyes.

I coughed the mouthful of the vol-au-vent into my handkerchief. 'He's a very fine cat,' I remarked rather stupidly, feeling that everyone was looking at me. 'He must be called after the one in T.S. Eliot's *Practical Cats*.'

''Macavity's a mystery cat. He's called the Hidden Paw,'' chanted Prim. 'I can never remember any more of it.' There was nothing hidden about this Macavity's paw. It was into the bowl of peanuts, Roger's trouser turn-ups, Prim's bag, even Geoffrey's glass of sherry in an unceasing quest for food. 'I love cats,' Prim went on, as she tried to tempt Macavity with a nut. 'I've got a beautiful fluffy pussy myself.'

Above her head Geoffrey and Roger caught each other's eye and tittered like schoolboys. I pretended not to notice. Mr Winnacott smiled and looked utterly baffled. Prim glanced up at me, her head turned away from the three men, and winked.

A woman with a sallow complexion and grey hair screwed tightly into a bun thrust her way into the circle. 'What's this mess on the carpet, Swithin?'

'Just a little accident with a vol-au-vent, my dear. Miss Swann, my wife Beryl.'

'Morning, Beryl,' said Geoffrey, the laughter leaving him abruptly. 'I must be going now. Mother-in-law for lunch. Pity she's such a tough old bird.' He attempted a smile.

102

'Is that supposed to be amusing?' Beryl Winnacott looked at him with eyes like stones. 'No doubt you think old age something to be mocked.'

Geoffrey opened his mouth to reply and then thought better of it. He included us all in a vapid grin and shuffled away. Beryl turned to Roger. 'I've just had your bill for the business of the churchyard boundary. It's quite ridiculous and Swithin has absolutely no intention of paying it.'

'Oh, but, my dear — '

'Be quiet, Swithin.'

'Actually, it's much less than I usually charge,' began Roger mildly. 'As it was church business, you know, I gave my own time free and — '

'Good heavens, so I should hope! But the amount is quite absurd. You must take it up with the Bishop.'

'Oh. Well. All right.' Roger left the room, looking annoyed.

'Goodbye, Freddie.' Prim smiled at me. 'I hope we shall have the pleasure of seeing you again some time.'

'Thank you. You've all been very kind.'

'By the way, Primrose,' Beryl ignored me, 'I notice that all the oasis in the church has gone.'

'I used the last bit on Friday in the arrangement on the font. There was only a small piece left.'

'I see. Well, I suppose the funds must be made to stretch for another block. Economy is evidently a virtue despised by the commercial classes.'

'I'll donate some myself,' Prim said crossly, to Beryl's departing back. 'That was a hit at me for having a father who was in the brewery business,' she added in a low voice to me. 'Her father was the rural dean. They never had any money. Poor Beryl had to wear hand-me-down clothes and give her pocket money to the poor in Africa. She's never forgiven me for having pretty party frocks and a bicycle with three gears. I don't know why I let her annoy me. I was going to warn you about the vol-au-vents. They're several years old. We all know not to touch them. Beryl gets them out of the deep freeze every Saturday night and puts them back in after lunch on Sundays. There's one with half a dead fly stuck on the side that I spotted months ago.'

I thought unhappily of the few crumbs I had managed to swallow. 'Life in the country is more perilous than I'd imagined. She's Mrs Proudie to the life, isn't she?'

'Oh, you like Trollope! What a pity you're going! In these parts book lovers are an endangered species. Why don't you come and have tea with me this afternoon?'

'I'd love to.'

'Yardley House, Mill Lane. It's just across the bridge. Anyone will tell you where to find it. Four o'clock?'

'Thank you.'

'Now, Miss Swann.' Mr Winnacott came up almost at a run. 'Do stay and have lunch. My wife would be so pleased.'

I saw Prim shake her head behind his back as she left through the open front door. The wind was channelled into probes that worked their way up my skirt and down my neck. I began to shiver. 'Well, how terribly kind but, actually, I think I'll do without lunch today. I'm not at all hungry.' As I spoke my stomach heaved slightly, remembering the vol-au-vent. I felt distinctly unwell.

He looked crestfallen. 'On Sundays we indulge in a small cold collation — to spare the servants, it used to be said, but these days we manage without help. To think that at the beginning of the century this house had a cook and several maids.' He waved his hands in a vague, embracing way at the hall, where we stood in the shadows of the stairwell. The massive ornamented staircase was of a peculiarly depressing blackened oak and the walls were painted maroon, hung with faded prints of birds flying in formation over grey estuaries. It had rained as we left the church and dribbles of water

104

from the coats of the congregation lay on the parquet floor. The ebonised hallstand held a stack of hymnbooks, a plastic rainhood and a small bottle of yellow liquid. It looked like a urine sample.

'Of course we are lucky to have all this space when there are families living in pitifully cramped accommodation. Or worse. Only yesterday I visited a family of six whose tied cottage is being taken away from them. The mother has died and the father taken to drink. I confess, Miss Swann, as I tried to console the poor man at his wife's graveside I found myself unable to answer satisfactorily his questioning of the Lord's purpose in removing his helpmeet and strength. It seemed capricious indeed.' Mr Winnacott massaged his teeth with his lips and his eyes goggled slightly as he stared thoughtfully at the floor. 'We are all in the dark, Miss Swann, all in the dark.'

A light was snapped on abruptly above our heads, banishing the gloom that had seemed to gather about us as he talked. 'You mustn't delay Miss Swann, Swithin.' Beryl folded the rainhood and put it into a drawer. 'She will be anxious to get home before the next shower.'

'Oh, my dear,' Mr Winnacott gripped my elbow, 'I have asked Miss Swann to partake of our nuncheon. I am sure if you enjoin your entreaties to mine she will yield.'

'It's very kind of Mr Winnacott but you mustn't think of changing your plans.' I hoped to soften Beryl's granite glare.

She closed her eyes and breathed out slowly. 'Of course, if Swithin wishes it. No doubt you want to wash your hands, Miss Swann. Follow me.'

It ought to be possible, I thought, as I lathered my fingers with Wright's coal tar soap, to decline unwelcome social engagements without causing pain, but I had not discovered how to do it. The look of gratification on Swithin's face as I entered the Rectory dining room, made up a little for the unspeakable dreariness of the occasion before me.

Conversationally, it was undemanding. Swithin — we were now on first name terms — talked. I put in a response when he paused. Beryl ate in silence when she was not fetching and carrying from the kitchen to the table, having refused my offers of help. She gave me a plate on which there was a slice of watery, tin-shaped ham, a tablespoon of cold mashed potato and another of beetroot. I declined the piccalilli that stood in its jar on the table. Swithin poured glasses of water. Chloë gave a howl from the cloakroom where she was to remain throughout lunch. We folded our hands and bent our heads to praise the Lord's munificence.

We had our heads down so long that I felt my neck getting stiff. It was very cold in the dining room and I longed to clap my arms to my sides and jump up and down. My seat was hard, the dining-room wallpaper repulsive. It was impossible to be grateful for beetroot that reeked of vinegar. I felt a pressure against my leg. I glanced down to see Macavity staring up at me with glowing brass-coloured eyes. There was a drop of saliva on his chin. My plate was hidden from general view by an arrangements of dried flowers, dead so long that they had become uniformly brown. Swithin's and Beryl's eyes were closed in fervent thanksgiving. I sneaked the ham on to the floor. Twisting his head from side to side, Macavity chewed it up, purring furiously.

After grace I ate the potato, rapidly turning shocking-pink, chopped the beetroot into little pieces, swallowed half of it and hid the rest under my knife and fork. At first I put the sore feeling in my throat down to the vicious acidity of the vinegar, but by the time I had toyed with prunes and custard I was conscious that my head was throbbing and my limbs felt heavy. I was hot and cold by turns.

Swithin was talking about the poems of George

Herbert, the seventeenth-century divine. 'The man had faith, you see. Absolute certainty. In a world where life expectancy was brief, disease rife, appalling suffering the lot of the common man, his belief was unshaken.'

'Don't you think that might be why?' I said, leaning languidly back in my chair so that I could stroke the cat's head with a finger. 'Because life was so harsh he needed to believe in something perfect and good.' Through a gap in the broken stalks of the flower arrangement I saw Beryl spit a prune stone into her spoon.

'Mere wishful thinking, you mean?'

'Surely absolute certainty *must* be self-deception. No one *could* be certain about the existence of God.' I hoped I was making sense. The room seemed to waver between light and dark.

'Allow me to say, Freddie, how delightful it is to me to be able to talk of these things. On the whole my parishioners are not interested in philosophy. In fact, even the Bishop — '

He stopped and looked in alarm at his wife who had flung down her napkin with an exclamation of anger. Her face was red with emotion. '*You* may think it clever, Miss Swann, to voice these unorthodox and — to my mind — ill-informed views but I think some consideration is due to Swithin's vocation.'

'But my dear,' Swithin blinked with fright, 'Freddie is entitled to her opinion. And I must say *I* think it sensible and honest — '

'Can I believe my ears?' Beryl pushed back her chair and stood up, the embodiment of affronted dignity. 'Do you dare to tell me that because I do not doubt the existence of my Maker I am neither sensible nor honest? I shall go upstairs to my room. Goodbye, Miss Swann. I shall not stoop to untruth by saying that I hope we meet again.' She swept off in a way that reminded me so forcibly of Mrs Proudie that I could not conceal a smile.

'Dear Freddie! You forgive her! I call that saintly. The whole thing was my fault entirely.'

'Really, I don't mind.' I didn't care two straws for Beryl's good opinion and my body was now as burdensome as though it were filled with hot lead. 'I'm so sorry. I must go home — I mean, back to Drop Cottage. I'm not feeling quite — I must have caught a cold.'

'You're unwell! Yes, yes, you must get to bed at once! What a pity that the car is at the garage! I shall escort you.'

'It's very kind of you,' I murmured, 'but, really, I shall be quite all right.'

'I insist! You are a stranger to these parts. I shall guide you.'

Half an hour later Swithin, Chloë and I stood in dense woodland at a point where two paths met.

'I'm almost certain this is right.' Swithin forged ahead down one of the axes. The paths were narrow and muddy. In several places we were forced to choose between wading through puddles or pushing through brambles. 'Come on, Freddie, *here* we are.' Swithin waited for me to catch up with him, his face hangdog. 'I recognise Barbara Watkins's cottage. See that bright pink through the gap? It *would* have been a short cut if only I hadn't been such a fool as to get lost.' Chloë ran back and forth, barking and wagging her tail, enjoying what must have seemed to her a game.

'Never mind.' My throat was so sore it required courage to swallow. 'Let's just go on.'

But this we were unable to do for, as we emerged from the trees, we came to a stream that tore along on its way to the river, just wide enough and deep enough to be uncrossable. The clouds that loomed low and inky chose that moment to drop their weight of water on our heads as we stumbled towards a place where it was narrow enough to jump over. Swithin misjudged it and landed up to his waist in water. I got very wet and muddy helping him out. Dead leaves that had fallen the preceding autumn clung to our shoes like skates and made the going treacherous. By the time I stood at the gap in the hedge leading to Drop Cottage my skin was crinkling and my hair could have been wrung into a bucket.

'Go in, go in,' cried Swithin, in an agony of concern. 'I will summon assistance.'

'I'll be all right. You go and get dry,' I croaked, flailing through the hedge. I staggered along the path, slithered down the precipice and teetered over the bridge. I barely had the strength to push open the front door. I dragged myself up the stairs, pulled off my clothes and got naked into bed where I lay shaking until I felt my bones must break. My flesh seemed to be sizzling on a gridiron. I flung back the bedclothes only to search for them ineffectually when, a few minutes later, I became colder than ice. A sharp blade attempted to separate me into my component parts.

I realised, with a sense of fright and shock, that Alex was in the room. 'How did you find me?' I asked through cracked lips. He gave me water, which I sipped gratefully. He smoothed back my hair and folded my bedclothes under my chin. 'I'm sorry,' I cried. 'I'm so very sorry.'

'It doesn't matter now,' he said, putting his arms round me and holding so tightly that I couldn't breathe. I struggled to push him away. His face contorted into the mask of Tragedy with eyes like slits and a mouth turned down with despair. Swiftly it drew back and shrank to nothing. I slept.

From time to time Alex returned to look at me, his face sometimes upside down, sometimes sideways, sometimes the right way up. Often he frowned and was angry, and at other times he was smiling and his eyes were kind. Once he rushed towards the bed with his fist upraised and I screamed until my throat caught fire.

Then I was floating above the bed, light as a mote of dust. I pirouetted on the breeze, out of the window and down towards the river where I became a bubble leaping on the water, part of the *corps de ballet* of foam. I was floating, flying, dissolving — Alex grasped me by the wrist and was pulling me down. I fought to free myself but water filled my lungs. I was drowning. 'You see, Freddie,' said Alex, his face very large, his expression pitying, 'you wouldn't trust me. *Now* see what you've got yourself into.' I could no longer see or hear but I felt hands pulling me, pressing me down beneath the surface of the water.

'Freddie! Wake up!'

I opened my eyes.

10

Primrose Yardley's face was calm and kind. The hand that held mine was cool. 'Drink up.' I could not identify the taste but it was sharp and refreshing. 'Lemon barley water. It's the best thing for a weakened state. Edward was talking about antibiotics but I told him you wouldn't need them. All those nasty side-effects.' I opened my mouth to ask who Edward was but I seemed unable to do more than caw like a rook through parched lips. I tried to sit up but I was too weak. 'I'll put a pillow behind you.' Prim propped me up and smoothed the sheets and blankets. I saw that the small grate in the bedroom was filled with burning logs and that the room was composed of friendly shadows. Water plipped in a familiar way into the saucepan in the corner. I was safe and protected from all dangers by this woman, almost a stranger. I wanted to tell her how grateful I was but instead I fell into a dreamless sleep.

When I opened my eyes again it was much later. An oil lamp cast a glow from the table by the fire. A man bent over me. At first I thought it was Alex and I put up my hand to keep him away but then I saw that he had a broad face with a fringe of tightly curling hair and was altogether different. 'Hello, Miss Swann. You're looking much better. Prim's right. You won't need those antibiotics after all. Just hold this under your tongue for me.'

I concentrated on keeping the thermometer in place. I remembered Dr Gilchrist's voice and was certain that he had visited me several times before but dreams and reality were hopelessly jumbled. 'Good! Just above a hundred. Much better. I'll keep an eye on you for a little while longer. But you're in capable hands. I've always told Prim the medical profession is in dire need of her.'

'Yes, but I'm not in dire need of it.' Prim moved into view from the chair by the fire. 'You'll forgive me for saying so but I don't think I could keep my temper for half a day with the bungling idiocy of the National Health Service. I haven't the right temperament.'

'There's nothing amiss with your temperament as far as I can see.' Edward Gilchrist smiled in a humouring kind of way and took his stethoscope from his bag. I bent forward, my nightdress over my head and squealed as he pressed something ice-cold to my back.

'I'm sorry. It's because you're feverish.'

'Warm it up, man!' Prim's voice was snappish. 'Have you no consideration for your patient?'

'Sorry.' I heard the sound of huffing. 'Is that better?'

'Much. Thanks,' I croaked.

'I don't know what you expect to hear anyway. It's clear she's on the mend. Another day or two and she'll be well enough to get up for a few hours.'

'As you say, Prim. I humbly submit to your prognosis.'

'Remember, make yourself all honey and you'll be devoured by wasps.'

'Now, is that fair? What more can a mere man do but admit his inferiority?'

'If you two have finished arguing,' I emerged from the folds of my nightdress, 'I'd like to lie down again.'

Prim arranged the pillows and sheets, looking fierce. 'Be off with you and let me tend to my patient.'

I tried to thank him but was overtaken by a coughing fit. Prim gave me some more barley water to sip and told me to lie quiet. Dr Gilchrist went away, promising to call again the next day.

'You've been so good.' I barely recognised my own voice which either squawked or growled. To my dismay a tear ran down my cheek. 'I'm sorry to make an idiot of myself.'

'You're just weak, that's all. You'll be as right as rain in a few days. I'm going to put you on a strict health regime, and I warn you, I won't stand any nonsense. Good food and plenty of sleep. Edward says you must have been very run down for a cold to become viral pneumonia.'

'Is that what I've had? Prim, what day is it?'

'Wednesday.'

'Oh, I feel so muddled — it was on Sunday that I became ill, wasn't it?'

'You were coming to tea, do you remember? Swithin came to my house to fetch me. You've been pretty much out of it since then. But the village has been alert on your behalf. There've been plenty of enquiries about your health. Roger Windebank, Swithin, George, Mrs Creech — '

'But I've never even met her.'

'None the less she called to see how you were. She feels obliged to keep her customers up to date. Not a word from Beryl.' Prim laughed. 'I don't know what you've done to earn her disapproval but I mean to take a leaf out of your book if you'll kindly give me the hint. I'd give anything to be cast into outer darkness.' I meant to laugh, too, but coughed instead. 'And, of course, Guy has been a positive nuisance. Every day, twice a day. Several times it's almost come to a physical fight to stop him coming up here. Those flowers are his.' I glanced at the bedside table on which a vase of freesias stood. 'He must have gone to Tarchester for them. You won't be able to smell them, probably, but I've enjoyed them very much. Anyway, I thought you'd rather have Guy's than Roger's. His are on the table downstairs. Mauve chrysanthemums. Not nearly as pretty.'

I caught her hand. 'Thank you. You've been *so* good.'

'As a matter of fact I've thoroughly enjoyed it. Not you being ill, of course, but feeling useful. I looked after both my parents until they died. Pa had a bad heart and died in less than a year. But Ma was an invalid for ten years, on and off. I'm ashamed to say that I often resented the curtailment of my freedom. When she died and I was free to do what I wanted, perhaps even find a career for myself, I immediately got depressed. I went to the Dolomites for a month and then to Paris and Rome. All the things I'd longed to do. I went to all the best restaurants and hotels but I didn't enjoy any of it. I couldn't get over not being needed. No timetable, no vital tasks, no identity. Just being me required more imagination and skill than I possessed.'

I put my hand on Prim's lean, large one. 'I think it's just that you've got a great deal to offer other people.'

'Nonsense! But you managed to say all that without coughing. You'd better try to sleep. I'll go down and get supper. Oh, don't worry,' she added, as I was about to protest at the giving of trouble, 'I'm going to have some, too. I've been staying here, you know, since Sunday. I've made myself a comfortable bed on that compost heap that does duty as a sofa.' She went before I could thank her again.

Alex's presence in the room had been a hallucination. Yet as soon as I was alone, the uneasiness returned. I knew it was irrational. Even if he did find me I had only to tell him that I could not marry him and that I really meant it. I tossed restlessly in bed, wondering what there was in my temperament that had made this such a difficult thing to do. The flaw was in me. I understood that much.

A month after meeting him, when I suspected that I was falling in love with Alex I was amazed to find how rapidly he had moved into my life and made his presence necessary. I found myself waiting with impatience for his daily telephone call to ask me how my work was going. He never let me get away with a vague 'all right'. He made me describe my satisfaction on a scale of one to ten and then to evaluate the changes. I could see that he was attempting to train my mind to have the same kind of concentrated focus as his own. It was stimulating and I was grateful. He showed me what I had suspected, that during the last two or three years my approach had verged on the mechanical. The human face had become irksome by demanding exclusion of so much else that was interesting. Two weeks after our meeting Alex had offered to support me financially for a period so that I could stop taking commissions and experiment. I would not agree to this.

He had already been more than generous. I had insisted that I could not keep the Gainsborough drawing and he had taken it back without protest. But the third time we had dinner together he had given me a tiny fob watch, its dial surrounded by pearls and the back enamelled in blue with a spray of flowers in diamonds. I felt that we were friends by then and it would be ungracious to refuse it. I wore it almost every evening and loved it. But two weeks later, when he gave me a miniature by the eighteenth-century painter Richard Cosway, I protested.

'If you like it and I like to give it to you, why shouldn't you have it?' Alex had said.

'I can't afford to give you anything in return.'

'What really bothers you is that I haven't asked you for the usual reward a woman bestows on a man who takes her out to dinner and gives her presents. For shame, Freddie! What a conventional idea!'

'Certainly I don't mean that,' I had answered crossly, though the fact that Alex had become intimate with my life and yet, after a month of meeting at least every three days, had not so much as taken my arm was now almost constantly in my thoughts. I had explored all the obvious theories, that he might be homosexual and needed a woman to present a front to the world, that he might not be particularly interested in sex, that he might even be physically incapable, but nothing he said convinced me that any of them might be true.

He never paid me compliments about my appearance, though he sometimes praised me if he thought I had expressed myself well in an argument. Once I had taken him up to my flat to see my work. He had spent a long time looking at it and then said that despite the restraints of having to gratify the sitter, it had about it a pleasing fluidity. There was something there to develop. He had asked to see the rest of the flat. I had shown him the bedroom and the kitchen. He had looked at them without comment and then we had gone out to dinner.

'So if I were enjoying your body you would feel happier about accepting these things,' Alex had persisted. 'But I told you that first day that I wouldn't touch you until you asked me to. It has led to a certain lack of gallantry with coats and climbing into taxis but otherwise I don't know that there has been any ill-effect.'

So I took the miniature and that evening when we said goodnight I kissed him on the cheek. He smiled but made no attempt to return the kiss, accepting it with a slight bow. I realised if we were to progress from friendship to a love affair it was up to me to instigate the change. I must seduce him. I enjoyed the extraordinary sense of freedom it gave me to be with a man who asked nothing in return for everything he gave me. I was grateful, and inclined to think his generosity must demonstrate something that could only be love. I could not help but be struck by the contrast with other men. I failed entirely to recognise that this, also, was his intention.

I lay on my side beneath the muslin canopy of the bed at Drop Cottage, watching the changing patterns of firelight reflected on the wall, and abandoned further attempts to come to a decision about the future. The next moment I was in a boat, trailing my hand in the

116

water. Fish were nibbling my fingers. At first it was a pleasant tickling but then it became a definite bite. I woke with a shout. A pair of greenish-yellow eyes, inches from my own, stared at me as I cackled like a hen with fright. My heart began to slow as I recognised the black and white cat from the Rectory. The insistent sucking of my fingers ceased the minute I put out my hand to stroke him and Macavity started to purr.

'How did that bad animal get in?' Prim frowned, as she put a tray on the table and helped me to sit up. 'He was here on the doorstep on Sunday when I came back with Swithin. He must have followed you home from the Rectory. He's been sleeping across your threshold ever since, a picture of devotion.'

'If he's devoted to anything it's ham.'

'And everything else in the edible line. There are paw-prints on the butter and all the corners of the loaf have been chewed.'

'Oh dear, I know one shouldn't feed other people's animals but don't you think we might — '

'Don't worry. Today he's had a whole tin of rabbit-flavoured Purr-e-Kat, a third of a pint of milk, the remains of some fish I cooked for him yesterday *and* half of Chloë's supper.'

'I'd forgotten about Chloë. How is she?'

'She's been up and down the stairs to see you. But Macavity's hissing seems to have demoralised her. Luckily she gets on very well with Balthazar, my spaniel. I hope you don't mind but I brought him with me. He pines if I leave him too long.'

'How could I mind anything when you've been so kind? Besides, I've discovered that I like dogs. I'd love to see Chloë.'

In response to Prim's call she appeared at my bedroom door. She whined affectionately and wagged her tail, but approached the bed with caution, keeping an eye on Macavity who lay stretched out, curling and straightening his paws as though riding an invisible bicycle. Chloë sank, groaning, on to the rug before the little grate.

'This is cosy, isn't it? No doubt Chloë's and Macavity's fleas are starting a new bloodline.' Prim put the tray across my knees. 'Potato and leek soup, the only vegetables Mrs Creech had.'

'Gosh, parsley in March.' I admired the dark specks floating in the soup.

'I'm afraid not. They're bits of rust. I ran the tap for ages but it wasn't any good. I might have overdone the salt. I get rattled doing things by gaslight. It's like living in a tent. I know it's romantic but somehow I seem to have lost my taste for that, over the years.'

'Was the woman who lived here called Anna?'

'Yes.' Prim looked up from her plate of soup, surprised. 'How did you know?'

'I saw her name scratched on the window. Did you like her?'

'Not really, if I'm truthful, but she was very attractive. She looked like a heroine from a novel by Sir Walter Scott. Long black hair, lots of tossing it about. Big dark eyes, tiny waist, retroussé nose. The only flaw was her voice, very high and childish. I found it irritating.' The picture I had of Anna underwent a complete revision. For some reason I had imagined her to have brown hair and that quiet gallantry that belongs to many unmarried English women of that generation — a refusal to allow loneliness to excuse flagging standards, a life painstakingly built round service to others and a pattern of domesticity at home. Good books, good works, good posture. 'Naturally she was very attractive to men. There was a doll-like quality about her that I think appealed. Amazing isn't it that even men of sense prefer to mate with their intellectual inferiors?'

'Do they?' Was I Alex's intellectual inferior? We were so different that the idea had not occurred to me.

'Men like women to be cushions, something they can leave an impression on. That's tough on me. I'm incapable of that kind of beguiling responsiveness.'

'I don't believe you. I thought Dr Gilchrist was in a fair way to being smitten.'

'Oh, Edward.'

'Don't you like him?'

'Yes. Yes, of course I do. One couldn't not, really, he's so obviously . . . good. But he isn't quite the hero of one's dreams. He always reminds me of a good-natured Hereford bull. It's the hair, I think. And I don't like weakness in men.'

'Weakness?'

'He drinks. Not when he's on call, naturally — though I think that sort of thing creeps up on you. Last time we were at the same dinner party he had to be driven home by the host. And at the Winnacotts' Christmas bash — more like a famine, really, two Twiglets and one cheese-and-pineapple stick each, plus the vol-au-vents, of course — Edward had obviously been drinking before he got there. He passed out on the sofa during the Sunday school's rendition of 'Little Donkey'. At first I thought his snores were the sound effects. Mrs Bagshot still hasn't got over telephoning Edward to find out the results of her pregnancy test only to hear manic laughter followed by a drunken version of 'I've got a lovely bunch of coconuts'. It's very bad for his reputation. And once you stop being able to judge it at parties it isn't long before you think a tot of whisky will be just the thing before you go out on your rounds. Not so much a slippery slope but a helter-skelter.'

'Poor Edward. Perhaps he's unhappy.'

'If he isn't now he soon will be.' Prim sat with her knees wide apart, her lower limbs clad in corduroy knee breeches that laced up the sides like Vita Sackville-West's. Her hair, apart from her Shetland pony fringe, was tucked behind her ears exposing a bone structure not unlike V. S-W's, a face very narrow for its length.

'I suppose there are worse things than weakness. Cruelty, for instance.'

'Oh, yes. But is love a matter of comparisons? I've always thought it was involuntary. At the beginning anyway. Afterwards, I think, for women it often becomes just a habit of nurturing. When the passion wears off and you see him as an ordinary fallible mortal, your maternal feelings come into play. However badly he behaves it's a reflex action to protect and forgive him. My mother was like that with my father. He used to make an ass of himself, having silly tantrums if everything in the house wasn't exactly right and throwing his weight about. Though my mother was the brighter of the two she used to say that when he was repentant she could never harden her heart against him. She was too accustomed to considering his comfort. Women are masochists by nature. They bend their necks to the yoke.'

'Do you really believe that men are inferior? That marriages only work because women sacrifice them-selves?'

'Hell, I don't know. These days there isn't time to analyse why marriages go wrong. They've hardly brushed off the confetti before they're heading for the divorce courts.'

'Haven't you ever been in love?'

There was a brief pause. 'Once, years ago. But I didn't have a mane of black hair to toss. When you're as plain as I am you can't expect reciprocity.'

'I won't have you call yourself plain. For one thing, your eyes are remarkable.'

'Thank you. Funnily enough, that's what *he* said. Do you know, it's one of the few things I remember him saying? There's vanity for you. I must say in my own defence, he wasn't a man who talked much.'

'Was that one of the things you loved about him?' I was surprised that someone as fluent in speech as Prim had been attracted to someone inarticulate. 'Don't answer if that's too inquisitive.'

'Oh, I don't mind talking about him. There's always a bitter-sweet pleasure in revisiting the past and recalling those tidal waves of the heart's blood.' Prim leaned back in her chair and her plate slid dangerously near the edge of her tray. 'But there's very little to say. I was in love with him. He was in love with . . . someone else. That's all there was to it.'

'So he never knew?'

'There was one evening when he was taking me home from a local dance — we'd known each other all our lives so there was nothing significant about that — but we were driving through the forest, which felt dark and primitive and the moon was up. I expect I'd had too much to drink. He was concentrating on the road and I was looking at him, thinking that it would be almost a pleasure to be cut into small pieces for his sake. The atmosphere seemed charged. He said, without looking at me, 'What's up?' My circulation surged like the National Grid when the Queen's Speech comes on. I put my hand on his where it rested on the steering wheel. I don't know what I expected. That he'd do an emergency stop and take me in his arms, perhaps. He didn't react. Obviously his hand wasn't a good conductor of high voltage. After a few seconds I took my hand away. We drove on in complete silence.' Prim smiled, her soup forgotten in the piquancy of revisiting the past.

'So nothing was ever said? That must have been very hurtful.'

'It would have been the better evil. When we got to Yardley House he turned off the engine. My hopes leaped up like sardines to a bobbing lantern, only to be cruelly destroyed. 'Dear Prim,' he said, taking my hand in his and patting it as though it were a Labrador's rump, 'I'm very fond of you. You're such a nice, peaceful person to be with. We've known each other such a long time. There's such comfort in that, isn't there?'' Prim began to laugh. 'A complete failure of intuition. It did the trick, anyway. I knew it was no-go. A treacherous tear ran down my face. That was when he made the remark about my eyes.'

'You must have been miserable.'

'Oh, I played my own version of a Greek tragedy for several months and then I suppose I just accepted it. The trouble was that I'd already formed the habit of loving him. And then when he went away — but you're coughing again. Bedtime.'

Prim refused to be drawn further on the story of her old love and produced a toothbrush, mug and a bowl to spit into. I was equally intransigent about the chamber pot that Prim declared she didn't in the least mind emptying. It took ages to get downstairs as my legs had developed a spirit of rebellion.

A path had been cut through the nettles to the privy and it now had all the accessories available to sanitation without plumbing, that is, a roll of lavatory paper and a shining new galvanised bucket. I remembered to duck my head as I went in. The spider had been busy, constructing a web of great virtuosity. I saw it sitting in the centre, striped legs stretched out. As I continued to shine the torch on it, it lifted one foreleg delicately. I wondered if a spider was capable of experiencing emotion. As days of work were destroyed in seconds did it feel frustration and rage? Did it triumph at its own cleverness as it watched a fly struggling? Or fear as the dark shape of a bird dropped down upon it? It seemed impossible that it should eat and breed and spin and kill in a state of impassivity, obeying only instinct.

Creeping sensations of chilliness cut short these

122

musings. I wondered how I would find the strength to get all the way back to my bedroom. My limbs were trembling with tiredness and my head was spinning. A bush beside me rustled and sprayed me with raindrops. Very close to my ear I heard the first few notes of 'Come Into The Garden, Maude.' I went up the stairs faster than Roger Bannister.

'What on earth's the matter with you?' Prim, who had been straightening my bed and emptying the saucepan that collected the rainwater out of the window, looked at me in surprise as I dragged myself, with panting breath, the last few steps.

'It's that blasted whistler again. He's taking years off my life. It's simply terrifying to know someone's so close and you can't see him.'

'Just a blackbird on its way back to the nest.' Prim didn't look at me as she hung my dressing-gown on the door. 'Is this your nightdress?' She held out the rose pink silk. 'It's exquisite.'

'It isn't mine.'

'Then it must be Anna's. Well, I'm going to wash it and you can wear it. No good letting something so lovely go to waste.'

'Why don't you wear it? I have no particular rights to it.'

'Because I've got shoulders like an Olympic breast-stroker. And I'm rather pigeon-chested to boot. But it would look wonderful with your hair.'

I thought perhaps Anna would not mind. I would prefer my things to be appreciated when I no longer needed them. If there is anything that binds one to life in this world, after death, I can't believe it's a piece of clothing.

'You're looking very serious.' Prim straightened the sheet across me. 'Is there someone you'd like me to telephone? Someone who was expecting you back in London, perhaps?'

'There isn't anyone.' Prim looked surprised. Possibly my tone had been unnecessarily vehement. 'The truth is — I've run away. It was very cowardly of me but I had to have time to think.' I laughed, then coughed. 'George thought I might have robbed a bank but I can assure you it's nothing like that.'

'Don't feel you have to explain a thing.' Prim was tidying my bedside table. She turned her bright, direct gaze to me. 'Honestly, you mustn't feel because I've told you so much about myself that you've got to do the same. I don't know many women of my own age that I feel I could really talk to, so I've bent your ear inexcusably.'

'I'd happily trust you with any secret. Only I'm afraid you'll think badly of me. It's strange that circumstances — well, your kindness, actually — have thrown us into such intimacy but we hardly know anything about each other.' Prim sat on the bed next to Macavity who lay on his back, paws in the air, snoring. 'Alex and I were supposed to be married last Saturday. I keep telling myself that I've done the right thing for both of us. Oh, God! I can't think of him without seeing his face — so shocked, almost frightened — as though he couldn't face the fact that I was leaving him. I feel sick whenever I think how much I've hurt him. I keep wondering what he's doing. Is he sitting in our house now, hating me, hating himself, drinking too much, lonely and comfortless, his self-confidence in ruins?' I burst into tears.

'You paint a dreadful picture. But unlikely. Remember, he *is* a man.' Prim's acerbity was a helpful check to the weeping that was making my chest fill with phlegm. She patted my hand and waited for me to stop crying. 'I knew you were in trouble. While you were feverish you kept apologising to Edward. 'I'm so sorry, I'm so sorry,' you said, over and over again. And now and then you shouted,

'Alex!' I wasn't sure if it was in love or dread. Perhaps it was both.' I sniffed and wheezed and blew my nose on the Kleenex Prim offered me, too exhausted to speak. 'Good. Now you'll feel better. Lean forward while I puff up your pillows. There, now you can lie down and be quiet and stop worrying. We'll talk about it in the morning if you still want to. I'm going to turn the lamp down low. If you want anything just yell. No morbid thoughts, now. Apparently Churchill always said, 'Bugger everything,' when he was on the point of nodding off and it enabled him to sleep like a baby.'

I did as I was told. No one had mothered me in this fashion since Mrs Pope had walked out of the house saying that the days of slavery were over and she wouldn't submit to it. An hour later she had returned, said she was sorry and asked Fay to take her back. But Fay had said it was good riddance to bad rubbish. Mrs Pope had looked up sadly at me as I leaned over the banisters. 'I'm ever so sorry, Miss Freddie, my lamb. I shouldn't have let her drive me to it. I feel that badly to be leaving you, really I do. But flesh and blood can't stand it.'

I had not been able to cry much after my mother died. I had been so frightened by my longing for her that I had tried to shut up my heart. I went through those first terrible months with a jaw that ached with tension and a chest that felt as though it was stuffed with something hard and prickly like sawdust. I felt out of breath all the time and my hands and feet were cold and tingling. Sometimes a sob had broken through despite myself. If I was alone I found walking fast up and down the room was helpful. If there were other people present I used to get a book and stare at the pattern of words on the page, without reading them, until some duty like school work or talking to people drew me back into the stir of the world. I think people

125

were surprised to be confronted by a small puppet with a face of wood.

When Fay came to the house in Cheyne Walk, the day after my mother's funeral, I recognised her scent at once. My father had been stinking of it for ages. She bent to kiss me and said in a cooing voice, 'Oh, you poor little girl!' Her hair stuck out stiffly like gold wings on either side of her face. I thought she looked very pleased about something. I dug my nails into my palms and stared at her shoes, shiny black with very high heels. Fay looked round the hall and up the stairs — my stairs. 'Heavens, Charles! What a lot needs doing to it! It's perfectly Victorian! But the bones are good.'

Then Mrs Pope came up from the kitchen basement and my father introduced them.

'I'm going to transform the house for Mr Swann,' Fay said, in bright, clear tones as though Mrs Pope were deaf or stupid or both. 'I'm sure you'll be able to help me a great deal.' Mrs Pope had looked very hard at my father and Fay. Then she put her arm round me and led me swiftly away, as though shielding me from evil influences. 'God, what a gruesome old bat,' we heard Fay say, as we scurried downstairs.

Four years later, when Mrs Pope went away I could allow myself to cry for her and, at the same time, let some of the much deeper sorrow well up like blood to fill a cut. It was agonising but it was also an alleviation of the grief that I carried constantly with me beneath the surface of my daily life.

'What's that?' I half raised myself on my pillow. A descending trill of notes sounded from the garden.

'It's a nightingale. Listen!' Prim held up a finger. 'How lovely! What does Thomson call her? 'A sober-suited songstress. Ships, dimly discovered, dropping from the skies.' Whatever can he mean?'

'I really believe it is.' I lay still, listening to the

arias, too wild and unresolved to be shaped by a human brain. The next moment, my dreams were a confusion of disconnected thoughts and tantalising images. Accompanied by the sweet, inchoate melodies, I slept better than I had for months.

11

'Let me do that.' Guy leaped up as I leaned forward to put my cup on the table. Prim, who had been moving rapidly towards me was thwarted as Guy slipped a cushion behind me. On the table beside the sofa was laid the apparatus of the sick — a thermometer, a jug of lemon barley water, a glass, aspirin and a box of Kleenex. In addition there was a vase of violets, *Country Life* and grapes brought from Tarchester by Guy.

It was three days later. I had been carried downstairs with great ceremony. In literature if not in life, illness carries with it overtones of purging and redemption. I had not been sick long enough to do my character a great deal of good but none the less I felt that significant changes had occurred in the course of it. For one thing I was dependent on the goodwill of those looking after me. I was as helpless as a baby and with childlike irresponsibility I found myself comfortably detached from the usual carking care. For most of the time I was able to live fairly happily in the present.

Guy had insisted on carrying me down the stairs and had managed it gracefully, without groaning or puffing. Prim had swathed me in wraps and massaged my feet to improve their circulation as she said they were looking rather white. The rivalry between Prim and Guy to be indispensable to me was so bitter that they had stopped speaking to one other. It had the indirect effect of curing me faster than anything else could have.

As Guy professed not to be able to cook, Prim was obliged to spend time alone in the kitchen while he and I talked. He sat at the end of the sofa and took my feet in his lap. My indisposition gave the whole thing a chaste, acceptable intimacy. Chloë and Balthazar, Prim's black spaniel, lay back to back on the rug. Macavity remained aloof, asleep on my bed. A damp log sizzled as it burned and the chrysanthemums on the table glowed a vinous purple.

'I shall be sorry when you're better.'

'Isn't that rather unkind?'

'You aren't suffering, are you? Just a little weak and missish. It was a bad dose of flu or whatever it was but you're on the mend. And I expect you're a trifle jaded after your narrow brush with matrimony. When you're better I'll take you out and show you things.'

'Things?'

'Ruined castles, grottoes, gorges spanned by high bridges as wide as a hand's breadth, waterfalls like plumes of smoke, lakes blacker than a starless night.'

'Really?'

'Well, there's the cement works at Eastbury. And some pretty ups and downs with sheep on, some of them ours.'

'Somehow I don't see you as a son of the soil,' I said, noticing the perfect symmetry of his face, thrown into chiaroscuro by the firelight. It is rare for the two sides of people's faces to match exactly. His mouth was wonderfully bowed like a girl's.

He pulled a face. 'I don't like farming, that's for sure. There never seems to be anything between crisis and tedium. Either the animals are dying of a virulent plague, the machinery is broken beyond repair and the weather is flinging down thunderbolts or else you can't do anything because it's too wet or too dry, the ground's frozen or the bloody stuff won't ripen. It's dull and smelly and dirty.'

'Couldn't you get in a farm manager?'

'Can't afford it. We can only just keep going as it is. Most of the valley's not fit even for grazing.'

'What would you like to be, if you could do something else?'

'I'd like to be a photographer.' I was surprised. Somehow I couldn't see Guy wandering through war-torn cities taking eloquent shots of children's emotionally ravaged faces against burnt-out buildings. 'Once I modelled macs and shooting sticks for a company that makes expensive togs for sporting gents. Quite boring but very well paid. It struck me then that the bloke behind the camera was having more fun than anyone. He made great play of being creative and temperamental. It was apparent that he was also making several, if not all, of the female models.'

'Aha! Now I understand.' Images of Nadar and Cartier-Bresson faded. 'You want to be a sort of David Bailey. Have you done anything like it?'

'As soon as you can totter on your pins, I'll take some shots of you. Nude would be best. It'll lend an air of artistic sensibility. I shall make my bedroom into a studio. You'll love the house. Girls always do. That reminds me. My father's giving a dinner on Saturday. Everyone will be a candidate for the undertaker's box of paints. The house will reek of mothballs and lavender bags. It'll be the sort of occasion that makes you want to stuff your napkin in your mouth to stop yourself screaming. We're one woman short so I suggested you. I told him how beautiful you are and he got quite keen. Say you'll come. It'll be the only thing that'll get me through it.'

'Well, thank you. You make it sound irresistible. Is your attendance at this grisly occasion absolutely necessary?'

'I've got to keep the old boy happy. He's quite capable of changing his will.' Guy lit a cigarette and looked serious for once. 'My father never tires of telling me that when he dies the whole place will go to Vere. Want a suck, darling?'

'No, thank you.' I waved away the cigarette smoke that seemed to be battling with oxygen for the exclusive right to enter my nostrils. 'Who's Vere?'

'My elder brother. He scarpered twelve years ago. It's a family trait.'

'What do you mean, scarpered?'

'Ran off at the age of twenty-three with — ah, no names, no pack drill. Whatever that means. I wouldn't mind a little pack drill with you, Freddie. In that context it sounds rather exciting.'

I gripped the poker which lay on the hearth beside me and raised my hand threateningly though really there was little I could do as he had hold of my feet. 'Be quiet or I'll box your ears. Go on telling me about Vere.'

'About ten years ago we had a letter to say he'd been killed in a railway accident in India. My father pretends to refuse to believe it. That's because he's dying for the chance to take his revenge on Vere. And also because he wants to annoy me about the will. I'll have to prove Vere is dead before I can claim a penny. It'll be a terrible nuisance.'

'You're making it up again! I wish you'd try to make some distinction between fact and fantasy.'

'I swear it's the truth.'

'Fathers don't take revenge on their sons these days, do they? It sounds like High Victorian melodrama. But don't tell if it's a painful family secret.'

Guy paused for a moment. 'Well, if I don't tell you someone else will. It's not exactly a secret round here. The woman Vere ran away with was our father's mistress.'

'Guy!' I waved the poker. 'The truth now. Or do I have to beat it out of you?'

'What are you two doing?' Prim, her face pink from the kitchen fire, came in to find that Guy had snatched the poker from me and was holding it over my head. We were both laughing.

131

'Now, Freddie, promise you'll whack me really hard. You know all public schoolboys get excited at the merest mention of beatings. You really are the most remorseless tease.'

Prim took the poker from him. 'Now we've *all* got black hands. Don't encourage him, Freddie. He doesn't need it. Look, you've got soot on your blankets. Really, it's like taking Sunday school except you two are worse than children. I would have thought some people had homes to go to.' She looked pointedly at Guy.

'Some people are dreadful spoilsports. I bet Prim was a horror at school. Head prefect, ink monitor, sneaking on the other little girls to the headmistress.'

'I bet Guy was expelled for trying to sodomise all the juniors. I never knew anyone so addicted to sex.'

'Has use of the second person singular become illegal or something?' I protested. 'Why don't you just be nice and talk to each other? You've both been so kind and I'm very grateful. Please, let's be friends.'

Guy and Prim regarded each other with hostility until Guy suddenly winked. Prim began to smile, reluctantly. 'Want some stew, you shocking reprobate?'

'Thanks, you dear old autocrat. I'll come and help you.'

I heard them arguing in the kitchen about who was to carry my tray. I looked around the room. The curtains trailed loose threads from their ragged hems, but they no longer blew about in the draughts. Prim had filled the broken panes with pieces of cardboard. A high wind sent whooshing noises down the chimney and rattled the front door. Balthazar's head was pillowed on Chloë's tail. The logs shifted as they burned, sending out wafts of apple scent. Cupid, accompanying a tinny bell, struck eight times with his arrow. A porcelain shepherd and shepherdess, which Guy and I had identified as either Chelsea or Derby, languished charmingly among lambs and flowers on the book-shelves. Poor Anna, I thought, having to leave this.

'Here you are.' Prim gave me my supper. 'Now, I want to see a clean plate.'

'You know, those breeches do nothing for you from behind.' Guy looked at Prim critically. 'What with the masculine attire and the commanding voice, I think you may well be metamorphosing into a sergeant major.'

'I don't care!' Prim glared at him. 'They're perfect for gardening. Unlike you, I don't think appearances are the most important thing about a person.'

'An exemplary attitude, of course. If true.' Guy looked at her quizzically.

'Well, I suppose I may be presumed to know — '

'Oh no, please!' I groaned. 'We were all getting on so nicely. I shan't be able to eat anything if you're going to quarrel.'

'We don't mean it really,' said Guy. 'It's just our fun.' He took hold of Prim. 'Give us a buss, my chuck, for old times' sake.'

Prim flushed redder and pulled away. 'That was ungentlemanly. Sit down and eat and shut up.'

I pretended not to have noticed. 'Prim, you must have known Vere. Guy's been telling me the strangest things.'

Prim sat in the armchair on the other side of the fire. 'Yes, I knew him.'

'Well, that's more than I did,' said Guy. 'I was twenty when he went away. After prep school he went to Winchester and I went to Harrow. The holidays were never long enough for us to get to know each other again. I hunted in the winter and played cricket in the summer. Vere used to go off on his own on his bike, or sit in his room, reading. Strange solitary fellow. A dark horse.'

Prim laughed. 'Do you remember that tennis tournament? The Parchments had one every year. It was the high spot of the Dorset season. Strawberries and

133

wine cup and dancing afterwards. Your father made Vere go to it when we were about sixteen. I never saw anyone play so badly. I don't think he had the least idea of the rules. Every ball was lodged into the wire netting or went miles outside the court. Once he hit it so hard it went up into the sky so high that I swear it never came down. He wasn't asked again.'

'I remember very well. Polly Parchment was fifteen. I was thirteen. We locked ourselves into the summerhouse and took all our clothes off. She had a bottom like two warm peaches. Now she's a gym mistress with thighs like duffel bags. Vere knew perfectly well what the rules were. He used to play tennis for Beech House, our prep school. He was pretty good. Then he decided it wasn't what he was interested in.'

'Looking back I can see now he wasn't really very happy, was he?' said Prim musingly.

'He and my father never got on. It's quite hard to be the black sheep in our family as we're all dyed deeply dark of hue but Vere always managed to behave worse than any of us. I remember the time he got drunk one Christmas at dinner. It must have been his last in England. He'd managed to hog a whole bottle of claret to himself. The candles had been snuffed so that we could admire the jolly flaming brandy. Vere suddenly stood up, leaned forward and threw up over the pudding. He doused the flames so we were plunged dramatically into darkness. When the candles were relit he sat down again and said to the old girl, Lady Frisk, who was sitting next to him, 'I beg your pardon. You were telling me about your horse. Three-quarters thoroughbred with a dished face and a tendency to windsuck. Or was that your daughter?' Then he keeled over into the nuts and raisins and had to be carried upstairs and put to bed. The summer after that he ran away.'

'Is any of this true?' I appealed to Prim.

'I can't vouch for the pudding story.'

'My father used to treat his mistress like a whore. Most of the time he was cold and insulting. But he liked her in bed. He used to tell us over breakfast what a good fuck she was. When he discovered that Vere had been making the beast with two backs with his light-of-love my father had another stroke. Couldn't speak or move for weeks. He gradually got better. He cried a lot, I remember. So perhaps he did care about her.'

'I doubt it.' Prim stubbed out her cigar with a force that was almost angry. 'I'd put it down to temper. Hatred is by far the longest pleasure, as the poet said. Your father's an expert. Though I felt sorry for him at the time. It must have been humiliating to be so publicly betrayed.'

'What a sad cynic you've become, Prim.' Guy laughed and gave my foot a secret, affectionate squeeze. 'But it's true that the milk of human kindness runs sour and watery in the paternal vein.'

I was silent, thinking of my own act of betrayal in running away. Prim's words had stung. Alex had been made to look a fool. And I had given him no opportunity to plead for himself or even to understand why I was leaving him. I decided then that I must go back to London and face him as soon as I was well enough to manage the journey. There could be no question of staying until the weekend. I owed Alex a proper explanation.

There was a knock at the door. My heart made a jump for my throat. Because I had been thinking of him I was convinced it was Alex. George's grinning head appeared round the door. ' "He that made it was to sell it. He that bought it did not want it. He that used it never saw it." What is it?'

'We don't know. Give up,' said Guy impatiently. 'What do you want, Brat?'

135

George looked black and raised his fist towards Guy. 'Don't call me names. I shan't give you the letter if you do.'

'Hand it over, you ass, and let's have less of your cheek.'

George dragged his foot across the room and stood before Guy, scowling terrifically. 'I'm *not* an ass. I'm cleverer than you, Mr Guy! Almost everybody is. Granfer says 'tis because of you the lambing's so poor this year. You only got an old ram and you didn't put him in soon enough. He says you're the worst farmer in Dorset and couldn't mend a fence to save your life. He says other folk must put your mistakes aright. So there!' George opened his eyes wide and stared defiantly at Guy, who looked back at him in some amazement.

'Does he, by God?' Guy began to laugh. 'The old devil! And he's always so obsequious, too. Well, he's probably right. Oh, do stop looking like a tragedy queen, George. You ought to be on the stage with your predilection for scenes.'

George raised his fist again. 'You making fun o' me, Mr Guy? I can knock any man's block off. See how strong I am?' He clenched his fist to demonstrate the muscle in his pitifully thin arm.

'All right, you're a regular turkey-cock. Here's tenpence and be off now.'

'The letter isn't for you,' said George after pocketing the coin Guy held out. 'Unless your name's . . . ' he consulted the envelope ' . . . Miss Swann.'

'Who could have sent it?' I tried to see the envelope, fearing that I might see Alex's neat, sloping hand.

'You haven't guessed the riddle.' George's eyes were pleading. ''He that made it was to sell it. He that bought it didn't want it. He that used it never saw it.''

I thought as hard as I could. 'A blind man's stick?'

'Not bad.' George was grudging. 'Happen it could be that. But it ent right. Give up?'

'Give up!' we chorused.

'A coffin! Here you are.'

The writing, large, upright and turbulent, was Viola's.

'I think Freddie's answer was more interesting,' said Guy.

'Oh, do be quiet, Guy.' Prim frowned at him. 'George, have you had any supper? There are some potatoes and stew left if you'd like it.'

'Would I, Miss Yardley? You bet!'

I opened the letter.

12

Darling Freddie, thanks for the postcard. I'm v. relieved you are in the land of the living. Hope you got there safely and the cottage isn't in too bad a state. Everyone's been asking me where you are and I tell them I think you've gone to Brazil. I was eating a nut at the time of the first telephone call and that's what put it into my mind. Anyway, Brazil is a good way off and no one I know ever seems to go there. I've suddenly become very popular. Even Jacquetta Kingsley, you know, that intense dark girl, tall and stretched-looking like an El Greco, rang me this morning to see if I knew anything and said she was asking Alex to dinner because she felt so sorry for him. Of course she wants to get her paws on him. But if you've changed your mind again, darling, don't fret. She hasn't got a hope.

Another sharp prick to my self-esteem. I was cast for ever as vacillating and capricious. I deserved it.

Fay has telephoned twice. She can hardly speak for temper. When I suggested Brazil she slammed the receiver down. I ran into Oonagh Fitzpatrick last night at the Pemberton-Broody private view. She said she thought Alex had some sort of Svengali hold over you. She was quite nasty about him and utterly sweet about you, trying to get me to admit that I knew where you were. I'm very conscious of the fact that I'm a most unsuitable confidante because I'm hopelessly indiscreet but I'm really trying hard. Henry was there too. He looked happier than I've seen him for ages. Whatever you say, he was in love with you and still isn't over it. I wouldn't be surprised if he isn't at the airport now buying a ticket for Rio de Janeiro. (Is that in Brazil?) Funnily enough the only person who hasn't contacted me is Alex. But the most interesting thing is that I'm being followed. No, honestly. There's a little bald man in a Gannex mac who follows me everywhere. He stands outside the house all day when I'm working at home and the other day I spotted him by the fish counter in Harrods food hall. When I looked over he pretended to be examining an octopus. I went upstairs to the Georgian Restaurant to meet Stella Partington for lunch and there he was again, staring at a row of pandas in the toy department. I don't know why Stella always wants to have lunch with me. I'm utterly dumbfounded by her smartness and when she tells me she's been round the world four times since I last saw her on a shipping mag-nate's yacht in the company of Rudolf Nureyev, Maria Callas and the Crown Prince of Romania I can never think of anything to say but gosh. Giles says that's why. Anyway, yesterday I saw him again — ancient macked super-sleuth — in the toothpaste section of Boots. So I'm going to have to be cunning about posting this in case a hand comes up out of the letter-box and snatches it. I'm rather shocked. I mean it's got to be Alex, hasn't it, that's put him on to me? I think it's more than a little sinister and double-handed of him. But as you once said to me Alex is a man who has to be master and only allows you to think that you're making the decisions. You said you found it rather sexy.

I stopped reading for a moment. Had I really thought that once? How elusive, how wayward is sexual desire. What had first disarmed my defences and dissolved my mistrust became in time the index of our incompatibility. Alex was the first man I had met who knew exactly what he wanted and who controlled himself so that he could control others. It seemed to me a rare quality in men. I think my father, for example, was quite unaware that Fay ruled him, even to extent of explaining to him what he thought about things. Alex's high degree of emotional cognisance was one of the surprisingly feminine aspects of his character. His self-command was miraculous. I had found this seductive without quite knowing why. Now I thought it had something to do with the pleasure of giving up responsibility for myself. He allowed me to be a child again and for a time I had enjoyed this. But after I had played for a while in his kindergarten, indulging whims and desires, the idea that I was an adult with a mind of my own had reasserted itself and I had begun to chafe against the kind, caressing hand of authority. And then I found that there was a tiger's claw in Alex's velvet paw.

'George dear, it isn't considered good manners to use your knife like a spoon.' Prim put her hand on George's arm which was cranking away like a piston, shovelling in food with the blade. 'Sit up and hold your knife properly, not like a pencil.' Prim tried to shape George's grubby hand round the handle of the knife. 'You seem very hungry. Didn't you have any lunch?'

'There was only boiled taters.' George spoke with his mouth full. 'Granfer had Spam but there wasn't enough for me. I didn't want the Spam anyway. It was black in parts wiv fur on it. The tin was blown.' I saw Prim press her lips together. 'I stole some raisins from the pantry afterwards,' George added, sensing sympathy.

'It's never right to steal.' Prim spoke absently. She went into the kitchen. George saw me looking at him and very slowly he dropped his left eyelid in a wink. He

140

looked so bright and devilish that I realised instantly where lay the resemblance that had been hovering at the back of my brain. 'Now,' said Prim, placing a bowl of rhubarb crumble in front of him, 'either use a fork on its own or the spoon and fork together. Never the spoon alone.'

'Why?' asked George quite reasonably, allowing some crumble to fall from his mouth.

'Because . . . I don't know why. It's just the way it's done. If you're going to get that scholarship to Tarchester Grammar you don't want the masters to disapprove of your table manners, do you?'

'Don't care.' George scowled and allowed custard to dribble down his chin.

'Don't care will be made to care. I don't believe I just said that. Exactly like Nanny. George, you should hold your spoon resting between your thumb and the knuckle of your first finger.'

'But that's like a pencil! You said not to hold me knife like that!'

I left Prim to wrestle with the arcane rules of polite behaviour and returned to Viola's letter.

Of course, sexiness is something more mysterious than the darling old Sphinx. I don't complain of this, but it does seem in extremely short supply. If anything were to happen to Giles — I can't bear to even think of it!!! — I should have to resign myself to celibacy. I mean there are so many attractive, interesting women around and so many rather awful men that clearly the most intelligent thing is to be a lesbian. But when Oonagh fondled my bottom last night it only made me want to giggle. I mean, is homosexuality involuntary or can you cultivate a desire for your own sex?

I did not know the answer to this.

Anyway, none of this helps your current predicament in the least. I wish I knew what you were thinking and feeling. I hate to think of you lonely and depressed.

It struck me keenly that I was neither of these things and then, more painfully, that I ought to be.

Be sure to tell me at once if there's anything at all I can do. And please write soon. Fondest love, Viola.

I turned the page and saw that there was a lengthy PS. It was written in ink of a different colour so I gathered there had been a lapse of time in the writing.

Well, yesterday I was congratulating myself on having shaken off Gannex Mac, having spent the morning shopping in Bond Street — the most delicious pair of shoes at Scarpino's but zillions more than I could afford — so I went to Fenwick's for a cup of coffee to mull it over before dashing back to buy them — pale grey suede with four-inch heels, not exactly useful, I know — anyway, not a glint of GM for hours then I saw this man loitering outside the shoe shop who looked vaguely familiar. A nose like a plum, one of those dark purple ones, Early Rivers, I think they're called. Then I remembered that I'd seen him staring at a display of knickers in Fenwick's. Anyway, Plum Nose is lurking outside in the residents' garden as I write this. I can see his shuffling about through last year's leaves. I feel I ought to rush out and warn him that the place is nothing but a dogs' loo. This must be costing Alex a fortune. It's like being in a spy film, quite exciting, but isn't it rather unkind of Alex to pursue you like this? Unless he seriously thinks you've gone mad and are a danger to yourself. I mean love is about letting the other person do what they want, isn't it? Best love, V.

I folded the letter. I understood what Viola meant about the kind of love that allows the beloved free rein to be themselves. But probably there were as many different ways of loving as there were lovers. And within those different ways as many complicated and contradictory sensations as there are seconds in the day. Constraints were not necessarily bad. Might one not, for example, be changed for the better by attempting to deserve a lover's good opinion?

'You're looking tired, Freddie.' Prim bent over me and pressed a cool hand against my forehead. 'I thought so. A little bit of a temperature.'

'I'll carry you up.' Guy tried to get between me and Prim.

'How kind but I need to go to the privy. And I'm going alone,' I added firmly. Prim brought me a pair of gum-boots and a torch. 'Actually, being waited on hand and foot is extremely addictive. You've both been angelically kind and I can't think how I'm ever going to return it.'

'I can.' Guy's whispering, as Prim went to fetch my coat, made my ear buzz.

'Don't do that! Honestly, do you never think of anything but sex?'

'Darling Freddie, you ought to be ashamed of yourself. It's you that has the one-track mind. All I was going to ask of you was your attendance at that dinner on Saturday.'

'Oh, all right. I mean, thank you.'

Here was another demonstration of a woeful inability to make up my mind when not half an hour before I had decided to return to London. But Viola's letter was a stark declaration of Alex's determination to get what he wanted. I was afraid that he would be able to talk me back into marrying him. I needed to be mentally and physically stronger before I confronted him.

I managed to remember the low beam just inside the

kitchen. I had heard variously pitched howls throughout the day and both Prim and Guy had bruises on their brows. Outside frost was falling and the little path Prim had made to the privy was slippery. The moon was up, gazing with lopsided calm across the valley, and stars sparkled like crystals of ice. The spider ran to the centre of its web as soon as I shone my torch on it. It never seemed to catch anything. It must have been my imagination that it looked thinner. I wondered if spiders felt cold. I don't know why this should have reminded me of the phantom whistler but it did. I heard nothing from him as I returned to the house. I had just sufficient charity to hope that he was well wrapped somewhere indoors.

''Bye, Miss Yardley. Thanks for the bit o' dinner. 'Bye, Miss Swann. Thanks for the bit o' fire. 'Bye, Mr Guy. Thanks for nothing.' George favoured us all with a grin before going out and letting the door bang.

'The little blighter. I wish I hadn't given him ten p.'

'Defiance is his only weapon, I suppose.' I swallowed the cough medicine Prim had poured into a spoon for me as though I were a child and waited until she had carried the dishes to the kitchen sink. 'He's a Gilderoy, isn't he? I'm amazed I didn't see it at once. He's got your mouth and bone structure exactly.'

'What an eagle-eyed little thing you are! Now I come to think of it, I expect eagles have eyes that are fearfully bad-tempered and unpleasantly orange. Yours are a fascinating greenish-grey, like a mossy rock under water and generally filled with sweetness.'

'If you don't want to talk about it, that's fine. But don't flirt, please. I'm still too weak.'

'Aha! That suggests a time to come when it will be acceptable. You're absolutely right. George is Vere's bantling. Dusty's daughter, Lizzie, was a comely lass. A generous armful.'

'What happened to her?'

'Drowned in the mill race. Must have been the end of everything for her when Vere went off.'

'Oh, poor, poor girl!' I suppressed the hard things I thought of Guy's brother. 'And poor George! He's bright though, isn't he? Is he likely to get this scholarship? An education might be the saving of him. He seems very unhappy living with his grandfather. Can nothing be done about his foot?'

'I'm not the child protection officer, you know.'

'But you're his uncle. Don't you feel some kind of responsibility for him?'

Guy looked at me in a considering way before replying, 'Yes. You're quite right. Slipping him change isn't enough, is it? But, you see, I owe it to Vere's memory not to queer the pitch further for him with my father. You must see that my position's delicate. I can't do much for George without acknowledging the relationship, can I?'

'What relationship's that?' asked Prim, coming in with the hot-water bottle, which she had wrapped in a shawl. 'All right, if I wasn't meant to overhear I'll pretend I didn't.'

'One can't expect to keep secrets in a house the size of a packet of tea. How on earth did they manage to have progeny?' Guy seemed keen to change the subject. 'It must have been like making love in the village street.'

'I think Sunday school was probably invented for the increase of the human race.'

Prim tactfully made no further reference to the conversation she had unwittingly overheard but I said, 'We were talking about George. I feel so sorry for him. Not enough to eat and having to spend his free time helping his grandfather in the mill. It doesn't seem a proper life for a child.'

'You're quite right. I've thought before that something should be done. He ought to have help with his school work so that he can get that scholarship. But

I don't suppose Dusty would pay for coaching even if he had the money. And no one knows who the father is.'

There was a pause. I did not look at Guy.

'Oh well,' he said, with a little sulkiness in his voice, 'what does it matter? I'm sure I can trust you to be discreet. George is Vere's child.' Guy looked at Prim in rather a challenging way and I realised that, however lightly he spoke of his brother, Guy was deeply attached to his memory. It was the other side of the joking, flirtatious Guy and the contrast made this evidence of greater seriousness, when it came, all the more attractive.

'Vere?' Prim looked blank and closed her eyes, something I'd noticed she did when thinking. 'Well, you could knock me down with a bargepole!'

'Aren't we mixing our metaphors?'

Prim hugged the hot-water bottle absently. 'Vere and Lizzie! There never was anything more unlikely!'

'I don't see why. Lizzie was pretty little thing. Perhaps not Simone de Beauvoir when it came to conversation — '

'Oh, for heaven's sake, Guy! I'm not talking about whether or not he fancied her.' Prim's tone was impatient. 'There are other considerations. It was an act of brutal callousness to leave her in the lurch. I'm surprised that Vere — oh, well, he was young. Poor Lizzie! I remember when they found her body, wreathed in weeds — no, I can't bear to think about it even now, after so many years.' Prim gave me the bottle to hold while she lit another cigar. It was evident that her thoughts were far away. Then she shook her head, as though banishing unpleasant ideas. 'So! What are you going to do about our little basket, Uncle Guy?'

Guy looked pained. 'I suppose I shall get no peace now until George is Senior Wrangler and Archbishop of Canterbury with a house on the Côte d'Azur. But, don't you see? If I start doing things for the boy everyone will want to know why. Vere made me swear that I wouldn't ever tell anyone. Doesn't giving my word count for anything?'

'Don't worry about that.' Prim spoke with firmness. 'You can use me as your agent. We'll work together but you can give me sole credit and I'll just have to live with the burden of undeserved glory when he's Master of Trinity.'

'Hang on a minute. Just what have you got in mind? Remember, my resources are limited.'

'You can afford to pay for some coaching. I'll go halves with you. And Dusty'll do what you tell him, whatever his opinion of your skills as landlord. You must make sure that he allows the boy time after school to do his homework.'

Guy looked depressed but did not demur.

'I wish I could help,' I said. 'I've only got forty pounds in the world to call my own. I daren't use my cheque book.' I explained about the joint account.

'You mean, even though you've told him unequivocally that you don't want to marry him he'll try and run you to earth?' Prim was incredulous. 'It sounds to me like persecution.'

'Perhaps it is. Only I'm so confused I can't tell what's right and wrong any more. All I know is that he's looking for me.' I told them about the relevant parts of Viola's letter.

'Good God! The man's a tyrant!' said Prim. 'Well, don't fret, Freddie. Guy and I will come to your defence. Won't we, Guy?' He saluted her, his expression ironical. 'You needn't worry about repaying me, Freddie, for any little thing I may have done for you.' Prim's fine brown eyes gleamed. 'Thanks to you, I'm beginning to enjoy a sense of mission and purpose that I haven't felt for ages. I shan't be able to sleep tonight for making plans.'

Guy sighed heavily.

13

'This is a very great pleasure, Miss Swann.' Ambrose Gilderoy got up from his chair with difficulty and moved towards us with the aid of two sticks, throwing his weight from one leg to the other to gain forward impetus. He gathered both sticks into the same hand so he could shake mine. 'How delightful of you to come to my little party. You'll find us sadly dull, I'm afraid. No one of your own age but my wicked boy and Werner, the son of my dear friend, the Baroness.'

Despite his infirmity it was easy to see that Guy's father had been a very good-looking man. His hair, dark-grey and brushed straight back from his high forehead, gave him an old-fashioned distinction. His frame was contorted but his face was still handsome and his eyes were bold and cynical, like Guy's. The paralysis on one side of his mouth made his smile sardonic. He tapped Guy's arm affectionately with a hand that shook little. The other was twisted, barely able to hold the handle of the cane. 'I mustn't give you the wrong impression, my dear. Just a little wayward-ness that the passage of time is bound to cure. We must not judge too harshly. Throughout history the scales have been weighted heavily in favour of handsome young men.'

Considering that Guy was thirty-two this seemed graciously indulgent.

'Thank you for the testimonial.' Guy's tone was non-committal. There was no corresponding cordiality in his expression.

'Come along my dear.' Mr Gilderoy rested his hand on my arm. I felt it tremble with effort. 'Let me introduce you to my other guests.'

Backs creaked and knees snapped like pistol-shots as several elderly men hoisted themselves from their chairs. As one always does, I forgot the names as soon as they were given to me. I was handed a glass of champagne and sent to sit on a sofa next to a woman with grey hair plaited into an insecure chignon who told me, with the air of conferring largesse, that her name was Lady Frisk. This was familiar. I remembered the story about Vere and the Christmas pudding. Lady Frisk asked me at once if I hunted and when I said I did not, lectured me on its beneficial effects for young women, provided one remembered plenty of Pond's cold cream if there was a wind and a hot bath the minute one got home. There was nothing like hunting, Lady Frisk said, for promoting a healthy mind. Lady Frisk's voice had a piercing tone, projected forcefully into my ear.

'You look very much in need of outdoor exercise, Miss Swann, if I may say so. Quite washed out. I suppose you are not anaemic? I recommend raw liver pulverised to a paste. A little nutmeg, pepper and paprika makes it palatable. My secretary can send your cook the recipe.' I opened my mouth to beg her not to go to such unnecessary trouble but she paused only to draw breath. 'With your constitution you should not indulge in rich foods and too much alcohol. Your complexion is as muddy as any I have seen.' I drew back as she leaned closer to allow her little grey eyes to wander over my face. 'A girl's greatest beauty is a clear skin. It is a mistake to try and cover blemishes with makeup.'

'I'm not wearing any.'

'Just as I thought.' Lady Frisk's chignon wobbled as she nodded. 'A touch of rouge would make all the difference. My daughter, Charlotte, has been brought up always to sleep in a mask of oatmeal and egg-white, and cotton gloves filled with a mixture of Vaseline and

149

the juice of a lemon to ensure white hands.'

'It sounds horribly uncomfortable.' I thought it was time I asserted myself a little. I resented so much unasked-for advice and, anyway, I concluded, looking at Lady Frisk's mottled cheeks and nose hectic with broken veins, it came without warranty. 'And supposing one were married? Might one's husband not reasonably object to so much mess on the pillow?'

'Ah, well!' Lady Frisk threw up her hands and flung back her head violently as though the sofa had given way beneath her. 'If you intend to practise the vulgar habit of sharing a bedroom, I have done with you!'

This was good news. I sipped champagne and looked across the room at Guy, who was whispering something in the ear of a woman with a red wig and bright pink cheeks. She smacked his hand with her evening-bag but looked pleased.

The drawing room of Gilderoy Hall was beautiful, with a handsome Adam fireplace and plasterwork on the ceiling and above the doors in the same style. The panels were framed with gilt and ebonised mouldings. The furniture was a harmonious blend of eighteenth- and nineteenth-century mahogany, the curtains a green brocade with handsome pelmets, the sofas and chairs comfortably upholstered in slip covers of faded chintz and needlepoint. A very good landscape of the school of Constable hung above the fireplace. The room was not quite grand but it was elegant, with that distinguished ease acquired when its decoration has evolved slowly over time. It had a masculine air, suggested not only by the absence of flowers and small ornaments but more blatantly by the prominence of a tantalus of spirits on a side-table, a pile of newspapers on the floor by the master's chair, the redolence of cigar smoke, even from the cushions of the sofa on which I sat, and a general impression of homely untidiness.

'Now, don't mope, Miss Swann.' Lady Frisk rapped

my knuckles painfully with her spectacle case. 'I cannot bear sulking. You must conquer pride and accept criticism from those who have more experience of the world.' She followed the direction of my gaze to Guy's companion in the red wig. 'That woman should be an example to you. She is certainly wearing too much makeup! One thinks of circus clowns!'

I was tempted to say that the woman *was* makeup. I could see from ten paces that her eyelashes were false. She must be several pounds lighter when she took everything off to go to bed.

'I always tell Charlotte a little *papier poudre* to quell shininess and a hint of rouge on the cheeks and lips is all a gentlewoman should resort to. Beauty comes from within. She has a raw egg beaten in milk every morning as soon as she wakes up.'

I decided that Charlotte must be an absolute ninny if she had nothing better to do than rub things into her skin and doctor her insides with quack remedies.

'Do tell me,' I asked, hoping for cheap revenge, 'what does Charlotte do?'

'She is studying for her Ph.D. in Astrophysics at Cambridge.' It was annoying. 'Who *is* that woman?' asked Lady Frisk, looking again at the red wig. 'One of Ambrose's *cercle amitié* one surmises. Of course, I am the first to recognise the advantages of a nearer relationship with our European neighbours but one need not have them actually in one's drawing room. She looks quite French to me,' she added, in tones of faint disgust. 'Ah, Baroness, how do you do?'

Lady Frisk nodded graciously to a woman of late middle age, who had just come into the drawing room with a walk so slow and stately she might have been following a coffin. She had sat very upright on the edge of her chair and closed her eyes. In acknowledgement of Lady Frisk's greeting the Baroness lifted her eyelids and lowered them again. She had an austere, bloodless face, like a portrait by van Eyck, with white hair tightly braided and fastened round her head.

A young man with blond curls, who had come in with the Baroness, bowed to Lady Frisk. 'So extremely delightful to see you again, Lady Frisk. I hope you are finding the veather enjoyable?'

Lady Frisk frowned at him. 'Certainly not. It is unseasonably cold and it hasn't stopped raining for a week.'

'Ah. Yes. The English veather. It is so bad as to be quite a joke, *ja?*' He laughed good-naturedly, displaying shining white teeth.

'I beg your pardon.' Lady Frisk looked more annoyed. 'I think the climate in Great Britain is superior to anywhere. We have the benefit of the Gulf Stream, of course, which Germany does not. Being an island has served to protect us from more than one kind of menace.' She got up and walked away, leaving the young man to stare after her in bewilderment. He had not yet learned that only the English may be rude about their own weather.

'Werner von Wunsiedel at your service, Fräulein.' I introduced myself and he brushed his lips against my hand. His chin was prickly and I saw that what had looked like a smudge of dirt was an incipient beard. 'Permit me to say that you are a decoration to the evening. These parties of Ambrose are so nice but not . . . young. May I sit next you on this fine sofa?'

'Certainly.' I thought I caught a flash of the Baroness's eye but when I looked again more carefully her face was as still and blind as a classical statue.

'It is very delicious for me to talk to a beautiful young English lady. Ve who have been born after the var can forget all those difficulties between us, can ve not?'

'Of course we can,' I cried heartily, immediately very conscious of them.

'Our parents are old enemies but ve new bloods are

152

citizens of the vorld!' He flung out his hand in a theatrical gesture, knocking the monocle from the eye of a red-faced old man who was bending to stub out his cigarette in an ashtray nearby. 'A thousand pardons, most excellent sir. The spectacle has received no hurt?' The old man backed away muttering something like 'infernal jackass' into his moustache. 'Now vat vas I saying, my dear Miss Freddie?'

'Um — something about being citizens of the world.'

'Ya, Ya! Ve do not think of disputing over boundaries.'

It seemed to me that, on the contrary, he thought of them a good deal. I allowed my glass to be filled again. I could see it was going to be an evening of unremitting work.

Werner fairly gulped back his champagne before giving me a significant look. It might have been my imagination but I thought the Baroness's deportment had taken a distinct list in our direction. 'Vat an extraordinary thing that ve fellow spirits should have met in just this vay in this so delightful house hidden avay in English countryside. Let us drink to Destiny!'

'Werner.' The Baroness's eyes were open and looking at him though she did not turn her head. 'Fetch me my furs.'

'Certainly, Mutti,' Werner got up and rushed away obediently to return with an ermine tippet but not before the Baroness, moving with surprising speed, had taken his place beside me.

'Thank you, dear heart. Now go and tell Madame du Vivier I hope she will favour us with her beautiful piano playing at some time during our visit.'

Werner went away, his expression a little sulky. The Baroness hung the wrap over the arm of the sofa. 'We were not introduced,' she said, turning her head towards me but looking at the toe of my shoe. Her eyelids were patterned with forked violet veins. 'I am the Baroness von Wunsiedel and Werner is my son. You are staying long in Dorset?'

'No. I'm going back to London in a few days' time.'

The Baroness made a small expansion of the lips that might have been a smile. 'Werner is a delightful boy but young for his age. Perhaps I have overprotected him. It is possible.' She acknowledged the fault with a slight inclination of her head. 'One in his position, his family, his birth — you understand. One must guard against bad influences. He is a little . . . headstrong, easily drawn in by the wiles of others. He is about to become engaged to the Princess Prenzlau. I thought you would like to know that, Miss Swann.' For a moment she lifted her eyes, the colour of a wintry sky, to mine.

Werner had returned from his errand. 'She says she vill be happy to oblige you. But really,' he lowered his voice, 'she plays so badly it is frightful to hear, like hitting the vood with a hammer.'

'Miss Swann, you look pale,' said the Baroness, ignoring Werner. 'You should go nearer the fire. Here there is a draught. Werner will sit beside me.'

I felt very cross to be ordered about but on the other hand I was heartily sick of the Baroness.

'Ah, Meez Swann.' The red wig, who was Madame du Vivier in person, claimed me as I walked away. 'You, I can tell, are not native of zese parts.' I hoped she was not going to remark on my shattered appearance. 'You have ze style. Such a charming dress if I may say so.' She lowered her voice. 'Not like zese dull women who come to dinner wearing ze cook's curtains.' She looked directly at Lady Frisk, who was clad in purple bombazine. I warmed to Madame du Vivier, although she was quite frightening close to. Her face powder was distinctly lavender and her eyelashes dragged themselves apart as she blinked. Her scent — something like frangipani — was so overpowering that I began to sneeze. 'Oh! you have ze rhume! Allow me to recommend one of ze excellent suppositories I have in my room upstairs.'

★ ★ ★

At dinner I was seated between the old man with the monocle, whose name was Lord Deering, and a slightly younger man called Montague Barst. At once they began to talk to each other literally over my head. I didn't much care. I ate the soup, which was what English hotels call 'cream' of cauliflower. Actually, it was quite good. When the attention of Montague Barst was claimed imperatively by Lady Frisk, Lord Deering asked me if I hunted. Again I denied it. I could tell he lost interest in me immediately but mindful of social duty he bent to his task.

'We had a good day out yesterday. Found three times, killed twice. Put my old mare over a stake-and-bound fence no one else would touch and she took it like a bird. Galloped a couple of rings, then left-handed by Bartleshaw Wood, down the old fosse-way. Ran it to earth down a blocked drain. Fox couldn't stagger another inch but, by golly, she gave us a good run for her money. Nearly came a cropper across a ditch with wire. Some of these damned farmers don't know what's what.' My sympathy was entirely with the fox. I stopped my ears mentally and found myself thinking about Alex.

It was the sort of evening that Alex, perversely, would have enjoyed because it would have taxed his social skills to the utmost. To him boredom was failure. The more unpromising the occasion, the greater the triumph. Alex disliked the country because it was too often cold, muddy and uncomfortable and he despised the hunting, shooting and fishing fraternity because he thought the enjoyment of killing harmless creatures puerile. He had once said that had the pheasant, fox or deer been similarly armed with shotguns or teams of

155

trained animals capable of pursuing and killing the hunters, then he might have seen something in it.

But he relished encounters with that section of the English upper class that despises the artistic and intellectual, to be found in droves wherever there are parks and trees. They were naturally suspicious of his conspicuous cleverness and alarmed by his eloquence. Alex bore himself like a gentleman, dressed soberly, eschewed ostentation, was polite to dotty aunts and dogs, yet he was not one of them. He was too smooth, too quick to comprehend, too alert. And there was that olive skin about the eyes. A disturbing hint of the exotic.

Alex was quite aware of this and he enjoyed the challenge of overcoming their prejudices. Middle-aged women were generally the quickest to lower their defences. He was too astute to compliment them on looks they knew had gone absent without leave decades before. Long married to inattentive husbands, they were flattered by the interest of an attractive, intelligent man. They had been uttering the same wearying platitudes since their first coming-out dance but Alex was adept at drawing from each banality the thread of an argument that he proceeded to explore and embroider. He did it in such a way that seemed to put into their mouths the wit and invention that was his alone. Women who had known, ever since their husbands had fallen out of love with them, that they were dull and plain were astonished to find themselves fascinating.

Young women, accustomed to masculine concentration solely on their outsides, were excited by attention to their insides. After conversation with Alex the most thoughtless schoolgirl was prepared to consider herself complex and original. He liked to probe people's psychological recesses and he had the gift of asking pertinent questions with a marvellous impartiality that was as effective as a truth drug. When occasionally I overheard these women telling Alex things they might

156

have blushed to reveal to their mothers or their husbands I was amazed.

Men were generally more opaque, groping in obscurity in matters emotional, and preferring a rayless landscape wherein to hide from unpleasant truths. But Alex's professional life had trained him to lead people along predetermined paths without them knowing it. By dint of a little subtle excavation in the regions of fear, doubt, and grievance, he exposed the evidence he was looking for.

When I asked Alex once why he bothered to do it, he said it made boring people interesting. I thought this reply disingenuous. I could see that it created a spurious kind of intimacy, where the candour was only on one side, and that it placed Alex in the role of mentor and savant that was gratifying for his ego.

When I accused him of this he said I was being naïve, that we all manipulate others for our own ends. I argued that if this was true, and I thought it probably was, the difference lay in our being unaware of what we were doing. Motivation was supremely important and there was a difference between instinct and calculation. Alex said this was specious nonsense and what was it that I was actually objecting to? Did I expect him to sit mute at dinner? Was I jealous of his interest in other people? Attractive though the idea was of devoting himself entirely to me he thought that I might come to find him tedious if he did nothing but work and confine himself exclusively to my society.

We had this conversation some six months after meeting, shortly after we had decided to get married. I was much struck by the way I was left with the feeling of being in the wrong. When arguing with Alex I found it difficult to keep hold of my own side of the case. When I thought about it more coolly, later, it occurred to me that Alex had resented my criticism and had swiftly turned the tables to demonstrate not only that I

157

took insufficient trouble with my fellows but also that I was in danger of being egocentrically demanding of his time and attention. I did not think either charge was true.

'My old chestnut now, eighteen, give or take a day, and getting thin about the withers but she's only ever given me one bad toss. Devil of a nasty place it was, ditch with a willow stump in it. Couldn't blame her for coming down.' I looked into the bloodshot eyes beneath the coarse curling brows of Lord Deering and wondered what possible fears and sorrows this man might have that I might plumb. He put a yellowed thumb nail into his mouth to scrape a piece of meat — we were now eating duck — from between his front teeth and I looked away hastily. 'Damn fool of a hunt servant forgot to block the earth so we put the hounds at one end and lit a fire at the other. Ha, ha ha! That gave the fox something to think about!'

I at once abandoned the task as being beyond my capability.

'I say, old man, don't hog all the beauty to yourself,' said Montague Barst turning from Lady Frisk to give me a sentimental look. Lady Frisk drew herself up and looked decidedly offended.

I was expecting to be asked whether I hunted but Montague Barst was a man of different ilk. With his dinner jacket he wore a daring waistcoat of dark green moiré and a paisley bow tie. Montague had a set in Albany and prided himself on being more intellectual than his country neighbours. He pursed his small mouth constantly, selecting the *mot juste*. We had one of those unsatisfactory conversations about current West End plays. As we had not seen any of the same ones it was very dull.

It was a pity because the dining room was charming, pale duck-egg blue panelling and alcoves of porcelain that looked interesting, and the food was the sort that

Mrs Pope used to make before Fay got her on to *cordon bleu*. It was simple and robust, with fresh ingredients, and I was able to eat a good deal of it. This was probably because I was, if not happy, more serene than I had been for a long time.

'By God, that was a test of the sweetness of one's nature.' Guy gave me a glass of champagne. We were in the billiard room, alone. Guy had offered to get another bottle of brandy and had taken me with him. He told Madame du Vivier, who had been hanging on his arm since the men had come into the drawing room, that he wished to show me the spectacular view of the valley. She had looked disbelieving and given me a smack on the bottom with her evening bag that had made me spill my coffee. The window in front of us was large, the billiard room being a Victorian addition, but as it was quite dark outside and the moon was obscured by cloud, I saw nothing but the vague outline of something massive, black against an indigo sky.

'You seemed to be having rather a good time.'

'Actually Madame du Vivier's quite a jolly old thing. We talked about you. She said you had *du chic* and there was something about your mouth that suggested you could be quite passionate.'

'How misleading appearances can be. I might have said the same, with as little real evidence, about her eyebrows.'

'Except that her eyebrows are only rather unconvincing pencil and come off at night and your mouth doesn't.' Guy kissed me swiftly on the lips. 'No. Still there.'

'Don't!'

'What's the matter? Do you think your betrothed might be out there, hiding in the bushes with field-glasses trained on our window?'

The idea was so horrifying that I took a step back. 'It's just that I feel it would be disgustingly disloyal of

159

me to flirt with another man, having hurt Alex so abominably.'

'You've thought about it, then. That's good. Madame du Vivier's theory is you can always tell a sensuous woman by the way she constantly touches and strokes herself, plays with her hair, that sort of thing. We noticed that nearly all the time you were fiddling with your ear.'

'That's only because I was trying to prevent myself hearing what that horrible old man was saying. I must say, considering she was practically undressing you over the pudding, she had some nerve talking about *me* being sensuous.'

'There's no 'practically' about it. I thought it was one of the dogs nuzzling my crotch under the table as they are wont to do but when I put down my hand I encountered Madame's hot little claw.'

'Oh, what nonsense! What a liar you are!'

'It's God's truth. I found this in the zip of my fly.' He held up a curved piece of purple plastic, a false fingernail.

'How delightful to see you enjoying yourselves.' Ambrose Gilderoy was standing at the door. I wondered how long he had been there, watching us as we laughed. 'I thought I'd come and see what had happened to the brandy. Though, God knows, Barst and Deering seem half-cut already.'

When Lady Frisk had been asked by Ambrose to take the ladies into the drawing room, Lord Deering had staggered across the dining room to open the door, his eyes wandering independently in alcoholic befuddlement, and said, very loudly, 'That's it, that's it. Always let the seasoned battle-horses take the lead.'

For some reason Lady Frisk appeared to hold me responsible for this remark for she delivered a homily over coffee, fixing me the whole time with her eye, explaining how careful she had been to warn Charlotte

160

of the dangers of flirtation and the reckless inflaming of men's appetites.

'*Sacrebleu!*' Madame du Vivier said, to the elderly woman with a flat face and bulging eyes, like a Pekinese, sitting next to her. 'What can *she* know of men's appetites?'

'I always find a suet pudding answers,' replied the Pekinese. 'With plenty of jam.'

Madame du Vivier looked bemused.

14

Ambrose took my arm and led me to the window. 'Turn out the light, Guy, so that Miss Swann can have a proper look at our valley.'

As my eyes got used to the darkness, I made out the irregular outline of the hill on the other side and saw the stars emerge in gaps between the clouds. At this point the valley was much wider than at Drop Cottage and the hills were loftier. The river was hidden by trees.

'There, now! Look at that!' Ambrose clutched my arm more tightly as the moon came from behind the clouds and dropped a glittering ladder of beams. The vast ruin of a great house standing above the black woods on the opposite hill was temporarily animated by the rays, and the gaps in its walls became lighted windows.

'Oh, how beautiful!'

Half fortress, half fairy palace, the springing arches of the Gothic doors and windows boasted of man's genius. The roofless walls told of his fallibility. I was surprised to find myself affected almost to tears by the sombre grandeur of the decayed building.

'Magnificent, isn't it?' The old man seemed to share my emotion for his voice trembled. 'Spokebender Abbey. One of the loveliest houses in England. Now nothing but a shell. One thinks of the vain bluster of Ozymandias. 'Look on my works, ye mighty, and despair!' '

Suddenly we were caught in brilliant light and the panorama before us was snuffed out. Miss Glim, her face blocks of brightness and darkness to my dazzled eyes, stood at the door. 'I beg your pardon, sir. I didn't know you was in here. I was looking for another bottle

162

of brandy for the men.'

'Quite right, Cissy. I have been neglecting my guests.' Ambrose's voice lost its elegiac tone and became brisk. 'That was a very good dinner you gave us. Didn't you think so, Miss Swann?'

I smiled at Miss Glim. 'I thought it was delicious.'

She didn't look at me. 'Will you be wanting me any more this evening? I can do the glasses in the morning. I'd be glad to get to my bed.'

'Of course, of course. You must be tired. Just take the brandy into the drawing room and I'll follow you. We'll leave these two young people together to enjoy the view a little longer. Romantic, isn't it?'

Miss Glim cast Guy a piteous look, as though she were a bird whose breast had been pierced by a thorn. Ambrose shuffled out of the room in front of her. She allowed the door to bang.

'I think we ought to follow them. Your father doesn't realise it but that poor woman is in love with you.'

Guy laughed. 'My father knows it all right. That little postscript was just to spite Cissy. He's a dab hand at that kind of thing.'

'I don't believe you. I think he's rather a dear.' I had been wondering on and off all evening why Guy hated his father. Ambrose was a considerate host, encouraging his guests to talk and seeming content to listen. And it was evident that there was poetry in his nature. There had been genuine emotion in his voice when he talked of Spokebender Abbey.

'I'll tell you a story. Sit down.' He pushed me gently into an armchair by the window and perched on the arm. 'Are you sitting comfortably? Then I'll begin. Only don't expect a fairy-tale. That house, Spokebender Abbey, was the seat of the le Maistre family for four hundred years. The Gilderoys are parvenus. We've only been here since 1746 when this house was built. The two families have always been friends and rivals, with numerous feuds and intermarryings. The last le Maistre to live there, Colonel Harry, was the same age as my father and they grew up more or less as brothers. They learned to fish and shoot and ride together, and went to the same schools. My father was always the cleverer of the two and won the Latin prizes, but Harry was better at all the outdoor things, a crack shot, all that sort of thing. My father went to Cambridge after that and Harry went to Sandhurst. At weekends they used to racket about London together.

'Then they fell in love with the same girl, a singer called Georgiana. I suppose it was because they were so used to competing with each other that they chose the same woman. She was pretty but my father says she had a voice like a screech owl. Anyway, there was a pitched battle for her favours and for a while it could have gone either way. Harry was taller, my father was handsomer. Harry was more dashing, my father better at wooing. Probably she was playing one off against the other to see how much money she could get out of them.

'Then the war came. Harry was called up at once. My father was exempt because he'd had rheumatic fever that was supposed to have affected his heart. Poor Harry, bivouacking on some dreary foreign plain, while my father and Georgiana had all the fun of London in the black-out. He must have felt as sick as a dog when the telegram came to say that my father and Georgiana were married. Perhaps Georgiana thought Harry would be killed. It's possible she really preferred my father. He can charm your soul from your body if he wants. Vere was born in 1942 and I followed in 1945. After the war Harry, now Colonel le Maistre, a hero with the scars to prove it, came home to Spokebender Abbey and everything went on much as it had before.

'Harry and my father were, so I've been told, very like each other — both arrogant and reckless and they liked to live hard. I suppose my mother's presence excited the rivalry. They despised anybody who wasn't prepared to live as they did and that was virtually everybody in the area. That must have been when the county started to talk of the two families as godforsaken reprobates. Hellfire Club, all that sort of rubbish. The parties they had were pretty wild by all accounts, though naturally the locals weren't asked. I expect a lot of the stories were made up.

'Anyway at some stage, not long after Harry came back, he and my mother revived their old love affair. She started to spend a great deal of time at Spokebender Abbey. So there was this *menage à trois*. I can imagine my father watching and biding his time and actually quite enjoying it. He gets bored easily. It must have made the time pass pleasantly.

'On Sundays there were regular card games and terrific drinking sessions. They always played for very high stakes to make it more exciting. My father suggested putting the two estates into the pool. Harry was drunk enough to agree. My father won Spokebender Abbey with a straight flush, and the next day he threatened to take Harry to court if he didn't pay his dues. Harry probably thought that the whole thing was an elaborate joke. It made a terrific local scandal once the two families' solicitors got involved but Harry kept on smiling through it.

'My father told Harry he could stay on as his tenant for as long as he cared to. But the minute my father had the documents of transfer of ownership in his hands he sent his men over to strip off the roof. Every tile, every piece of lead. The whole building down to the coal bunker open to the skies. And there was nothing Harry could do to stop him.'

My champagne suddenly tasted sour. 'I can't believe anyone could be so . . . vindictive!'

'How little you know of the world, my sweeting. Of course, once there was no roof Harry had to move out.

God, can you imagine how angry he must have been? I'm surprised he didn't kill my father. But he had his revenge. My father evidently thought he had dealt their little *tendre* a fatal blow as everything Harry had was tied up in the estate and my mother had no money of her own. It seems he underestimated a genuine passion. Perhaps my mother was sorry for Harry. Or she disapproved of what my father had done. I've no idea what sort of woman she really was. Anyway, when Harry left he took my mother with him.'

'I don't know who to feel most sorry for,' I said slowly. 'But I suppose it must be for you and your brother.'

'I would have been much more upset if Nanny had been the one to go. I don't think I saw much of my mother. We spent all our time with the servants and the horses and dogs. We didn't feel deprived. In fact, we were pretty happy then, freer than most kids. Nanny tried to discipline us but she was a soft touch. A bit simple.' Guy laughed, his handsome face lit with amusement. It seemed altogether ridiculous to see him as an object of sympathy. 'My first memory was of Vere's dog. He was called Raffles and he ate one of Nanny's gloves. He threw it up again soon after, minus the buttons from the cuff. Vere came into the nursery several days later and said he'd found the buttons in the garden. He held them up to show us and then, while Nanny screamed at him to put the filthy things down, Vere dropped them into his mouth and swallowed them. He said he wanted to see what Raffles had felt like. There was a terrible to-do and the doctor was sent for and Vere was beaten for it. Vere told me years later that they weren't Nanny's buttons at all but two chocolate drops. When I asked him why he hadn't told the grown-ups that it was only a joke, he said it was to get his own back. I couldn't see that. After all, Vere had the beating and the row and the purgatives. But that was

166

Vere for you. He always was odd.

'My mother had already left by then, I think. My father had the first of several strokes when he found she and Harry had gone off together. But his will to win was stronger than the paralysis. He got over it very fast that time, with no lasting effects. And when the news came, two years later, that Harry had died of alcohol poisoning in some dreary hotel in an out of season resort on the Italian Riviera he must have triumphed. He used to tell us, Vere and me, that our mother was a low-bred harlot who'd returned to her roots. Vere remembered her much better than I did, of course. He used to go very white when my father said that. I think he used to cry at night but perhaps I only imagined it. Nanny was very nice to us and used to call us her poor little ewe-lambs. Strange, now I think about it, as we were both boys. Vere got very silent and secretive then, I suppose as self protection.'

'Whatever you say, it sounds very sad.'

'Your solicitude does you credit, my darling, but it was all a long time ago and I've fully recovered from any childhood hurts.'

I wondered if that was true. 'I must go home.'

We collected Chloë from the kitchen. She seemed very pleased to see us and followed me about, licking my hands. The kitchen, large and old-fashioned, with a cooker and fridge on legs and cream-painted cabinets with red Formica tops, was warm and tidy. It smelt of food, shoe polish and ironing. I noticed on the floor near the door a row of men's shoes, gleaming, neatly arranged on newspaper. Some newly laundered shirts hung on coat hangers above an electric heater. There were stacks of clean plates and rows of knives and forks spread on the table, partly covered by drying-up cloths. There was no sign of Miss Glim, just a solitary mug left to dry on the draining board. I hoped the cup had not been bitter because of me.

167

Ambrose was in the hall, saying goodbye to those guests who were not staying in the house. Lady Frisk frowned at me as Guy helped her into yards of ancient musquash. Ambrose bent to kiss her hand with old-fashioned gallantry. Again I wondered if everything Guy had told me was invention. My eye passed beyond him to the wall where the painting of a young woman hung half in shadow. She was fair and had Guy's curved mouth and the same generous space between brow-bone and eyelid. It was not very well painted but it had caught the air of amusement and raillery that was the essence of Guy's charm. Ambrose turned his head quickly to see what had attracted my attention. He gave a little sigh and a slight shake of his head as if to suggest that her loss was still painful to him.

'Thank you for a delightful evening,' I said, as he took my hand.

'Guy, go and entertain Madame du Vivier and the Baroness. I want to importune Miss Swann for just five minutes. You'll indulge an old man, my dear?'

I tried to look pleased, though I was aching with tiredness. He leaned on my arm as we crossed the dining room to a door behind a screen. He opened it and switched on the light.

A breath of cool, scented air touched my face at the entrance to the conservatory. There were no palms or ferns or wicker furniture, only two long benches of sand in which dozens of flowerpots were sunk to the brim. The colours in those pots were like little heaps of jewels — tiny brilliant petals like mounds of rubies, sapphires, garnets and amethysts set among leaves of emerald, silver and gold. I was enchanted. 'How wonderful!' I said. 'All the world outside grey and dull, still in the grip of winter, and in here a treasure house.'

'This is the Canadian Bloodroot, *Sanguinaria canadensis*.' Ambrose pointed with his stick at a pot of scalloped grey leaves holding pearly buds and

168

cup-shaped pure white flowers. 'The roots are crimson. It likes peat. Here is the miniature lupin *lyallii*. The flowers are so intensely blue one thinks of brilliant skies and hot seas. This little gem with its pink, papery bracts and tiny scarlet flowers has the common name of Pussy-paws. Charming, isn't it? It comes from Mount Rainier above Washington.' The ferrule of Ambrose's stick flashed in the lamplight as he pointed from plant to plant. I scarcely listened, I was too intent on absorbing the variety of form and colour. 'I shall give you these, my dear.' Before I could protest Ambrose had picked several heads of something that looked like an anemone. It had soft blue petals suffused with violet. 'Keep them cool and they will last two days. No, don't thank me. It is most fitting. They are exquisite — like you.'

'I'd love to paint them,' I said. I touched a bud with my fingertip. 'What a pity they will die so soon.'

'Fleeting beauty is the most precious.' Ambrose's eyes were on my face. 'There is so much that is coarse and obvious and omnipresent. You have a leaf in your hair, Miss Swann. Allow me.' He touched my temple and swept down my cheek with his hand. I felt at once the unmistakable sexuality of the gesture. He smiled. It was Guy's smile but infinitely darker and more dangerous. 'Let me show you my latest invention.' He picked up a glass dome like a large bell jar, which was attached to the wall by a long rubber tube. 'See that moth?' I saw a flutter of delicate yellow wings. 'They lay eggs on the leaves. Very annoying.' He put the jar on the bench enclosing the moth and the flowers and turned on a tap. 'There. A little gas and gradually the insect will feel its wings grow heavy. See how it tries to beat them. It can no longer rise. Its head is drooping. It is suffocating slowly. The air that was once the medium of flight is death to it.'

He laughed. 'It's fun to see them go, isn't it?'

Ambrose turned his eyes to mine and I saw pure enjoyment there.

★   ★   ★

Guy pressed the starter button, engaged first gear and we shot forward to overtake Lady Frisk's Austin Princess with only inches to spare, the drive being cut out of the hillside and having a frightening drop on one side.

'Must we go quite so fast?' The headlights caught snatches of bush and tree, gravel and dizzying precipice in flickering succession as though we were looking into one of those Victorian toys that spin round fast to give an illusion of movement. A zoetrope, I think it is called.

'I always try to beat my own record. Don't worry. I could do it with my eyes shut. Look!' Guy closed his eyes. 'All right! Have a care for my eardrums. Your lungs must be getting better if you can scream like that. Eyes wide open, see?'

He drove with exaggerated care all the way back to Drop Cottage. My progress down the path was impeded by the weaving of Macavity against my legs, no doubt intending to tell me that he had not been fed for three hours. My coat was so muddy by now that I slid down the slope with scarcely a care. Guy insisted on holding my hand across the plank bridge though I was getting much less afraid of it. The cottage was in darkness. Prim had gone back to Yardley House the day before. I missed her very much. She was insistent that I must be in need of peace and solitude. I suppose she imagined I wanted the chance to be alone with Guy. He shouldered open the door that, despite Prim's efforts, still grated against the floor. There was a glow from the remains of the fire. Guy found the matches and lit the gas lamps.

'Goodnight,' I said. 'Thank you. It was an amusing evening.'

He took me in his arms. 'Give me a proper kiss. Oh, I know. You're blacker-hearted than Duessa, guiltier than Eve and unfit for dalliance with the worst of men. You look very decorative in your sackcloth and ashes, though. Just put your lips to mine for a minute in a nice sisterly way to thank me for my forbearance.'

I offered him my cheek. Guy pressed me to him in a long and passionate embrace, his mouth on mine. I tried to push him away, at first because I thought of Alex and then, more energetically, because I found myself thinking of Guy.

Guy let me go suddenly and said, 'Ha! Admit it! You liked it!'

'Yes. Yes, I did. Unfortunately.'

'Why unfortunately, my little melter of hearts?' Guy started to take hold of me again but I backed away.

'Because it means I'll have to leave here. And I'll be very sorry. Despite the leaking roof, filthy weather, mud, privy, pneumonia and everything. I'll miss you and Prim and Dr Gilchrist. And the animals. But I'll have to go tomorrow to save myself from getting into a worse mess than I'm already in. Somebody once said that a good conscience is a continual feast. Well, now I know exactly what he meant. If I went to bed with you I'd absolutely hate myself.'

'Uh-uh. Tomorrow's Sunday. No trains.' Guy smiled wickedly at me. 'So this is to be a war of attrition. All right. I'll take away that kiss for consolation. Goodnight, Elfrida darling.'

He closed the front door behind him and I heard him whistling 'Your Tiny Hand Is Frozen' along the path. The trouble was I *had* enjoyed being kissed by him. I saw a rectangle of white on the table. It was a letter from Viola. Presumably George had brought it while I was at Gilderoy Hall. I stood directly beneath a lamp in order to be able to read it.

171

Darling Fred, I thought I ought to warn you at once. I nearly yelled aloud when I saw a photograph of you on a poster at the bus-stop near Marble Arch. It says, 'Have you seen this woman?' and there's a description of you and a photograph. It's rather smudgy but quite a good one, you'll be pleased to hear. I couldn't see what you were wearing. I hate the thought of you being sprung on and marched away by two burly con-stables. I was planning to come down to Pudwell the minute my lectures finish and give succour but unluckily something's come up. Giles has been asked to write a couple of articles on a church in Florence which is stuffed with paintings by Raphael. He wants me to go with him. It would fit very nicely into my dissertation as it happens and normally I'd leap at it. But I hate to leave you so beleaguered. I've said I won't go unless you tell me you're all right. Could you ring me at the flat tomorrow? There's a man on watch outside even as I write — big cheeks and blub-bery lips like Alfred Hitchcock — but I suppose Alex hasn't tapped the telephone. I wonder if he's coming to Florence with us? Alfred Hitchcock, I mean, not Alex. Please don't forget to ring. Be of good cheer, and don't get depressed, Best love, Viola.

It wasn't depression I felt but anger. How dared Alex treat me like this?

As I lay in bed listening to Macavity's purring, Chloë's snoring and the plinking of the water in the bucket — it had begun to rain again — I thrashed through it all once more in my mind and found that anger went some way to cool the flood tide of guilt that had made it impossible for me to think rationally. I had made a terrible mistake in believing that I wanted to marry Alex. But once I had begun to be doubtful, the only possible course of action was to refuse to go ahead. It would have been far, far worse to have gone through the ceremony only to regret it later. Now this was obvious and irrefutable. However, the actual wedding had become so momentous, elaborate and wide-reaching that none of us had been able to think beyond it for some time. The number of decisions to be made — what colour the page-boys' sashes were to be, the quantity and kind of canapés to be served before the wedding breakfast, who was to be asked to stay at the house and who was to be put up at the hotel, what to do about Aunt Minna's dog during the service — had obsessed everyone who had had anything to do with it and the real purpose of the wedding had been buried in trivia. It had become sufficient unto itself, as unstoppable as the car of the Juggernaut, and for a while I had believed I must be prepared to throw myself beneath its wheels.

Now I was sure that I had done the right thing. I had not wanted to stop loving Alex. For a long time I had struggled to suppress the misgivings that forced themselves into the forefront of my brain. I had been prepared to cheat myself in order to go on loving him. Each time I questioned the probity of his affection I had felt a thrill of terror at the idea of being without it. Now I asked myself why I had needed it. Had there been some singularity in Alex's passion that had precisely coincided with some deficit in me?

I stirred uneasily. I felt resistance from Macavity who thrust his legs hard into my back. Chloë grumbled in her sleep. The drips faltered. I did not know the answer.

15

'If it's made you change your mind about staying then — selfishly — I'm glad.' Prim stood at the sink in the kitchen at Yardley House, peeling potatoes. 'Although I agree that putting up posters is unfair coercion, you must admit that the man's certainly keen to get you back. He must love you a hell of a lot.'

'But I don't think that *is* love.' I was sitting at the table, labelling jars of Prim's home-made marmalade, jams and pickles for the next church bazaar. I was enjoying myself, embellishing the labels with pictures of the various fruits and vegetables. 'Don't ask me to define the wretched emotion because I couldn't begin. But I'm sure it must have something to do with wanting the person you love to be themselves. If you can't trust them that far, or if you don't respect their ability to make proper decisions, then you don't really love them. How does that sound? Pure cant, I suppose. Why is it impossible to talk about things like love and God and the eternal verities without covering oneself with embarrassment? Is it because we daren't reveal ourselves even to those who are closest to us by talking about what's most important?'

'Hang on, there are several separate questions in that little lot.' Prim pushed her fringe back from her forehead. A streak of sun through the open window made her face very bright. 'For a start, you're only talking about the most perfect love. I admit it would be the ideal to let your other half have his or her way in all things. But supposing you happen to love someone who isn't perfect and who may wander into error if you don't bloody well keep them up to scratch? Let's take adultery, since that seems to be the major bone of contention between couples. There must be millions of wives who've had to surreptitiously manage their husbands, to remind them of the consequences of tumbling into any available bed. If you let men do what they want, ninety-nine out of a hundred will behave without any regard for self-preservation whatever. Let alone in *your* best interests.'

'Don't you think you're exaggerating just a little?'

'Okay. How many men do you know who would be likely to refuse an opportunity for sex with no strings attached and the likelihood that their wife or girlfriend would never find out?'

'Mm. Well. Of course I know mostly painters and writers and actors and they're a notoriously libidinous lot. I don't think it would be fair to take them as a yardstick. They're all as insecure as eggs balanced on wires. And they consider themselves duty-bound to drain life's cup.'

'How many?' Prim persisted.

I couldn't think of one, actually, when it came to it. Henry, who had been my lover before Alex, had sworn that he was unable to write a line unless he could be confident that he was going to see me every day, if only for five minutes. I was his muse — his Laura, his Celia, his Maud Gonne, his Fanny Brawne. As he was, I thought, quite a good poet, I had taken seriously the responsibility for his output and had very nearly given in to his demand to let him move in with me, though the idea of Henry maundering gloomily about the flat, wanting to make love all the time when I was trying to paint had not been enticing.

It had been almost a relief when I discovered that he had been spending every afternoon, while I was working, in bed with the hat-check girl at a night-club called the Blue Kangaroo. It had been, he told me, purely in the nature of an experiment, to see how emotionally involved he could become through solely

175

physical communication with someone dissimilar in intellect and temperament. When I asked him about the results of the experiment he said they were disappointing. Melody — that was the name of the hat check girl — had a line in pillow talk that was crude and alienating. She called him 'Hunky' and 'Big Boy' and various other epithets that put him off. Henry was offended when I was unable to stop laughing. The absurdity of this was of great assistance in getting over the shock of his infidelity for, naturally, I was hurt.

'I think my father might turn it down,' I said at last. 'He'd be too frightened by what Fay would do to him if she found out he'd been unfaithful.'

'Exactly. Your stepmother's made it clear what he's allowed to do and what he isn't. No conspicuous trust or respect there.'

'Swithin Winnacott probably wouldn't.'

'Mm.' Prim stood still for a moment thinking, a snake of peel dangling from her hand. 'You could be right. He seems to lack the male predacious instinct. All right, but he's the exception that proves the rule.'

'And there's Edward Gilchrist. I really don't think he'd stoop to such a thing.'

I had met Dr Gilchrist several times as a patient and I had liked him more the better I got to know him. I was under no illusion that he came only to inspect my lungs. That he was in love with Prim was obvious. He had large blue eyes that were incapable of dissimulation, and when he looked at Prim they grew soft. When he was talking to me his expression was jolly and his voice was matter-of-fact. When he addressed Prim he looked hangdog and there was reproach in his voice. Love is popularly supposed to transform the plainest into beauties but I think it has to be returned to do that. Unrequited love makes the very worst of us. We behave like beaten curs, hoping to be thrown a bone of comfort. Dr Gilchrist did not actually slink and sidle in

176

Prim's presence, but the spring went out of his step.

'Perhaps not. I can't tell.' Prim cut an eye out of her potato with a vicious stab. 'He is as other men, I suppose.'

'Actually I don't think so. He's more intelligent than most. And he doesn't flirt.'

'No. Except with the bottle.'

'Poor Edward.' There was a short silence. 'I suppose I don't feel as disapproving about drinking as you do. Because of my mother. She drank herself to death but I still loved her more than anyone else in the world.'

Prim looked aghast and put down the potato peeler. 'If I've said anything about Edward's drinking that's hurt you, I'm terribly sorry. I had no idea.'

'Of course not. How could you have? But, you see, because of that I can't see it as a vice. Weakness, yes, but I can love someone whose weakness is their own worst enemy. It isn't quite pity, it's more . . . sympathy.'

Prim stared at the pan of potatoes. 'The trouble is, other people's weaknesses frighten me rather. That must be some kind of insecurity. Paradoxically the more security you have the more frightened you are. It's because you haven't been tested.'

'Perhaps I should thank Fay for that. Driving me to independence, I mean.'

'Was she really so terrible? Tell me about her.'

I tried to be fair as I described to Prim what had been Fay's effect on my childhood. Now I could see that it must have been extremely tiresome to inherit a silent, introverted, grieving child. Fay was an interior decorator of the smartest kind. People's sensibilities were not spared. When I was older but still living at home she used to take me with her sometimes to make notes of her ideas. She would walk into people's drawing rooms, wrinkle her nose — and a very sharp nose it was, too — and say 'Quite horrible. All this must go. I see Empire.' And go it did. The room would become a monument to Napoleon with gilt-and-mahogany columned and pedimented furniture and curtains embroidered with bees and laurel wreaths. People were too frightened of her to protest that they had only wanted her advice on the colour of the lampshades. Of course, it looked wonderful after she had finished with it but her clients must have had permanent backaches from the hard, upright chairs and headaches from trying to read in semi-darkness. Fay hated strong lighting as it was historically incorrect.

The minute she came to live with us, the day after my mother's funeral, she began to redecorate our house. I was moved up to the top floor. It was a lovely room with a good view of the river and Fay did the whole thing in French Rococo. My bed was a *lit à la Polonaise* in yellow-and-white striped silk. I had a green *chinoiserie* chest of drawers that was unusual and valuable but I was not allowed to put anything on it in case I ruined the lacquered surface. The carpet was palest cream and I had to take off my shoes before going in so as not to make marks on it. My bedroom was frequently shown off to visitors so it had to be kept immaculately tidy. If there was so much as a comb on the French gesso-and-gilt dressing table Fay would be angry. Looking back I can see that it was a beautiful room but as a child I longed for my old bedroom and the brass-and-iron bed with the squeak and the lumpy mattress I used to jump on, the comfortable chair with the missing castor that my mother had covered with blue velvet, the flowered bedcover, the desk covered with ink stains and my old pink eiderdown that shed a few feathers daily. When I lay beneath the silk curtains of my elegant new bed — on my back so as to avoid imprinting the embroidery of the pillow-cases on my cheeks — I could see a wicked old man's face glaring down at me from the ruched bit in the centre of the canopy and I spent long hours suffocating with fear beneath sheets so finely woven they were as cold and slippery as glass.

'I remember being convinced that there was a man with shears lying under my bed,' said Prim, after I had described my night terrors. 'I had to jump from my bed into the middle of the room so that he couldn't cut off my feet at the ankles. I'd forgotten all about that until now. I suppose all children have these terrors that they never speak of. I think it was amazingly insensitive of your stepmother to change things. Blast! There goes the telephone again.'

While Prim went to answer it, my thoughts continued on the subject of Fay. By marrying my father she had dropped caste quite as much as my father had when he married my mother, so I suppose she must really have loved him. Her friends were quite grand and she entertained a great deal. Through Fay's contacts, my father was offered consultancies and appointed to directorships. Money ceased to be a problem. I was bought clothes by the armful, though I was hardly ever required to be sociable.

I lived most of the time downstairs in the kitchen with Mrs Pope. Uncle Sid came to visit me from time to time. I tried to keep him and Fay apart because it was obvious even to a child that they wouldn't get on. Once, on Mrs Pope's day off, I looked out of my bedroom window and saw Uncle Sid coming up the street with his jaunty walk and his wide-awake hat tipped over his eyes. I ran downstairs but Fay was at the door before me. Uncle Sid was holding a parcel in his arms.

Fay said, 'We have a regular fishmonger. You need not call again.' I suppose she could smell the prawns.

'I come to see me niece, little Fred,' he said, with that slow shake of his head when something was troubling him.

'Hello, darling Uncle Sid.' I pushed past Fay and took his hand.

'You had better come in.' Fay made no attempt to hide her surprise and disgust.

The three of us sat in the drawing room. Uncle Sid's face looked very red against the pale green walls and cream sofas. Fay kept the house very hot. He wiped his face with his handkerchief. 'Warm for the time of year, ain't it?' he said.

'Is it?' Fay said. She lit a cigarette and looked bored.

'I shouldn've recognised the old place,' Uncle Sid looked around him in wonder. 'Quite like a hotel, ain't it? But Sylvie had a way of choosing things that was very much 'er own style. They didn't cost nothing but they was individual. I remember an old sofa with roses on it. Weren't it pretty, Fred?'

'It was lovely.'

'If you've still got it, ma'am, stored away somewhere, I should like to 'ave it. I can see my Sylvie a-laying on it as clear as I see you now.'

'That old Victorian thing?' Fay waved a hand dismissively. 'It went to the rag-and-bone man.'

We had none of us anything more to say. Uncle Sid went away soon after. A few days later a terrible smell in the drawing room alerted Mrs Pope to the parcel of prawns that Uncle Sid had left beneath the sofa.

It wasn't long after that that I came down with a bad attack of scarlet fever. Though at first my head ached and my throat hurt dreadfully, after the fever went I rather enjoyed being ill. Fay got in a woman to clean so that Mrs Pope could look after me. We played Snakes and Ladders and Snap and cut out paper dolls together while I tried not to scratch the bright red rash that had come out all over me and we watched with fascination as the skin peeled from my body in papery shreds. Fay didn't come near me. She was never ill herself and thought other people made a great deal of fuss about nothing. My father came in once or twice a week and stayed for an awkward five minutes. We had nothing to talk about. I expect in my feeble and bedridden state I was an unpleasant reminder of my mother.

In those days scarlet fever was considered a serious illness. When I was declared better the doctor gave the order that my room was to be fumigated and anything that could not be disinfected was to be burnt.

'Not Evangeline!' The doll my mother had made was always with me. I used to take her to school in my satchel and sleep with her on my pillow at night.

'Course not, lovey.' Mrs Pope had kissed me. 'I'd as soon think of burning the house down!'

But when I carried her downstairs on my first day up, I met Fay in the hall.

'Give me that doll! I told Mrs Pope to be rigorous. That woman has no idea of the meaning of the word!'

'No!' I clutched Evangeline tightly and glared at her. 'Mummy made her and you're not allowed to touch her!'

'You *horrible* child!'

It was out now. All the feelings of hatred and jealousy that we had barely suppressed seethed in our words and our faces. There was a tussle. Fay lost her temper and slapped me hard. I fell against the banisters. My father came out of the drawing room to see what the noise was about. I wiped away the blood that was running from my forehead into my eyes and looked beseechingly at my father. He retreated and closed the door. In that moment of despair Fay managed to grab Evangeline. She positively ran down to the basement. I followed her, shrieking, to see Fay open the lid of the boiler and throw Evangeline in.

'Ha!' she cried in triumph. 'That'll teach you to be disobedient.'

'You are ugly and bad and I hate you more than anything in the world! I'm going to pray every night for you to die but God won't have *you* in Heaven because

181

that's where Mummy is — ' I became incoherent with grief.

Though Fay's eyes were furious she twisted her mouth into a smile. 'Your precious mother was a drunken sot!' She tossed her head and, panting a little from emotion and the unaccustomed exercise, walked back upstairs.

I ran to the boiler and opened the lid. Evangeline's kind blue eyes stared up at me in pain and terror. Flames licked her face cruelly and her quilted rosebud mouth crumpled and turned black. I put my hand into the fire and pulled her out but only one leg came. The rest fell back in and was consumed. I knelt, sobbing, on the floor and kissed the leg and the shoe and my hand which stung unbearably.

It was winter and after an hour or so it began to grow dark in the boiler room. All defiance had gone, I was exhausted by grief. I crept upstairs fearfully, wondering what punishment would be mine. The door of the drawing room was slightly open. Several people, friends of Fay's, were drinking and smoking and talking. My father was standing in front of the fireplace, laughing at something one of the women was telling him. She turned her head, saw me and screamed.

I ran up to my room and locked the door with trembling fingers. My own appearance in the mirror frightened me. My hair was wild and my face was streaked with blood and tears. My hand throbbed agonisingly. I lay down on the bed. Some of the blood and soot went on the pillow but in the circumstances it didn't seem to matter much. I waited in the darkness for the pronouncement of my doom.

No one came. It was Mrs Pope's afternoon off. When I opened my door to her the next morning she was horrified by my dishevelled state, the cut on my head, the red swollen hand, the crumpled clothes I had slept in. When I showed her Evangeline's leg Mrs Pope turned bright red. 'The master shall hear about this,' she said darkly and went downstairs.

I don't know what she said but it was effective. My father came down into the kitchen later that day and handed me something wrapped in Harrods paper. 'Go on, Freddie. Unwrap it,' he said, with something of a tired sigh when I stared dumbly at the parcel. A doll with long red hair and a blue satin frock lay in the box. Her lips were parted and showed two bright white teeth. 'She reminded me of you.' He patted me on the head, hurting me because of the cut but I knew he didn't mean to. 'Pretty, isn't she?' I nodded. 'Much prettier than the old one.' I looked at him with a feeling of hopelessness. If I had a million years in which to do it I could not have explained why prettiness was neither here nor there in the matter of love. 'Won't you try to be a good girl now? It makes my life very difficult when you and Fay quarrel. She's done her best to be kind to you.' His face was solemn. 'Don't you want Daddy to be happy?' He took hold of my hand, making me cry out. 'Oh, God! Sorry. Listen, Freddie, you've got to make an effort to get on with her. In a relationship between two people there has to be giving. You can't always have your own way. Do you understand?'

I understood, all right. I had learned a valuable lesson. God cared nothing about justice. He was indifferent to questions of right and wrong. Fay flourished while my mother was dead. Against adults, no matter how wicked, children are powerless. The disappointment that attended this realisation hurt me more keenly than the stinging of my hand.

16

'That was Beryl.' Prim had come back into the kitchen. 'She wanted to know where the rags for cleaning the brass in church have gone. I threw them away last week because they were black and in holes. Beryl feels that as she provided them it was up to her to decide when they should be dispensed with. She carried on as though I'd chucked away a copy of the Gutenberg Bible. That woman is a complete arsehole! Sorry, but to have to waste my time with utter trivia . . . ' Prim swore more colourfully. I didn't mind. Prim's language was tame by comparison with most of the painters I knew. 'Anyway, what were we talking about? Oh, yes, Fay. What does she think about Alex, by the way?'

'Oddly enough, she's besotted with him. She never stopped telling me that he was an exceptional man and, in so many words, that I didn't deserve him. I suppose she can take comfort now in a certain savage satisfaction that I've proved her right. And, if nothing else, Alex's behaviour since I ran away confirms that he *is* remarkably different from other men. But I always knew that. In fact when I met him I was so captivated by his originality that it didn't occur to me to question what the implications of his behaviour were. He was so much in charge that I gave up operating as an independent person. It was blissful, not to put too fine a point on it.' I sighed and applied myself to the labels once more.

Prim refilled my wine-glass. 'I do wish I could draw like that. Those labels ought to be exhibited, they're so beautiful. Were you always good at it?'

'It's something I've always enjoyed doing. I hated school so I drew all the time to get through the tedium.

184

Going to art school was like breaking out of gaol. Although it was hard work of a different kind. But I knew at last where I was going. It was a relief. And then when I left I was intoxicated by the joy of independence.'

'What was it like?' Prim ran her hand through her long fringe, making parts of it stand up like a crest.

'My mother left me the little money she had. By the time I was twenty-one and allowed to spend it there was enough — thanks to my father's clever investing — for a deposit on a flat and a few months' living expenses. While everyone else was taking LSD and experimenting with lifestyles I was beavering away on my first commissions. I got a reputation then for being sensible. I'm sure I wasn't any more mature than the rest of them but I was much more organised and hard-working. The men I knew were — like most young men — dilettantes and poseurs, looking for some kind of emotional and spiritual location. Sometimes I felt more like a mother than a girlfriend. Alex was physically twelve years older than me and a thousand years older in knowledge of the world. He had complete authority. It was heaven to be with him, to give up stern endeavour for frivolous pleasure, knowing he'd take care of things.'

'Forgive the blatant curiosity but you know how I like to get down to fundamentals — what was he like in bed?'

I paused in the middle of drawing a strawberry and thought back to the first time we had made love. Six weeks had gone by — six weeks in which Alex and I had spent every available moment together. We went to the theatre, the opera, the concert hall, the cinema. We visited exhibitions, museums, private views, even a poetry reading. We had done the complete tour of all Alex's favourite restaurants twice. Alex liked to order for me. He said my difficulties with eating came from some complex psychological problem in my childhood that he intended to unravel. He made a game of it and when I could not eat he said it was because he had ordered the wrong thing, thus absolving me from guilt. I felt as though a weight had been lifted from me and I began to lose my dread of food.

I don't remember a time when we had nothing to say to each other. Often we argued. Alex always won and because I was in love with him I didn't care. I was proud to be with him, proud of having been chosen by him. I saw the way men held him in esteem even if they did not always like him. And women were fascinated by him. It was Alex's absolute self-possession that attracted them. It was quietly done. He was too intelligent to show off. I saw that they were envious.

I thought how surprised they would have been if they had known that Alex had never even touched my hand. It was clever of him. Because he didn't, I began to want him to, very much. He allowed me to kiss his cheek at the end of every evening. He did not kiss mine. The idea of our making love began to haunt my thoughts as, no doubt, he knew it would. If he seemed to be looking at me with something like desire my heart-rate would increase until I was afraid he would detect my state of suspense and expectancy. The sense of anticlimax, when he went on talking of other things, increased each time.

The trouble was that I had never seduced a man and I had no idea how to go about it. It might have been pride or vanity that stopped me unbuttoning his coat and taking off his tie — the convention that women are objects of desire, flattered or suborned into sex. I suppose there was also an element of fear that Alex, who always implied that he had calculated on a certainty, would be disappointed in me as a lover.

When things had reached a pitch of tension between us that was both exciting and nerve-rending we were invited by one of Alex's fellow barristers to a party at which there was dancing. We were put on the same table but not together. It wasn't a very good party, the guests were dull and the food duller, but I was happy because Alex was there. During dinner, while the band played the usual sixties hits and people hopped about with more enthusiasm than grace, we talked dutifully to our neighbours. Later on, when weak coffee and petits fours were served, they began to play Cole Porter songs, the lights were dimmed and the mood became sentimental. I signalled across the table to Alex that I wanted to dance. He allowed me to put myself into his arms on the dance floor. The minute I felt his hands on my back my skin grew hot and cold by turns and my knees weak. For twenty minutes we circled the room oblivious of our surroundings, shivering with desire. At least, I was. Alex broke the spell.

'Let's go,' he said, in a voice that was remote, almost stern. In the taxi he was silent and stared out of the window, keeping very much in his corner. He came up to my flat with me without my asking him and I thought that at last he would not be able to stop himself making love to me. But I had underestimated his iron will. He stood in silence, hands in pockets, with his back to me looking out on to the street. I went into the kitchen to get a glass of water. When I came back he turned and said, not smiling, 'I'd better go. You don't want me, do you?'

I was so surprised by what seemed an admission of vulnerability that I put both my arms round him and pressed my face into his shirt front. 'Please,' I said, holding him very tight. 'Please!'

He took my face between his hands and began to kiss me. Suddenly we were tearing off our clothes. Our desire was so overwhelming that zips and buttons were infuriating. We made love on the floor of the sitting room rather than waste time going into the bedroom. Our longing, fed by the speculation of the past six weeks, was so fierce that it was over for both of us in about eight seconds. Ten minutes later we made love with scarcely decreased urgency in the bedroom and several times after that, during the night.

Even as I remembered those days I felt a faint prickle of the old desire. I glanced at Prim. She was looking at me curiously.

'Oh, much as other men,' I said.

'I don't think I believe you. There was a soupy smile on your face while you were thinking about it. Actually, from the little you've said about him, I rather like the sound of your Alex. Perhaps it's just that I fancy being swathed in wonderful clothes and taken to Cartier's. By all means tell me to go to hell if I'm being too nosy. I've always been much too blunt. My mother used to complain about my frankness all the time. And my bad language. Poor Mother! She wanted everything in life to be sweetly scented and starched and tidy. And she managed to have it like that, mostly. Unfortunately illness doesn't come attractively presented. I did my best but she never forgave me the indignities of sponge-baths and bedpans.'

'She was very lucky to have you. And this house.'

I looked around the kitchen. Yardley House had been built at the beginning of this century in brick and stone and oak, in the style of Lutyens, with strong medieval and Arts and Crafts influences. It was not, to my eye, beautiful, being a pastiche of too many fashions, but I appreciated the substantial craftsmanship of its construction, the high quality of the materials used, the comfortable proportions of rooms — memorials to Prim's mother's taste in overstuffed sofas, écru linen and expensive fawn carpets. The drawing room and the dining room were dignified and formal with oak furniture, all matching and evidently made for the house. I liked the cosy little sitting room where Prim generally sat, with its books and water-colours and cretonne covers. The house was filled with the sound of

188

ticking clocks and smelt of lavender. Fay would have despised it as revoltingly drab and bourgeois but to me it suggested a certain kind of English life, a world in which things stayed the same and, despite births and deaths, world wars, a Labour government getting in, there was always thin bread and butter for tea. There was a sort of gallantry about it.

The lawns outside were well tended as they had been, no doubt, from the day they were sown and the circular fish pond at the end of the rose pergola was sensibly netted against herons. Twin borders of iris with knobbly rhizomes, the leaves tattered and mottled with brown after the winter, ran down to the orchard beyond.

The kitchen where we sat was my favourite room. It was well lit with large windows overlooking the garden. It had an Aga and a white sink with wooden draining boards either side, large cupboards with space for everything and a red tiled floor that Prim's daily polished with Cardinal. Balthazar had his basket in a recess made specially for dogs in the lower part of a large oak dresser. I was amused to see his eyes gleaming in the darkness as he guarded his lair. Even Chloë, for whom he had a warm regard, was growled at if she went too near. On the dresser shelves was a superb eighteenth-century green-and-white Wedgwood dessert service, decorated with shells and seaweed that I very much admired.

'It is heaven, isn't it?' agreed Prim. 'I bought it after Mother died to cheer myself up. This is such a worthy house. I thought it introduced a welcome element of frivolity.'

'You really are a good housekeeper.' I looked at the speckless Aga and the gleaming windows, at the vase of narcissi on the starched seersucker tablecloth. I found it endearing that Prim did not extend this perfectionism to her own appearance. Her hair was frequently uncombed and every piece of clothing had a hole in it.

It was as though she did not see herself at all. Her lack of egotism made me re-evaluate the emphasis I placed on my own appearance. As far as I could judge I was not narcissistic, or anything near it, but Prim's indifference even to a haircut made me ashamed of anything that might be called vanity.

'I haven't got enough to do, that's my trouble.' Prim bent to take the casserole out of the oven. 'I know it's pointless to keep on polishing the same old surfaces just for me to look at but I hate doing nothing. And it seems rather criminal to read novels during the day. The emptier your life is the more you have to structure your time. So it's hospital visiting on Mondays, Wednesdays and Fridays, painting class on Tuesdays, and on Thursdays I go into Tarchester for shopping. I usually go to the cinema as well. It's the high point of the week. Of course there are other things that come round regularly, monthly meetings of the Civic Society — a lot of dear old men doing their best to keep the fell hand of urban development at bay — and the Red Cross committee — quite amusing to watch the grim battle for supremacy that goes on — and there are church things that I can't say I enjoy but Swithin has to be supported. And now and then an invitation to dinner or drinks or something like that. Not exactly Jennifer's Diary, is it?' She removed the lid of the casserole.

'Suddenly I'm starving. What is it?'

'Pheasant with chestnuts and celery. Actually I cheated and used a tin of unsweetened purée as you can't buy chestnuts at the moment. You're supposed to cook them in stock then smash them to a pulp with cream and sherry to thicken the sauce. I defy anyone to tell the difference. At the last minute you put in slices of orange. Another half an hour, I think.'

'I feel incredibly spoilt. You really ought to be fattening up a nice husband. And perhaps a brood of children as well. Your talents are wasted.'

'Anyone at home?' Dr Gilchrist's face with its short turned-up nose, that made him look boyish though he was nearer forty than thirty, appeared round the back door. 'Hello, you two. I've just been to look at Mrs Washbourne's leg ulcers and as I was passing I thought I'd call in. You're looking in the pink, Miss Swann, if I may say so without seeming to boast.'

'Come in, why don't you?' said Prim, rather pointedly, as Dr Gilchrist was already standing in the kitchen and had closed the door behind him.

'Thanks, I will. Oh my goodness, what a wonderful smell!'

'We were just about to have lunch,' said Prim untruthfully.

'Oh. Well. I won't hold you up then.' I was moved by the look of ravening hunger on his face though Prim's eye was flinty. 'Actually, I brought you something. I found these this morning as I was walking across from the surgery and I thought you might enjoy them.' Dr Gilchrist put a handkerchief, made into a parcel, on the table. It was filled with odd-looking mushrooms with wrinkled, honeycombed caps. 'Morels,' he said with an inflection of pride.

'How delicious!' I said. 'In London they're considered a great delicacy. I thought they only grew in France.'

'Oh no.' Dr Gilchrist's expression grew eager as it always did when he was explaining something. His love of imparting information was unusual in a doctor. 'It's just that the French and the Italians — and the Germans for that matter — have a much greater appreciation of fungi. It's a pity the English fight shy of them. They've got more protein than vegetables and plenty of vitamin D. Of course, they haven't got any chlorophyll so they can't manufacture their own carbohydrates. That's why they have to live off other plants or animals, preferably in decay.'

'I didn't know you were so knowledgeable about these things,' said Prim, lifting a mushroom to sniff at it.

Dr Gilchrist smiled at her. His hair was a little too long and curled over the collar of his shabby coat. 'There's a great deal we don't know about each other, I dare say.' I felt certain he was thinking it didn't matter, that he knew enough to love her and that he might have said so had I not been there.

'I thought mushrooms came up in the autumn,' I said.

'Most of them do. But besides morels you might find velvet shanks about now. They grow throughout the winter. Yellowy-orange and sticky, growing in tiers on the side of tree trunks. And next month there'll be some St George's mushrooms. A large white cap with a good strong flavour.'

'How can you be sure they're edible?'

'It's one of those things where an ounce of practice is worth a pound of precept, as they say. You have to examine them closely with the help of an expert. They all look different, feel different and smell different. But it's subtle. It takes time.'

'Would you show me? If you're not too busy?'

'Willingly. There's nothing I enjoy more than a fungus forage. You're taking up Nature in a serious way, then?' He liked to tease me about my metropolitan insularity.

'I may be. I've decided to stay on here for a bit.'

'Three cheers! We shall love having you.'

'Thank you. As I'm to be a regular I insist you call me Freddie.'

'Delighted. Edward to you.' He put his large warm hand in mine briefly.

'The only difficulty is I've no money. Only thirty pounds in the world. I don't suppose it's possible to sustain human life on morels.'

Edward looked sympathetic. 'Won't you tell me what the mystery is?' He glanced at Prim, who was prodding the potatoes, now boiling fast. 'You'll give me a reference, won't you, to say that I'm to be trusted?'

'Freddie can judge for herself, I should think,' snapped Prim. Then she added, perhaps feeling that she had been ungracious, 'I don't think it will hurt to tell Edward.'

'All right. There isn't really a mystery. It's just that I've behaved very badly and I don't much like people to know.' I explained briefly about Alex.

Edward screwed up his eyes as though in thought. 'I see. Mm. Tricky.' He was silent so long that I was afraid I had disgusted him by my treatment of Alex and I began to regret having taken him into my confidence.

'I know it was a mean, rotten thing to do,' I said humbly. 'I ought to be thrashed for not knowing my own mind. And I can't really explain what made me do it — in a way that anyone could understand.'

Edward looked surprised. 'Of *course* you're sorry for it. But once you realised it was a mistake what else could you do? I'll lay good money you had a proper reason. You don't *have* to be able to justify your feelings, you know. It's enough that you feel them. Or should be.' He hesitated. 'Sometimes when people have had extremely critical parents they imagine that they've got to acquit themselves of blame . . . ' He let the rest of the sentence go and smiled kindly at me. 'Now, let's think what we can do to improve your finances. Aha! I have it. You can paint a portrait of Prim for me.'

'Certainly not.' Prim began mashing the potatoes with tremendous force. 'Don't be bloody ridiculous. I'll lend Freddie the money.'

'Thank you, dear Prim. If I borrowed from anyone it would be you. But we all know what a mistake it is to allow money to come into friendship. No, I'll have to get a job. Perhaps I could work as a waitress or a shop assistant in Tarchester. Though there's the difficulty of getting there. I sold my old car when Alex gave me a

Mercedes coupé as an engagement present. I feel, morally, it belongs to him. If only the buses weren't so absolutely hopeless.'

'They aren't *that* bad.'

'I call two a day absolutely pathetic. Even worse than the trains. I wonder you all put up with it. Nothing after six o'clock and no trains at all on Sundays? It seems quite ridiculous. Why are you laughing, Prim?'

'I suppose Guy told you that?' She took a leaflet from a drawer and put it in front of me. It was a railway timetable. 'I'm sorry,' she said. 'He really is a bastard but you must admit it's funny.'

I was indignant. 'Look at this! Not only trains from half past six in the morning until eleven at night, one every hour at least, but six, no, seven trains on Sundays!' I was amazed at Guy's ability to lie so coolly. It had never occurred to me to doubt what he told me on the subject of transport, though I had been suspicious of almost everything else he had said. 'And I suppose his mother didn't run away with his father's best friend and marry a fisherman and a necrophiliac and die of catscratch fever in Naples, either!'

'Well, as far as I know, that's all true. It's what Ambrose told me, anyway. Don't look so upset, Freddie. Guy has always been something of a shit. It's part of his charm. He only wanted to keep you here. You ought to be flattered. It's much more trouble than he usually takes.' There was some acidity in her voice. 'Now where's the oven-cloth gone? Oh, bloody hell! Balthazar's pinched it, I bet. He's like a magpie, always trying to line his nest, though he's got a perfectly good blanket. Yesterday I found my dressing-gown and my father's old golfing socks in there.' She approached Balthazar's den and put in her hand only to withdraw it quickly when he began to growl. 'Oh, all right, you idiot dog!' She fetched a biscuit, enticed him out then rescued the oven-cloth while he was crunching it up.

Seeing Chloë's sad brown eyes she went again to the biscuit box. 'I don't know why I pander to Balthazar's bad behaviour. I need my head examined.'

'It's love,' said Edward. 'Tolerance isn't weak or mad. On the contrary, I think it's a sign of mental health.'

Prim was frowning as she took the casserole from the oven. I could see she felt that Edward might be aiming a hit at her and she didn't like it. But looking at his guileless expression I was sure that he had not been thinking of himself.

'Oh, bugger!' Prim stumbled over the supine form of a large, long-coated tabby called Teeny, who was lying with her nose and tail, and the maximum surface area possible in between, pressed against the warm enamel. 'Nearly dropped the fucking thing!'

'You might think of joining the army,' said Edward mildly. 'I believe it's the thing there to swear every other word.'

'I like swearing,' said Prim, sticking out her chin. 'It makes me feel young and dangerous.'

'To me you are both those things,' said Edward. 'Even without the language.'

Prim looked annoyed then began to laugh. 'You'd better stay to lunch,' she said, removing the lid from the dish and bathing us in rich, scented steam.

17

Chloë and I walked back to Drop Cottage alone. Edward had some patients to see before evening surgery and Prim was expecting George for tea. She had asked me to stay but I knew she wanted to begin the metamorphosis of mutinous savage into polite scholar and I thought this was better done without an audience. Also, I wanted to think about the future.

'Freddie!' A voice hailed me from a distance and I looked up to see Swithin Winnacott hurrying along the lane towards me.

'Hello, Swithin.' I waited while he got his breath back. His face was glistening with exertion. He pulled up the flaps of his deerstalker and fastened them across the top of his head. 'How are you?'

'A touch of catarrh but otherwise well. I'm just on my way to see Mrs Washbourne.'

'I know. The leg ulcers.'

'You *are* catching on to village life. Poor woman, I'm afraid she isn't very happy.'

'Are they very painful?'

'It isn't that. Last time I called to see her she was dancing to the gramophone. I could see her hopping about quite clearly through the window. When I rang the doorbell she shouted to me to come in. She was lying on the sofa. She told me that she hadn't been able to put a foot to the ground for a week. The record was playing so loudly, we had to raise our voices. She said she needed music to cheer her up, she was so depressed by being bedridden. Naturally I didn't let on that I knew this was a little fib. She must be starved of attention. That's very sad, I always think. Perhaps her family don't appreciate her as they should.'

'I should think not if they have to run round after her when she isn't ill. Does she get sickness benefit?'

'Oh dear. You know, I hadn't thought of that.' Swithin's brown eyes were downcast as he contemplated Mrs Washbourne's probable fraudulence.

'What a nuisance money is. It makes quite reasonable people behave very badly.'

'You're quite right, Freddie. We're all beset by temptation. Who knows what unsatisfied longings Mrs Washbourne may have?'

As I had never met her I could form no idea of these. 'Actually, I'm badly in need of money myself. You don't know of any jobs going, do you? Something unskilled, no matter how lowly.'

'Does that mean you're going to stay with us for a while? I'm so glad! But, oh dear, a job. We need a new sexton, of course. But it's only fifty pounds a year.'

'I'd never be able to dig a grave for anything bigger than a guinea pig. What does a sexton do, exactly, besides making clever remarks about worms and mutability?'

'Well, apart from ringing the bells he looks after the fabric of the church. That doesn't amount to much more than listening to the death-watch beetle. There's never any money to do anything. These days graves are dug by mechanical diggers. Much quicker, but noisy. It's taken the philosophy out of it somehow.' Swithin looked at his watch. 'I must run. I've got the school governors' meeting tonight. Beryl will have got supper early and she'll be cross if I'm late. But, don't worry, Freddie. I'll give the matter thought. Remember, the Lord will provide. So they say.' I turned to look after him as he rushed away, his mac tangling round his knees. I noticed that he was wearing one brown shoe and one black one.

So, grave-digging was out. It was extraordinary how ill qualified I was to do anything. I could not take shorthand or type, file or do accounts. Actually, I could barely add up, maths being a definite weakness in my intellectual makeup. I had absolutely no idea how commerce worked. Words like turnover, marketing, retailing and stock-taking might be sorcerers' cantrips for all the meaning they conveyed. I realised that my previous existence had been absurdly narrow. I had neglected the rich diversity of the world in favour of hard cash.

I looked up at the dove-grey, cloud-filled sky in symbolic acknowledgement of the sudden expansion of my ideas. A few icy drops of rain fell on my upturned countenance. 'Freddie,' I said aloud, 'you have been an utter fool.' There was the sound of a stifled sneeze behind me. I whipped round and stared into the undergrowth that bordered either side of the lane. There was a violent shaking of branches to my left. Chloë barked and made threatening little rushes at the source of the commotion. 'All right,' I said with pretended ferocity. 'Come out now! No more silly games!' More shaking of leaves. I strode over to the bush. A small rabbit with starting eyes leaped out almost on to my shoes and bolted away down the lane. I shouted after Chloë until I was hoarse, and luckily she returned with empty jaws. A sharp wind blew up the collar of my coat into my face and whipped my hair into a tangle. I trudged towards home — as I now thought of Drop Cottage — wondering how I was going to make sense of my life.

A large brown bird flew suddenly across the lane in front of me, making me jump. ''Behold the fowls of the air, for they sow not, neither do they reap nor gather into barns.'' I said, as this single fragment returned whole to me from infant scripture classes. It was comforting if true. The whole passage, I recalled, was about not taking thought for the morrow and being as beautiful as a lily without trying. But what about those strictures to furnish lamps with oil and multiply one's talents? It was all very contradictory. And what I had seen of birds during my brief sojourn in the country suggested that they put a lot of hard work into harvesting in their own style. Would the Lord provide, I wondered. It said something, perhaps, about my feelings of guilt and shame that I was perfectly certain He would not.

As soon as I got home I lit the fire and fed Chloë with the remains of the pheasant Prim had given me. I called Macavity but he was nowhere to be seen. This was so unlike him, particularly when there was food about that, despite the rain that was now coming down in a steady stream, I went out into the garden. The wind dropped suddenly and, very faint and far away, I heard something that might have been mewing. I struggled through an overgrown hedge to find myself in a little square, surrounded by dense yew on all sides. In the centre was a stone table beneath a bower of woven branches and leaves. As I looked at it the back of my neck prickled with shock. On the table was a plate heaped high with food. I crept forward, almost sinking to my knees in awe and stared at the beans, vegetables, dumplings and brown bread and butter. Wisps of steam spiralled slowly in the damp air. The Lord, in the teeth of my scepticism, had provided. And, my goodness, He hadn't wasted any time in doing so.

For a few seconds I felt as though I had been slapped for my idle profanity. Then, as I stood staring at the manna beneath its bower of greenness, it struck me as improbable that Heaven would be so scrupulous as to provide a knife and fork and a green Utility plate. I pronged a butter bean and ate it. It was warm and quite delicious. I lifted the lid of an enamel can. The hot liquid smelt strongly of some herb — perhaps camomile.

An indistinct noise from somewhere to my left

distracted me. I called Macavity's name several times and he answered me with a heartfelt yowl. In the middle of wet bushes at the end of a steeply sloping path was a small wooden hut. I pushed open the door. It was a terrible mess of newspapers, heaps of mud, stones and leaves. There was also a cardboard box tied up with string and it was from this that the mewing came. I undid it and let Macavity out. He was so pleased to see me that for some time he ran round me, pushing his head hard against my knees.

I felt very angry with the perpetrator of this cruelty. Luckily Macavity had eaten a large breakfast that morning but I hated to think what would have been his fate if I had not found him. It occurred to me that whoever had fastened the string might not be far away. By all the evidence he or she was deliriously insane. I went quickly back to the cottage with Macavity in my arms.

He gobbled some of Prim's pheasant greedily and then rushed to the sofa by the fire, stretching himself out so as to take up a great deal of room as befitted one whose nerves had been so recently racked. I squeezed in next to him and put my mind to the business of making some money.

It struck me as I sat staring into the flames, sipping tea from a charming Rockingham cup, that apart from the breathing of the animals it was extraordinarily quiet. There was the occasional crackle from the fire as the flames reached a sappy bit of cortex and the odd squawk from a bird outside. Otherwise all was still, the river being too far below to be audible from inside the house. The rain had almost ceased. As I listened to it the silence began to ring in my head.

In London there was the constant buzz and rumble of traffic. And one was surrounded by, almost confined by, other people. Now, as the sky began to darken, I sat in a silence that almost hurt my ears. A lonely evening stretched ahead. Hours would go by during which I would strain to read by the light of the gas lamps. I might cook something like cheese on toast or an omelette, the limitations of budget and equipment discouraging anything more adventurous. Finally I would go to bed rather early because the light was too dim to read by comfortably and there was nothing else to do. Being alone brought unwelcome and unpleasant aspects of one's character to the surface of consciousness. It was the psychological equivalent of those fasting diets one went on to rid the body of impurities.

I felt suddenly that I could not stand myself in so undiluted a form. Thoughts circled, half formed, in my brain and I was made restless by their dull futility. Perhaps I was not fit company for my fellows. Out in the wider world the rest of mankind was consorting together in convivial harmony. I was alone, a failure. Worse, I was selfish and cruel. I deserved to be an outcast and pariah. Dr Johnson said, rather unsympathetically, that the solitary mortal is certainly luxurious, probably superstitious and possibly mad. When I had telephoned my father to tell him that I was not going to marry Alex, Fay had snatched the receiver from him and screamed down it that I was insane. Perhaps she was right. How satisfied she would have been, could she have known of my present despair.

When she had met Alex and me by chance at the Berkeley — it must have been only ten days after that first meeting at the opera — she had stared at us with an expression of disbelief that was quickly replaced by one of frantic curiosity. She had telephoned me the next day and cross-questioned me about where I had met Alex and how often I had seen him. I told her I hardly knew him and she had seemed grudgingly satisfied. I didn't tell her that we had spent three evenings together that same week. But when by chance, two months later, we had run into my father and Fay at a drinks party, it must have been obvious even to the asparagus rolls that we were desperately in love. Fay had sipped her champagne with an expression of one forced to drink vinegar and she had looked tired and middle-aged beneath the careful makeup. Alex told me afterwards that Fay had telephoned him several times during the preceding weeks, after that meeting at the Berkeley, to ask him to dinner. He had been obliged to make all sorts of excuses. I had asked him with some indignation why he had not told me before and he had replied, quite reasonably, that he had thought it would make me cross.

Alex took command of the situation as he always did and asked my father and Fay to join us for dinner at Claridges. I was surprised that she consented to come. Then I saw that she could not help herself. She was enormously attracted to him. Alex put himself out to be utterly charming. My father and I might have been sitting at another table for all the part we took in their conversation. Alex did not *quite* flirt with her. That would have been too crude a description for the respectful concentration he bent on her. He applied his interest like a poultice on a thorn and drew out all her hopes, fears, vanities and disappointments which he anointed with the salve of his sympathy and admiration. By the end of the evening, when I was beginning to yawn, Fay was bright-eyed and expansive.

After that she wrote him little notes and rang him up regularly and every few weeks they lunched together. That Fay was in love with Alex there could be no doubt. My father must have realised it but he resorted to the age-old masculine device of pretending that he had noticed nothing. He might even have been relieved. Fay took to treating him like a elderly relation whose moods had to be tolerated and comforts considered even though he merited little genuine interest. She was much kinder to him than before.

When I asked Alex if he expected to be able to continue this state of play indefinitely he said he thought it perfectly possible. Fay was the sort of woman who preferred admiration to sex. She was essentially cold and self-absorbed. He taught her to see herself as his equal — she was ten years older — and accomplice, well-matched in experience and sophistication while I was a decorative child — a Sleeping Beauty, an *ingénue*, his consolation for being too scrupulous to have an illicit liaison with Fay. It seemed to me an odd little comedy of feigned intentions and secret satisfactions.

I wondered why he thought it worthwhile. Alex was unblushingly matter-of-fact about it. My father was a rich man and Alex had no intention of allowing Fay to persuade him to disinherit me. When I pointed out that Alex was paid enormous fees and, because he had insisted that I put my prices up, I was earning more than I had ever done before, Alex said simply that one could never have too much money.

He was clever with Fay. Sometimes when she had had too much to drink she would practically confess her love. Alex always managed to avoid a declaration while giving her the impression that he, too, yearned. She became emotionally dependent on him for a fix of sexual excitement without the mess and untidiness of the physical act. I think Alex enjoyed his power over her. Whether he found her attractive or not, I had no idea.

Thinking of Fay, who was definitely not in harmony with the rest of the human race, something like a sense of proportion returned and the absurd paranoia that oppressed me in my solitude receded. The difficulty was that I had never been really alone. In London there were always things to do and people to do them with. They might not be particularly stimulating but one could be entertained. An indifferent play, an amateurish private view, a companionable supper with friends, these things filled one's time effortlessly. In the country it seemed that you had an ocean of emptiness to fill. I felt that I must manage my time better and spend it in rewarding ways. Here was the perfect opportunity to read Gibbon's *Decline and Fall of the Roman Empire*, something I had always promised myself I would do. I could begin *A la recherche du temps perdu*. I could cultivate my mind to the finest tilth, free from interruptions. But all I wanted now was go out somewhere and be frivolous.

I was forced to admit that I missed Alex. I missed having someone around who — after himself naturally — thought first of me. I had grown used to his attention and now I felt the lack of it acutely. But if you cannot be happy in your own company there must be something wrong. I tried to visualise a state of being poised somewhere between the tumult of the world and the isolation of the poet's trance — autonomous, content and free of illusions. For a moment I had it, a condition of existence free from speculative, deceiving dissatisfactions with oneself and the world. I would fix my mind upon it and not allow myself futile cravings for the distractions of society.

There was a knock at the door. Chloë got up barking and I was on my feet just as quickly. I was so pleased at the idea of seeing someone that I almost ran to the door. It says something about the depths to which I had plunged that my joy was scarcely diminished to see Dusty Miller on the step. He thrust his mealy cap to the back of his head with a whitened hand by way of greeting and handed me a piece of paper.

'Dearest Freddie, As you've decided to stay after all I thought we'd better fix the old place up. Dusty will mend the roof. I've got to go to Bexford to sell some cows but I'll be back. Guy.'

'You're going to repair the thatch? How kind of you.' I wondered at the speed with which the news had travelled.

''Tisn't kind. Maister Guy's the boss.' Dusty spat with some force, luckily into the bushes outside the door. 'When Maister says jump I'm obloiged so to do.' Dusty's eyes were alight with injury. ''Tisn't as though I weren't run off me feet anyways. Maister Guy says to put a notice in the paper for a mill hand as George ent to be worked at nights.' He spat again into the hapless bushes. 'Got ideas of edicating him. Hoick!' This was the sound he made when clearing his throat to expectorate and it was not attractive. 'I never had no edication.'

'I'm sorry you've got to do extra work on my behalf.' I was quite insincere in saying this but I thought I ought to make an effort to be on good terms.

'Thatching's very hard on the hands, so 'tis,' he whined, and I tried to look sympathetic.

'Just a minute,' I said as he pulled his cap forward over his brow and turned to go. 'You say you want someone to help you in the mill. Why not me? I'm as strong as George, I should think.'

Dusty turned back and looked at me in surprise. 'A bit of a chiel like you? You'd be dead before the day was done.' He was shaking his head in a cloud of flour when he stopped to reconsider. 'I suppose now you could watch the machines and that. At any rate, you've got two good legs on you.' He stared down at them in a way I didn't quite like. 'What for d'jer want to do it, though?'

'For money, of course.'

'Don't tell me a maid wi' duds what a queen might hanker arter hasn't got money. That's a good one, that is.' Dusty bared his gums and a few solitary teeth in a show of mirth.

'No, really, I do need money.'

'How much?' Dusty looked cunning.

'What were you going to offer in the advertisement?'

'I hadn't made up me mind.'

I didn't believe him 'What about two pounds an hour?'

Dusty appeared to be doubled up with silent laughter. 'One pound.'

'One fifty.'

'Done!'

I knew then by the grin on his face that I had sold myself too cheap. But it was work. After Dusty had gone I was surprised to find myself light-hearted. From eight o'clock on Tuesday morning — I had asked to have Monday off to buy some working clothes — I would have a new identity. I reflected on the romantic associations of milling and imagined women in vaguely biblical costume grinding corn by hand, one stone upon another, centuries before refinements like the wheel were thought of. The mill had been the centre of rural life from the infancy of agriculture until this century. In songs and fables millers were traditionally dishonest misanthropes. There was the old saying that nothing is braver than a miller's neck-cloth which takes a thief by the throat every morning. Dusty seemed to fall neatly into character. I felt myself to be entering the very web and woof of rural life. I looked forward to tasting the rude but poetic satisfactions of being a mill-hand and indulged in a pastoral pipe-dream until it was time to go to bed.

18

'Honestly, Freddie, I wonder if living at Drop Cottage has turned your brain.' Prim and I were clearing out the shed that overlooked the river, erstwhile prison house of Macavity. It was Monday, my last day of lotus-eating before I became a hireling. 'He's such a nasty old man. And you'll break your back working for him. You're still coughing. I don't know what Edward will have to say about it. I almost hope he'll forbid it.'

'Now, Prim.' I raised an admonitory finger. 'This is my first step on the road back to independence and already you're trying to frighten me with tales of bogeymen. Delightful though Edward is and much as I respect him, he has no authority over my actions.'

'You're quite right. I'm sorry. I've always been bossy. Take no notice.' Prim's expression of contrition lasted for perhaps a second before her gaze sharpened. 'But, for goodness' sake, don't let Dusty take advantage of you. And remember, always bend your knees and keep your back straight when you have to lift something heavy.' When she saw me smile she began to laugh. 'I know, I ought to get a job where tyranny is a virtue. Senior matron or colonel-in-chief. I don't have enough scope on the church bazaar committee. Think of my hips in uniform, though.'

'You aren't a tyrant, just immensely kind and unselfish. How could I have managed without you?'

On the long list of Prim's good deeds the last was to drive me into Tarchester so I could buy some suitable working clothes. Tarchester was an attractive town with a predominance of beautiful stone buildings and the usual unfortunate sprinkling of ugly modern shop-fronts and jarring twentieth-century architecture, so beloved by town planners. We had found a useful surplus store in a back-street where I had bought a large pair of jeans, inelegant but with plenty of room for bending about in, cheap rubber-soled shoes, a navy reefer coat and a thick fisherman's jersey of oiled wool. I also took the bellows to be repaired and bought a pretty cream-and-green enamel kettle, rejecting sensible stainless steel as being contrary to the whimsical romanticism of the cottage.

We had lunch in the Tudor Café, fake horse brasses, reproduction Windsor chairs and embroidered pictures of ladies in crinolines standing among hollyhocks, but the lasagne was home-made, if not something an Italian would have recognised. We had a squabble about who would pay. I threatened to walk home if she refused to be my guest, on the grounds that I wanted to celebrate being the mistress of an income again.

When we got back to the cottage I told Prim about Macavity's imprisonment and she had wanted to see the hut. Now that I had leisure to look at it properly I saw it was a sort of belvedere built on a crag of rock, a viewpoint from which to admire the spectacular scenery of the valley. The ground dropped steeply away from it down to the river. The little house was hexagonal in shape and the door had once been painted blue. The windows, nearly all cracked or missing, were leaded lights, and years ago someone had taken the trouble to fashion the outside into a rustic conceit by nailing split logs to the walls.

'You know this could be very pretty.' I trod down the brambles to examine the narrow cantilevered balcony that projected above the drop. 'Some of the logs have rotted away but they could be replaced. I wonder what this is that's grown all over it?'

'It's a honeysuckle,' said Prim decidedly.

'How clever of you to tell when there aren't any flowers. Let's have a bonfire and get rid of all the rubbish. However did all this mud get in? All these little heaps decorated with stones and feathers. And there's another thing. There's a sort of shrine in the garden, in the little hedged square up there. Yesterday it had a plate of food on it. When I looked this morning it had gone, even the knife and fork. I couldn't have imagined it, could I?'

Prim smiled. 'There isn't anything holy about it. It's an alfresco dining room.'

'Ah! So you *do* know about it!'

'Barbara Watkins puts food there every day for Lemmy.'

'Lemmy?'

'He's rather eccentric. He doesn't like being indoors. He isn't quite like other people. Oh, don't worry,' she said quickly, seeing my face, 'Lemmy would never hurt anyone. He's the gentlest soul alive. In many ways I sometimes think he's the most truly good person I know. He certainly isn't a fool. Just — different. He lives in the woods near the Abbey. But he likes this garden for some reason. Bar's fed him for the last couple of years ever since she came to Hintock Cottage. There's a gap in the hedge where your gardens meet. She asked me the other day if I thought you'd mind if she went on using it and I said I was sure you wouldn't.'

'Of course I don't mind.' I was silent for a while thinking. 'Is Lemmy the phantom whistler?'

Prim nodded. 'He has an extraordinary ability to imitate sounds. Once I put my gramophone on the window sill and played some Mozart — it was the Sinfonia Concertante. Lemmy sat in a tree, listening, and afterwards he whistled the whole of it from beginning to end, note perfect, as far as I know.'

'Why on earth didn't you tell me?'

'I almost did but you seemed so tense and unhappy when you first came. I was afraid you'd be frightened by the idea of someone creeping about the garden, someone not entirely — conventional. He does look rather wild. He doesn't like having his hair cut and his fingernails get very long. Bar's incredibly good with him and tries to get him to dress properly but he won't wear clothes unless he's in the right mood.'

A naked eccentric prowling about the garden! I hardly dared to look round for fear of meeting a pair of demented eyes glaring at me from a bush. I had no feelings of ownership about the garden. As far as I was concerned the entire village was welcome to perambulate in it at their leisure but the idea of being watched was unpleasant. 'Are you certain he isn't violent?'

'Absolutely. If you happen to see him he'll be much more frightened of you. Don't be put off by his appearance. Just talk to him calmly and he may decide to trust you. Really, it's all right. I'm very fond of him.'

'Mm. I'll do my best. Do you think Lemmy's responsible for shutting up Macavity?'

'Oh, no! He adores animals. Besides, Lemmy wouldn't come in here. I told you, he has a phobia about being inside.'

'Do you mean he lives out in the woods even in winter? Without any clothes on?'

'He has blankets. And Bar's made him a cloak of hen's feathers. It took me months to collect enough.'

I laughed. 'You know, this place is a perfect rest-cure for anyone suffering from a surfeit of town life. All right, I'll remember to speak very gently to him and try to win his confidence. I just hope he won't spring out on me suddenly and imperil our friendship by making me scream.'

As I went back to the house to find matches for the bonfire I could not prevent my eyes darting right and left, and when Macavity strolled out of the undergrowth to remind me that it was tea-time I jumped high in the air and frightened us both. I washed the cobwebs from an ancient basket and put in cups, milk and sugar plus a bar of chocolate and some apples. I thought suddenly of Alex. How he would have despised such simplicity.

Being with Alex was like skating very fast through the most beautiful landscape — exhilarating and spellbinding with just a suggestion of danger. Like all lovers I was terrified that the bliss might not last. A tiny fissure in the ice — it could not be called a quarrel — came a few weeks after Alex asked me to marry him.

The day had been one of brilliant light but London had been hot and stinking of exhaust fumes. I decided to take a sketchbook and a picnic and drive up to the Norfolk coast, really just for the pleasure of walking by the sea. I telephoned Alex to tell him I wouldn't be back until late. He had sounded put out. 'What on earth do you want to go all that way for? Can't you go to Kew if you've got a craving for Nature? Besides we're going to the Standings' for dinner.'

'It wouldn't be at all the same thing. I want sky, clouds, water, seabirds.'

'As far as I know Kew has its quota of clouds and sky.' I heard him talking to someone else in the room and then he came back on the line. 'My secretary informs me there are lakes and black swans. I should have thought that would be more interesting.'

'I want to go and see Uncle Sid.'

'I didn't know you had an uncle living in Norfolk.'

'I told you about him. My mother's brother. The one with the rundown smallholding.'

'Ah, yes. I remember.' Perhaps I imagined a note of disapproval.

'And I want to walk on the sand and look at worm casts and razor shells. Smell the salt and watch the waves breaking. All right, I know it sounds childish, but it'll suit my mood exactly. And I'll make sure I get back in time to change for dinner.'

'You're right, it *does* sound childish. In fact, whimsical in the extreme.'

211

'I just feel like some fresh air.'

'But you don't like the country.'

'I've never said that. I just don't spend much time in it.'

'I don't like the idea of you dashing about in this freakish mood. I'd better come with you.'

'It'll be a bore for you. Honestly, I'll be fine by myself.'

'I'll be round in half an hour.'

So we went to Norfolk in the Rolls, chauffeured by Bax, Alex's driver, stopping on the way for lunch at an expensive hotel. No further mention was made of calling on Uncle Sid. When we reached the pinewoods that marked the landward boundary of the beach Bax put up two deck-chairs in the shade, a table for Alex's briefcase and newspaper and a bucket of ice for the champagne. After we had walked a few hundred yards Alex remembered something important about the next day's meeting and returned to his deck-chair to make notes. I walked half a mile to the sea, wading the icy creeks and watching the colours of the wet sands change from mauve to pink to gold.

Alex was absorbed in his work when I returned. I had cut short my walk, feeling guilty about Bax sitting in the car reading the *Daily Mirror*, no doubt very bored. I wondered if either of them had been aware even of the cry of a seagull. Bax still had his cap on. He looked very pink in the face. Alex grumbled on the journey home that he had sand in his socks. They had spent an uncomfortable afternoon to accommodate my caprice. Of what could I complain?

I had to walk slowly back to the belvedere because of carrying the teapot. A Thermos flask was evidently too newfangled for Viola's godmother. Prim had built an impressive pyre and we had tea by a good blaze.

Naturally our fronts were rapidly scorching while our backs, and particularly our bottoms, grew damp and chilly. Until the advent of central heating this must have been a familiar sensation for everyone throughout the cold months. Prim's face, as the light of the fire gilded it, was plain and beautiful by turns, her brown hair gleaming and her eyes bright. Above us the cottage was hidden by projecting rocks and stands of trees, their bare branches turning black as the sun left the valley and details were obscured by a seeping twilight. Chloë and Balthazar ran excitedly up and down the path as a flock of birds, probably rooks, made a noisy return to their nests. I thought how beautiful it was and wondered that I had been content so long to live without such scenes as these.

'I haven't seen Guy for two days,' I said musingly, watching the cardboard boxes turn from red to black to silver. 'He said in his note he'd gone to Bexford to sell cows. Can one sell cows on a Sunday?'

'I don't know. But that's typical of Guy. Just when he seems to be a regular fixture, he disappears without warning.' Prim hesitated. 'Don't be cross with me for interfering, but I wouldn't get too fond of him if I were you. He can be very charming — all the Gilderoys have the power to captivate — but someone always seems to get hurt and it's never Guy. Sometimes I think he's missing a moral sense, other times I think he's just hopelessly shallow. But then he can surprise you with a demonstration of real sensitivity and perception. Perhaps he simply doesn't *choose* to care.'

'I think he was deeply wounded as a child by his mother going off.'

'It could be. But then that might be just what he wants you to think. Odd, isn't it? Most men are transparently simple to read, but Guy is opaque. And that makes him dangerous.'

'It would if you fell under his spell. I haven't done that.'

'But you *are* a touch enamoured. Oh, you needn't

213

answer. I'm being nosy again. I'll tell you something for nothing. I once had a brief fling with him myself.' I did my best to look surprised though it had been obvious to me from first seeing them together that there was or had been something between them. 'I wasn't in love with him or anything like it. I told you about my unrequited passion. The blighting of all my hopes.'

'I hope it wasn't as bad as that. You were very young. There must have been other men.'

'No. Oh, I've been to bed with a few, but I wasn't in love with them. They never measured up. I couldn't get rid of the idea that he was the only man for me. I can see now that I became obsessed. Perhaps it was a way of dealing with the pain of rejection.'

I thought at once of Alex. Supposing he was unable to stop loving me because I had rejected him? How awful if I had blighted for ever his ability to love. The moment I thought this it seemed conceited and silly. Prim had been a vulnerable innocent girl. Alex was vastly experienced, adult, cosmopolitan. But supposing Alex had rejected *me*? I simply could not imagine what my feelings would have been. I saw clearly for the first time that his fixed passion for me had been a vital element in our affair. I had found someone wanting me so much extraordinarily seductive. I felt hot suddenly, detecting in myself a despicable weakness that could only be called vanity.

I shifted uncomfortably, moving on to my knees to dry the seat of my jeans. 'Do you think not having one's feelings returned is sometimes an added inducement to love?'

'Making the other person seem infinitely superior you mean? But I think he *was* superior to other men.' Prim laughed. 'That's love for you. You can't ever quite accept that your feelings aren't reciprocated. You're convinced that one day they'll realise they can't live without you. It seems so right, perhaps even ordained.

You feel angry that they're too blind to see it. I think I sometimes came close to hating him.'

'Wasn't it La Rochefoucauld who said that love viewed from outside looks more like hatred than love?'

'And Ovid who said that love was a kind of warfare. Perhaps it all boils down to rampant egotism. But, anyway, it didn't happen. He loved someone else and I had to get on with things as best I could. I tried all sorts of things, writing poetry, getting drunk — and going to bed with Guy. Come to think of it, that was the only thing that helped at all.'

This time my surprise was genuine. 'How could that be?'

'It gave me something else to fret about. The chilli juice in the elephant's eye. I only slept with Guy once. He pursued me for the space of a week, with soft words and flattery. I'd never been subject to blatant wooing. I was lonely and miserable and I wanted to escape from feeling so much. Also I was a virgin and tired of being one. So I thought, what the hell? I expect he did all the right things. I was too inexperienced to know, of course. But I hated it. I felt myself being pushed immense distances away from anything I believed in. Afterwards Guy was sweet, kissing me and telling me that I was incredibly voluptuous and I'd made him very happy. He really was persuasively enthusiastic. So I thought it was because it was my first sexual experience that I'd felt so lonely I wanted to howl.

'I told myself I must try to get rid of the old love and abandon myself wholly to this one. Also Guy was by far the most attractive and interesting man for miles around. But I never got the chance.' Prim looked at me with eyes full of derision, whether for herself or Guy I couldn't tell. 'He was going away for a month to stay with some cousins in Scotland but we arranged to do all sorts of things when he got back. The usual nice but dull men asked me to go with them to the local hunt ball. I said I was going with Guy. I persuaded my father to increase my allowance so I could get us both tickets. I managed to work myself into quite a state of anticipation.

'I was looking forward to showing off my conquest of one of the most eligible bachelors in South Dorset. My reputation had been embarrassingly unsullied until then. I bought a new dress that made me look quite slim. I went to the hairdresser's in Tarchester and had a deep fringe cut and the ends set in flick-ups.' Prim laughed. 'Do you remember that hideous fashion? Well, the days went by and I took to haunting the study where the telephone was. Only the sodding thing never rang. My father said as he'd paid for the tickets I was jolly well going to go. He insisted on driving me there himself. I walked in, feeling anxious and miserable and the first thing I saw was Guy smooching with Tania Heythrop from the riding school. The humiliation was excruciating. I spent the evening fighting off the drunken advances of Geoffrey Searle. His chin was shining with butter from the hollandaise. It was Hyperion to a satyr, all right.'

'Oh, Prim, what torture to be young!'

Prim looked amused. 'It was, it really was. I cried for hours when I got home and it took me a long time to stop minding about it. Do you know, Guy actually had the astounding cheek to try again — oh, it must have been about five years after that disastrous evening. He looked so affronted when I turned him down that I couldn't help laughing, which annoyed him even more.'

I laughed too, infinitely touched by this tale of youthful suffering. But at the same time I understood that she intended to warn me of the undesirability of allowing myself to be entangled in Guy's lures. A freezing wind got up quite quickly after that and blew sparks and burning cardboard about, threatening the continued existence of the belvedere, so we raked out the centre of the fire and packed up the basket. A helpful burst of rain extinguished the last stubborn flames. Prim had to go up to the Rectory to take the Bible-reading class for Swithin, who had a bad cold.

'It's such a waste of time. Only Mrs Morris and Tom Browse ever come to it. They can practically recite the entire thing verbatim from Genesis to Revelation. They like to compete with each other to show off. But Swithin sounded so wretched I didn't like to say no. You'd think Beryl could do it for once, but Monday's her evening for ironing the altar cloth and Swithin's surplice and what-not. It's Lamentations, isn't it, that talks about affliction and misery, the wormwood and the gall? That's Beryl to a T.'

'I'm afraid I don't know. It's probably me who's most in need of Bible classes. But,' I added quickly, 'I must get to bed early to be fresh for tomorrow.'

'We finish at eight. How early can one go to bed? No, I'm kidding. It's the most agonisingly dull evening and, anyway, if you were there I couldn't keep a straight face. It's when Mrs Morris says, 'Excuse *me*, Mr Browse,' with a triumphant look on her face that I get worried I'm going to giggle.'

We returned to the cottage, washed up the tea-things then walked together with the dogs as far as the telephone box. Prim and Balthazar went on to Yardley House while I persuaded Chloë to wait for me on the grassy verge. One of the panes of glass in the telephone kiosk was missing and a penetrating draught blew into my ear. A piece of chewing-gum was wedged into the receiver. I held it as far as I could from my mouth and dialled the number. I imagined the bell ringing in the pretty drawing room, which was lit by a Venetian window that looked out over the fountain. Just as I decided to ring off Viola answered it.

'Hello?'

'Hello, darling. It's me, Freddie.'

There was a pause before Viola said, with an unusual reserve in her tone, 'Hello, Marjorie, how are you?'

'It's Freddie!' I said, louder, bringing the gum dangerously close to my lips. 'I got your letter and I just wanted to say you needn't worry about me. Of course you must go to Florence with Giles and actually I'm loving it here. It's the strangest, most wonderfully odd place and I'm longing for you to see it.'

'Oh, good. I quite understand.' Viola still sounded odd, very distant and formal. 'I'm glad you like it.' A pause. 'I'm sorry, Marjorie, but I can't talk now. You see,' she laughed artificially, 'I've got someone here — '

Just as I realised what she was trying to tell me I heard a muffled exchange and Viola shouted 'No! Give it to me!'

A masculine voice said, 'Freddie! It's you, isn't it? What the hell are you playing at? Where are you?'

I dropped the receiver and stared at it as it swung like a pendulum on the end of its flex. I could hear Alex's voice shouting tinnily in the confines of the telephone box. For several seconds I was stupefied by shock. Then I slammed the receiver back on its rest, flung open the door and had run twenty yards down the road before I asked myself what the hell *was* I playing at?

My heart beat so violently I felt faint. I was terrified But why? I was perfectly safe, more than a hundred miles away and there was no chance that Alex could trace the call. This was the man I had been preparing to spend the rest of my life with but now the sound of his voice affected me as though the ground had opened to reveal a pit of burning coals and Satan himself had asked me to jump in.

I walked back to Drop Cottage. The trees scraped their branches together, groaning in the rising wind and I heard the repeated cry of a vixen seeking her mate. Usually I delighted in these intimations that Nature's irrepressible forces were at work but now I scarcely noticed them. I felt sick, distressed and angry but whether with Alex or myself I could not tell.

19

I don't know how long I sat on the window seat, watching night steal across the valley. I grieved for the rage and desperation I had heard in his voice but all doubts about whether I had done the right thing were resolved. I clung to the certain knowledge that if I had married Alex he and I would be in a different kind of hell by now, from which escape would have been much more difficult.

When it became too dark to see I put a match to the fire and the gas lamps and at once the cottage was filled with a soft radiance. It would be difficult to reconcile myself to the cold glare of electric lightbulbs when eventually I returned to London.

I put down some meat for the animals. Chloë wolfed her plateful straight away but there was no sign of Macavity. Remembering the events of the day before I was suddenly fearful. I opened the back door and called his name several times. When there was no response I shouted louder but this brought on a fit of coughing. By the time I had control of it, my eyes were streaming.

'It weren't the cough that carried 'er off, it were the coffin they carried 'er off in,' said a childish voice from one of the bushes directly in front of me. I heard sniggers.

My first reaction was apprehension. I had not bargained for meeting Lemmy in the dark. I pushed wide the door so that light streamed on to the bush. I remembered that Lemmy must be humoured and spoken to kindly and quietly. It isn't every day you converse with a naked stranger. I would keep my eyes on his face. 'Do come out. I'd very much like to meet you.'

'Dew come eout,' said the sing-song voice in imitation of mine.

This was tiresome. 'Don't let's be silly,' I said more firmly. 'If you won't come out I'm going back indoors to get warm.'

More titters. I felt annoyed. I strode to the bush and pulled aside the branches. Three pairs of eyes looked up into mine. One pair filled with tears and their owner opened its mouth and began to scream. 'All right, all right,' I said quickly. 'Come on, you lot. Out of there.'

'It's *our* den,' said the largest child, thrusting out his lower lip.

'This happens to be *my* garden,' I replied, before reflecting that this was not true. 'Now, come along, for goodness' sake, and let's stop him screaming.'

' 'Tisn't an 'im, 'tis an 'er,' explained the third child, who was neither screaming nor thrusting out a lip.

'Well, fine. Would she like a biscuit, do you think?'

The noise stopped as abruptly as if the screamer's head had been cut off. All three tore out of the bushes.

'Is there only one?' said the largest. The whites of his eyes glistened dazzlingly in his mud-daubed face. He had a flat nose like a boxer's and ears that stuck out.

'One biscuit, do you mean? No, you can all have one.'

'Bicket,' lisped the screamer pathetically. She was an odd sight. A baby's woollen bonnet, much too small for her, was knotted under her chin. It had been put on back to front so that the neck hole hid most of her grubby little face except her nose. On her top half she wore a jersey much too large for her so that the sleeves dangled empty to the ground. Her bottom half was bare but for a large towelling nappy that had slipped to her knees. 'Bicket,' she said again, and there was in her tone something so dismal and without hope that any inclination I might have had to smile was dashed.

'First you must tell me what you have done with my cat.' I addressed the boy.

'Nothin'. We haven't never seen your cat.'

'Wasn't it you who shut him up in the box yesterday?'

'He was our prisoner,' said the third of the trio, a girl. Her appearance was as dishevelled and unappetising as the others but I recognised in her tone an attempt to appease. 'We was goin' to let him out again later.'

'It was very unkind of you. Animals don't like to be shut up in boxes. Supposing you had forgotten about him? He would have died from hunger and thirst.'

'He was our prisoner,' said the girl again. 'We was playin' cowboys.'

'I never saw no cat,' persisted the boy, allowing his thumb to stray up to his mouth then putting his hand swiftly behind his back.

'Well,' I put on my sternest face, 'no biscuits until you tell me where he is now.'

At this the youngest began to scream so loudly that I put my hands over my ears.

'Honest, we haven't seen him today,' said the older girl, tugging at my sleeve. 'We come back to let him out but all the things was taken out of our den and the cat were gorn.'

I didn't know whether to believe her but the baby was screaming so piercingly that I gave in. I ushered them into the cottage and made them wash their hands. It took a kettle of hot water and several latherings of soap before they were anything like clean. I held the baby under one arm to dry her red, chapped hands. The sweat stood out on my brow as she struggled and kicked and yelled for a biscuit.

'Here you are.' I put the packet of chocolate digestives on a plate. I was about to offer them round but the boy grabbed two and thrust them both into his mouth, glaring at me defiantly.

'Here, Wills, that's rude. You didn't orter,' reproved the girl. 'Here, Titch,' she said, taking one off the plate and giving it to the baby. The baby stopped screaming,

222

put the biscuit to her lips and began to suck on it with a faraway look in her eyes. Her bare legs were thick with dried mud to the knees. 'Ta ever so, Miss,' said the girl, taking one for herself. She ate the biscuit very fast and then fixed her eyes on the plate.

'Would you like another?' I asked.

She looked up at me, almost disbelieving. 'Can I?'

'Go ahead.' I was touched by the naked desire on her face and the way her hand shot out to hover over the plate even while she waited my permission. I had never had anything to do with children but I thought these three were probably not typical.

'Can I stroke your dog, Miss? Ent she lovely!' She stooped to pat some chocolate into Chloë's gleaming coat. Chloë advanced towards the baby, her eye on the biscuit but a shriek stopped her in her tracks.

'Help yourself, Wills.' This time he took only one, watching me all the time. The baby plopped down suddenly on to the kitchen floor, her legs stuck straight out in front of her and continued to suck at the biscuit until it disintegrated into sludge. She started to cry again. Chloë made for the sitting room and did not reappear. I gave the baby another biscuit, feeling guilty. She ought to be eating apple purée or mashed carrots or whatever one gave little children.

'I hope your mother won't mind you eating so many biscuits.' I offered the plate once more.

'She won't mind,' said the girl. 'She don't mind what we eat, speshly if we're give it.'

'Are you brother and sisters?'

'Yep.' They were eyeing the last biscuit.

'Would you like some toast?' The two older ones nodded eagerly. The baby was in a world of her own. There was chocolate even in her eyebrows. I cut a slice from the loaf I had bought that morning in Tarchester, and skewered it on the fork.

'Didn't you have any lunch?'

'Nah. Mum's sick again and she don't like the smell of chips when she's sick. She says it makes her feel like she's got a finger in her froat.'

There was no arguing with this.

'What's the matter with her? Has she seen a doctor?'

'She don't like doctors. She says they come to nose. Like the so-we-shall lady.'

'Do you mean the social welfare people?'

'Mum says we mustn't let her in. She wants to take Mum's best friend away.'

'I'll stop her comin' in,' said Wills, straddling his legs, raising his fists and contorting his face into a grimace. I gave him a piece of buttered toast. He bit off a huge piece with a ferocious snarl. 'Ent you got no jam?' he asked, wiping his lips and cheeks with the back of his hand.

'No. Don't do that. Take smaller bites and then you won't get it all over you.' I attempted to dab at his face with a damp cloth but he ducked away from me and went to stand on the doormat to eat in peace.

'Who's your mother's best friend?' I asked the girl.

'Vod Ka. She has to have it for her health. Only it ent been doing the trick lately.'

'What's your name?'

'Frankie. It's short for Frances. Mum were in love with this bloke called . . . ' she searched her memory ' . . . Frankie Vorn. She wanted to call Wills after him but Dad said no. He liked the name Willyum. So she called me after him instead as Dad had left home by then. Ta very much.' She took the slice of toast I offered her.

I felt a little guilty, questioning her. She seemed only too willing to tell me all her family's secrets. She ate her toast in tiny bites, running her tongue carefully round her lips afterwards and watching my face, as though hoping for approval. She had long dirty hair, a sharp nose, a pointed chin and deep-set eyes. When she wasn't watching me, she looked round the kitchen with grave curiosity, fastening on each object in turn as though committing it to memory. The alertness of her gaze gave her foxy little face an attractive eagerness. I smiled at her.

'What's your'n, Miss?'

'It's Freddie.'

Wills guffawed. 'Don't be daft. That's a boy's name!'

'That's rude, that is, Wills.' Frankie was indignant. 'And what if 'tis? So's mine a boy's name. What's it short for, Miss?'

'Elfrida.'

'El-fri-da.' She said it thoughtfully. 'That's a real lady's name. Is this a real lady's house?' She looked round the kitchen again, puzzled.

'I don't think so. It's just a cottage. What's your idea of a real lady?'

'Mum saw one once, goin' by in a car. She had a hat on and white gloves. Mum took her bike to one side to let the car go by — ever so big and black it was, one of them walruses — and the lady waved her hand. Mum said if she'd been born wiv a hat and gloves she wouldn've needed her best friend.'

Wills guffawed again. 'Not a walrus, you silly baby! She means a Rolls Royce!' He wrapped his arms across his chest and bent himself up with mirth. 'A walrus! Ha, ha!'

'Shut up, you!' shouted Frankie, her face dark with anger. 'You horrible boy, you know nothin'! You just think yore clever, so there!' She stuck out her tongue as far as it would go, then looked at me and bit her lip.

'Now let's not spoil things by quarrelling,' I said, my voice automatically sliding into schoolmistressy tones. 'Who'd like another piece of toast? Oh my goodness! What's the matter with the baby?'

She was leaning forwards slightly from the hips and had become a frightening shade of scarlet. Wills said

'Pooh! Stinks!' and opened the back door.

'She's just fillin' her nappy.' Frankie looked amazed at my ignorance. 'We didn't bring another 'un. I don't suppose you've got none?'

'No.' I looked at the baby. Wills had, if anything, understated the case. 'What shall we do?'

'We'll have to take it off her and she'll have to have a bare bum to go home. Have you got a plastic bag?'

I found a carrier bag and handed it to her. She struggled with the baby who began to kick and scream. Wills went outside and I would have gone with him but it seemed unkind to leave Frankie alone with the horrid task. Eventually we stood the baby in the sink and washed her poor red bottom with warm water. I felt I had aged years by the end of it.

'Why don't you throw that revolting thing away?' I suggested pointing, to the nappy, heavy with ordure.

'Roof will kill me if I do that. We haven't got enough as 'tis.'

'Who's Ruth?'

'My big sister. She don't come out to play wiv us. She has to take care of Mum. Mum has the frights a lot and Roof is ever so good at makin' her better.'

Poor little thing! Looking after a mother with delirium tremens was a cruel lot to have drawn.

'How old is Ruth?'

'She's twelve. Wills is ten, I'm eight and Helen's eighteen months. Only we always call her Titch.'

'Ellen? That's a pretty name.'

'Not Ellen. *Helen*. With a haitch.'

'Helen. I see. Well, Frankie, we'd better think about getting you home.'

Frankie's mouth drooped. 'I don't want to go, Miss. I like it here. Even though you ent got a fridge or a toaster or nothin', I reckon it's very nice. I think Mum'd like it too.'

'Oh, well, when your mother's better, she could

come and see it, perhaps.' I disliked myself for the feeling of deep reluctance with which I issued this invitation.

'Oh, Mum don't go out anywhere.' I felt an equally painful twinge of shame when I heard an eagerness to reassure in the child's voice. 'She ent even been outa bed for days.'

'Who looks after you, then?'

'Roof.'

'What about your father?'

'Mum's kicked him out for good an' all. Last time he came she fell for Titch and she says he's no bloody use for anythin' but gettin' girls up the spout.'

We wrapped Titch's bottom in an old towel I found in a drawer. I cleaned off as much chocolate as I could and put on her bonnet the right way round.

'I don't know how we're going to carry the baby over the bridge and up the bank.'

'Oh, we never come that way. There's a path froo the woods. I'll show you.'

'Do you mean to say that all this time I've been struggling up and down that blasted path at risk of severe injury when there's an easier way? Why did no one tell me?'

I saw why a few minutes later when the torchlight fell on the entrance to what was virtually a tunnel through the undergrowth. The floor was a fetid stream-bed clogged with swampy mud.

'We made it,' said Frankie with simple pride. 'Wills cut the branches so you can get froo wiv only bending a bit. It's nice and cool in summer.'

I had to bend quite a lot. Brambles tried to tear the skin from my forehead and twigs to gouge out my eyes. Luckily the stream never got more than a foot deep. I balanced Titch across my knees and crouched over her. She was a dead weight and quite silent. It was three times the distance of the other path. I thought of it several times, almost with longing.

We reached the top. My muscles creaked and twanged as I straightened up and handed Titch to Frankie. There was no sign of Wills. Chloë resisted Frankie's blandishments and kept firmly on my other side. It was a dark night with thick clouds covering the moon. The torchlight shone on puddles that rippled beneath the wind. We walked quickly. After a while Frankie started to pant so I took the baby back. It was an unusual sensation to have soft little arms about my neck. From time to time I felt her mouth against my cheek. She began to suck it. Frankie walked beside me, shining the torch anywhere but forward on to the road and continued to talk without pause.

'Wills says there's crocodiles livin' in that hedge but I don't believe him.' None the less she pressed closer to me whenever the wind rustled the branches. 'Can I come again? I won't bring Wills, but I have to look after Titch because Roof can't manage her as well as me mum.'

'Don't you think Wills will want to come?'

'Dunno. I 'spect he will if there's grub. I thought you wouldn't like boys.'

'I don't mind them.'

'Can we come tomorrow, then?'

'I've got to go to work. I've got a new job.' Then, remembering the children's awful hunger, I said, 'All right. Tomorrow at five o'clock. I'll get something for tea.'

'Right.' After a pause, 'We didn't do anything to your cat, honest. And I won't let Wills touch him again. I'm ever so sorry we put 'un in the box.'

'That's okay. As long as you understand it was unkind.'

'This is where we live,' said Frankie abruptly. I could

see no lights or sign of habitation anywhere.

'Shall I come with you to the door?'

'Nah. Mum'd hear you. She gets wild if she thinks folk are comin' to nose. Give us Titch.'

I put the sleeping baby into Frankie's arms. 'Goodnight, then.'

The child did not answer but staggered into the darkness with her burden. I walked home, thinking about what she had told me of her life. It seemed to be a rough and hostile world — a mother who got wild and had frights, an older sister ready to come to blows if she had gone back without the dirty nappy. Wills, aggressive and self-absorbed, who had not waited to see his younger sisters safely home. Perhaps that was too much to ask of any ten year old. I tried to remember what I had been like at his age but I could not remember that I had ever had to be responsible for anyone. Except, of course, my mother.

I ought to get in touch with the social services at once. Probably they would take the children away and put them into care. One read awful things in newspapers about such places. Siblings separated, too few people to look after them, stern unaffectionate house parents and sometimes worse — physical and sexual violation. But enough food and clean clothes. What was most important? On the whole my instinct was biased in favour of mothers, unless there was danger of harm. I would do nothing before I had consulted Prim.

After supper, I worried again about Macavity as a change from worrying about the children. I nearly believed Frankie. But, in that case, where was he? A cheerful mew from my bed, when I stumbled up the stairs, put me in the picture. His sleek body lay curled on the eiderdown, his head on my pillow. As I bent over him he purred and stretched out a paw to acknowledge my presence but his eyes remained closed. He had simply not been hungry. He was changing character, from a sly desperado to a pampered favourite. Already he looked fatter and glossier. I resolved that he would not return to Beryl's niggardly regime. If necessary I would take him back to London with me.

20

'Freddie! Over here!' I pushed through the undergrowth towards the voice. Alex was leaning against the trunk of a tree that blossomed about his head. A breeze ruffled his hair. He looked rejuvenated, happier than I had ever seen him. A lamb gambolled at his feet and birds flew about his head. He smiled radiantly. 'Come here, my darling.'

My heart swelled with compassion and sorrow for the suffering I had caused him. He held out his arms and I ran into them. He bent his head to kiss me but the second our lips met he groaned and pushed me away. Before my appalled gaze his mouth was blistering and peeling as though it had touched something corrosive. His eyes were agonised as he withered and shrank to the size of a child. The groaning became a shrill scream, which turned into the bell of my alarm clock.

The horror of the dream oppressed me for at least three quarters of an hour while I washed, dressed and boiled water for tea. Dusty had said nothing about lunch so I packed a bag with sandwiches and fruit and as an afterthought put a packet of chocolate digestive biscuits into my pocket in case I should feel weak at the end of the day. The fisherman's jersey was rather scratchy and the coat felt heavy. I gave Macavity, who was not yet up, a fond pat of farewell and set off with Chloë to walk to the mill.

It was a bitter morning after a night of hard frost. Ice-embedded gravel cracked beneath my feet and the puddles were frozen hard. The birds were silent beneath the white sky. A primrose bent its head beneath a weight of crystals. At the stroke of eight I knocked at the mill door. No one answered so I went in.

The noise of rushing water that had been apparent from outside was much louder within. The stone walls and floor sent back the echo of biting cogs as three iron wheels, one revolving vertically, the other two horizontally — I learned later they were called the Wallower, the Pit and the Great Spur — turned a wooden shaft as thick as a man's waist. Behind them was a stone wall that stopped half-way, allowing a view of the massive wheel, about fifteen feet in diameter, that was the primitive power at the building's heart. It was black, sodden with water to its wooden core and decked with slimy weeds. As the buckets spewed out with a roar the flume that drove it, it shook off a vapour of shining droplets.

Accretions of meal had dimmed all colour. Even the air was crammed with fine drifting particles. A steep open stair led to the floor above. As I looked up Dusty's feet appeared on the topmost step. Despite his crookedness he descended with the speed of an athlete and consulted his watch. Then he looked at Chloë. 'Ye's brought that dog, then. If it sees to the rats it can bide.'

I gave Chloë a look to impress upon her the necessity of 'seeing to the rats' for both our sakes.

'Ye can make a start here.' Dusty pointed to a wooden chute by the three shuddering wheels. 'The meal'll come fast down. Fix one of these here sacks to them clips. When 'tis full shut off the chute wi' this,' he pointed to a lever, 'and pull 'un out wi' sack barrow. Full bags ower by door. Next sack on clips. Take bodkin while t'other'n fills and stitch top of first sack. Ye've to work quick, mind.'

'So when it's full I pull this lever down to close the chute?' I smothered myself in a storm of meal. It clung to my eyelashes, went up my nose and down my throat.

'Push up to shut 'un,' Dusty said when he had finished cackling. 'And don't open so sudden or ye'll have 'un all over the blooming floor. Let it come gradual.' I tried to brush the meal from my clothes but it stuck fast. 'Ye's not going to wherrit about a bit of dust on thy duds, I do hope,' said Dusty. 'I'll go up top and start the grinding.'

He pulled on an iron bar. The wheel increased its rate of turning and the slapping water began to boom. The noise of revolving machinery pounded in my ears. I pulled the lever down. At first there were only trickles and runs but suddenly the meal began to flow fast in a stream and the sack grew swollen.

As soon as the speckled meal reached the top I closed the chute and struggled to push the barrow beneath the sack. Sweat burst out on my forehead as I wheeled it — I discovered later that they weighed two hundred-weight apiece — to the other side of the room. I ran back, fastened the new sack to the clips and opened the chute. I began to stitch the top of the first bag but the second one was nearly full before I had reached half-way. After a further tussle with the barrow it occurred to me that it would be easier to put it under the sack while it was empty.

I became heated with exertion, threw off my coat and jersey and applied myself. But I could not keep up with the stitching. The fifth sack was overflowing before I had finished closing the second and in my agitation I stabbed myself with the bodkin. When Dusty came down to see how I was getting on I was ashamed of the drifts of meal about the floor, spotted here and there with blood from my finger.

He seemed to derive pleasure from my incompetence. 'Ye's made a bruckle het o' it! I knew how it'd be, letting a maid at the work.' I heard this clearly for he had slowed the monster to a stately revolution, in which mood it yielded no more than groans and trickles.

'I've got the hand of it now. It's just the sewing that's hard.'

Dusty looked at the two sacks I had managed to

cobble together. 'Ye want bigger stitches. Like this, see?' Expertly he thrust the bodkin through the hessian with a snaking movement. 'Now us'll scoop this lot up into next bag.' He gave me a broom to sweep the floor.

'Won't it matter about blood getting into the flour?'

'This here's a provender mill. Animal feeds. 'Tis more'n ten years since we ground flour for the baker. Folks nowadays wants it wi'out the wheat-germ and that, so as it's soft and white and swaddled in plastic. Flour's all ground in big roller mills, these days. Maister Guy talks of shutting up the mill. In me granfer's time it were the body of the village as the church were the soul. But females are the devil for wasting a man's time wi' talk. I want to see a clean floor next time I'm down or I'll be turning 'ee off.'

I worked hard for the next two hours and got quicker at sewing up the bags. I found I no longer needed to concentrate on what I was doing and could allow my mind to wander. I smiled as I tried to imagine Alex's horror if he had seen me hot, dishevelled, badly dressed and up to my eyebrows in meal. He would have concluded I had gone mad.

When at first I had accused Alex in my own mind of imperiousness, I had acknowledged that he was twelve years older and that he knew more than I did about the things over which he exercised divine rule. In fact I had found his high-handedness seductive. But as time went on I felt less disposed to be seduced.

At first the incidents were so trivial I could easily dismiss them. There was the time he had ticked off one of the senior clerks in front of me for having dirty fingernails. Ted was always friendly and chatty whenever I came to meet Alex at his chambers. He had been unable to hide his humiliation. Afterwards, as we sped away in a taxi, I protested against this unkindness. Alex said it was patronising to expect people to have standards lower than one's own, that he himself never had dirty fingernails and as he was much busier and had much more to occupy his thoughts than a clerk, it was reasonable to pull him up on something that reflected badly on the chambers. But not in front of me, I had objected. Alex had taken my hand and explained patiently, but with a hardening of purpose as though imparting a useful lesson, that it was my presence which would ram the lesson home. After that there was always a sense of strain between Ted and me, and though we tried to recapture our former camaraderie, he could never bring himself to look me in the eye.

It could not be said that Alex was unfeeling or emotionally repressed, yet he was easily in control of himself and his chief efforts were directed towards the regulation of others. His appetite for success was such that everything that touched him, however minutely, had to be transcendent. At first I admired this quest for perfection. His fine discrimination added to my enjoyment of everything from the operas of Handel to the design of a matchbox cover. But when it extended to people I felt the beginnings of uneasiness.

I saw that one of the reasons that our love affair was so harmonious was because Alex was orchestrating it. He decided where we were going to go, what we were going to do and whom we were going to see. Naturally he consulted me, but in such a way that it would have been disagreeable of me to refuse. The places, the diversions, the people were entertaining and Alex always had a persuasive reason for choosing them. Either he thought they would be a useful contact or get me a commission or, more engagingly, he longed to show me something delightful. But they were all settings in which Alex showed to advantage. And almost without exception, unless we were staying in the country houses of his friends, they involved the dispersal of cash. Alex was generous and had good taste. Of course I enjoyed being given beautiful jewellery and clothes and staying in the best hotels. But I am not addicted to luxury.

Alex used to say that it was an inalienable part of loving someone to want to know their past. I might have taken this as a warning if I had believed it to be true, for I very much disliked hearing about Alex's former girlfriends. I honestly don't think it was jealousy so much as his assumption that I would be jealous and therefore needed to hear him dissect their characters for faults and highlight their failings as lovers. It took me a long time to identify why this was repugnant to me. In those last weeks when I was trying to make sense of the dread that filled me when I thought of marrying Alex I could only conclude that it had something to do with the impression he gave of the bleak separateness of relationships between men and women once the fraudulent flush of passion had gone out of them.

'Shut 'un off,' shouted Dusty, sticking down his head into the hole above the stairs and making me jump. ''Tis time for a stop.'

With his neck thrust out, stone-coloured hair hanging from his grey mealy brow and his mouth agape, he looked like a medieval gargoyle. He ran down the ladder and I followed him into the dark, gloomy kitchen. Everything, even the ceiling, was painted ox-blood red. He took a pan caked with brown dribbles of grease and put it on to boil.

'Red's me favourite colour.' Dusty sounded defensive. I expect my face betrayed astonishment at the style of decoration. 'Besides, I got a lot o' paint cheap after the war. I'll make us a drink of tea. Ye's not partickerler how it comes, I hope?'

I am, but I shook my head obediently. I was almost mad with thirst but the tea was so repulsive I had to be stern with myself to get it down. At the bottom of my mug were two tea-bags, effusing bitter gushes of tannin. Dusty gulped his tea like a sea-lion swallowing a fish.

'Have you worked here all your life?' I felt some sort

of conversation was required.

'Since a boy. Fifty-five year, come Michaelmas. Old Maister Gildry were boss then. Jolyon Gildry, that was. Maister Guy's granfer. A devilish hard man.' Dusty shook his head and blew through his lips like a horse. 'He rode a great black mare wi' a whip under his arm. He caught one of the hands having his way wi' a maid in the brake-fern and he whipped the man till his shirt were red. I mind he turned out the gamekeeper's wife nigh on a se'night after her man died. And she with five chiels under ten and no place to go.'

'He sounds a monster.'

'Aye, right eno'. But we respected him. You couldn't get a seat in church when he died. He were like the king of the place. Maister Ambrose now, he were quite different. A teuny man even afore he had his apoplexy. Didn't want to do wi' coarse folk like us what made the money for him to spend on women and wine and song. There won't be many to hear his funeral rites. He's hated far wuss than old Jolyon ever were.'

'That's seems unfair. I thought Mr Gilderoy was . . .' I remembered the gassing of the moth ' . . . courteous and charming.'

'Aha. And the devil seems charming when he comes a-calling. How else will he coax out thy soul?' Dusty tapped his nose which was glowing red through his mealy complexion, where he had wiped it on his sleeve. 'Don't you go there too often, young leddy, or your own kin won't know you. 'Tis said Maister Ambrose has the art of shape-shifting. He stands on the hillsides come Walpurgis Night and howls like a wolf. Now if 'ee's done talking, we'll up and at it. A woman's sword is her tongue and she don't let it rust.'

By one o'clock my back was aching and my fingers were sore from handling the rough hessian. Dusty and I had lunch together in the kitchen. I was ravenous. I had eaten my sandwiches, apple and banana before Dusty had finished warming his own lunch, which consisted of a soup plate full of sauerkraut. He had ten catering-size tins of the same on the dresser.

'That's an unusual thing to eat,' I said.

'I go to cash-and-carry in Tarchester. They sells off cheap what ent popular. Folks round here don't seem to go for this.'

'I'm not surprised. It's pretty disgusting, I think.'

''Tis cheap eno'.' Dusty ate with a grinding, sideways motion like a sheep, to synchronise his remaining teeth. 'A bit on the vinegary side, perhaps.' He got up and examined some of the buckled, rusty tins on the dresser. 'Sweet peppers. That'll do for pudding, I reckon.'

Watching Dusty eat so much unpalatable tartness while my own stomach was growling with unsatisfied longings was more than I could stand. 'I'm going to see Mr Winnacott. He's in bed with a bad cold. I'll be back by two.'

I put on my coat and discovered the chocolate digestives in the pocket. I took the path through the woods, nibbling as I went. The sun had thawed the ground and was casting flickering shadows of new leaves among the unfurling ferns. A butterfly with orange tips to its wings skittered between the tassels of nettle flowers. Fallen tree-trunks were veiled in emerald moss and there was white blossom in the naked thorny hedges. Chloë chased a yellow-banded bumble bee until it swooped out of her reach. A squirrel bounded across the path in front of me, its dandelion clock tail held up in an elegant curve.

★　★　★

The master bedroom of the Rectory was a sad contrast to so much wild beauty. It was furnished with massive pieces of a Victorian mahogany suite that seemed to suck in light. The walls were papered with William

Morris's dingiest print, and the floor was covered with brown linoleum. Swithin's face was a paler shade of the olive-green sheets and pillowcases. Apart from his nose which was blue.

'This is kind, Freddie,' he said in a weak voice, holding out a limp, icy hand. A stiff breeze tore at brown-striped curtains until they swelled like sails at the mizzen.

Despite the fisherman's jersey I shivered. 'Would you like me to close the window?'

'Would you?' Swithin looked guiltily at the door. 'Beryl likes plenty of fresh air. I must admit I'm feeling rather chilly.' He coughed twice, dolefully. The grey blankets looked thin and the shiny green eiderdown meagre.

'You poor thing!' I saw he was in need of sympathy. 'What a very bad cough.'

Swithin brightened. 'It *is* rather a shocker. I don't remember ever having been so unwell. My temperature was a hundred and three the day before yesterday.'

'Goodness! You must have felt terrible!'

'Yes, but I mustn't bore you with the sorry tale of my affliction.' He looked at me hopefully. I questioned him about each symptom and soon he had a little colour in his cheeks and his voice was restored to more or less full volume.

'How are you feeling now?'

'Awfully weak. Beryl believes in starving fevers. I'm not sure a chap can be expected to get better on a diet of dry toast and Bovril alone.' I pulled the biscuits from my pocket. 'Oh, Freddie, my favourites! You're too good.'

We finished the packet between us and talked about the weather, my job at the mill and the difficulty of finding locum clergy at short notice.

'The crisis in the Church of England is not going to go away,' said Swithin. 'People no longer consider

239

churchgoing an essential ingredient of respectability so we're relying on more tenuous benefits. I hardly think guitars and cups of cold coffee in the vestry plus a sing-along during the harvest festival supper will do it. Who wants to be poor and meek and mild and inherit the earth these days when they can get drunk for two weeks in Marbella instead?'

'You mean it's materialism that's the problem?'

'Partly. It's becoming a much more here-and-now culture. But also people know more. Television has convinced them that the earth is round and we're creatures of evolution. Nothing to do with serpents and sinning and all that. You can't fill their heads with a lot of mumbo-jumbo and superstition and expect them to toe the line for fear of repercussions.' I was surprised into silence for a moment. 'I'm sorry, my dear Freddie, I shouldn't have said that. It's because I'm not well and I'm rather . . . you know, depressed.'

'Of course you can say it if it's what you think. I shan't report you to the Bishop, I promise.'

Swithin laughed weakly. 'I've already spoken to him. His advice is to pray. But, you see, that's just what I can't do!' His voice grew high with anguish. 'I've tried for ten years to get God to help me but He refuses. Either He's a sadist or He doesn't exist! There! I've said it at last!' Swithin smiled at me triumphantly then burst into tears. I sat on the bed and patted his hand and gave him sheets of lavatory paper from the roll that stood next to a sticky spoon on his bedside table. 'I'm terribly ashamed,' he sniffed. 'Fancy weeping like a child.'

'It's partly this wretched flu. I cried like anything, even though I had Prim looking after me beautifully and I was warm and had lovely things to eat and interesting conversation.' I paused, realising this was tactless. 'One just feels sad and hopeless. But also, if I became convinced I could never paint again, for whatever reason, I should want to cry like anything and that's a much more trivial thing than a priest losing his faith.'

'Doesn't it sound Victorian?' Swithin was making a valiant effort to control himself. 'Remember the chap in one of Mrs Gaskell's novels who had doubts? *North and South*, that was it. He had to go and live among the smoke-stacks of the North as punishment. The filthy air killed his poor innocent wife. I ask myself every day if I ought to give up my ministry. But I believe it would kill Beryl if I did. Isn't it better that I should go on without faith, just doing what I can? But the hypocrisy!' Swithin gave a moan and put the sheet to his eyes.

'Part of the problem is that you're terribly depressed — probably much more so than you realise. Faith is largely a matter of intuition, isn't it? When you're depressed you can't believe in anything much, certainly not your intuitive feelings.'

Swithin stopped crying and looked at me. 'Do you know, that makes sense? Of course intellectually one must have doubts but the whole point of faith is deciding to believe despite them. I think you've got something there, Freddie.' I smiled encouragingly. His face fell again. 'But what's the good of faith if it deserts you when you most need it — when you're depressed, that is?'

'Well, you've got me there, I must admit. I'm not a theologian. I don't know if there *is* any good in it. But faith must be the most important thing there is in human existence. Unless it's all a lie. It's got to be more difficult than being buoyed up through every misery because your faith sustains you. That wouldn't be any kind of real, testing commitment, would it? But if you go on struggling to believe and pray through doubt and depression, well, then, I'd say that was pretty much the real thing. I'd call that faith.'

'You mean I've got it but I'm too depressed to recognise it?'

'What do you think?'

Swithin drew his lower lip back and forth over his teeth while he considered. Then he lifted red-rimmed eyes to me. 'I don't know, Freddie. But suddenly I do feel rather better. Oh dear, this is rather shaming. It ought to be the other way round. I should be consoling you.'

'I happen to know about depression because when I came here I was so depressed I doubted everything.'

'What got you back together, so to speak?'

'Lots of things, really. My friendship with Prim for one thing. It's extraordinary how close to her I feel, though we've only known one another a few weeks.' I did not mention Guy but, of course, he was a contributory factor. 'The great beauty of my surroundings. And the cottage. I feel — don't laugh — some sort of communion with its last owner, almost an obligation to go on looking after it because she isn't there to do it any more.' Swithin's round brown eyes were solemn, without a suggestion of mirth. 'And there are things that have drawn me in and made me feel I have some small claim to belong here, like Chloë and Mac — animals becoming dependent on me. And now the children.'

'Children? Tell me more. My dear, I'm feeling *so* much better.'

The door flew open. 'Who closed that window?' Beryl was exactly like my old headmistress, the embodiment of Blame. She stalked across the room and threw the window wide. 'What is this?' She lifted the empty biscuit wrapper between thumb and forefinger as though it were forensic evidence. 'Perhaps you meant well, Miss Swann,' she looked at me with cold eyes, 'but a healthy stomach is undermined by snacking. There is no nourishment in a biscuit. And,' her accusing eyes looked down at the floor, 'there are *crumbs*.'

21

By four o'clock, when Dusty gave me permission to go, I felt as though I had been trudging over sand dunes beneath a merciless sun in the teeth of the simoom with a dried fig in my mouth instead of a tongue, but I refused Dusty's offer of beer because I hate it. What I longed for was a cup of Broken Orange Pekoe or Lapsang Souchong. I might as well have howled for the moon.

I went first to the post office, which was just round the corner from the mill. It was a pretty cottage with a large bow window with dimpled glass and a bell that tinkled as you opened the door. Mrs Creech, of whom I was not very fond, looked up with start as I came in. I caught sight of myself in the mirror in which she hoped to catch shop-lifters when her back was turned. I was the personification of Harvest and Horticulture. My hair stood up in pale coils, my clothes were shroud-like with meal. Mrs Creech might, with perfect justification, have called me a cream-faced loon. Her expression indicated that her thoughts were tending this way.

'I heard you were going to work for the miller. I said, 'That can't be right. Miss Swann is a lady, whatever else she may be.' I don't heed the tittle-tattle that comes into my shop. I speak as I find, and what I say is, charity costs nothing. 'Depend upon it,' I said this morning to Mrs Hopper, 'Miss Swann has her reasons for entertaining single men at all hours of day and night.' '

I was too tired to be indignant. Mrs Creech knew everyone's business, which she distributed about the village in poisoned morsels. The first time I went into her shop she had screwed up her eyes to examine my clothes and jewellery and from her obsequious manner it was clear that she considered I had the potential to be a big spender. My dishevelled, floury appearance changed her attitude from sycophancy to suspicion bordering on contempt.

I bought a large loaf of bread, butter, strawberry jam, a packet of chocolate cup-cakes and a bag of apples. It seemed to lack a certain style. I added a bag of Iced Gems to the pile. I wondered, aloud, what children liked to drink. Mrs Creech, who had a flexible neck and never took her eyes off me all the time she was wrapping the loaf and fetching the jam from the shelf, said she couldn't say, she was sure. It all depended how they were brought up.

'What children are these?' she asked, a thirst for knowledge getting the better of disdain.

'Actually, I don't know their surname.' Mrs Creech tucked her hands into her sleeves of her peach-coloured hand-knitted cardigan, supporting her large breasts on her arms while she stared at me with unfriendly curiosity. 'There are four of them and the eldest is called Ruth. There's a boy called William and a younger girl called Frankie.'

Mrs Creech turned down the corners of her mouth. 'If it's those Roker children I should think gin would be what they're most accustomed to drinking.' She looked at the food I had bought with something like regret. 'If you'll take my advice you'll search their pockets before they go. Their mother's not a whit better than she should be. No doubt she's had her troubles and I'm the last person to gossip — 'Mrs Hopper', I said only yesterday, 'judge not lest ye be judged'. It can't be easy bringing up four, single-handed,' here she lowered her tone and leaned forward, her eyes hard with malice, 'and a different father for each one of them, if what I've heard is true. It's not to be wondered at that she's turned to drink in the circumstances — but I should be failing in my duty if I didn't warn you that those children are savages. Mr Creech chides me constantly, saying that I'm all heart and too soft by far and no one is fonder of children than I am, but speaking for myself, *I* would not allow the little hooligans over my threshold. The boy has been in trouble with the police already.'

I was too spineless to argue with her. Also, I felt I could not afford to quarrel outright with her as she was my only source of supplies. In a feeble act of defiance I spurned the cheap bottle of squash she offered me and bought lemonade, milk, cocoa powder and a bag of sugar.

I tottered down the lane, Chloë running ahead, full of friskiness after her long nap. I could hardly hold up my head and every muscle trembled with fatigue. Frankie was sitting on the front-door step, with Titch asleep on her knee. Her face cracked into a grin when she saw me but all she said was, 'I told Wills there wouldn't be nothink to eat till five. He's gone to set snares in the woods for rabbits.' I shuddered and pushed open the front door with the last shreds of strength. 'Course he never catches 'em. He's only a stupid boy.'

'I'm very glad to hear it.'

'Is it wrong to catch rabbits, then?'

'Well, I suppose, if you're very hungry — I don't know — I couldn't do it myself and I'm sure there's a kinder way of killing things than trapping them in snares. One might shoot them.'

'What about wringin' chickens' necks, then? Is that wrong?'

I was touched that Frankie evidently regarded me as an arbiter of morals. I hoped I would not fail her. 'I think it's rather a horrible idea, don't you? It must hurt a lot. I'd rather eat something else than do it.'

'Supposin' there wasn't nothin' else?'

'Mm. I don't know. The chicken and I would have to die a slow, lingering death together from starvation, I think.' I smiled at her. I could not expect her to

245

sympathise with my revulsion for killing. 'People brought up in towns, like me, see things rather differently from country people.'

'Wills got us a chicken for Christmas. He said he caught it in a snare and wrung its neck but we found out arter he'd pinched it from the butcher's in Tarchester. Mum said he was a bleedin' little feeth. Was it better to steal the chicken or snare it and wring its neck?'

'Stealing is always wrong.' I attempted to bypass the conundrum. 'I'm simply dying for a cup of tea. Let's get the kettle on.' Frankie followed me into the kitchen, uncharacteristically silent for nearly a minute.

'Even if Titch needed medicine to stop her dyin', would it still be wrong to steal it?' Frankie's earnest face, pale and angular, was turned up to mine.

'I think it would be all right then, probably. That would be an exception.'

'But what if Titch was only ill — not dyin' but she had a bad, bad belly-ache?'

'Oh, Frankie, I don't know. I expect, yes, it would be better to steal the medicine than let her suffer. I'm afraid I don't have all the right answers. There are lots of things I'm not sure about. Let's say, in general it's wrong to steal and we must only do it in exceptional circumstances. I mean, when we really can't help it.'

Frankie sucked her lower lip, crinkled her forehead and withdrew her gaze from my face to the mid-distance as she digested this. 'But you're grown-up. How old do you have to be to know about things?'

'Even very old people don't know everything. Grown-ups make mistakes all the time, even the cleverest and best of them.'

'Have you made any?'

'Oh, yes. Hundreds. Thousands, probably.'

'Tell me what they are.'

Frankie was leaning hard against me, pleating

between her fingers a corner of the paper bag that held the loaf. I saw that her scalp where the thin hair parted was far from clean.

'It would take much too long, and I'm very tired. Will you be a good girl and help me get tea ready?'

Frankie was a willing assistant, not objecting to washing her hands thoroughly before wiping the table clean and putting out the pretty blue-and-white plates and cups with windmills and tulips on which was the most expendable china the cottage possessed. She put them down very carefully, with the picture the right way up. I lit both fires, cut up slices of bread and butter and put the jam into a bowl with the silver jam spoon I found in the back of a drawer. I made a pot of tea for myself and drank two cups, scalding hot, straight away. Frankie wanted lemonade. Titch was fast asleep on the sofa and did not stir even when I tucked a blanket round her. Her cheeks were chapped and mucus had dried on her upper lip. Her mouth made sucking movements as she slept.

'Does she still have a bottle?' I asked Frankie.

'She did've but we lost it in the river yesterday. It rolled down the bank and Wills tried to get it out but the water took it. That's why she's tired. She screamed and screamed all last night 'cause she always has her bottle to go to sleep wiv. We had to shut her in the bathroom so that Mum could get some peace. We could still hear her though the bathroom's right at the back.'

The Roker domestic arrangements did not bear thinking about. I could go some way to an immediate practical remedy, however. I took my purse from my bag. 'I'll finish laying the table. You run to the post office and buy her another bottle.' I put the cakes, biscuits and apples on plates. I was about to shake up the cushions but the chair seemed to beckon me with promises of softness and rest. I sat down. Chloë flopped down beside me. I closed my eyes for a second.

I was swooping over a long empty road, a white ribbon that unfolded mile after mile before me. Then it became a river of meal, gushing so fast that I could not keep my feet. I was stumbling, tumbling, rolling with the roar of the river in my ears. I was drowning in meal. I saw Alex on the bank setting huge man-traps with iron teeth. I waved my arms at him to attract his attention but he was too busy with something that struggled in his hands — a bloody mess, that screamed and screamed —

'You better wake up, Miss.' I opened my eyes. Frankie was leaning over me, pulling at my sleeve. 'That wasn't a nice dream you was havin', was it? I have bad dreams, too, and then I shout for Wills.'

I sat up. My eyelids were heavy, my mouth was dry, my heart pounding. 'Wills?' I was surprised. 'Does he comfort you?'

'Nah. He tells me to shut it and go back to sleep. But it makes me feel better when I hear his voice. I got a lovely bottle, look.' She showed me the cardboard box with pride. Then her eyes flew to the table. 'Can I have somethin' to eat?'

'Help yourself to jam.'

'Is the spoon to put it on wiv?' Frankie looked at it doubtfully.

'Put it on the side of your plate, then use the knife to spread it on your bread.' Frankie followed my instructions, cupping her hand under the spoon to avoid dropping jam on to the table. Unconsciously she stuck out her tongue and imitated with its tip the motion of her knife blade.

'Who's Alex, then, what you was calling out? Is that your brother?' Frankie having eaten two pieces of bread and jam rather fast, sat licking her fingers.

'I haven't any brothers. Or sisters either. I've always felt very sad about that.'

'That's one, then. Them mistakes you was talkin' about. You don't want to have 'em. I wish I hadn't got none. Roof's always tellin' me to do things and she's only four years older'n me. She makes me do things she don't like doing, like sticking the coat-hanger down the drain when it gets blocked. It stinks. She copies my mum. 'Get your arse off that chair and give me a hand or I'll give you what-for.' She only says that because Mum says it. Titch ent so bad but she's a nuisance. I get tired of lugging her about and when she screams I could kill her. And I hate Wills. Them cakes look good.' When I told her to help herself she took one and peeled off the wrapper fastidiously. She bit into the icing. 'Ooh! This is der-licious!' Chloë started to bark and the baby jerked out her arms and began to cry without opening her eyes. 'See what you done, Wills? You woke her up!' Wills had walked in without knocking. He ignored Frankie's remonstrance and fixed his eyes on the table. He stretched out a black hand towards the cakes but Frankie snatched them away. 'No, you don't! You gotta have the bread-and-butter first. She won't have you here again if you don't do it right.'

More heated words were exchanged between brother and sister. Wills called Frankie a silly fucking cow, Chloë barked, the baby screamed and I had a moment's regret that I had allowed myself to have anything to do with any of them.

'Hello?' Guy stood in the doorway. 'Is this is private madhouse or can anyone join in? Freddie, my darling, you look most original, like a floury Dorset bap. Who are these blackened infants? It must be a scene from *The Water Babies*.'

'Just a minute.' I put my hands to my head. 'Frankie, go into the kitchen and fill Titch's bottle with milk. Chloë, be quiet!'

Wills had fallen silent on seeing Guy and began to edge round the table towards the kitchen door.

'I know you, don't I?' said Guy. 'You're the little perisher who let my bull out the other day. I caught you pinching wire out of the hedge. All right, don't snivel.' Wills had uncharacteristically started to knuckle his eyes. I was amazed. He had so far seemed frighteningly impervious to human weakness. 'If you're going to cry you'd better go because I can't stand the racket. Otherwise sit down and be quiet.'

'Have some bread and jam,' I urged, moved by pity for the crestfallen Wills, who crouched on the edge of his chair, wearing a hunted look. He picked up two slices, slapped a spoonful of jam in between them and put the entire thing in his mouth at once, chewing fast and looking warily at each of us in turn in case we might be moved to prise his jaws apart and extract the contents. Jam and bits of bread bulged out between his lips.

'For God's sake!' Guy turned his back on Wills and bent over my chair. Before I knew what he intended he had pulled me to my feet and into his arms. Then he kissed me long and hard. 'Mm, you taste like breakfast cereal, something Swiss and wholesome. Look what a mess you've made of my clothes! I know! You've been rolling in the granary with Dusty. Have you missed me, you bad unfaithful woman?'

'I've got a job at the mill,' I explained, extricating myself from his arms and picking up the baby who had managed to kick her way out of the blanket and was in danger of screaming herself off the sofa.

'You're joking, I hope?'

'I'm not. I needed money and the job happened to fall into my lap. It's tough but I can manage it.'

'It's completely unsuitable — a waste of your beauty and brains.'

'Don't be silly. I can hardly be a model or a film star in Pudwell which is the only use for a face nor can I split the atom or discover DNA. I'm grateful to have found something I can do that doesn't involve training of any kind.'

Guy continued to look disapproving but I was distracted by Titch, who had clutched my hair and was trying to stuff it into her mouth. Frankie returned with the bottle and at once the baby gripped it with both hands and clamped her mouth to the teat. Her eyes rolled up into her head while she sucked frantically. 'This child's starving.' I lowered myself back into the chair with Titch still on my knee. 'Hasn't she had anything to eat today?'

'I tried to give her some pilchards but she kept spittin' 'em out and screamin' for her bottle.'

'Pilchards? Surely that's not what babies have for breakfast?'

'Mum used to give her porridge but we've run out. We been using up things from the pantry 'cause Mum ent been to get her money. There's only pilchards, corned beef and a jar of pickled onions left. And a bottle of somethink called Thousands of Islands. It's not a very nice pink.'

'Oh, Guy!' He was watching me with something like a smile on his face. 'We must help them. Their mother isn't . . . very well. Their sister is looking after them and she's only twelve. What do you think we ought to do?' I tried to signal my concern with my eyes without Frankie seeing.

Guy frowned. 'Aren't there people whose job it is to look after the indigent? Social workers, or somebody like that.'

'Oh, no.' Frankie looked frightened. 'Oh, please — no! Mum says they'll take us away. The so-we-shall lady is ever so cross when she comes. She isn't nice to Mum and then Mum gets angry. Last time Mum frew a ashtray at her. The lady went away with a fag-end in her hair only she didn't know.' Frankie tugged at my arm. 'Please, Freddie, *don't* tell the so-we-shall lady. I know

251

she'll do something bad to Mum to pay her out for the ashtray.' Tears stood in Frankie's eyes.

'All right, Frankie,' I took her hot, sticky hand in mine to reassure her. 'Don't worry. We won't let her do that.' Rash words, I realised, as soon as they were out. What other course was there? 'But you must see that something will have be done. I'll go back with you and talk to your mother.'

'Better not,' said Guy, sitting down on the sofa, leaning back and crossing one elegantly trousered leg over the other. He lit a cigarette. 'Remember the ashtray.'

Really, as an adviser he was hopeless. For the first time I regretted not having a telephone. I thought of walking up to Prim's but remembered that she spent Tuesday evenings at a bridge class in Tarchester, preparing herself, so she said, for a lonely spinsterhood. Swithin was bedridden with his cold. I was certain that Beryl would unhesitatingly put the whole thing into official hands. Edward Gilchrist's evening surgery in Tarchester didn't finish until seven o'clock or thereabouts so he would not be home for another hour. 'Wills! I said, my attention suddenly diverted. 'Where are the cakes and biscuits?'

The plate was bare, licked clean of crumbs. Only a rim of icing round his mouth attested to their former existence.

'You greedy bastard!' Frankie was irate. 'I only had one!'

'I haven't had none.' Wills spread his hands and assumed an air of injured innocence.

'Don't be silly,' I said, very annoyed. 'Of course you have. And I meant you to. But not all five! *And* you've eaten all the bread and butter and the Iced Gems. You'll have an upset stomach, scoffing like that.'

'I never get ill,' declared Wills.

'That ent true,' said Frankie. 'What about the time

you ate Mum's headache pills? You was sicker'n a dog then. And you messed your pants. We had to have all the doors and windows open for ages.'

Wills got up, clenched his fists and advanced towards Frankie.

'Wills, if you hurt your sister I shall send you home at once,' I said, in my sternest voice. He took hold of Frankie's hair and pulled it hard, making her scream. 'Stop it at once, you bad boy!' I struggled to get up but was encumbered by the baby on my knee.

'Cut it out, you little horror,' said Guy, casually, 'or I'll take a stick to you.' Wills let go of Frankie and ran back to his chair where he sat looking cowed and rather white. Clearly masculine authority was the only kind Wills recognised. Guy gave me an amused look. 'Are you really going to go on working for Dusty?' It was evident that the children's plight interested him not at all. 'That means I'm your boss. You must do exactly as I say or I'll have you dismissed without a reference. First I'll give you a rise. How much is that old skinflint paying you?'

'One pound fifty an hour. But really, Guy, we must do something — '

'I bet he was going to tell me two pounds and keep the difference for himself. All right, you get another pound an hour from now on. I shall come down from time to time to make sure you aren't slacking. Punishment for bad workmanship will be a session of correction in the loft with the mill owner. Perhaps a delicious little whipping. Mm, how I look forward to it.'

'You mustn't whip her!' Frankie looked at Guy, her expression furious. 'She's my friend! I won't let you!'

'He's only teasing,' I reassured her. 'He's my friend, too.'

'Is he?' Frankie looked at each of us with a puzzled expression. Then her face fell into disappointment. 'Are

253

you sweethearts, then? I thought you didn't have nobody.'

'Would it matter if we were?' I asked, wondering why it troubled her.

'No. Only . . . men don't like kids, do they? They want you out the way. When Dad came back that time Mum fell for Titch, he locked the bedroom door all the time to keep us out. Before he came Roof and me used to sleep in Mum's bed wiv her 'cause she don't like the dark. And Uncle Billy — Mum's friend when Wills and me was little — used to give us money to go out all the time.' She sighed. 'They don't wanna bother wiv us.'

'Then they're very silly,' I put my arm as far round her waist as I could reach, hampered as I was by Titch who lay across my knee, panting with the effort of so much concentrated sucking. '*I* like children and *I* want to bother with you.' The statement, prompted by pity and sentiment and full of good intentions, was punctuated by a torrent of milky liquid blurting from the baby's lips.

'She always does that when she has a full bottle. Oh, lor'! All over your sweater.' Frankie was contrite. ''S my fault. I orter've watched her.'

'Oh, help! Can you get a cloth — ' I stopped speaking as Will got up and was spectacularly sick over the table.

'I must tear myself away, regretfully, from this delightful tea party,' Guy stood up, too. 'Very Roman. Perhaps you could build a small vomitorium and make it a regular thing. I'm going to find something to drink. See you later, Freddie.'

I watched him with reproachful eyes as he scampered down the gangplank and swam ashore. Frankie and I mopped and soaked and sponged. Prim had left a bottle of disinfectant from her spring-cleaning and soon the sitting room smelt like a sanatorium. The two sick ones were at first inclined to whimper and be sorry for themselves but by the time their cheeks had returned

254

from eau-de-Nil to rosy they were hungry again. We gave Titch the buttered crust from the loaf to suck. Wills said he hated tomatoes, which was all I had apart from some stewed shin of beef for Chloë and Macavity's supper. I found myself in a moral dilemma. Ought I to give it to the boy as he was higher in the chain of being, though less deserving? The problem was unexpectedly solved by the return of Guy, bearing three parcels of newspaper. A heavenly scent of frying oil and vinegar overlaid the Dettol.

'Fish 'n' chips!' screamed Frankie and Wills in ecstasy. I could have screamed with them when I saw the bottle of champagne under his arm.

'As I was on my way home to plunder the cellar I happened to meet the fish-and-chip van,' Guy explained, as Frankie ran to get plates. 'I thought it might solve the immediate problem of feeding the troops.' He looked modest as I expressed my thanks. 'You can tell me how grateful you are later. Let's get this lot fed and back home where they belong.'

It was only after we had eaten the fish and chips that I remembered Ruth and her mother, perhaps at this very moment dining on an ancient tin of corned beef and furry pickled onions.

'Now, look here, Freddie,' said Guy severely, when I brought the matter to his attention, 'you can't hold yourself responsible for every waif and stray. If you want to set up a soup kitchen you must register yourself as a charity and raise funds. I refuse to fuel the paupers of Dorset. Look at Africa. It's been proved that it doesn't work just giving people handouts. You must encourage a spirit of independence. And as far as I'm concerned,' he added, seeing that I was about to protest, 'you must accept this battered cod as the widow's mite — a gesture humble in fact but great in significance. And my last.'

Twenty minutes later we were in the Land Rover with

255

Wills, Frankie and Chloë in the back, and Titch in the front on my knee. There were two more newspaper parcels on Frankie's, which I had paid for. Guy said he supposed I meant to crush him with a sense of his own sordid parsimony but I said it would take more than the expenditure of ninety-five pence to do that.

'Isn't this nice?' said Frankie, from the back seat. 'I'm enjoyin' myself.'

I was glad to hear it. I was extremely tired and very cold, as Guy had insisted that we drove with all the windows open in case anyone wanted to be sick again. He parked where Frankie told him to and I walked with the children down a winding path that led to a building made of corrugated iron with a rounded roof. I couldn't see clearly in the gloaming but it looked ramshackle. There was a collection of rubbish outside the front door, including an old bath and a bedstead. I knocked at the door.

'Sod off, whoever you are!' said a woman's voice. 'Or I'll get the perlice.'

'It's us, Mum!' shouted Frankie, opening the door. Horrible smells, of unwashed bodies, inadequate drains and boiled vinegar, issued from inside.

'Who've yer got wiv yer?' yelled the voice. 'We don't want no one here. I ent well and I don't want to be disturbed.'

'It's all right. I've only come to see if I can help.' The room was so dark I could see very little. There seemed to be a rack of nappies drying by a smoking stove.

'We don't want yer help. Fuck off or I'll throw!' I saw a figure with wild hair gesturing in the gloom.

'We've brought you some supper.' I advanced, intending put down the two parcels on the table but something flew through the air and caught me sharply on the browbone. It was a boot.

'You didn't orter, Mum! She's my best friend in the world and you've gone and hurt her.' Frankie was in

256

tears. 'Oh, Freddie, you're bleeding!'

'Never mind.' I gave the parcels to Wills who was standing in the doorway with his mouth open. 'Explain to your mother that it's all right. Don't worry, Frankie. I'll see you tomorrow.'

The partner to the boot caught me a stunning blow on the back of my head as I turned to go. I ran back up the path and got panting into the Land Rover.

'Not a success, I take it,' said Guy calmly as we drove home. 'I can't say I'm surprised. Now you know how injured missionaries feel when their gospels are rejected. Perhaps in future you'll limit your zeal for Poor Law Reform to bringing relief to grateful and deserving young men. Let's get back and open the champagne.'

'It isn't my feelings that are injured so much as my head.' I said, feeling something warm and wet trickling between my fingers.

'My God, you *are* hurt!' said Guy, when we got back to the sitting room of Drop Cottage. 'The blighters! Here sit down. I'll get a cloth.'

When he saw that the back of my head was also bleeding he suggested calling the police.

'No, we mustn't do that. It was my fault. The poor woman must be absolutely desperate. You should have seen that terrible house.' Without warning I burst into tears. 'Oh, don't take any notice. I'm just dreadfully tired and my head's throbbing.'

Guy spoke soothingly, dabbed at my wounds and gave me champagne. Then he sat down on the sofa next to me and held my hand. For several minutes we sat in companionable silence. I felt the tensions of the day recede.

'How were the cows?'

'Cows?'

'The ones you went to sell.'

'They went like lambs to the slaughter.'

This jarred. 'The Land Rover didn't really break

257

down, did it? That day we had lunch with the Deacons. It was a ruse to get me to stay.'

Guy smiled and lit a cigarette. 'And are you sorry you did?'

'You behaved very badly.' Guy blew out smoke and smiled a little more broadly. There seemed little point in upbraiding someone who didn't care what I or anyone else thought of him. Besides, as it turned out, I was actually grateful for the result though I disapproved of the method. 'What I like about living here is that the real world, with its misery and cruelty and disappointments, seems very far away. I could almost dispense with time altogether — at least, I mean the awareness of time. Of course, I'm getting older by the second and everything's in flux but there's nothing to remind me of it. That sense of urgency and the pressure to succeed that I felt all the time in London has gone.'

'Really? It hasn't left me at all. If I don't get my just reward now I can't answer for the consequences.' He took hold of my chin with his other hand and turned my face so that I was looking at him. I pushed his hands away and stood up.

'Thank you for everything you've done. I'm going to bed now. Alone.'

Guy looked up at me. I detected something like anger in his eyes. 'I'm becoming accustomed to my role as nurse and I hardly like to importune one so enfeebled, bodily and mentally, but I very much want — to put it mildly — to make love to you. I get the feeling that the idea isn't wholly repulsive to you. I don't mind girls being a bit neurotic, often it adds to their charms, but I'm getting tired of the shadow of Alex looming like a portent of doom every time I try to kiss you.'

'I'm awfully sorry. I mean, if I've misled you. You've been so kind and I do want — oh, damn it, it's quite impossible. I'm not fit to have a love affair with anyone. I couldn't live with myself. I hardly can now. It would be unforgivable. I've hurt Alex so badly. Don't you see that?'

Guy got up. He looked unmistakably furious now. 'Perhaps if you change your mind you'll let me know. You ought to get yourself sorted out, Freddie. You're very lovely but sooner or later people will get fed up with your preoccupation with your conscience. It's a crashing bore. Goodnight.'

22

'You don't mean to say you took any notice of that?' asked Prim with asperity, twenty-four hours later.

We were sitting by the fire, finishing the champagne, having escorted the children home. Prim had called providentially to bring me half a dozen eggs and had stayed to help me scramble them for the children's supper. Tea had been more successful than on the previous day as I had dealt it out in limited quantities over a period of time. Prim was as inexperienced with children as I was, but she had a sterner eye and Wills was more inclined to do her bidding.

'Well, I thought he was probably right,' I said, in answer to Prim's query about Guy. 'In fact, I know he was. I have, I realise, become revoltingly self-indulgent, boring everyone who's patient enough to listen with tales of my blotted copybook. As though it can possibly matter to anyone else. Actually, I was ridiculously hurt, which is always a sign, you know, that someone's put their finger accurately on the tender spot. Not only that — I'm going to miss him. After he'd gone I thought — oh, bloody hell, I did like him, you know.'

'My dear Freddie, of course you did. You needn't be ashamed of it. Guy's an absolute charmer. His being a rat is part of it.'

'Is he a rat?' I sighed and wondered how a blob of Titch's banana had got on to the toe of my shoe. 'My judgement's all to pieces — no, there I go again. I've made a resolve not to bleat any more. All right, he's selfish, I suppose. But just when you decide he's a brute he does something beyond the call of duty, like bringing fish and chips for the children and driving them home.'

'Ah! But did he do it for the children or because he

knew it would soften your heart, that's the question.' Prim lit a cigar. It always made me smile to see her do so because it looked so incongruous with her white teeth, healthy complexion and shining hair. Edward lectured her about throat cancer which, I thought, was one of the reasons she made a point of smoking in his presence. 'The thing is, Freddie, he wanted to hurt you because you disappointed him. He thought he was in luck yesterday and when you rejected him he said the first thing that came into his head to avenge himself. You're in the state when any reproach hits its mark, that's all. Why on earth should you feel guilty because you didn't want to go to bed with him, whatever the reason?'

'If he assumed I would that makes it rather worse, doesn't it? I must have led him on.'

'I never heard such rubbish! Ever since the so-called sexual revolution, flower-power and the pill and all that, every woman's been under intolerable pressure to throw herself on her back for any passing bucko who fancies her. Before that women were in thrall to their parents and the disgrace of being 'cheap' and having an illegitimate baby and now they've passed the handcuffs to men. You didn't want to sleep with him. That should be enough. Guy had no right whatsoever to feel resentful.'

I smiled. 'I'm feeling better already. Yes, of course you're right. I really must pull myself together and start thinking sensibly. I'm going to put it behind me and not give it another thought. Well, not too many, I hope. Now, more to the point, we must do something about the children.' I had told Prim what the children's circumstances were and Prim's first idea was that we ought to call a child welfare organisation immediately. I explained my reluctance. 'Frankie says that her mother hasn't had anything but water to drink for two weeks now, ever since she fell ill. Isn't there a chance that she may be able to get things going again and look after the children herself? It would be so sad to break up the family. She can't be entirely without redeeming qualities.'

'I've never spoken to Mrs Roker but I've seen her about the village. Improbably blonde hair, high heels and rather a lot of bust showing. Poor thing, I suppose her appeal for men is the only power she has. We shouldn't assume, you know, that the social service people will want to rush in and take away the children. Why shouldn't they want to keep them together as much as we do? And they've better resources.'

'That's perfectly true. But Frankie says they've already threatened it.'

'Supposing that baby's health is being permanently damaged because of malnutrition?'

'I think Ruth is capable of feeding her if she has the means.' We had sent the children home with a basket of things like bread and milk and porridge oats for their breakfast. 'From what Frankie's told me she's very conscientious and bullies the children into cleaning their teeth. That reminds me, I must get them some toothpaste tomorrow. Frankie says they've run out.'

Prim looked amused. 'You really have taken them to your heart. Well, on the whole I'm inclined to think you're right. Let's keep the Rokers going through this current crisis if we can. Luckily at this time of year the hens lay like mad. I'll make a cake for their tea tomorrow.'

'Oh, Prim, you are a dear! I felt sure I could rely on you to help.'

'And my deep freeze is stuffed with pheasants. Roger Windebank's wife refuses to eat them at any price and he, poor deluded man, is trying to shoot his way into the upper-middle classes.' She looked doubtful. 'Do children eat pheasant, do you think?'

262

'I'm the last person to know. I've never had anything to do with them.'

'It looks like you're in for a crash course.'

'It would be so much easier if we could go to the house and talk to Mrs Roker. If you can call it a house. It's round and made of corrugated iron.' We had only taken the children as far as the top of the path for fear of missiles.

'What a townie you are never to have seen a Nissen hut! There were thousands of them built round temporary airfields during the war. I've got an idea. Barbara Watkins — she's actually your next-door neighbour though you can't see her house from here — teaches art and drama at Tarchester Primary where the Roker children go. Perhaps Mrs Roker will trust her. I can't imagine anyone not liking Bar. Why don't we consult her?'

'Excellent idea. When?'

'Time and tide wait for no man. Rather an obvious remark, now I think of it. Get your coat on.'

Eight o'clock seemed an odd time to call on someone unannounced but I deferred to Prim's superior knowledge. We took Chloë and a torch and set off through the woods. I had seen glimpses on my walks of a bright pink house through the trees. Now it was too dark to see much at all but Prim got us on to the right path and before long we were tapping at a door.

'Who — is — it?' sang a female voice.

'Prim.'

'Darling, how heavenly! Come in. It's on the latch.'

A pungent breath of incense brought back my cough. The room was heated to tropical temperatures and lit by lamps draped with scarves. The walls were glazed in bright orange and decorated with brilliant trees, flowers, animals and birds. A tiger peeped shyly through giant leaves in the manner of Rousseau. The colours were so vivid, even in the dimmed light, that several seconds passed before I noticed my hostess. She lay in the shadows on the floor, curled in a tight ball with her knees under her chin, her bottom towards us. She was completely naked. 'Five — four — three — two — one,' she chanted, as though she were a rocket about to go off.

'I hope we aren't interrupting anything,' said Prim. 'I've brought Freddie to meet you.'

Before I could stop her Chloë had sauntered in and given Bar's bare buttocks a friendly lick. Bar uncurled swiftly, rolled on to her knees and shook out her waist-length hair, which was an odd colour, somewhere between apricot and orange, like smoked salmon. 'Hello, Chloë, good girl!' She bent to pat Chloë's head. 'Fancy seeing you!'

Bar had a charming face, round and rosy with large sparkling eyes and a tiny plump mouth between two transient dimples. Her breasts were firm and — I reminded myself that I was not at a life class and looked at the room instead. It was bare of furniture except for a small table, crowded with objects, that stood at the edge of a large chalk circle. At the centre was a black cooking pot, something like an old-fashioned cauldron.

'I'm celebrating Eostar. I was just being an egg on the point of hatching. I'll consider it done. Let's have a glass of wine — oh, wait!' she said, as Prim took a step forward. 'You mustn't walk through the circle! You'll be psychically scorched. Just a second and I'll come out.' She stood up, took a knife from the table and swept it from the floor up to a few inches above her head, across and down again. 'You probably can't see it but the circle is made of blue fire and I've cut a door in it with my athame — that's a consecrated knife that's been magically cleansed.' She stepped carefully through the opening she had traced. I looked carefully but I could not see even a wisp of smoke. Chloë was sniffing at the objects on the table, showing particular interest in a loaf of bread. Her psyche seemed as yet unsinged. 'It's wonderful to see you, Prim darling.' She flung her arms around Prim's neck. 'How do you do, Freddie?' She put a hot hand in mine. 'I've already heard a great deal about you and my curiosity's thoroughly whetted.'

'How do you do? I'm afraid I'm not nearly as interesting as Mrs Creech imagines.'

'She didn't say you had glorious red hair. And I bet it's natural. I'll let you into a secret. Mine's dyed.' I raised my eyebrows in what I hoped was a fair imitation of surprise. 'I dye it to accord with the mood of the year. It's flesh-coloured at the moment because the year is newborn. Really it's a very boring dead vole shade.' I couldn't help noticing that Bar had dyed her pubic hair to match. 'Let's go into the kitchen and have a glass of something.'

We shuffled sideways round the edge of the chalk circle. The kitchen was painted dark blue with suns and moons and planets circling overhead. A comet with a long, multi-coloured tail shot over the modern electric cooker and a zigzag of lightning struck the Morphy Richards toaster. Bar poured three glasses of a brown liquid from a large bottle labelled Malt Vinegar and cut several slices from something resembling a thick green pancake with the same knife she had used to cut her way out of the circle. It seemed a useful tool, dedicated to both the sacred and the mundane.

'What is it?' Prim voiced my thoughts.

'It's a sort of cake made with eggs and apples and tansy leaves. In the Middle Ages people thought that eating a lot of fish during Lent gave you worms so they ate tansy cakes, which was supposed to get rid of them. 'On Easter Sunday be the pudding seen, To which the tansy lends her sober green,' ' she sang sweetly. 'Now do try a piece. And drink up.'

'Can it be good to drink vinegar neat?' Prim asked doubtfully. 'I know about Lord Byron, of course, but I think even he combined it with potato.'

Bar laughed, her dimples appearing and disappearing delightfully. 'This is my own birch sap wine. I got that old bottle from Dusty. Don't worry. I sterilised it well.'

I took a cautious sip. It was sweet and quite pleasant but I thought in the bouquet there lurked a trace of pickled something.

'If we're going to stay more than five minutes I must take off a few layers.' Prim removed her coat and jersey. 'I shall need basting, otherwise. I don't know how you can stand the heat, Bar.'

'Isn't it marvellous what psychic vitality can do?' I noticed a Dimplex electric fire in the corner of the kitchen, incandescent with kilowatts. 'Take everything off, darlings, why don't you?' Bar spread her hands in an expansive gesture and her breasts shook. She was well-covered without being fat, with pretty pale skin and more dimples at her elbows and knees. 'You've no idea how much better you'd both feel to be at one with Nature.'

'It would take more than having no clothes on for me to be at one with Nature.' Prim's tone was caustic. 'There's a great deal of Nature I don't approve of — old age and death for a start. And wasps. Also, I don't particularly enjoy seeing mounds of tremulous flesh. When they're my own, that is,' she added politely.

'We witches like to work magic in the nude.' Bar's large eyes were serious. 'Clothes impede etheric energy. We call it going skyclad.'

'That's a charming notion, Bar, dear, but whatever its appellation I should be very embarrassed to be discovered by a chance caller wearing nothing but crumbs in my navel.'

'No one *does* call.' Bar sighed. 'You're the first visitors I've had all week. It's all very well outrunning the wind with the Horned God but I'd like to be able to handfast with someone, preferably near my own age and with a full complement of faculties. Of course I rejoice in the countryside but, golly, it's lonely!'

'Handfast? What does that mean?' I asked.

'It's the witch word for marriage.'

'I've never met a witch before.'

'That's because you haven't been in a proper psychic state. It's one of the resolutions of our creed.' Bar stood up, held out her arms and recited in a sing-song voice, ' ''May those who have never walked barefoot never find the path that leads to my door.' '

Keeping her arms high Bar closed her eyes and lowered her head as though in prayer. Prim and I sat politely to attention, waiting. It was one of those occasions that bring home the value of etiquette in normal life. We sat so long in silence that I began to wonder if Bar had forgotten we were there. I did not dare to catch Prim's eye. My leg was uncomfortably warm from the heat of the electric fire but whenever I tried to change position my chair, which was made of ancient wicker, made a violent creaking sound that seemed intrusive to the prevailing mood of spiritual exaltation. I heard a crunching noise from beneath the table. I looked down to see that Chloë was making fast work of the loaf of bread she had stolen from the consecrated table.

'Ah-h-h-h-h!' said Bar at last. She flung back her head, dropped her arms, opened her eyes and breathed in and out vigorously as if she had been running. 'I understand now! The Goddess has told me everything.' She looked at me with mingled sorrow and surprise. 'You were chosen to be the bride of the Lord of Death, to be sacrificed upon his altar. But the Goddess loves you too much to see you condemned. She has sent you to me to lead you back to joy. You've allowed sexual desire to be a force of oppression. You've been his sexual instrument.'

'Well, that may be putting it rather strongly — ' I began.

'Naturally you don't realise it yet. You've evidently got a very good psychic centre. But the Lord of Death chose you because you were a creature of the world. Now that you're beginning to rub off its tarnish you'll be released from perverted desire for a union with the Hunter God himself.' Bar looked triumphant.

'Oh, good,' I said lamely.

'It's the most tremendous honour. I must say, I'm jealous. But I suppose it's something to be chosen to help bring it about. I knew at once that astral forces had brought you to my door.'

'Actually it was Prim's idea to come.'

Bar smiled at me kindly. 'Of course, Prim was selected as a tool for the purpose.'

'Well, that's excellent, Bar, and I'm glad to have been of use,' Prim spoke briskly, 'but leaving the astral plane for a moment we've come to talk to you about something else. You know the Roker children?'

'Ruth Roker's gone on to the comprehensive. Frankie's in the third form. There's a boy. Let me think. William. Not one of my successes. He always draws pictures of people being tortured or stabbed or blown up. And he steals the brushes and poster paints. When I asked the children to imagine themselves being an important grown-up, all the other children wanted to be princesses or astronauts but William wanted to be a terrorist. Ruth was an odd girl. Uncommunicative, but there's something interesting there. Quite a good little drawer. Neat little houses with flowers round them. Nothing original but few children are at that age. Hopeless at acting. Quite wooden.'

'We're worried about them. Did you ever meet Mrs Roker at a parents' evening?'

'Blonde hair. A lot of makeup. Drinks. I felt sorry for her. Last time she had to be driven home semi-conscious by Mr Batts, the woodwork teacher.'

'That's the one. Well, the children aren't being looked after properly. Thanks to Freddie, they aren't going hungry but something must be done — and quickly. Either we report the matter to the social services or we talk to Mrs Roker and find out whether she's really ill or just coming off the booze. She threw a pair of boots at Freddie. We thought, as she knows you, you might be able to find out what the problem is.'

'I'll try, darlings. Of course I'll try. I'll go tomorrow after school.' She turned back to me, her eyes bright. 'It must have been quite something making love with the Lord of Death, however energy-sapping. You mustn't think it's vulgar curiosity. Well, not entirely, anyway. Witches consider sexuality sacred. It's an act of worship, an affirmation of Earth's fruitfulness.' She looked gloomy. 'It's a pity there's so little of it.'

'But what about the Horned God you mentioned?' I asked, wanting to turn the conversation from my own doings. 'Is that the same thing as the devil? Or is that the Lord of Death?' I was getting confused.

'Satan is a Christian idea. We're pagan. The Horned God is half man, half beast. The Greek Pan, the Celtic Cernunnos, Antlered Herne. The Lord of Death is the part of him that dies with the old year — he expresses all the negative violence of the world. There *are* Satanists, of course, but they're not witches. Witches are entirely beneficent, you know.'

I felt I didn't know anything. The combination of occult and alcohol and a hard day's work at the mill was making my head spin. I had not realised that the sedate traditions of village life concealed such a ferment of nonconformity.

'Come on, Freddie, we'd better go,' said Prim. 'You look all in.'

'That's the aftermath of sexual congress with the Forces of Darkness,' explained Bar sympathetically. 'All

269

that re-emergence of the intuitive self. It's very draining.'

We staggered home beneath a weight of parcels and bottles that Bar had generously pressed on us for the Roker children. I wondered how they would like ash key pickle, nettle mousse and yarrow tea.

'I suppose Guy told her about Alex,' I said, with something of a sigh. 'I know neither you nor Edward would gossip and he's the only other person who knows.'

'I doubt it. God, these bottles are heavy.' Prim shifted her basket to the other hand. 'Guy and Bar had a passage of love last year and they haven't been on speaking terms since.'

'Then it was just a coincidence.' Possibly the incense had narcotic powers. I was almost ready to believe in Bar's divinations.

'Of course it was,' said Prim firmly.

★ ★ ★

I didn't see Bar again until two days later. It was Friday night. Frankie had been waiting for me on the front doorstep as usual when I returned from the mill and that evening Titch had held out her arms when she saw me and cried, 'Bicket,' which had become her name for me, I suppose because she associated me with food.

When she did not scream she was adorable. She would sit on my knee and scan my face with solemn eyes of stormy grey, surrounded by dark lashes clumped together with the residue of the last gush of tears. Her cheeks were fat and soft, her delicate skin flushing pink and white almost as she breathed. She liked to explore my face with her fingers and repeat the words for nose, mouth, eyes and teeth as I said them. Then, prompted by some reflection, her face would suddenly break into a smile. It was irresistible. I had to kiss her, which made

270

her laugh. 'Bicket kiss!', according to Frankie, was her first actual sentence.

'She looks better, don't she?' During these sessions Frankie always stood very close to me and pressed her body against my arm. 'Ruth washed her hair, too.' I had given Frankie the remains of my shampoo. 'She didn't half scream when it went in her eyes, though.'

I winced and made a mental note to buy some baby shampoo.

'Frankie, do you think your mother's getting any better?'

Frankie's ears and the tip of her nose grew red, which I had noticed was a sign of great emotion with her. Then she put her face close to my ear and whispered, 'She said I wussn't to say so's you'd go on givin' us food. She didn't believe me when I told her you wasn't rich and worked in the mill. She went to get her money today. We had hot dogs and mushy peas for dinner. And Arctic Log.'

I had wondered why Wills had refused a second potato. As I expected, the children were obstinate in refusing Bar's wholesome organic woodland gleanings, preferring tomato ketchup and sausages with plastic skins. Wills had gone away as soon as he had cleared his plate, saying he was going to see what his snares had caught. My pleasure at the lifting of responsibility far outweighed my resentment at Mrs Roker's attempt to make me a milch-cow.

'I'm really glad your mother's better.' I kissed Frankie on the nose to show her I wasn't cross and she put her arms round my neck and kissed me so hard my cheek felt bruised.

'Can I still come?' she asked, still in a whisper.

'I'd be very sad if you didn't.' Frankie leaned against me and rested her head on my shoulder. I was so moved by her desperate need for affection that I felt my eyes fill with tears. 'Come on,' I said. 'Let's walk home the long

271

way through the woods and see if we can see any fox cubs.'

Of course we didn't but we glimpsed something that might have been a bird or a bat, flitting through the trees and Frankie nearly trod on a hedgehog so our quest for natural history was satisfied.

Afterwards, back at Drop Cottage I prepared myself for forty-eight hours of relaxation. I was stiff and sore after four days of hard labour. Usually I went to Yardley house for a shower or bath but for some time it had been my ambition to make use of the ancient tub that hung from the ceiling of the outhouse beneath the cat-slide roof. I managed, with the help of my newly-constructed muscles to get it into the sitting room and after half an hour of boiling kettles it was three-quarters full of steaming water, into which I sprinkled epsom salts. The fire was well stoked and the front door wedged shut. I put Mendelssohn's violin concerto on the gramophone, flung off my clothes and got in. It was indescribable bliss. After Chloë had had a go at drinking the bath water and given up, presumably because she didn't like the taste of the salts, I was able to drift away into a state where thought was suspended in favour of sensation.

I must have been lying there unmoving, eyes closed and head lolling, for perhaps a quarter of an hour, mental activity confined to a fragment of brain that idly pursued the notes of the music, when I heard a log fall in the grate. I opened my eyes. Bar was sitting with her feet up on the sofa, conducting the concerto with one hand and holding a glass of wine in the other. To my tired brain and rambling senses she seemed to be an apparition. I could easily have believed that she had materialised in a puff of smoke or a shower of stars.

'I helped myself, darling. You don't mind, do you?'

It is always disconcerting to find you have been under observation without your knowledge. The feeling of exposure is naturally much worse when you have no clothes on. 'Not at all.' I folded my arms across my chest. 'How long have you been here? I must have looked so silly.'

'You looked perfectly sweet. Trances are good for you. Mind-cleansing. I can see your aura is very wobbly round the edges. I couldn't open the front door so I came in round the back.'

'Why didn't Chloë bark?'

'Witches have a special communication with animals. Also, I happened to have a biscuit in my pocket.' I looked at Chloë who refused to meet my gaze. 'I've come to set your mind at rest about the Rokers. I went to see them last night after school. Ruth didn't want to let me in but she didn't dare say no. Poor child, she's very protective of her mother. Of course, it ought to be the other way round. Mrs Roker was sitting up in bed, looking chirpy, if yellow, and guzzling a bar of chocolate.' I had sent three home with Frankie for the older children as a particular treat. 'She was truculent at first but then she softened up and seemed glad to have someone to talk to. She told me she'd been under the weather but was feeling much better. I gather, from oblique hints, she's given up drinking. I couldn't see any bottles anywhere. What she needs is dandelion tea. It's very good for jaundice'

'You don't think she should see a doctor?'

'Certainly not. She needs a good diet and fresh air, not unwholesome chemicals with damaging side effects.'

Though acknowledging that Bar's view of things was strictly tailored to her beliefs, which of course is true of all of us, I felt enormously relieved by her account of Mrs Roker. No sick person could eat a whole Mars bar.

The bath-water was cooling rapidly. 'Be a dear and bring the bottle and another glass, would you?' I asked. While Bar was in the kitchen I leapt from the bath, dried myself, and had my dressing-gown buttoned before she returned. There was a knock at the front door. I removed the chair I had jammed under the handle and opened it a crack.

'Good evening, Miss Swann.' It was Mrs Creech. She looked slightly dishevelled and was panting. 'My word, that's a very nasty journey. I'd not have undertaken it if I'd known. I've mud all over the back of me legs. You ought to get it seen to, really you should.' It had not occurred to me before that the path was a useful deterrent to prying callers. 'I do hope I'm not interrupting anything.' She was craning her neck, attempting to see into the sitting room.

'No, of course not. Be quiet, Chloë.' She was doing her imitation of a highly trained police dog confronted by a criminal, crouching down on her front paws, hackles raised and lips drawn back over her teeth.

'That's a nasty, vicious animal you've got there. I'm surprised you feel safe with it. But, then, as you live alone perhaps it's as well . . . '

Mrs Creech's eyes took in my dressing-gown. I opened the door wider so that she could see I was not entertaining the husbands of Pudwell. 'I'm collecting for Christian Aid Week.' She gave me a small envelope. 'Also, I've a petition here to get the council to move those gypsies on.' Her thin lips puckered with disgust. 'They leave litter and lower the tone of the village. And since their children have been attending the school the incidence of head lice has become quite chronic. Though you aren't, properly speaking, a resident, I'm sure you'll be glad to lend your support.'

'Oh, I really don't think I know enough about it — they've got to live somewhere. Perhaps litter-bins and shampoo?'

Mrs Creech's eye fell on Chloë, who had stopped barking but continued to snarl. 'They steal pet cats and dogs and eat them, you know.' I could see from her expression that she thought in Chloë's case this would be a good thing.

'I'm afraid I must know more about it before I can decide.' I closed the door a couple of inches until it met Mrs Creech's foot. 'I'm having an early night — just on my way to bed.'

'Here we are, darling.' Bar emerged from the kitchen with a tray, her breasts quivering as she moved. 'I've taken off my clothes, too, as I know how shy one feels at first.'

Mrs Creech's eyes and mouth grew wide, and she threw up her hands as though to blot out a vision of Sodom and Gomorrah. Her Christian Aid envelopes drifted about the room like autumn leaves.

23

The morning was uncharacteristically brilliant. New leaves, dyed sulphur-yellow by the sun, fluttered like tiny pennants on the soft wind. Birds performed a sublime choral work against a backdrop of thrilling blue, the colour of the Delftware bowl I had filled with primroses and moss that stood on the window-sill. Pink and white apple-blossom unfurled almost before my eyes. Even Macavity, who had remained on my bed during the cold, gloomy days, was moved to potter about the garden.

'I've come to do yer roof.' Dusty stood at the front door, bent beneath a weight of ladders. 'Where's that little beggar, George? He were supposed to give me a hand.' He threw down his burden with a crash and spat into the nettles. 'That path's a real booger, ent it? There's a very tidy boongalow empty by the cross-roads. Some folks'd rather be awk'ard at any price. I'll get me tools.'

He reappeared with an assortment of ancient iron and wooden implements, rakes, combs and shears, the sort of things on display in a folk museum. He went away and returned with several armfuls of what I thought was straw but Dusty informed me was Abbotsbury spear, a type of local reed. 'Ye'll not find better thatch'n this,' he asserted, kicking the pile of tarnished gold with his foot. 'We'll patch first and then us'll ridge.'

I knew nothing about the craft of thatching but when Dusty brought a bundle of sticks sharpened to a point and told me they were spargads, I remembered Marty South in Hardy's *The Woodlanders* working by firelight until dawn, making the same article to earn money for her sick father. I was moved by this link with literature but Dusty was unimpressed.

'Aye, I mind talk o' that book-writing man. Lived over Bockhampton way. Folks come from Americky joost to see the old house where he was raised. I don't hold wi' them kind o' books. Make-believe — where's the purpose o' that? There ye are, ye young rascal. What's 'ee been doing, eh?' It was quite obvious what George had been doing. His beauty was spoiled by a swelling eye and a bleeding lip. 'Ye've been fighting again, ye little hooligan. And ye've had the worst of it, I should say. How come ye want to go provoking lads bigger'n ee?'

'William Roker called me a cripple,' George looked fierce as he repeated the insult. 'But I made his nose bleed. I shouldn't wonder if I ent broke it.'

'Well, get along now and bundle that reed or I'll break yous 'n' all.'

George applied himself to the task with what looked to me like expertise.

'How are you getting on with your school work?' I knew better than to offer him sympathy for his bruises.

'All right. I don't mind it. I'm having extra lessons. Mr Gildry's paying.' He stopped what he was doing to look at me. 'Why should he do that, now?'

'I don't know,' I lied. 'I expect it's because he doesn't want to see you waste your talents.' George gave me a look of disbelief and spat. 'If you do that again I shall be cross. It won't do at the grammar school, you know.'

'I know that. I know most things you don't because you're only a girl.'

I restrained myself from smacking him. 'Girls are as clever as boys, you know.'

'Course they aren't! If you're so clever tell me the answer to this: 'When it goes in 'tis stiff and stout. When it comes out 'tis flopping about.'' He grinned at the expression on my face. 'You've got a dirty mind! I know

277

what you're thinking. Well, it ent that. It's cooked cabbage!'

I left them to it. There was an old bench near the enclosed garden, overgrown with brambles but with a wonderful view of the upper part of the valley. I spent a few minutes cutting away the worst of them, then sat down to enjoy the changing colours on the hillside opposite as puffs of clouds drifted slowly past the sun. I admired the effect of lambent leaf-shadow against the trunk of an oak that grew beside the bench. A robin hopped about beneath it, eyeing me boldly. At least, I thought he was looking at me but this proved to be a feint for he pounced on something hidden among the weeds and flew off to the outhouse, carrying a worm. He returned to repeat the performance with a beetle. I went to see what was so alluring in the shed. A brown bird, presumably its mate, fluttered out into my face. On a shelf, in an empty Sharp's Kreem Toffees tin, was a nest with five greyish-white eggs, freckled with brown. They were warm to touch. The shed contained a selection of garden implements. I took a spade back to the bench and turned over a spit of ground to provide the diligent parent with more worms.

As I looked at the newly exposed soil, an idea was born. It spoke beguilingly of juicy carrots, tender beans, crunchy lettuces, new potatoes tasting sweet and earthy. Food, cheap and plentiful, could be mine for the outlay of a few pence. But how long must I wait before I could reap the rewards of this modest investment? My only experience of horticulture had been at prep school when we grew broad beans in jam jars filled with sand and pink blotting paper. I remembered that my pallid shoot, over-zealously watered, had turned brown and died long before anyone else's. The sun warmed my face while I allowed the idea to grow. The handle of the spade was worn smooth with much handling. I felt inspired. What did my inexperience matter? I could master what generations had learned before me.

The robin came back to spur me on. He had needle-thin legs that looked too fragile to support his stout body and coral-coloured chest. I dug with enthusiasm, moving my excavations to a more open site away from the oak tree, fired by visions of the bounty that might be mine. Over lunch I digested the relevant chapter of a book called *The Golden Treasury of Gardening*, which I found on the shelves in the sitting room, that guaranteed a vegetable Utopia regardless of skill or knowledge.

At two o'clock Chloë and I raced down to the post office. I was scarcely able to contain my excitement. It was like beginning a painting in the old days, the thrilling sense of possibility, the excitement of the mysterious act of creation with its slow, dream-like florescence of half-ideas punctuated by violent flare-ups of inspiration. When Mrs Creech saw me, her expression became vindictive and she and another customer had a whispered conversation over the bacon-slicer. While Mrs Creech talked, they both stared at me and their eyes and mouths grew wider and wider until they looked like the Tenniel drawing of Tweedledum and Tweedledee frightened by the monstrous crow. I caught the odd phrase, 'naked as the day she was born', which must have referred to Bar, and 'a woman of insatiable lust', which presumably meant me, but I was too exhilarated to care. I bought packets of runner-bean, beetroot, pea, carrot and lettuce seeds plus a bag of wizened-looking tubers labelled Sutton's Foremost. As an afterthought I bought string, bamboo canes and a packet of mixed sweet peas. I panted back to Drop Cottage with my purchases to find a strange man standing in my garden. I knew at once who it was.

Lemmy was standing just beyond the plank bridge, watching Dusty who was half-way up a ladder pulling out armfuls of reed. He was exceptionally tall, straight-backed and broad-shouldered, no doubt tough-ened by the rigours of an outdoor life. His hair was dark and dirty and hung on his collar. Luckily he was wearing clothes, a pair of blue trousers stained and ripped at the knees and a dark red shirt, far from clean. His toes poked through canvas shoes. His feet were filthy. I was delighted that I had managed to approach him without being seen. I remembered Prim's injunction to speak quietly and calmly.

'Hello,' I called, from the other side of the bridge. I made my voice as soft and friendly as I could, though I was rather out of breath. He turned quickly and looked at me with an expression of alarm. Or was it confusion? It was difficult to tell for the lower part of his face was concealed by an unkempt black beard. 'Don't worry,' I said quickly. 'I want to be your friend. I hope you'll think of this garden as your own and come and go just as you like. I know all about the food Bar puts out for you.' I stopped, embarrassed. 'Putting out' food made him sound like a dog. If I had known what an intimidating masculine presence Lemmy was, I should have felt even less relaxed at the idea that he was wandering about the place, watching me. The expression in his eyes changed to extreme wariness but at least he did not run away. Because of the beard I couldn't tell whether he was hostile or frightened, or possibly both. I started to approach cautiously, keeping a smile on my face. He watched me moving nearer and continued to look bewildered. Prim had said that he was perfectly intelligent but I began to wonder. 'Prim's told me about you,' I went on in a voice as much like oiled silk as I could make it, grinning ever more brightly. 'I feel this place is as much yours as mine really — I mean, you've been here so much longer.' I paused. Chloë, who had lingered behind me in the lane, chasing a rabbit, came racing down the bank and bounded over the bridge to hurl herself on the intruder. But the moment she came within a few feet of him she hesitated. She began the strangest high-pitched howl, almost like a child screaming. For a moment I was frightened, thinking she was ill, perhaps having a heart-attack. She threw herself on the ground at his feet, still howling and whining and wagging her whole body with what I realised seconds later was joy.

'Chloë!' Lemmy lifted her into his arms, no small feat for she was a large dog. 'Dear old girl! Dear old girl!' Prim had told me that he loved animals, and I saw that this affection was returned tenfold. Chloë licked his face, still howling with excitement. He put her down and patted and stroked her as she threw herself at him again and again, yelping and whining. Finally he knelt and embraced her. I saw that his eyes were filled with tears. I was rather touched.

'I like animals, too,' I said. 'Not that I've ever had much to do with them. Chloë's the first dog I've ever looked after. Prim said you had a great affinity with animals.'

'She did?' Lemmy looked nonplussed.

Perhaps I was being too complicated. Lemmy had been an *enfant sauvage*, isolated from human society for a good deal of his life. He might not understand words like 'affinity'.

'You like animals and they like you,' I prompted gently. 'Actually that's rather an understatement. I've never seen Chloë like this with anybody.' It was difficult to steer a middle course between being simple and being patronising. 'Isn't it marvellous that spring has come?' I went on, striving to find a subject that would be of interest to him. Presumably if one lived out of doors the weather was of supreme importance.

'Marvellous. Yes.' I thought I detected a twitching deep within the beard that might have been a smile. I walked across the bridge towards him at a slow, steady pace so as not to frighten him into flight. He stood up, keeping his hand on Chloë's head as she pressed lovingly against him, continuing to whine. His fingers were filthy, the nails rimmed with black.

'I've decided to restore a small area of the garden,' I went on. As a conversationalist Lemmy lacked the most rudimentary skills but he was certainly looking at me in a more friendly way. 'I'm going to grow vegetables. I'll give you some if I'm successful.'

'That's very good of you.'

His voice was low and attractive. It was impossible to tell what he was thinking with that ridiculous beard. I longed to reassure him. I remembered his taste for music. I could not whistle to save my life but perhaps singing might do as well. A snatch of one of the Savoy Operas came to mind. ' "Then a sentimental passion of a vegetable fashion must excite your languid spleen, An attachment *à la* Plato for a bashful young potato, or a not too French french bean!" ' I trilled and, seeing something like amazement in his eyes, immediately regretted it. 'It's quite a well-known song. I thought it might amuse you.' I blushed.

Much to my relief he did laugh, then. It was a pleasant sound, deep and hearty, of real enjoyment. I felt encouraged.

'That was very . . . good of you, Miss, er — '

'Swann. But do call me Freddie.'

'Thank you.' He bowed his head courteously.

'I hope I can call you Lemmy.'

'Certainly.'

Now I was sure I could see a smile lurking in the beard.

'Goodbye, then,' I said, as we seemed to have reached conversational stalemate. He bowed his head again and walked away. Chloë went with him, without a backward glance.

As I raked over the virgin vegetable patch to make a fine tilth for sowing I mulled over the encounter.

Because I had been afraid of alarming him I had been too self-conscious. I picked up bits of brick and shards of china and decided that in future I must be more natural and not try to force a conversation. I must let Lemmy dictate the course of our relationship. I tied the canes together in the middle of the square to make a wigwam and pushed the sweet-pea seeds into the ground, three to a cane, with my blessing. I watered them in and stood back to admire the effect. My goodness, gardening was therapy! I hadn't felt so pleased with the world for months.

An hour later and I had planted circles of radishes, lettuces and carrots which I intended to interplant with love-in-a-mist, cornflowers and night-scented stocks, as suggested by *The Golden Treasury*. I stretched and heaved a sigh of satisfaction. A pair of hands covered my eyes so quickly that I had no chance to turn round. I stood still, willing myself to play the game like a sport, though it is one I always find irritating. Lemmy? Surely it couldn't be Dusty? Suddenly I had a terrifying conviction that it was Alex and I twisted violently to free myself.

'Hello, my darling.'

'Guy!'

'Pleased to see me?' There was no denying it. I was. He was looking particularly agreeable, in a pink-striped shirt and jeans, the sun turning his shining hair to the colour of brass. Unlike poor Lemmy, Guy's elegant hands were clean, his fingernails well manicured, his boots polished, no doubt by Miss Glim.

'I thought you'd sacked me.' I attempted coolness with just a hint of censure.

'That was a moment of madness.' He took my hand, turned it over and kissed the inside of my wrist. I tried to ignore the galvanic effect on my treacherous central nervous system. 'I behaved selfishly and stupidly. I knew it the minute I got outside the door but I was too much of an ass to come back and apologise.' His eyes were uncharacteristically serious as he gazed into mine. 'I'm so sorry, Freddie. Of course I want to make love to you but if I'm only allowed to talk to you and admire you and hold your hand, that's better than nothing.'

I was astonished. Experience had taught me that men are simply not interested in friendship with women. If you don't want them to enjoy you sexually they're damned if they'll enjoy you at all. Of course, sometimes they hang on, pretending pleasure in your *bons mots*, just in case you weaken.

Guy put his arms round my waist and pulled me to him. 'Am I forgiven, Freddie? Just to be with you, holding you like this, is happiness. Can I help it if other thoughts come involuntarily to mind? You shouldn't have that face if you don't want me to desire you.' As abruptly, he let me go and took a step back. 'There! Best behaviour! Now, we'll talk of other things. What's it like working for that old devil at the mill? I don't like the thought of you breaking your back with those heavy sacks.'

'I'm getting better at it. I don't mind the work. It's dull but I can think about something else. I can't get used to the rats though. Yesterday I lifted a sack and one jumped out of it. I'm afraid I screamed and ran upstairs. I know they won't hurt me. It's the way they move I can't get used to. Dusty's mad keen to set traps for them but I dread one being caught more than anything. It seems so unfair when they're only trying to live, just as we are.'

'He's a shocking old villain, isn't he?'

'I'll thank 'ee to mind who ye're calling a scamp and a villain, Maister Guy.' Dusty's head appeared over the rooftop behind which he had evidently been crouching to hear what we were saying.

Guy laughed. 'Get on with your work, you old reprobate! Come on, Freddie, put down that hoe and come for a walk with me. I've got an idea.'

He led me through the garden and into the woods. We began to descend the long zigzagging path that ran below Bar's cottage and came out much further up the river. A blackbird cried, 'Chink, chink, chink' as he hopped in front of us. He seemed agitated. Then I saw the yellow eyes of Macavity peering furtively from a bush, like a cutpurse.

'Where's Chloë?' asked Guy. 'I thought you two were inseparable.'

'She's gone off with Lemmy. I'm trying not to feel hurt.'

'Ah, so you've met the phantom whistler. I hope he didn't frighten you.'

'Not at all. He was more civilised than I'd expected. Fully dressed for one thing.'

'Once I caught Mrs Creech trying to beat Lemmy's naked buttocks with her umbrella. Instead of running away the poor fellow was skipping round in a circle trying to protect himself with his hands. He could have laid her out with a single punch to the jaw. But he has no instinct for self-preservation.'

'What did you do?'

'I seized the umbrella and threw it over the hedge. Lemmy saw his chance and hopped it.'

'Nudity seems very much in vogue in Pudwell.'

'Not half as much as I'd like.'

The earth smelt sharp and ripe. Bluebells lifted their dusky violet heads in preparation for blooming. Scattered about my feet were wild flowers of every colour and shape whose names I did not know, young shoots thrusting up with soft, pale leaves, delicate buds blossoming, fern fronds unfurling. The light was green, flitting over the ground in splashes. We were descending in single file as the path was narrow. Frequently my skirt, which was longish, cotton and flimsy, caught on a thorn and I had to stop to untangle myself. Once I got left behind and ran to catch up. Guy was waiting for me, leaning with folded arms against a tree. He reminded me of that famous sixteenth-century miniature by Nicholas Hilliard of the young blade, at ease, rakish, dangerous. I hoped there was nothing metaphorical about the bramble bushes.

'Now you know where we are.' Guy took my hand. We had reached the floor of the valley. Before us lay the river but here its torrents were calm, its eddies smooth. Hardly a ripple disturbed the glassy surface as it rolled by. Only the twirling leaves and sticks on its surface indicated the speed of its passage. To the left and right of us the land rose steeply and the river ran through broad streaks of brilliant light and shade.

'Gilderoy Hall is almost directly above us but you can't see it from here. This is the boathouse.' Guy indicated a large hut almost hidden by trees, its exterior ornamented prettily in the Gothic style. There was a rowing boat tied to the jetty. 'Let's go out on the river.'

'This is a wonderful idea.' I sprang rather clumsily into the boat. 'You are clever.'

Guy did not contradict me. The presence of blue canvas cushions on the seat in the stern prompted the flicker of a suspicion that there was more premeditation about our adventure than he would have me suppose. Guy undid the rope. At once the boat began to slide gently along with the current. He dipped the oars into the water and we shot into the middle of the river. It is impossible to sit in a small boat and resist trailing a hand in the water. It was warm at the surface but two inches below it was extremely cold. Weeds of startling emerald lay horizontally, straining at the roots, slimy to touch, breaking in handfuls. Where the oars disturbed the olive silkiness, the sun scattered spangles of light, dazzling my eyes. Guy rowed expertly. It was a pleasure to watch the rhythmic movements of his shoulders and arms as he bent forward and pulled back in one flowing action. He caught my eye and winked. I decided to take an intelligent interest in my surroundings.

'What are those white flowers on little stalks over there? They're so pretty.'

'Water crowfoot. In a few weeks it'll be a sheet of white and green. It's caviare to a swan.'

'Why is the river smooth here and so turbulent below the cottage?'

'It divides just above the boathouse. This part is controlled by sluices to feed the mill. It joins with another river and eventually completes a large loop. Whereas your part of the river goes down to the sea.'

'Did you learn to row when you were a boy?'

'Vere and I virtually lived on the river when we were kids. There were always atmospheres in the house. It was wonderful to get out on the water, even in winter when the reeds were frozen and splashes burned your skin with cold. Every summer we swam and rowed and fished — Vere gave that up after a bit, he didn't like to see the fish gasping, he always was hopelessly sentimental — and we camped on the islands. There are three further up. Vere built a pirate ship. It was really a raft with an old sheet as a sail. He told me he was going to sail out to sea and commit daring deeds. I really believed him. I begged him to take me along but he said you couldn't have adventures unless you were alone. Well, in the end he had all he could want.'

There was a pause.

'Do you miss him terribly?'

'Yes.'

We didn't say anything after that. My thoughts became intertwined with the creak of the rowlocks, the slap of the water against the sides, the sunlight flashing through the trees, the motion of Guy's body, forward, back, forward, back. I remembered Maggie Tulliver's disastrous journey down the river with Stephen Guest in *The Mill on the Floss*. Her upbringing and her own

287

code of conduct had told her that they should not travel further, that they could not do so without destroying the happiness of those they loved. But the enchantment of the gliding motion, the fascination of the rushing water, scarcely changing to the eye yet violently in flux, the sedative powers of wild beauty had brought about a paralysis of will, dissolving conviction, discounting consequences, disconnecting time.

I withdrew my hand from the water. The cushions were yielding, the wood smelt pleasantly of preservative, faintly tarry. The air quivered with warmth. I closed my eyes. A pigeon cooed in the trees, and far off I heard a cuckoo. What were the notes supposed to be? C to G sharp. I tried to echo them accurately in my mind.

'Freddie. Darling Freddie.' I opened my eyes. Guy was beside me. He put his arms round me. A voice in my head that I recognised as my good friend in times of difficulty and danger instructed me to resist. He kissed me very gently. You must stop this, said the voice of sense. 'I can't help it, darling. I do love you so much. God, you can't know how desperately I love you!' Guy's voice was low yet it drowned mine entirely. We kissed with increasing fervour until I turned my face away with a sigh of despair at my own hopeless lack of will. 'Guy, I don't want — '

'Oh, shut up.'

'But don't you see how messy, how intolerable, this makes my life?'

'I don't care.'

'All right, no reason why you should but — '

'If you don't shut up right now I'm going to strangle you with the painter.'

I shut up. Seconds later I found myself drifting down river in a rowing-boat, making love with a man I suspected of deviousness and mendacity, in full view of anyone who cared to watch. So much for the old cautious, sensible Freddie. I enjoyed every moment.

24

'Hello?'

'Hello, Fay. It's Freddie.'

I heard a sharply drawn breath. Then Fay said, 'Get me a cigarette, Charles. It's Elfrida.' I waited, listening to sounds of Cellophane being rustled and the click of a lighter. The telephone box smelt foul and there was a tide of sweet wrappers, newspaper and a rotting banana skin at my feet. 'Where are you?' asked Fay at last.

'In a call box outside Pa — a railway station.'

'I see. It's very good of you to get in touch,' Fay drawled, with sarcasm, and I thought I detected pleasure, too, in her tone. She was exultant because at last I had done something to justify her dislike. I understood that because I had several times found myself wishing that Alex had done something dastardly so that I could prove to myself and the world that I was right. 'I suppose you're bored with your little holiday and you thought you'd like to take up with everything where you left off. But I'm afraid you've got a shock coming to you, Elfrida. It may have amused you to behave like a spoilt, narcissistic little tramp but no one else is laughing.'

'I honestly never thought it was amusing for any — what do you mean, 'tramp'?'

'You don't expect me to believe that there isn't some other man involved? Some wretched queer who wants to hold your hand and recite his poems and thinks you're a vamp in bed because you let him put his hand up your skirt. You don't deserve a proper man like Alex. You can't expect someone of his age and experience to be satisfied with the occasional chaste peck and the promise of more to come. Of course he's going to

289

demand his rights. You *are* a bloody little fool!'

I began to see. Of course Alex and Fay would have analysed my behaviour in minutest detail. I think Fay got a prurient thrill from discussing sex with him. It was the closest she wanted to get to the real thing. They would have talked over my freakish conduct in the days before the wedding.

Six weeks before the great event we had received the keys of our new house in Melbury Street. Though it was empty and the decorators not due to begin work until the following week, Alex said he wanted to call in immediately to check a few details the architect had forgotten. It was such a lovely house that I was at a loss to understand why my spirits, already unaccountably depressed, sank even lower as soon as I saw it. When I imagined living in it with him I seemed to feel a tightness around my chest as though the oxygen had gone out of the air.

'Come into the dining room a minute,' he said. He closed the door and began to kiss me. I recognised the preliminaries to making love. I returned the kiss but mounting dismay made it an effort of will. 'Let's take possession of the house now,' he said. My reluctance intensified and I tried to free myself. 'Don't be a silly little Puritan,' he murmured, kissing my neck and pressing me hard against him. 'No one can see in and so what if they did?'

'I don't think it's that. I just don't want to.'

'You will.' He unzipped his flies and lifted my skirt.

I was aware of a feeling of actual dislike that grew with every caress. I tried to pull away but he laughed and held me tighter, hurting me. The pain made me angry and we began to fight. Alex tore my shirt open and pushed me against the wall. He was intensely excited by my resistance. The angrier I became the more he liked it. In the end I stopped fighting him and gave way because of an inexplicable feeling of shame.

'I was right, you see,' he said, as he rolled off me finally, and we lay side by side on the dusty floor. When I stared mutinously at the ceiling and said nothing he took hold of my chin and turned my face towards him. 'Don't think I'm going to let you play fast and loose with me, Freddie, because I won't.' He wasn't smiling. I forced myself to look into his eyes and thought, for a brief second, that I was looking at my enemy.

That evening Alex flew to Zurich for several days and I had time to make plans for the house and teach myself not to refine on a very small point. But when I met him at Heathrow and drove him back into London I knew at once that the feeling I had so carefully crushed — an unwillingness to make love that, if I let it, grew almost to panic — had jumped out like a grinning jack-in-the-box.

We went back to his flat. He pushed the door shut and started to kiss me.

'Alex, I think I need a bit of time to myself. I expect it's all the fuss about the wedding. I do wish we'd been firm and not let Fay make it into a such a circus. I spent all morning writing gushing letters of thanks for perfectly hideous presents from people I can't remember ever having met.'

'Poor darling. What a bore for you.' Alex took off his coat and tie. 'But the thing's done now. Anyway, these occasions are rites of passage, that's all. What does it matter whether a lot of people come or a few? You wouldn't want a dreary register-office affair with a dull restaurant lunch for a few friends afterwards.'

'Actually, I think that's just what I would like.' I moved away from him and went to stand by the window. 'Just the people we're really fond of. No strain, no . . . showing off. That's what it seems to have come down to. Fay wants to make our wedding the smartest of the year — the most beautiful flowers, the biggest guest list, even the most famous organist. She wants to

291

inspire greenest envy in the hearts of her friends and promote you in the eyes of yours. Isn't that a very long way from two people deciding they want to spend the rest of their lives together because they love each other?'

Alex came over to me and began to unbutton my coat. 'Aren't you being rather childish? It's a perfect opportunity to do some entertaining. Anyway, we can't do anything to change it now. Be a good girl and shut up and let me make love to you.' I kept my arms folded over my chest. I tried to think of an excuse for not wanting to. He frowned. 'I suppose this is an attempt to inject a bit of drama into the thing. Fay warned me that you'd probably play up to get yourself centre stage.'

I slapped his face hard, then stood trembling with shock, as much because of my own reaction as with indignation at the unfairness of the accusation. Alex took hold of me and pushed me down on to the floor. I am ashamed to say that I lost my temper and bit him. This excited him to a frenzy. Now, looking back, I realised he had made the remark about Fay because he knew it would make me furious. Already he was acquiring a taste for violent sex. Again the utter humiliation of the thing made me stop fighting eventually and his satisfaction was crowned by victory.

Afterwards he apologised so charmingly and was so affectionate that it would have seemed priggish to complain. My own pride forbade me to make too much of it. Sexual games were probably inevitable in a long relationship. What disturbed me far more was that throughout I had felt nothing but revulsion. Worse, I identified feelings of something like fear. I told myself I was tired, worried, over-anxious. I knew that Alex loved me. But during those acts of lovemaking I absolutely hated him.

I spent long hours trying to define this feeling. I tried to explain that what was to him exciting was to me alienating. Perhaps I was too oblique, from a reluctance to hurt him. For there were still times, when we were not making love, when I felt a resurgence of my former passion for him. Love dies lingeringly and when it does there is still the habit of loving, which is hard to break.

Alex's response was to reinterpret what I was saying to show that I was confused, self-contradicting and wholly mistaken. I admitted the first two charges but became seriously angry as I fought for the legitimacy of my own point of view. It always ended in the same way. The minute I lost control of myself Alex forced me to make love. The more I protested the more he was gratified, sexually. So I started to avoid being alone with him, which didn't help my case.

I felt sick now as I remembered those occasions of sexual appropriation. Of course, Alex would have found an explanation for my defection that would put him in the most favourable light. He had probably enjoyed presenting himself to Fay as a man of unbridled appetites and imperious ways.

'You're quite wrong, Fay, if you think that I left Alex because of a squeamishness about sex. Or for any other man. I tried to tell him — '

'Oh, don't give me that little-girl-hard-done-by act! I've heard it all. I've put up with your simpering wouldn't-harm-a-fly ways for twenty-two years and had to listen to people telling me how lucky I was to have such a charming stepdaughter. Lucky! Hah!' Fay was almost screaming now. I could tell by the way numbers and epithets rolled off Fay's tongue that she had spent sleepless hours rehearsing what she wanted to say to me. It seemed only fair to let her get it off her chest so I waited. 'Let me tell you what I think of you. It never occurred to you, did it, that I might not have *wanted* a child hanging round my neck day and night? I've endured your obstinacy, your ingratitude, your airs and graces, that judging, condemning look of yours until I've wanted to — throttle you! My God, if I'd known *then* what it would be like I'd never have married your father.' Fay's voice had a wobble in it, induced by the pathetic picture she was drawing of herself as victim. 'You've *never* missed an opportunity to defy me — ' I held the receiver away from my ear and watched a pigeon, its beak smeared with tomato sauce, struggling to eat a bit of hamburger bun that had been thrown down on to the pavement. ' — complete disregard for myself I was determined that this wedding was going to make everyone sit up — ' the pigeon snatched whole the fragment of meat and ran round in a circle trying to swallow it. ' — all the *months* of work, the embarrassment, making me look a com*plete* fool — ' It tackled the bread again, shaking its head and pattering on rose-pink feet among the squashed chewing gum that lay like lead coins on the concrete. ' — all my friends — a laughing-stock — *thousands* of pounds — ' The pigeon gave up and flew off.

'I'm so sorry, Fay. I realise that it was dreadfully expensive — '

'Is *that* all you can say? You're sorry? My hat *alone* cost three hundred pounds!'

'Well, you've still got it,' I said reasonably. 'It'll be useful for Ascot.'

'I give up! I absolutely bloody give *up*!' Fay began to sob. 'The girl chucks away everything I've done for her and tells me I can wear the bloody thing at *Ascot*! It would *choke* me to wear it!'

'Can I speak to my father?'

'No, you can *not*!' Fay shouted. There was some murmuring in the background. 'I won't have you undermining me, Charles! If you cared *twopence* about me you'd refuse ever to speak to her again after the way I've been treated. You've *always* been too soft on the girl. This is all *your* fault! I warn you, if you take her part against me it will be for the *last* time. I won't stand for it!' More murmuring. Then Fay spoke again. 'Your father doesn't want to talk to you, Elfrida. He's bitterly hurt by your behaviour. I hope you're satisfied!'

I put the receiver down.

* * *

'Everyone seems to think you've gone to Brazil with that idiot Gideon Duff — that bloke with the huge house in Scotland and the teeny-weeny brain. I told them you wouldn't be such a fool.' Oonagh Fitzpatrick tipped back her full brandy glass and drained three-quarters of the contents. She lit a cheroot. It was five o'clock in the afternoon on the same day, Sunday, of my abortive attempt to speak to my father. We were sitting in her filthy, freezing studio in Battersea, warmed only by the grudging heat of a stinking stove. I could not understand how Oonagh retained not only her balance but also her health on the diet of poison she insisted on. I never saw her eat anything like fruit or vegetables. Her preference was for black coffee, spirits, tobacco and game crawling with maggots and she chewed hashish all day while she painted, yet her skin was clear and her eyes bright. 'A stickleback has larger temporal lobes than Gideon Duff. If you ask me it's not a guilty conscience you're suffering from but something like wounded pride.'

Oonagh and I had been at art school together and we had kept up the friendship, despite our different characters and attitudes. It was difficult to say quite why the affection had lasted. I admired her uncompromising attitude to the truth and she . . . actually I had no idea why Oonagh liked me. She was unfailingly rude but, then, she insulted everyone.

Oonagh's appearance was startling. She was tall with cropped hair bleached white, a craggy face with a long, bony nose and was so thin as to be completely flat-chested. She always wore men's uniforms; today she was dressed as a member of the Luftwaffe. She described herself as gynandrous — being of doubtful sex — and wore a monocle to encourage the notion that she was a lesbian as this frequently made men want to go to bed with her. She always used men's lavatories as a point of principle, though she never explained what the principle was.

Oonagh was the daughter of an Irish peer. I had once been to stay at the castle near Tullireen and had had to spend two days in bed when I got home, recovering from sheets you could have wrung a cup of water out of, a drawing room so cold that the flowers froze in their vases, filthy kitchen habits and starvation. One of the cook's less nice ways was to put the dirty plates on the floor so that the dogs, of which there were many, all huge, could lick them clean. Oonagh insisted that dogs have incredibly clean mouths and antiseptic saliva but I was unable to eat anything after that.

I had gone that Sunday to see Oonagh because she was likely to know where Alex might be found. She had a large social acquaintance and adored gossip. Not much happened that did not come sooner or later to Oonagh's ears. I was profoundly troubled by what I had allowed to happen on the river with Guy the day before. The feeling that I had callously betrayed Alex made me sick of myself.

And there was an additional pain, only too well deserved, in that the moment Guy had had his way I was tossed aside like a plaything of which he had tired.

Guy and I had returned to the cottage, drowsy with sun, fresh air and exercise — he had made me row back to the boathouse on the grounds that he was always fagged after making love. I was an inexpert rower and it had taken us twice as long to cover the same distance. Also it had been against the current. Guy had leaned back against the cushions watching me with an expression I didn't quite like. When I accused him of gloating he said it was solely adoration lighting his eyes but it looked to me like exultation, akin to crowing. We had walked hand in hand up the path to find Frankie waiting on the doorstep with Titch asleep on her knee.

'Get rid of them,' said Guy.

'No. Hello, darling.' I gave Frankie a kiss and ushered her in. Frankie looked hard at Guy and then at me with a knowingness I disliked to see on the face of a young girl.

'He don't want us here.' She had come into the kitchen with me. 'He wants to be on his own wiv you.'

'It's all right, Frankie. Where's Titch?'

'I parked her on the sofa — ' There was a scream. We ran in to find Titch face down on the floor. There was blood on her chin but luckily the cut was small.

'You might have watched her,' I said reproachfully to Guy, who was standing by the window, reading a book of poetry and ignoring the child's sobbing.

'I really don't like Kipling very much. Too much jog-trot about the rhythm.' Guy frowned, displeased. 'Does that child do anything besides scream?'

It was not a good beginning to the evening. Guy refused tea and Prim's seed-cake. 'I think I'll go home and change. That idiot Roger Windebank is coming for drinks. My father's tinkering with his will again. I'd better go and make sure they don't do anything hare-brained. If he's going to cut Vere out, I want to make sure I stay in. Goodbye, my ravishing water nymphet.' He kissed me on the lips and gave my bottom a squeeze, then left without a backward glance.

'Is he comin' back?' asked Frankie.

'I don't know.' I felt suddenly depressed.

'They're buggers, aren't they, men?' Frankie sniffed, no doubt in imitation of her mother.

'Absolute buggers!' Then I collected myself. 'Well, no, perhaps some are but there are very many excellent,

kind, honourable and brave men.'
Frankie looked disbelieving.

* * *

'What do you think of it?' Oonagh took a painting from
the floor and stuck it on an easel. She stood back,
blonde-thatched head on one side, to assess it. It had
been executed with a palette knife in slashes of red,
orange, yellow and black that had dribbled into each
other. It looked to me like a particularly nasty, festering
wound. 'What does it make you think of? I only thought
of the title this morning while Fergus and I were making
love.'

Fergus was a park-keeper Oonagh had picked up a
few months ago. He was good-looking and a deaf-mute,
which she claimed made him the ideal bed-mate. When
she felt like sex she would go to Hyde Park where he
would be labouring among the bedding begonias and
beckon. Afterwards they waved to each other as he
picked up his hoe and left.

'Mm. Very interesting. It makes me think of
something violent, hot, messy. Sexual, obviously.
Perhaps overtones of war?'

Oonagh looked at me reprovingly. 'I wonder on what
you base that judgement? Actually it's called *Icequake*.'

'Sorry,' I said humbly. I fell back on the old formula
that never fails to please any artist. 'I think it's quite the
best thing you've done.'

'Really? Good. Anyway, I was saying? Ah, yes. This
need to flagellate yourself over having chucked Alex. It's
nothing to do with feelings of guilt. You made a mistake
and you don't like facing up to that. You don't like all
those people knowing that you, beautiful, clever,
talented Freddie Swann, made an ass of yourself over a
smooth-tongued, manipulative shyster.'

'That's very hard on Alex.'

'Why is it hard? All lawyers are shysters. The legal system is such that it operates by persuasion. A good lawyer depends on eloquence, not candour. Alex is a supremely good lawyer.'

'Oh, well, I can't defend his profession, but I really do mind having hurt him. There is a part of me that loves him still, a part that's grateful for the excitement, the fun I had being with him. I expect you're right about the humiliation of a public *volte-face* but that isn't all of it. I loved being with Alex. As long as life was uncomplicated and we didn't need to profess our beliefs about important things we were well matched.'

Oonagh shrugged her shoulders. 'In other words, the relationship was one of shattering superficiality. How commonplace. So you think he's dreaming away his misery in some opium den, or pickling his sorrows in neat liquor because you've rejected him. Is he loading the chamber of his revolver as we speak or knotting the rope — perhaps filling his pockets with stones or making a suspension of quicklime and arsenic?'

'I don't know where to find him. He isn't at the house in Melbury Street. And the name's been changed on the bell of his old flat. I've got to see him. I didn't give him the chance to tell me what he thought of me and I know I owe him that, at least.'

I remembered the afternoon, two days before the wedding, when I had known that I could not marry him. At least, my reason was still dithering but whenever I thought of it I was overwhelmed by such physical pain that I knew I had to put a stop to it.

I had driven to the house in Melbury Street where we had arranged to meet to discuss the decoration of the hall. It was a miracle that I ran no one down. Even then half of me did not believe I was really going to do this thing that would have such terrible consequences. Alex came to the door, his face half serious, half mocking. He took me in his arms on the doorstep. 'And how are you, my bad, capricious girl?'

This referred to the row the evening before. I knew that he intended the kiss to convey whatever penitence was due, if any, on his part. I allowed him to kiss me but at his touch the sensation of horror at what I was about to do made my knees weak.

I walked ahead of him into the drawing room. Oh, what a pretty room it was! I looked with regret at the marble fireplace with its carving of oak-leaves and at the french windows that led into the garden.

'I'm not going to marry you. I'm so sorry.'

I had not planned what I was going to say and even if I had done it wouldn't have been any use. Once I began to speak I was incapable of anything but the barest utterance for the blood bursting in my ears and the twisting of my guts.

'Don't be silly.' Alex had frowned and sighed. 'Now, look, don't, for heaven's sake, let's row about something so absolutely trivial. All right, if you must have it your way, we'll ask him, though I really don't think he'll feel comfortable.'

The 'he' in question was Uncle Sid who had written to say that he wouldn't come to the wedding because he didn't have the clothes for it but he'd drop in for a few minutes to feast his eyes on me and gladden his heart after I was married. I was to remember, however things turned out, that I was more precious to him than his own arms and legs. I was not to worry about him for he was going to sea with a fishing fleet to fulfil the old dream before he got past it and would be away for several months. He enclosed the brass pixie that was to be my wedding present with an additional note of explanation.

I had said that we must ask him to stay as soon as he returned to Norfolk but Alex had demurred. He and Uncle Sid had had a brief meeting during which my uncle had been plainly ill at ease and Alex had been obviously bored. 'What on earth would we do with him? I can't quite see him at the Ritz. Nor do I fancy having the drawing room smelling of cow dung.' We had quarrelled, with the usual physical fight that had ended in sex.

'Never let it be said that I don't give way to your moods. Even at your most tiresome I find you utterly irresistible.' He held out his arms and smiled.

'No.' I put out my hands to hold him off. 'It isn't any good. I mean it. I'm not going to marry you. I've made the most terrible mistake and there's no chance that you'll ever forgive me. But I can't go through with it. I really mean it.'

I forced myself to look steadily at him. Alex had tried to light a cigarette. The lighter wouldn't work so he threw it into the fireplace. Then for a time, perhaps a minute, he had walked about what was to have been our new drawing room, holding his hands to his temples. His eyes had looked very large and dark against the whiteness of his face. A pitying, cowardly part of me longed to say that it wasn't true, that everything would go ahead as we had planned. I would make myself be happy. What was happiness anyway? Did I expect a fairy-tale marriage with a flawless Prince Charming? For a moment I seriously thought I might be going mad.

Then he had come up to me and put his face very close to mine. The light from the uncurtained french windows had fallen directly on to his face and I saw that there were beads of sweat on his upper lip. 'By God, Freddie, this isn't funny! Don't make me angry with you!' He had breathed rather hard and the tendons of his neck had stood out as he tightened his jaw. 'If I thought you really meant it I might really . . . ' He lifted one closed fist and held it on a level with my face.

The feeling of dislocation from reality grew worse. I saw that the shadow on the left side of his face was composed of burnt umber and violet. I shut my eyes to stop myself observing him with a painter's eye. 'I do mean it,' I said, and the next moment I was spinning across the floor. Because I had not seen the blow coming I had gone down hard. I really had not expected him to hit me. But even as I struggled to rise, holding my hand to my bleeding lip I could have sobbed with gratitude for that punch. It made it so much easier to walk away. But I wasn't angry. I knew it was far, far less than I deserved.

As soon as I got out of the room I ran across the hall to the front door, pulled it open and flew down the front steps. My car was parked outside. I got in, slammed the door and locked it. My legs were jelly, my hands trembling so much I could hardly get the key in the lock. As I started the engine Alex came out and bent down to look in through the window. He tried the handle, then banged on the window. 'Freddie, darling, for God's sake, don't do this to me — ' I put the car into gear not looking at him and drove away, tears of sorrow and pity and terror pouring down my face.

Now, as I crouched over the stove in Oonagh's studio, I felt sick again, remembering his face. 'I just ran away, you see. I was afraid he'd talk me out of it but it was childish and stupid of me.'

'Ah! There you've put your finger on it. Childish, yes. And why? Because Alex was the father figure you've been searching for ever since your own father abandoned you for your stepmother. You were looking for someone to have authority over you, to tell you what to do and to take all your troubles away. Alex was an excellent parent, letting you out on leading strings for little adventures but ready to haul you in if the world grew nasty. He sanctioned your behaviour and he worshipped you. He was both master and slave. All little girls want Daddy's approval as much as they want him to make sense of the world for them. It must have been orgasmic.'

I frowned. Oonagh's description of our relationship was revolting. But was it true?

'Do you know where I can find him?'

'I might. You'll have to let me make a few telephone calls. Let's go to Joe's.'

Joe's was a seedy drinking club patronised by those who wanted to be thought eccentric. I wasn't keen but I couldn't think what else to do. I wasn't in a mood to be sociable. I only wanted to see Alex or, as second best, to talk about him. I knew this was unpardonably egocentric. We went to Joe's.

As soon as we got there Oonagh went off to telephone. A man I vaguely knew, called Jasper, buttonholed me at once to tell me about his latest project to revive cottage industries in outlying areas. He was building a silkworm farm and intended the whole of North Wales to be given over to the production of silk. He had hit some snags to do with climate, he told me at length.

I leaned against the bar, sipping slowly at a rapidly warming glass of wine that tasted of acetone, nodding and smiling and remembering that this time yesterday I had been on the river with Guy. I had a violent stab of homesickness for Drop Cottage, for the children and animals and all the inhabitants of Pudwell, especially Prim. Even Mrs Creech had her attractions in that she was far away from the noise, the smell of exhaust, the grime, the ubiquitous concrete. The superabundance of strangers physically so close, but so unlike in tastes and ideas depressed me.

'Is it true that you and Moncrieff have split up?' asked Jasper, apropos of nothing he had been talking about.

'Yes. So what happens when the caterpillar's finished pupating?'

'The emerging moth would break the filament so we kill them with steam at the chrysalis stage. So Gideon Duff's got what it takes, has he?'

'No. At least, I'm not in a position to say. I hardly know him.'

This was true. I had met him a few times at parties and he pretended to have fallen in love with me. Gideon had long golden curls and a high voice and had been expelled from Harrow for buggery. He was arrogant and spoilt and frequently drunk. He had challenged Alex to a fight but Alex said that fighting bored him and had walked away. Gideon had burst into tears of rage. He was not the sort of man it is easy to know.

'I must say I was surprised when I heard it. Always thought he was a fag. He didn't seem enough of a man for you, anyway.' Jasper looked at me speculatively. 'I never did like that slick bastard, Moncrieff.' He laid a damp hand on mine. 'Why don't we go back to my place and I'll show you some cocoons?'

Oonagh had returned from telephoning. I tugged at the braid on her sleeve to attract her attention. 'I think I'll go.'

'You can't. I've arranged to have dinner with some people at Il Coccolo. Come on, they're expecting us. 'Bye, Jasper.'

We left Jasper looking around disconsolately to see whom he might inveigle into a little cocoon-inspecting. A taxi tooted violently as we crossed the road. Another driver let forth a sentence of invective. A beggar and an ancient dog on a string limped by on the opposite pavement. Two young men with Mohican haircuts abused them roundly and tried to kick the dog.

'God, Oonagh, I don't think I'm up to dinner.'

'Rubbish. You'll love it when you get there. Don't be such a baby.'

Il Coccolo was crowded. Alex and I had been there frequently in the early days of our dalliance, when it had

304

seemed bright and lively. Why had I never noticed the smell of stale food gusting up from the grating in the pavement outside, the hackneyed muzak, the surliness of the waiters, the garish gilding on the *faux* pilasters between the mirrors, whose silvering was turning black with the breath of the diners?

'Freddie!' Melanie Shaft flung her arms round my neck as Oonagh and I walked in. It was good of her to be so affectionate as she was one of the disappointed wedding-guests and must have been annoyed to find herself unexpectedly with a free weekend. She was fair and tubby and very good-natured. 'Angel! We've been so worried! It was so dramatic of you — we've talked about practically nothing else since. Oh, but, darling, did you know — have you two made it up?' She glanced fearfully to the other side of the room. The restaurant was crowded and the mirrors that lined the walls from ceiling to dado made distinctions confusing. It took me a moment or two to discern from his reflection that one of the men sitting with his back to us was Alex.

The adrenaline reaction was so swift that I felt at once as though I had been plunged in ice and for a moment the room grew dark. The heat returned to my body in rolling waves. He was talking energetically, using his hands to emphasise the point he was making to a girl with bright red hair, cut in a sculptured bob with long pieces at the sides. Zara Drax-Eedes. I was astonished to see them together. Zara had always let it be known that she and Alex didn't get on. She had a forceful personality — some might say pushy — and a violent temper. Once she had thrown a glass of wine over him during a row. He had always spoken scathingly about her, describing her as bird-brained despite her pretensions to wit and intellect. He seemed to have revised his opinion of her wit, at least. Zara said something that provoked a burst of laughter. I saw him take her hand and slowly and tenderly kiss each knuckle. He had got to the fourth when he raised his eyes and saw my reflection watching him.

I don't know how long it took him to turn in his chair for I had walked through the door and was out in the street before I knew what I was doing. I hid in a passageway next to the restaurant to give myself time to think. I couldn't talk to Alex in front of Zara. We had never been friends and the present situation was unlikely to change that.

Alex came out into the street and stood looking to left and right. I was about to emerge from my hiding-place when Zara came zooming out. I leaned back into the shadows. There was an overflowing dustbin next to me that smelt vile.

'You bastard, Alex!' Zara's voice, always shrill, had an edge to it like a drill. 'Never do that to me again!'

'Do what?' Alex sounded annoyed. He paced about a bit, looking into parked cars. 'Bloody hell, where is she?'

'I'm warning you, Alex.' I could see Zara's face clearly in profile. Her nose turned up at the end. She was just the smallest bit chinless. 'If you have anything more to do with that woman I'll give you up for good. I mean it! It's her or me. If it isn't over with Freddie, say so now! I'm not going to play second fiddle to anyone. Nor am I used to having men run out on me at dinner. Daddy'd be livid if he knew.' Daddy was Sir Percy Drax-Eedes, an Appeal Court judge. Her voice softened. 'He's really come round to the idea of you and me. You know how useful he could be to you, darling. I was just about to tell you before she came in and spoilt everything — he's talking about moving into the dower house. That means if we got married we could live at Cheveley.' I assumed that Cheveley was the Drax-Eedes seat, of which Zara had frequently boasted. 'Think of the entertaining we could do there! Why throw all that away on someone who's shown before all the world that she doesn't care about you? We could be so happy.' Her voice sharpened a trifle. 'I'm going back in now. I shall sit down and count to ten. If you aren't back by then — with a smile on your face — it's all over between us. I hope you know me well enough by now to believe me.' She waited. 'Alex!'

'Yes?' He sounded fed up.

'I'm going to start counting the minute I sit down. If you let her make you unhappy again you're a fool. And I don't want to marry a fool. Ten seconds, remember.'

I breathed in the odour of stale fish and tried to make up my mind. I had nothing to offer Alex in exchange for Cheveley, Sir Percy's patronage and the delights of Zara's bed and conversation. Alex stood hands in pockets, looking around him for perhaps seven seconds before saying, 'Fuck!' loudly and going back into the restaurant.

25

'Was it a coincidence? I mean, it's pretty extraordinary that you should have run into each other.' It was late on Monday evening. We were in the clean, orderly kitchen of Yardley House and Prim was whipping egg whites for meringues.

'Oonagh set the whole thing up, I'm sure.' I was rolling pastry for jam tarts.

'Well, forgive me for being critical of a friend but wouldn't it have been kinder to warn you?'

'She knew I'd have refused to go if I'd known Zara was there. Oonagh likes drama. She's easily bored.'

Prim gave the eggs an extra hard beating to express the indignation she was too polite to put into words. 'He's a fast worker, you've got to give him that. What's it been? A month since you left him? And he's virtually engaged to someone else. Well, I think you can stop fretting about his broken heart.' Then she glanced at me. 'Oho! What are you looking so hang-dog about? Freddie! You haven't — not Guy! After all I said — oh, what a clot you are!'

'That's putting it mildly. If I was confused before I'm now practically deranged. But,' I held up the rolling-pin, 'don't feel you have to offer sympathy. Remember, I've done with complaining. While I was sitting on Paddington station, waiting for the next train to come back here, I decided it is an essential part of maturity to take responsibility for one's own actions. Guilt is simply a childish refusal to accept the consequences of one's behaviour. Now I know Alex is all right and it's the most enormous weight off my mind. He'll be very happy with Zara, I think. She's as ambitious as he is. And she's got red hair. That seems to be important.' I smiled at Prim to convince her I was genuinely relieved. 'Perhaps all our choices are dictated by the trivial. I allowed Guy to make love to me because I like his face and I was desperately attracted to him. I know he's selfish. Probably he's never cared for a woman in his life. Anyway, as soon as we'd made love he pushed off. He made the excuse that he had to talk to Roger Windebank but he could have come back after that.'

'What a pity we can't have children without them.' Prim threw in some sugar and at once the egg whites became dense and smooth and shiny. 'I fear I'm getting broody. I used to wake in the night and wonder what mark I could make in the world. Where was that lump of granite waiting for me to transform it into *La Pietà*? Now I lie there and think what George and the little Rokers might like for tea.'

'How's George getting on?'

'He won't admit it but I think he's actually enjoying the poetry. When he forgets to be a bandit, he's touchingly responsive to Longfellow. I suppose Hiawatha is a good role model. Tough yet tender. A warrior with a code of conduct.'

'Who are you talking about?' Edward Gilchrist had put his head round the door. 'Doesn't sound like anyone I know in Pudwell. If only a Victorian genre painter could see you two! I never saw such a charming picture of domesticity. It would be called *Hearth and Home* or *The Conscientious Chatelaine*.'

It was not difficult to guess that Edward longed to put Prim into that role in his own domain. 'We're talking about George,' I said. 'He's my employer's grandson. Prim's taken him under her wing. He's a clever boy but he's been pretty much neglected. He's having maths and history coaching. And Prim's reading poetry with him, besides trying to tame the savage.'

Edward sent her a tender look. 'Nothing like *The*

Fighting Temeraire and *Drake's Drum* for putting the right stuff into a boy.'

'After Hiawatha, I thought of looking at Clare.' Prim began to heap egg-white into fat swirls on a sheet of baking parchment. 'And perhaps Housman. The glories of nature and all that. George seems to have enough of the right stuff already, if by that you mean a desire to do battle on every possible occasion.'

'It's because of his foot.' I was cutting out fluted circles of pastry. 'It's such a pity! It's going to be so difficult for him to forget it. There's something of a rebel angel about him. He's a handsome boy. Beautiful, when he isn't scowling. Prim, perhaps you should read a little Byron with him. The perfect role model. He didn't let a club foot stop him from attempting deeds of glory as well as being a fine poet.'

'Good idea. I will. And the fact that women were crazy about Byron might give George confidence. I think women rather like a weakness they can mother and make allowances for.'

I thought of Edward's drinking and wondered if Prim might come to see it as an appeal to her superior female strength.

'That's the boy I've seen limping about the village?' asked Edward. 'I've wondered about him. He's not one of my patients. You know, it might be possible to do something about it. It ought to have been picked up before. With *talipes equinovarus* — that's the medical term for club foot — manipulation or strapping or a combination of both is best begun before the age of two. But there are several other things that could be done — transferring a tendon from another bone, for example — to make it possible for him to use the foot properly with only the slightest limp.'

'Edward! Do you think so?' Prim paused in the meringue-heaping. 'It would really change that boy's life. He's horribly sensitive about it. Once, when we were reading together by the fire, I took his tea over to him, as I might do for any guest, and he got furious because he thought I was treating him like a cripple. I thought he was going to hit me. Oh, if you could only do something for him!' Her eyes were bright as she stared at him across the table, a large blob of egg-white adhering to the bib of her apron.

Edward's pink face deepened to puce. 'Of course, I'll do my best. But it's awkward to make a beginning. Doctors aren't supposed to tout for trade. Somehow you'll have to persuade his parents to bring him into the surgery.'

'Both his parents are dead.' Prim looked thoughtful. 'Such a sad story. His mother drowned herself and his father — well. There's only George's grandfather. Dusty's ignorant and stubborn but Freddie might be able to persuade him.'

I saw Balthazar walking over to his basket within the dresser, his gait nonchalant, Edward's car keys in his mouth.

'I'll certainly try,' I said, when we had prised the keys from Balthazar's jaws and retrieved my bag from his sanctum. 'Theirs isn't a very good relationship. George is cheeky so Dusty hits him, and that makes George more defiant. But it's not every man who would bring up an orphaned grandson single-handed. It's hard to like someone who spits so much but we seem to get along in a strange way.' I yawned, pretty convincingly. 'Gosh, I'm tired. I'd better get to bed. Would you mind finishing the tarts, Edward? Prim'll show you how. Thank you for supper.' I kissed Prim, who was looking suspicious.

'I'm sorry I can't offer to see you home,' Edward said, not looking sorry in the least, 'but if I'm appointed guardian of the tarts . . . '

'Certainly not. Goodbye, you two.'

The night was clear and brilliantly starred. I

wondered if there would be a frost. Bad luck on the fruit farmers if there was. I had had a chat about these things with Will Dewy, the taxi driver, who had driven me to Pudwell from the station the night before. He was a cider-maker between September and November, with his own press that he carted between orchards. It was extraordinary how interesting one's surroundings could become, taking into account the subtle changes of weather and the patterns of Nature.

It was deepest black in the shadows where birds were brooding on nests, moles were tunnelling and foxes and rabbits were engaged in a race to the death. Insects toiled away, gathering food and building egg repositories. And much further away, on the seashore, lug-worms were digesting sand, and crabs and sea urchins dined and were dined upon in their turn. Like humans, they were dependent on the cycle of the seasons but it seemed to me that in some ways they were better off. In the process of what we were pleased to call civilisation we had lost our ability to live in the moment, and to depend on instinct, yet we were helpless in the face of natural disaster and even in the ecological messes of our own making. What we had done with our scientific discoveries and technological advances was to highlight the precarious and temporary nature of our existence.

The pale shape of an owl flashed across my path. Chloë would have been thrilled and given it a good barking. I missed her terribly. I heard a chirrup behind me. It seemed late for a chirruping sort of bird to be out. I walked faster. It chirruped along with me. I felt uneasy. Even clothed, Lemmy had been quite . . . well, if not actually frightening, then intimidating. The wildness of the beard, the dirty clothing spoke of an uncompromising anarchy that was all very well by day. Somehow at night, out of shouting distance of the nearest house, which I realised was mine and empty of succour, the idea of him was thoroughly alarming. I recognised *The Barber of Seville* and broke into a run. There was a pattering sound behind me. I prepared to scream but it was Chloë, bounding in large strides and wagging her tail as though pleased to find me sporting enough for after-dark games.

I waited until I had jammed the chair beneath the handle of the front door and lit the lamps before saying hello to her. She jumped up, licking my face. I gave her something to eat but I could see she toyed with it only out of politeness. However deficient in comforts Lemmy's forest fastness might be, it had a supply of dog-food. I was delighted that she seemed willing to accompany me to bed. I put the candle on my dressing table and then my already over-exercised heart began to thump again. I could hear regular breathing only a few feet from me. I held the candle high. Someone was lying in my bed. I tiptoed over. Guy lay flat on his back, fast asleep. Macavity was curled on his chest, practically chin to chin.

'Who? What? When? Oh, my God, what is it?' said Guy when I shook him.

'It's all right. It's only the cat.'

'Bloody hell! I thought it was some foul fiend come to drag me down to begin serving my sentence in boiling pitch.'

'If so, it would have been only what you deserved.'

'Where on earth have you been?'

'I might ask the same of you.'

'Ah! Just a minute, while I throw off the toils of sleep. You sound distinctly peeved, dear Freddie. And you look just like Brunhilde, standing there with your hands on your hips.'

'Peeved is putting it mildly. You rat! Clearing off the minute I was so stupid as to let you make love to me then turning up two days later in my bed as though I'm

313

to be grateful for any crumbs you might care to throw in my direction — '

'Hang on, hang on! Now sit down and shut up a minute, will you, and let me explain.' He grabbed my wrist and pulled me down on to the bed beside him. 'I know it looks bad but once you've heard the circumstances you may feel you've been just a bit hasty. As it happens, I was coming to see you yesterday when I met Mrs Creech. She said you'd gone to London for the day and wouldn't be back till late.'

'How on earth did she know that?'

'It would be quicker to ask what that woman *doesn't* know. Anyway, you'll agree there wasn't any point in my trailing all the way up here to sit and twiddle my thumbs. Today I *had* to go to Bexford and anyway you, I assumed, were earning your daily bread at the mill. I came here as soon as I got back — about seven o'clock — and spent three riveting hours sitting on the sofa admiring the damp patches on the wall. Then I thought I might as well get in some sleep.'

'We must just have missed each other. I went to supper with Prim. Well, that's all right as far as it goes. But what about Saturday? Wasn't it pretty mean to go off like that and leave me to conclude that once you'd got what you wanted you'd lost interest?'

'You *are* in a miff! You'd look good in a helmet with horns. All right, I can see it might have looked like that. Of course I meant to come back, once I'd squashed any ideas my father might have of dividing my inheritance among his less than savoury friends. You idiot! My heart and mind were absolutely set on a repeat performance of that glorious afternoon! But when I got home I found that something had happened that made it . . . well, pretty nigh impossible to get away again that night.'

'This had better be good.' I said severely. 'Remember, I know that you can lie with the best of them.'

'If you're not going to believe what I say . . . ' Guy

314

adopted a tone of pique. 'Damn it, I can prove it to you! Come up to the Hall on Thursday. It's my father's birthday. He always has a party and this year there's a special attraction. God, I've missed you!' He pulled me towards him and pressed his mouth briefly to mine. I resisted but not fiercely. 'Do I detect a wilting of the Valkyrie impersonation?'

'Oh, Guy! Stop playing games. What are you talking about?'

'You remember the story of the Prodigal Son? You're going to be privileged to see a re-enactment of it in twentieth-century costume. When I got home on Saturday afternoon I found that the fatted calf was looking glum. There was an addition to the cheery get-together in the drawing room. It was my brother, Vere.'

26

'A glass of champagne, my dear?' Ambrose waved a stick at the tray held by Miss Glim. She had smartened herself up for the occasion and wore black with a white apron and cap. I noticed that her feet, shod in black lace-ups, were enormous. I took a glass and thanked her. She looked down at the tray, her expression bitter. Ambrose laughed. 'I'm delighted you've come, Freddie. Guy talks of no one but you. I really think his presence on this day of celebration is conditional on your being here.' Miss Glim looked wretched.

'Happy birthday.' I kissed Ambrose's cheek as *esprit de corps* seemed to be raging. I had already had my own cheek brushed by two pairs of lips whose owners were quite unknown to me.

'Thank you, but I can't pretend to be of any interest myself. You've heard, of course, what we're really celebrating?'

The entire country knew. By Tuesday morning the word had gone out from the post office that the heir to the Gilderoys had come home and aprons were flung off, babies were abandoned in prams and cakes left to burn in ovens while people ran to tell their neighbours the great piece of news. Further afield telephone bills soared, the post was late and queues in shops grew long as every customer had something to say about such a mouthwatering nugget of news. Nothing so exciting had happened since Mrs Batt's daughter, Marlene, had become engaged to Mick Jagger. This later proved to be untrue. Marlene was affianced to Mike Jiggers, a gas-fitter from Tarchester.

'You must be overjoyed to have him home.'

Ambrose put his hand to his eyes. 'As you might

expect, Freddie, I feel, well, humbled is not too strong a word. To have my eldest son returned to me from the dead to brighten my remaining years — hah! the poetry of the thing! Biblical allusions are irresistible. There has been much babble this evening of sheep and folds. What do twelve years of silence matter — during which time he might have communicated the fact of his continued existence — when we can enjoy the thrill of this dramatic dénouement?'

For an instant his eyes were bright with anger. Then he smiled and rested his hand caressingly on my arm. 'May I say how very beautiful you look this evening?' His expression was appreciative but cold. I saw how Guy would look in forty years. 'You will wish to view the phenomenon. He is much fêted but we may just catch a glimpse of him through the excited throng.'

We went into the drawing room. Because our progress was slow I was able to examine the lost lamb before we were introduced. I saw that Ambrose's description was intended to be ironical. Vere stood very much alone in the crowd. People looked and wondered but they preferred to appraise him from a distance, as I was doing.

He was a large man, taller and broader than Guy. He wore evening dress like the other men but evidently not his own for the trousers and cuffs were several inches too short and the jacket gaped between buttons. I saw him twist his head and tug at the collar of his shirt. His hair was dark and had been cut unfashionably short, which made him look rather tough, someone not to be tangled with.

The resemblance between the brothers was unmistakable. Vere's complexion was brown and the lines were clearly marked on his face. One would have guessed at more than the three-year difference in age. But he had the same bone structure, the same curved mouth. His eyes were different, I saw, as we came closer. Guy's were keen, assessing, derisive. Vere's, several shades darker, were uncommunicative. His thoughts were apparently elsewhere. It was obvious that he wished himself away with them.

'This is my son, Vere. Our charming new neighbour, Miss Freddie Swann. Forgive me, I see some new arrivals.'

Ambrose turned away, leaving us alone. Vere turned on me incurious eyes that suddenly quickened with interest. He took the hand I held out to him. 'We've already met, though we weren't introduced. You were kind enough to promise me some vegetables if you were successful in growing them.' He smiled and immediately looked younger.

The moment I heard his voice several images in my brain shattered, reassembled themselves and I recognised him. 'Oh, but the beard — your clothes — your hair!' I was mortified. I tried to remember what I had said to him. I had given him *carte blanche* to visit the garden. Made idiotic remarks about vegetables. And grinned excessively. I could not quite suppress a groan when I remembered that I had sung a few lines from *Patience* to put him at his ease. 'You must think me quite mad.'

'Oh, no. I realised you'd mistaken me for someone else.'

'I thought you were Lemmy.'

He frowned. 'Lemmy? Wasn't he . . . I remember now. The wandering hermit. Well, no one can accuse you of being a false flatterer.'

'I'm terribly sorry, but you were looking pretty wild, you know. And I'd been expecting to meet him.'

'Wild is moderate in the circumstances. When I tried to convince Miss Glim that I had right of entry she tried to telephone the police. Even my father didn't recognise me. I got off an ice-breaker in the early hours of Saturday morning after twelve weeks at sea. There wasn't enough water on board to shave and the weather was so rough that if we'd tried to cut our hair we'd have gouged our eyes out. I got straight on a bus at Southampton. Then I noticed that people were sitting as far away as possible, trying not to catch my eye in case I was drunk. I'd forgotten how clean and tidy England is.'

'Was that your job? Breaking ice, I mean.'

'No. I just wanted to see the Arctic. I wouldn't be very good at it in the metaphorical sense either, would I?' He glanced round at the guests, who were staring fixedly at us while they talked, presumably about Vere. 'I don't know what else I expected.'

'People are diffident, I suppose. It's hard to know what to say to someone who's been away such a long time. Small-talk seems irrelevant but they're afraid of asking questions that might be — awkward.'

'Yes, of course.'

Vere frowned and looked down at his shoes. They were brown, I noticed, scuffed and down-at-heel. Guy's must have been too small for him. His eyes were distant again. He had departed in spirit. There was a silence. His manner was quite different from Guy's, polite, cool and a little stiff.

'If you knew I'd mistaken you for someone else why didn't you tell me so at the time?'

'I hadn't slept for forty-eight hours and it was a shock to see home again — I was immersed in retrospection. I didn't expect to see anyone. I was taking a short-cut down to the river. Also,' he hesitated and smiled, 'I was intrigued. I enjoyed the song.' He laughed and looked altogether different.

'What's funny?' Guy came up to us. 'Hello, Freddie, light of my life.' He kissed my cheek, lingeringly and put his arm round me. I could see that the other guests were very interested indeed. 'Don't flirt with her, will you, Vere? It would be a shame to wreck the joys of brotherly

319

love, so newly recovered.' Guy was smiling but his eyes were more observant than affectionate. I knew he rarely showed his real feelings. When he had told me that Vere had come home he had seemed genuinely pleased. But Vere's sudden materialisation would affect Guy's prospects. Miss Glim came up to us with a plate of canapés. I took one to appease her though I wasn't at all hungry.

'Thank you, Cissy.' Guy chose one with a radish made into a rose. 'And very pretty, too. You're a woman of many talents.' Miss Glim sent him a look blent of love and something close to despair.

'Thank you, Miss Glim.' Vere took a stuffed prune. She turned down her mouth until it was rectangular like a letter-box and moved away.

'I'm afraid Miss Glim has room in her heart for one only,' I said.

'I'm already resigned to the leg and the scraped piece of toast.' Vere seemed amused.

'You're looking particularly scrumptious, Freddie,' Guy put his hand on my waist and ran it down over my hip to my thigh as though I were a horse and he was checking my muscle tone. 'Beautiful dress. Let's escape back to the cottage as soon as dinner's over. I want to take it off you.' Two women standing near us raised eyebrows and exchanged glances. I shook my head slightly at Guy. Vere seemed not to have heard. He was staring across the room to the window, cradling the stuffed prune in the palm of his hand.

'Well, Vere! So *there* you are!' Lady Frisk's emphasis suggested that she had spent twelve long years in fruitless searching. She prodded his dress shirt. 'Naughty boy! And what have you been doing all this time?' Vere opened his mouth to reply but Lady Frisk went on, 'I consider it thoroughly irresponsible of you not to let your father know. But you young people are all the same. You expect only to please yourselves. Why, if I behaved as I liked the county would be in an uproar in a moment. My duties as chairman of the Conservative Association, president of the Women's Institute, and school governor, besides all my charity work, leaves me little time for self-indulgence, I can assure you! I am obliged to employ a secretary, so onerous are my duties. At this very moment, late though the hour is, she is composing my newsletter for the Civic Society. But I never spare myself.' Lady Frisk's voice was loud and those standing near us had stopped talking to enjoy Vere's raking-down. He bent his head to look down at her, occasionally opening and closing his mouth when he thought she might give him a chance to speak. 'My dear Charlotte was shocked to the core when I told her that you were *not* dead, as we all thought. I was obliged to explain to her that young men do sometimes behave as though they have no one to consider but themselves. But I am afraid it will take some doing to reinstate yourself in Charlotte's good opinion.' Vere twirled the stem of his glass between thumb and forefinger and looked grave but I was sure he wasn't listening. I turned away to speak to Baroness von Wunsiedel who was trying to attract my attention by tapping me impatiently on the shoulder.

'How are you, Baroness?'

The Baroness, magnificent in grey silk and sables, inclined her head to acknowledge my interest in her state of health but did not enquire after mine. 'We are delighted to see you again Miss Swann. We had not expected your visit to be of such duration. You had said that you were expecting to return to London before many days.'

'I changed my mind.' I was under no obligation to justify myself to her.

She lifted her heavy lids to engage her eyes with mine. 'Werner is here. He also will be delighted to see you.

His engagement with the Princess Prenzlau has been arranged.'

'I hope they'll be very happy.'

'It is quite what we expected for Werner. They will make a perfect couple. Her good sense will restrain his youthful enthusiasm.'

'Not altogether, I hope.' I was annoyed by her assumption that I was only waiting for an opportunity to throw myself at her son's head.

The Baroness made a supreme effort and opened her eyes fully for quite two seconds to discharge a dart of enmity. 'The Princess is modest and virtuous. She has no need of coquetry. Blood is everything.'

'I think good nature is much more important.'

'Of course Miss Swann. You cannot afford to think otherwise.'

Dinner was announced while I was thinking of a reply to this.

'Why the face like a thundercloud?' Guy took my arm and we walked together to the dining room. 'Aren't you having a perfectly lovely time?'

'I am, of course. But I should enjoy myself even more if I could give the Baroness a good push from the top of the hill.'

'I pity the poor Baron from the bottom of my heart. I expect he died from frostbite of the reproductive organs.'

'Don't you ever think of anything but sex?'

'Men are supposed to think about it. That's what they're for.'

'I wonder what Vere is thinking of. Not that, certainly.'

Vere had found his place at the table, which had been extended to seat more than twenty guests. He stood behind his chair staring at an arrangement of pale yellow tulips and paper-white narcissi. Their scent, always on the edge of sickliness, approached us in waves. Alex, who took wine-drinking seriously, would have disapproved. I was pleased to find that I could think of him without guilt or anger.

'I did the table plan,' said Guy. 'You're next to me so I can stroke your thigh between courses.'

Werner von Wunsiedel was on my other side. No doubt Guy wanted to make mischief with the Baroness.

'Vat good fortune, Miss Freddie!' Werner seized my hand in his and pressed it hard against his lips. 'You must allow me to say that your enchanting appearance vas one of the most happy memories I took back to Berlin.' His blue eyes were glassy with sentiment. I was glad to see that he had shaved off his beard.

'Thank you. How did you find Berlin?'

He looked surprised. 'I vas taken there by aeroplane — ach, no! You mean how does the experience of Berlin seem to me? Very dull. Many long dinners. Very stiff. You English can be formal, too, but always there are the little jokes that make happy. And the girls are so much more pretty.' He looked at me and drew in his breath quickly, making a snorting sound. I realised he was already a little drunk.

'How is the Princess?'

Werner stopped smiling. 'She is very, very healthy, I thank you. She eats only vegetables and never drinks alcohol. She rises at six hours in the morning to say the prayers, then an hour vith the clubs — you know, she sving them round her head — and ven there is not a dinner she goes to bed early vith *ein Kräutertee* . . . how do you say? A herbish tea.'

'Goodness, she must be bounding with energy.'

'The Princess does not bound. She dislike all frivolness. Particularly jokes.' Werner stuck out his lower lip and looked brooding. My attention was distracted by Madame du Vivier, who was sitting a few places away on the other side of the table. She was waving a lace-gloved hand enthusiastically. A long chestnut curl

323

flopped over her eye. I waved back.

I remembered that Werner was interested in politics. 'It's such a pity about the Berlin Wall.'

'Ach, *ja*! The Communists are caged like rats. They know nothing but propaganda.' Werner began to lecture me. The two middle-aged women seated next to Vere were talking across him while he crumbled his bread and stared into space.

'The division has made Germany veak.' Werner was still talking. 'I bring you into a secret, shall I?' His blond curls brushed against my temple as he whispered, 'A new movement is upstanding. Perhaps one may say not new. Let us better observe that the Phoenix has risen. You understand me?'

'Really?' I had no idea what he was talking about. 'This soup is delicious. Cucumber, isn't it?'

Werner downed a glass of white wine in one swig. '*Quite* delicious. But, then, Miss Freddie, you are one of us? Like our good host, you think as ve about the future of Germany?'

'The Common Market, you mean? I really know very little about it.'

'Too, too charmingly modest. It is ever the English manners. But your heart,' he banged his chest, 'is sad for Germany.'

'Well, naturally, we all hope for a better understanding between countries — peace in Europe and so on.' Vere had removed the centre of his roll and was busy shaping it into a dense grey cube. Where had he been during the intervening years? And what had happened to the woman with whom he had run away?

'So kind, dear Miss.' Werner put down his wine-glass and took one of my hands between both of his. I saw that Vere's attention had been caught by this action. 'Let us have this good understanding! I long to understand vith you, every smallest bit!' He ran his tongue over his soft boyish mouth. 'You will not startle if I say again

— the Phoenix is risen.' He seemed to have got much drunker in a very short space of time. His eyes focused on the tip of my nose and crossed slightly. I shook my head and smiled, having no idea what he was talking about. He inserted the tip of his long nose into my ear like a humming bird's beak into the throat of an hibiscus and hissed, 'The Third Reich is risen!'

I think I jumped then. I was horrified. 'Mr von Wunsiedel — '

'Werner, Werner!'

'Werner, then. I really think we ought to talk about something else — ' I looked anxiously round the table in case any of the other guests had heard him. They were almost exclusively of the generation who talk of 'Jap' and 'Hun' and have *not* forgiven and forgotten. Perhaps the strain of being engaged to a humourless health fanatic had driven Werner off his head.

'Do not be vorried. Here ve are with friends. I vant to share vith you the joy of this rising.' I withdrew my hand, which was growing damp in his and attempted to recover from the unpleasant shock of his disclosure. He had suggested that Ambrose — I could not believe it. Guy had said something once — but I had not believed him to be serious. Ambrose was listening attentively to the Pekinese-faced woman who was sitting on his right. At least, so I thought, but as I stared at him, wondering if it could be true, he turned his eyes swiftly in my direction and lifted an eyebrow enquiringly. I looked away. Werner ran his fingers from my elbow up to my shoulder to attract my attention. 'You have heard of Wewelsburg?'

'Wasn't that the castle in Germany which, um, Hitler tried to make a sort of Camelot?'

'Ja, ja, you have it! But all those stories the Christians steal from the *Volk*. The Holy Grail is of the Aryan knighthood, much, much older. I vill explain every-thing.' Werner made an expansive gesture and upset the glass of wine which had just been filled for him. A crimson stain spread over the tablecloth. There was commotion as well-meaning guests heaped salt, white wine and water on it, making a dreadful mess. I had a moment of madness in which I was tempted to chuck on some of the croûtons that had come with the soup.

'How are you getting on with Werner?' Guy turned to me with a strict observance of etiquette as the soup was removed to be replaced with a piece of fish with a ball of tomato ice. 'Quite a little philosopher isn't he?' He put his head close to mine and whispered. '*Sieg Heil!*'

'You know about it? I'm simply amazed!' Werner's attention was fully engaged by the gallant attempts of the woman on his other side to scrub red wine from his trousers. 'The man is a neo-Nazi!' I said in an undertone.

'Of course he is. Ow-w-w! This tomato stuff plays hell with your fillings.'

'Don't you find that a little shocking?'

'You know, you're a perfectly delicious combination of sophistication and naïvety. Why should I be shocked?'

'But he suggested — I thought he did — that your father was — a sympathiser.'

'That's putting it mildly. Given the chance my father would empty England of any Jew, gypsy, Slav, Communist or mental defective by breakfast time. He used to be hot against cripples at one time but, of course, he's had to change his tune.'

'You mean he thought that Hitler was right?'

'My sweet Freddie, hundreds of thousands of people thought Hitler was right. You don't suppose that losing the war changed their opinions, do you? Why should it? It was a conquest of military strength, nothing to do with the triumph of a particular ideology. Nazism had to go underground for a time but there'll always be those who believe in eugenics and pure blood. There's a very rational argument for it.'

'You're not telling me that you . . . ' I could hardly bring myself to say it.

'Don't be silly. Of course I'm not a Nazi. If I believe in anything it's the advancement of me. I think all fanatics are desperately hurt or weak people needing to bolster themselves up with some fantasy or other. I suppose you wouldn't be shocked if you were sitting next to the Archbishop of Canterbury and he chatted to you about heaven and hell and loaves and fishes and the resurrection? That's as fantastic as anything the Nazis believe.'

'Yes, but Christianity doesn't require you to round up non-believers and butcher them.' Guy looked sceptical. 'Well,' I realised the weakness of my argument, 'not nowadays anyway.'

'You've forgotten Northern Ireland. No one could begin to quantify the blood shed in the name of Christ.'

'Ah, but Christ didn't say that's what people ought to do.'

'I don't think the Utopia planned by the German *Volk* included death camps and gas chambers. People forget their ideals in the pleasure and expediency of doing away with their enemies.'

'But your father believes in it?'

'And so do three-quarters of the people sitting round this table. You don't and I don't and Vere doesn't — at least, I assume not, unless he's changed greatly. I don't think Lord Deering believes in anything but a bright frost-free morning for hunting. We can count out Lady Frisk, too. If she believes in anything it's in the transcendence of the English upper classes. What a shock she'd get if she realised she was dining with the chief members of FOE.'

'FOE?'

'Fascists of England. Neat, isn't it? I made it up myself as a joke but Father thought it was quite good.'

327

'I don't know how you can be so light-hearted about it.'

'Look at them. Most of them, except Werner, are tottering towards the grave. All so crotchety and full of foibles that they can't agree over the colour of the society's writing-paper. About as dangerous as a basket of kittens. My father was persuaded to take up fascism by the Baroness to take his mind off my mother leaving him. It could just as well have been canasta. It gives him the illusion of power, that's all.'

I looked at Werner, who was pursuing the ball of tomato ice round his plate with his fork. He was little more than a boy. I guessed twenty-one or thereabouts. When we were art students there had been a lot of extravagant talk about anarchism, nihilism, revolution and anything that made us seem more exciting and adult. Probably fascism served the same purpose for him. I glanced round the table at the other guests. They certainly could not be excused on the grounds of youth. But, apart from the Baroness, they looked jolly and benevolent. Mademoiselle du Vivier's curl was lying on the tablecloth.

'You've been sheltered from reality.' Guy went on. 'You've moved with arty, fashionable, liberal thinkers all your life. That's London for you. Everyone knows what they ought to be thinking and doing. Fashion and modernity are the currency. And not believing in things. I bet none of your friends believes in censorship, capital punishment or apartheid.' I had to admit that none of them did. 'Now it's frowned on even to be a Marxist. And religion is hopelessly *vieux jeu* — except perhaps Roman Catholicism, for stylists hooked on the ritual. It's part of your creed, not having one.'

'Do you mean that ethics aren't as important to people who live in the country?'

328

'Oh, no. You're saying that people who don't think as you do aren't ethical. But they are, according to their own lights. And there are plenty of right-wing racists in cities. But there's less individualism. People group in like-minded shoals in towns. In the country, being thinly spread, you're more mixed together. I don't suppose there's another arty, liberal agnostic in the parish besides you.'

'Well, there's Prim. Perhaps not arty but I'm sure she isn't a racist or a bigot. Though she is a committed Christian, so I suppose I'm not allowed to count her. And there's Bar Watkins.' I was definitely cheating here, hoping that Guy would not know about her arcane practices.

Guy laughed. 'Bar believes in almost everything to the point of mania. I think we must exclude witches.'

'She's very interesting.' Accepting that I had no hope of winning the argument, I changed the subject. 'And her skin tones are marvellous. I'd like to paint her. I admire her lack of inhibition.'

'Oh, so do I!' he agreed. I remembered then that Guy had a romantic interlude with Bar. Was there anyone by whom Guy's fancy had not been caught? Miss Glim put down a plate of *noisettes* in front of me. The smell of hot lamb fat mingled with the cloying sweetness of the narcissi. I felt a little sick.

'Vell, vell, Miss Freddie, here ve are again.' Werner bent towards me. 'How delightful! Such a vonderful house! So pretty country. Vill you come for a valk vith me tomorrow? Ve could go down to the river and celebrate the coming of spring, the birds making love and the flowers that smell so sveet.' He closed his eyes and inhaled rapturously.

Miss Glim's hand bearing a jug of mint sauce appeared between us. Werner's nose twitched. He opened his eyes and started back.

'I'm sorry but I have to work. All my daylight hours are accounted for.'

'And vat is this vork that takes you so cruelly from me?'

'I'm a mill-hand.'

'Vat? You joke vith me?'

'No. I work in the mill down by the river. Sewing up sacks.'

'Grosser Gott!' Werner snatched up my hand and dribbled over it. I tried to snatch it back but his grip was determined. 'To think these little fingers do something so indelicate!'

'I hope not actually that,' I murmured.

Vere was looking at us. There was something of a smile at the corners of his mouth. Werner thrust out his right arm in a Nazi salute. Conversation dropped away round the table and several people half rose from their chairs and hesitantly raised their right arms.

'Da!' Werner's index finger stabbed the air. 'The moon is risen!' There was a glimpse of silver between imperfectly drawn curtains. 'This is not, as the astronomers in their ignorance believe, the first moon. No, it is the fourth! The three moons — how do you say, 'beforetimes?' — crashed to earth. Between the third and fourth moons the island of Atlantis, home of the great varrior nation, was destroyed!'

Werner was off again, hacking his way through a thicket of ancient myths and complementary fabrications. Like Alice, I was being asked to believe six impossible things before breakfast. My mind wandered. The noisettes were replaced by a quivering mound of crème caramel.

'How are you, my little cosset?' Guy put his hand on my knee.

'Not hungry.' I had dealt with the lamb and vegetables by cutting them into small pieces and hiding them beneath my knife and fork and a convenient sprig of parsley. 'And rather tired. The combination of a hard day's work, ministering to my adopted family, followed by you know who,' I whirled my eyes in Werner's direction, 'has almost finished me off.'

'I have it in mind to deliver the *coup de grâce* myself.'

27

After dinner I put the greatest possible distance between myself and Lady Frisk. The Baroness selected a hard-looking chair in a remote corner. I saw her eyes close and her head sink slowly forward. I must have followed suit for the next thing I knew my coffee was cold and Madame du Vivier was sitting beside me.

'My dear friend, Werner has been telling you our little secret, *n'est-ce pas?* We have agreed zat you are most *sympathique*.'

'I think I've probably given the wrong impression — '

'No, no. You were quite right. We must not be too conspicuous. It is not everyone who understands our great plans.'

'Well, no. I'm afraid since the war — '

'Ho! Zat!' Madame batted it away like a troublesome insect. 'It is nozing but a leetle incident. We are talking of *zousands* of years of 'istory.'

'Miss Freddie?' Werner stood at the door of the drawing room. 'Ambrose would like to talk vith you.'

The Baroness's eyes were open. 'Werner, go upstairs and find my book about the Franco-Prussian war. Madame du Vivier will be most interested.'

'*Ganz bestimmt*, Mutti. Come, Miss Freddie.'

I followed Werner into the hall and paused to look again at the painting of Guy's mother. It wasn't very good — imitation Sargent but without the charm and eloquence of expression. The late Mrs Gilderoy looked supremely self-confident, her beauty spoiled by a hardness of the mouth. On the opposite wall hung a portrait of a man in army uniform of dark coat and bright red trousers. The pose was relaxed: he sat with one knee crossed over the other, very much at ease, in what I decided must be a conscious imitation of Tissot's famous painting of another military dandy, *Frederick Gustavus Burnaby*. The scar down his cheek, from temple to chin, gave the left side of his face an interestingly ravaged look, while the right side was smiling and debonair. His eyes were bold and black. The portrait was entitled *Henry le Maistre, Colonel, 11th Hussars*.

'Ah, Miss Glim.' Werner stopped her as she crossed the hall. 'Be so good as to fetch from the room of the Baroness a book you vill find beside the bed. She is expecting in the drawing room.' Miss Glim looked hot, her cap was crooked and she was carrying a loaded tray of plates. She gave him a speaking look but put down the tray and went upstairs. I noticed that she had changed her lace-up shoes for zip-up corduroy slippers.

'Miss Freddie!' Werner waggled a finger and looked coy, which should have warned me.

A door beneath the stairs revealed another flight of descending steps, presumably leading to the cellars. They were well lit and swept clean, and though I do not much like cavernous places, there was nothing particularly sinister about them. At the foot of the stairs was a stone chamber cut out of the rock. The walls were lined with wine bins, most of them filled with cobwebbed bottles. The next room was the same. It was not the setting for seduction, being cool, comfortless and sour-smelling, but when Werner began to giggle excitedly I became suspicious.

'Now, look, Werner,' I spoke crossly, 'I don't believe Ambrose is here at all. For one thing he couldn't manage the stairs.'

Werner looked pained. 'My dear Miss Freddie, of vat thing do you accuse me? This is vat I vish to show you.' He opened a third door, revealing another cellar, empty of bins. It contained a circular table and twelve chairs upholstered in red velvet. The walls were decorated garishly with runes and hieroglyphs and a very large, very bad portrait of Hitler. 'It is the stronghold of our faith.' Werner spoke in a hushed voice. 'A tribute to the sacred room in Wewelsburg. You know the story of King Arthur and his Knights of the Round Table? He vas king of the ancient Teuton races long before the English steal him as the Christian knight of chivalry. Here on this table is the place for the Holy Grail. Ven it is found there vill be the rebirth of the old virtues, valour and nobility and pure blood and all such as that!'

I tried not to hurt his feelings by laughing. I knew he would be embarrassed to remember this in a few years' time. 'Thank you for showing me. I think we'd better go back and join the others. I'm afraid your mother suspects me of trying to compromise your reputation.' A blast of Wagner, the overture to *Tannhäuser*, made me jump. Werner had switched on a tape-recorder that stood on the table, incongruous among the trappings of ancient legend. He locked the door and put the key in his pocket. 'Werner! Don't be an idiot! Open the door at once!'

'Oh, Miss Freddie, don't be cross vith me, please. I vish I could make you understand how I long to be in the arms of a soft and lovely girl!' He looked despondent. 'The Princess, of course, is all that is noble but it is like having to hold a pillar of stone. She has a chin like the Habsburgs and she chew the raw garlic to clean the blood. My horse is more pretty than she. I confess ven I imagine the marriage night I am afraid . . . ' Werner drew in his breath, threw out his hands and let them fall to his sides. 'Miss Freddie, vill you let me kiss your dear lips and press your sweet, sweet body so that together ve can make a vonderful music and fly ourselves up to the great shining moon in a symphony of love?'

'No.'

'Oh, ho! Don't be shy, my beautiful *Liebling*.'

He advanced towards me, arms outstretched. I heard a whirring, humming sound behind me. For a moment I was frightened. It came from a glass-panelled door that gradually filled with light from the top. The door opened and out stepped Vere.

'Off you go, Werner,' Vere had to duck his head to get into the sacred chamber. 'By popular request you're to entertain the ladies with some songs. Madame du Vivier is running through the accompaniment on the piano. Hurry, man,' he added, as Werner looked mulish, 'your audience awaits.'

Werner got into the lift. There was a whizzing of machinery as he was borne upwards.

'Let's turn this row off.' Vere switched off the tape.

'Don't you like Wagner?'

'No. I don't like my emotions being worked upon.'

'It was very good of you to come to my rescue. It was silly of me to get myself into this situation.'

'I imagine you were quite safe. He's just a romantic boy. His mother has a great deal to answer for.'

'Usually I defend mothers, who get the blame for everything, but I have nothing to say on behalf of the Baroness.'

Vere smiled briefly. He looked around. 'This was a perfectly good wine cellar before I went away. It was lucky I discovered the lift this morning.'

'Has the house changed much?' I felt some hesitance about asking such a direct question. Vere had an air of reserve about him that discouraged impertinent curiosity.

'Hardly at all.' Vere frowned and stood looking down at his shoes. To break the ensuing silence I was about to suggest that we went back to join the others when he said, continuing to address his toe-caps, 'I hoped that some things would be different — ' He broke off with a sigh. 'I was expecting too much. People don't change as they get older. They just become more . . . whatever

335

they were to begin with. My father — ' he stopped again.

Because I had so frequently been a confidante, as part of my work, I knew that the best way to encourage the naturally reticent was to go straight to the point before they had time to retreat. 'Why did you come home?'

'I was homesick.' He laughed. 'Ridiculous, isn't it? I've been homesick for twelve years. Not a day's gone by without my thinking of the house and the hills and the river. The beauty of it. I've seen all the wonders of the world, just about, but none of it matched what I remembered here. I suppose there was no investment of feeling anywhere else. What I mean is, all the best of me was here, hope, passion, faith — joy, if you like.' He looked at me and shrugged. 'How stupid that sounds.'

'Not stupid. Sad.'

'Sad?' He looked alarmed and swung round, turning his back to me to study the painting of Hitler.

'You didn't intend to come back, then?' I went on bravely, not wanting to lose the opportunity now that I had my foot wedged, metaphorically, in the door.

'When I left England I told myself that it must be for good. It was the price I had to pay to make up for the pain I was causing.' He laughed suddenly. 'Guy tells me you're a painter. What do you think of this monstrosity?'

Together we studied the slicked-down hair, the snout-like nose, the small red-lipped mouth and the absurd moustache. 'Terrible though it is, it has caught the madness of repression.' I pointed to the tiny wild eyes. 'As though play-acting were a refuge from unbearable anguish — perhaps of being a small dull ugly man.'

'You believe he was prompted to do what he did because of low self-esteem?'

'What else can one think of someone who builds giant arenas and holds massive parades and does everything with hysterical exaggeration? I know the

336

received view is that he was a brilliant manipulator of crowds, but when I watch his face in those films of the rallies, I imagine I can see a euphoria that has nothing to do with calculation. I think he really believed it. Until he found himself alone with a cyanide pill.'

'If only it weren't so easy to cheat oneself.'

'Then you'd have come home sooner?'

He looked at me in surprise. 'Yes. That's what I was thinking.'

'What changed your mind?'

'I really don't know. Six months ago I was planting mahogany trees. Neat rows of healthy foliage under a blazing sun in a sky the colour of lapis lazuli. A bird flew by, a scarlet ibis, brilliant and exotic, and I thought what I'd give to see a small brown sparrow. I remembered those lines by Shelley — And nearer to the river's trembling edge/There grew broad flag-flowers, purple pranked with white,/And starry river buds among the sedge,/And floating water-lilies — well, you know it, I expect. I thought of damp woods of oak and ash and beech pushing out from a carpet of wild garlic and dog's mercury. And the English sky full of clouds, dark one minute, luminous the next. The softness, subtlety, the diversity. I thought of the river — *my* river. I wanted to see primroses, apple-blossom and pussy-willow. I wanted to see rooks and starlings nesting, hear the moorhens calling among the reeds, see the kingfisher flash over the water. The desire to come home became compelling. I took a long time selling my house, tying up loose ends, saying goodbye. The trip on the ice breaker was an attempt to convince myself that I was master of my fate, that I wasn't in a hurry. But all the time the longing was . . . ' He paused. 'Do you know, the Nazis should have had you on their side. They wouldn't have needed bright lights and sinister equipment. You could make the Laconians garrulous.'

When he was teasing, the resemblance to Guy was striking. 'The Laconians? Something to do with 'laconic'?'

'They were famous for their pithy speech. Philip of Macedon sent them a message — 'If I enter Laconia I will raze it to the ground.' They sent back a reply. 'If.' '

Vere had successfully diverted my attention. 'Look, I'm taking up far too much of your time. Let's get out of this spiritual Golgotha.' His voice was like Guy's but deeper, slower.

'But I'm really interested.'

'I've talked too much about myself. You must be cold and bored. Shall we take the lift?'

'We'll have to. Werner has the key in his pocket.'

Because the lift was small we had to stand squeezed together, chest to chest. I had to look upwards to avoid the imprint of a pearl stud on the end of my nose. Vere stared over my head.

I felt conversation was imperative. 'Are you going to stay long?'

'I hope for good. Are *you* going to stay long?'

'I honestly don't know. The intention was a few days, originally. I'm marking time, really, while I sort myself out.'

'You don't look in turmoil.'

'Good.' There was a pause. Vere looked down at me. I knew the generous thing to do would be to reveal a little of myself in return. 'I've lost faith in my ability to make decisions.'

'Oh?'

'I prided myself on being decisive and collected and a good judge of character. I made a mistake — I won't bore you with the details — and it's been a blow to my self-confidence.'

'I think that may be a very necessary process in the evolution of the human spirit. G. K. Chesterton said that the men who really believe in themselves are in lunatic asylums. I've often found the thought comforting.'

'I hope I don't sound insanely self-indulgent.'

'Now we've both apologised for talking about ourselves. What a diffident pair we must be.'

As we were cranking slowly upwards I noticed that Vere had forgotten to shave part of his chin. A triangle of black bristles showed above his collar. He must have sensed that I was looking at him for he put up his hand and felt the place.

'I'm not much good at this sort of thing any more. I've spent the last few years in Venezuela, helping to set up a farming cooperative. Black tie was not called for.'

'Did you like it?'

'Good people. Beautiful country. But hard.'

'What are you going to do now you're home?'

'Guy and I have had several conversations already about my taking over the running of the estate. It was his idea. One of the things that most worried me about coming back was that Guy might resent my stepping into his shoes and I was determined not to do it. But he insists it's up to me as elder son and all that. I think my younger brother must have turned into some kind of saint.' I thought otherwise, knowing how much Guy disliked everything to do with farming and work. 'Naturally I shall see he doesn't suffer financially.'

Guy must be unable to believe his luck, I thought. I changed the subject. 'Chloë was your dog, wasn't she?'

'I hated leaving her behind. Guy promised he'd look after her. I didn't expect her to be alive still. I'm amazed she remembered me. She seems very fond of you.' Since Vere's return, five days ago, Chloë had apportioned her time pretty evenly between us, turning up at the cottage at various times and staying a few hours before returning to the Hall. 'I think her loyalties are painfully divided.' For the first time it struck me as odd that Chloë showed no affection for Guy. 'It's rather a lot of

339

running about for an old dog,' Vere went on. 'Perhaps we should try to persuade her to stay with you. Her protection might be useful. Can you get the door open?' We had arrived at the top of the shaft. I couldn't and we had to manoeuvre carefully to reverse our positions without touching each other. 'There's a knack to the mechanism. There!'

The lift shaft came up into a sort of scullery next to the kitchen. Miss Glim was standing at the sink, up to her bony elbows in suds. What could it be like to spend one's life making do with what was left over from more fortunate lives, working hard so others could fritter away time in idle enjoyment? And to love someone who would only offer scraps of affection when it suited him. I felt terribly sorry for her. I hoped she had not noticed that I had eaten hardly anything of the last two courses. 'Thank you for an excellent dinner, Miss Glim,' I began. 'I can't imagine how you did it without help.' She continued to probe a glass with the dish-mop as though she couldn't hear me. 'Wasn't it delicious, Vere?' I turned to appeal to him but he had gone.

28

'Why didn't you tell Vere you hate farming? He thinks you're being splendidly noble.'

It was Saturday morning. I was sitting on the window-seat to catch the best of the fitful sunlight, mending the curtains. The embroidery of acorns and oak leaves was subtle and the silk velvet delicate. I had to be careful not to rub bare patches in the pile with too much handling. Guy sat at the table eating toast and Bar's elderberry jelly.

'It makes him think better of me and that makes me feel better about me. Where's the problem?'

'It isn't the truth. It's unkind of you to deceive him.'

'Oh, Lord! Not your prickly conscience again. You know, you're destined to be an old maid. No man's ever going to live up to your finicky moral standards. Be human, Freddie. We all lie and cheat every day of our lives. You were sweetness itself to Dusty just now, though you can't possibly *like* the miserable old bastard. Just because you want him to carry on repairing your roof, you offer him tea and praise like any middle-class woman buttering up a minion. You don't really care tuppence about him as long as he does the job.'

There came a hammering sound from above our heads and a drift of plaster dust floated down on to my sewing. I wondered whether I could ask Dusty to be a little less forceful without offending him. Guy was right, of course. Some degree of hypocrisy is unavoidable in human relations.

'But your own brother. Someone you love. Isn't it in some way an act of betrayal to mislead them?'

'I don't know what you're talking about. Anyway, Vere and my father are engaged in their own excoriating version of the truth game. I shall keep out of it. At breakfast this morning he asked Vere whether he was attempting to rescue the estate from penury in the hope of ingratiating himself.'

'What did he mean?'

'Oh, Vere has been hard at work ever since we agreed he should take over the running of it. He sits up all night studying the accounts. Then my father asked if Vere thought the family could afford to support destitute hangers-on who had tried their luck elsewhere and failed. He's trying to decide whether to cut Vere out of his will to spite him, or to leave him in to spite me.'

'Is that really how he feels? I'd have thought your father would be overjoyed to have Vere home.'

'Only because you don't know my father.'

I had to admit that this was true. 'What did Vere say?'

'That he was only concerned with running the estate and any conclusions my father might draw from this were his own affair. Nor did he particularly care what they were. Vere hasn't changed at all. Too proud to make the soft answer. I suppose you approve of that.'

'I wish you'd stop trying to make me out a prig.' I looked angrily at Guy, who was piling translucent garnet-coloured jelly on to his fourth slice of toast. 'And don't eat all the jam. It's for the children's tea.'

'That boy, Wills, will be eating jam courtesy of Her Majesty soon enough. Deacon caught him trying to take the battery out of the tractor. He's a born thief.'

'You didn't ring the police?'

'No. I pleaded for your *protégé* so Deacon gave him a good hiding instead. But next time it'll be handcuffs.'

'I feel so sorry for Wills. He's utterly lost. There's no one to whom he really matters. I try with him but he despises women.'

'I feel sorry for Wormwood Scrubs. Now, do put that silly curtain down and let's go and make love.'

'But it's nearly lunchtime.'

'Bring some sandwiches up.'

'I didn't mean that. It isn't a suitable time for making love.'

'Why ever not?'

'Well, Prim's coming for lunch for one thing. And I've got plenty to do.'

'We'd better be quick, then.'

'I can't make love in the same spirit as fitting in an appointment with the dentist. Besides Dusty could look in through the window at any moment.'

'So what if he did?'

'Doesn't anything matter to you but sex?'

Guy rested his chin on his hand and looked thoughtful. He looked so handsome when he was serious. His face in repose had a sort of highminded nobility about it. 'I can enjoy a good game of cricket,' he said eventually.

I couldn't help smiling but I shook my head. 'It's no good, Guy. I like you — too much really, for my own good. But we want quite different things.'

'I suppose you mean babies.' Guy looked gloomy. 'What women see in them I'll never understand. Smelly, demanding and dull.'

'No, not that. Not yet anyway. I want to be able to trust someone. I want to know that I haven't got to watch out for myself when I'm with them, that they'll tell me the truth. That they're incapable of doing anything that seems, by my standards, cruel or mean or dishonest.'

Guy looked at me pityingly. 'Shame really. Such a lovely girl. But touched in the head.'

I held up a strand of cornflower blue silk against the light so that I could see to thread my needle. A pair of eyes stared back at me from the holly bush outside the window.

'Christ! You made me drop my toast on my trousers, screaming like that!' Guy was indignant.

'Damn! I've cut myself with the scissors!' Blood welled up from the wound between my thumb and forefinger and ran across my palm.

'Quick! Get a cloth.'

'It isn't a deep cut. My handkerchief'll do.'

'I meant for my trousers.'

When I had tied up my hand I went out into the garden, leaving Guy fussing about his trousers. Inside the little hedged square, as I expected, a man was crouching over a plate of food on the stone table. He had brown hair curling down to his shoulders. His back was towards me, the spine like a knobbed stick, shoulder-blades sharp, the ribs clearly outlined beneath the taut brown skin, which was covered with pale weals and blotches of scar tissue. The joints of his knees were thicker than his thighs.

'Lemmy,' I said softly. He sprang up on to the table, as lithe as a cat, and turned to face me, still holding the knife he had been using to cut up his food. He was naked except for a garment that might once have been jeans but was now shorts. 'It's all right,' I took a step back to reassure him and smiled. 'Friend.'

For what might have been half a minute we looked at each other. Lemmy's face was remarkable. The lower part was covered by matted dark hair but the forehead was unusually broad and marked by strongly arched brows. This, combined with his small stature and the pointed ears that projected through his hair, made him look puckish, like a dryad or a faun. His eyes, so dark as to appear black, flitted across my face and up and down my body as if committing every inch of it to memory.

'I know you come into the garden,' I said. 'I've been looking forward to meeting you.' He continued to stare, but his eyes did not meet mine. I dared not advance because of the knife. I wished Prim had told me how much he understood of what was said to him. 'Friend,' I said again. 'Pretty garden. Lemmy safe.' I was not striking the right note. He looked wary. I tried again. 'Pretty flowers.' I pointed to a clump of speedwell growing in the grass.

His features lit with intelligence and he leaped from the table to land beside the patch of blue. 'Common name, germander speedwell,' he recited in a high toneless voice. 'Latin name *Veronica chamaedrys*, family *Scrophulariaceae*. A native perennial. Very common all over the British Isles. Grows to ten inches. Flowers March to July. Tincture of speedwell is good for gout, rheumatism, eczema and purification of the blood.'

Lemmy approached me stealthily, holding the knife. I stood still, rather frightened. When he got to within two feet of me he stopped and again ran his eyes over every part of me until they returned to my hair. 'Ah!' It was almost a sigh. 'Marigold, mandarin, marmalade. Orange, apricot, peach. Carrot, pumpkin, chestnut. Coral, topaz, cornelian. Beautiful hair. Lemmy wants to touch it.'

He put up his free hand and stroked it gently. Then he took a handful and twisted it round his fingers, examining it closely. I felt extremely nervous. He put his mouth to it and began to suck a strand.

'Lemmy!' Prim had pushed her way through the hole in the hedge. 'Don't do that. People don't like having their hair chewed.'

Lemmy dropped his hand at once and stepped back. 'Lemmy didn't know.'

'Put down the knife. You're scaring Freddie.'

'Sorry, sorry, sorry. Lemmy won't hurt you.' He flung the knife away from him. His eyes dropped to the handkerchief wound round my fingers, through which spots of blood had appeared. 'Lemmy will make it better.'

He walked round the square with a curious gait, standing on tiptoe, knees bent, with his arms stretched out behind him. Then he snatched something out of the hedge with a yelp of triumph. 'Here it is!' He ran back to me holding a cobweb, now crumpled into a greyish ball. 'Take off that cloth.' He laid the cobweb delicately across the wound with the tip of his finger, taking care not to touch the flesh. 'Now, plantain leaves.'

There were a few clumps springing up in the turf. Lemmy put several leaves into his mouth, chewed them, then spat them out as a dark green ball. It was a severe test to allow them to be pressed lightly over the cobweb. The handkerchief bound the poultice in place.

'You'll find it'll work,' said Prim. 'Lemmy could teach Edward a thing or two. Now, Lemmy! Remember what I've said about standing up straight. You look prehistoric, cowering and slinking like that. Head up, shoulders back.' Lemmy did as he was told and at once looked more human. 'Where's the new shirt Bar gave you?'

Lemmy looked round vaguely. 'Left at home.'

'That's no good, is it? Freddie will think you're not in possession of all your wits. Which is far from the case. You know it's important to look like other people. What have you got for lunch?' She went over to examine his plate. 'It looks like a beetroot omelette. Bar's so original. I wonder if these leaves are supposed to be in it or if they fell in by mistake.'

'Hedge garlic. *Alliaria petiolata*. Family *Cruciferae*, the cabbage family. A native biennial. Good for abscesses, whitlows and pus generally.'

'All right, thanks, that'll do. I'm hoping to enjoy my lunch. I'll leave some cake by the pond this afternoon but don't forget or the birds'll have it.'

'Thank you for looking after my hand.' I smiled at him but his eyes were fixed once more on my hair. Slowly he put the knife to his mouth and began to suck the blade.

'Where does Lemmy come from? Was he born in the

village?' I asked, as I pursued crumbs of mud in the leeks I was preparing for lunch. I had bought a quarter of a pound of bacon for the leek pie, which these days seemed the last word in extravagance. Prim was sitting at the kitchen table. Guy had gone without leaving a note. I refused to let myself be disappointed. It isn't men who make one miserable, I reminded myself, but our own unrealistic expectations of them.

'He was adopted as a baby by the schoolteacher and his wife, in the days when there was a village school in Pudwell. Lemmy is astonishingly well educated, if that's what you call accumulated information. He has a photographic memory. He can recite whole books about anything that interests him. I think they drilled him from when he was a very small child. They weren't ideal parent material, too old and set in their ways. Very strict. But it wouldn't be right to blame them. There was something different about him from the beginning. I can remember him as a child, always alone and jeered at by the other children. Perhaps he was too clever. When he was fourteen the school house was burned down. Lemmy's parents died in the fire. Lemmy was saved but after that he refused to be in a house again. He escaped from every institution they tried to keep him in. Once he was eighteen the authorities gave up and he's gone wild, just like a garden, you might say. Poor Lemmy! He doesn't seem unhappy, exactly, but it seems a waste of a good brain. And a good person. When you get to know him better you'll see how gentle and kind he is. What's this?'

Prim picked up a piece of paper from the floor.

'Probably my shopping list.'

''Can't face lunch with Hauptsturmführer Yardley — I'm not in the mood to be lectured on my duties and responsibilities . . . ' It's a note from Guy. There's more. You'd better read it.' She put it on the table. 'Well! Eavesdroppers never hear good of themselves. Nor, it seems, do people who read letters not intended for them.' Prim laughed but I could see from the set of her lips and the brightness of her eye that she was wounded.

'Oh, don't take any notice of Guy.'

'I suppose I am rather too inclined to give my opinion. I mean to help, but I ought to remember that other people don't want my advice.'

'Prim! You're not going to allow yourself to be upset by anything that arch-seducer might say? He's cross because he wanted — well, I needn't spell it out. I don't think you're bossy in the least. Just very, very kind and thoroughly sensible. You're the first person I'd come to if I wanted help.'

'Thank you. This pie's going to be delicious. What else are you putting in it?'

'Eggs and cream and a bay leaf. I made the pastry this morning. I found the recipe in this nice old cookery book. It was printed in eighteen sixty-five. Isn't it romantic to think of all the women who have searched its pages for inspiration? Perhaps Viola's godmother made this very pie.'

Prim was turning the pages but I could tell her thoughts were elsewhere. 'What hurts is that I stupidly thought there was something like affection between us — because of the past. I know I'm very critical of Guy but actually I'm always quite pleased to see him, if I'm truthful. One wants a *little* soft focus in one's life. I know I'm not the sort of woman men fall in love with. I'm too prosaic. And obviously too domineering. You're beautiful and enigmatic and vulnerable. Guy must really dislike me to deny himself the opportunity of being with you.'

'That isn't true. Men *do* fall in love with you. What about Edward? He's really in love, with a wholehearted-ness that's worth having. I don't think Guy feels affection for people of either sex, actually.' I reflected briefly on his readiness to deceive his brother. But perhaps men were all like that. I had so little useful experience, that was the trouble. Uncle Sid was the only man I had ever known who had tender feelings for people and animals and was not afraid to express them. No doubt this made him eccentric. 'Sometimes I'm convinced Guy's entirely and utterly selfish. Then I remember that he's paying for George's coaching and I have to readjust the image. It isn't every brother who'd take responsibility for a love child.'

'I still find it hard to believe that Vere fathered that child then abandoned him. It's out of character.'

'But it *is* good of Guy to pay for the coaching.'

'You saw him, I suppose, at Ambrose's party?'

'Guy?'

'Vere.'

On Tuesday morning Mrs Creech had gone to the unprecedented length of delivering Prim's weekly grocery order herself, in order to be the one to drop the bombshell of Vere's return from the grave. That afternoon Prim had been waiting with Frankie and Titch on my doorstep when I arrived home from the mill and we had discussed the electrifying news exhaustively over tea and late into the evening. Prim's face had been flushed but her voice calm when she said how delighted she was and how much she looked forward to meeting him again as he was such an old friend. I had drawn my own conclusions as to the identity of Prim's youthful and unresponsive love. Unlike the other inhabitants of Pudwell she showed no sign of impatience when a week went by without Vere once showing himself in the village. I could not help noticing, though, that she had taken to wearing mascara.

'Yes. I saw him.'

'How does he look now?'

'Well, of course, I don't know what he looked like before. I got the impression he was keeping his feelings on a tight rein.'

'He never did give much away. Not willingly.' She tugged at a piece of wool that hung from a ragged sleeve. 'When the rest of us were babbling about our ids and egos Vere always kept quiet. He'd make jokes if you tried to get him to say what he felt about things. But when you knew how to read him, there was no more transparent man on this earth,' Prim smiled to herself, and her secret was evident in the softness of her eyes. 'I believe he's really — Who's that?'

She swung round in her chair in response to a knock at the back door.

'That'll be Dusty, wanting tea,' I said. 'Let him in, will you, while I put the kettle on?'

Prim opened the door.

I heard Guy say, 'Prim! What a stroke of luck!' I bent down to make a fuss of Chloë, who had come running in, very pleased to see me. I was trying to think how I might warn him that reparations were due to Prim. 'I've just been to your house but you weren't there. Naturally, as you're here.' Then I realised it wasn't Guy. The voice was deeper, more resonant. It gave an awkward laugh. I straightened up and turned round.

Prim stood by the open door, her face flaming. 'Hello,' she said at last, in a voice that lacked its customary briskness. 'Come in.'

The room seemed darker with Vere standing in it, his head nearly touching the rafters. He put his arm clumsily around Prim's shoulders and kissed her cheek. 'You're looking very well,' he said. 'Marvellous!'

'Thank you.'

'Hello,' I said. 'Mind your head on the beams. Lovely day, isn't it?' I added fatuously to give Prim time to compose herself.

'Well, yes.' Vere bent to look through the window. 'Actually, it's just starting to rain.'

'Oh.' My wits deserted me.

'How are you?' Prim paused. 'It's been a very long time.'

'Hasn't it! Much too long!' Vere assumed a heartiness that was misplaced, I thought. 'My goodness, you've done something to your hair, haven't you?'

'Well, I've had it cut a few times since you left.'

'And you seem much bigger. You've grown!'

'Only outwards.' Prim was gaining composure by being caustic, while Vere was making sad work of the reunion.

'It's wonderful to see you! Marvellous!' Vere seemed to have run short of adjectives. To give them the illusion that they were not being observed, I peered intently at the leeks blanching in the pan. 'Well, well!' Vere blundered on. 'What have you been doing with yourself? How are your mother and father?'

'Dead, I'm afraid.'

'Oh! Dear! I'm terribly sorry!'

'It's quite all right. You weren't responsible.'

I took pity on Vere. 'Would you open this bottle for me?' I handed him the corkscrew. 'Prim and I were just about to have a glass of wine. Won't you have one?'

'Thank you.'

'I'll get another glass.' Prim escaped from the kitchen.

'You have put the old place to rights.' Vere looked round the kitchen, at the shining cups and plates on the dresser, the scrubbed table, the morels drying on strings along the beams.

'You knew Viola's godmother, then?' Seeing Vere's look of incomprehension I went on, 'I do wish I'd met Anna. Of course, you probably don't know. She got Alzheimer's, poor thing, and died some time ago. I expect it sounds silly and far-fetched but because I wash my face at her sink, stir her pans, read her books, mend her curtains and lie in her bed I have the unconquerable feeling that, in some way, I know her intimately.'

'Who's Viola?'

'Anna's goddaughter. She left her the cottage. It's

such a dear, strange little house and full of such lovely things. Our tastes are remarkably similar. I know it's stretching it rather far but I do think we would have had an affinity.'

'Do shared tastes guarantee compatibility?'

'Perhaps not that. But don't you feel drawn to people who like what you like?'

'I hadn't thought about it before but now I'm sure that I do.'

Vere stood, head slightly bent, hands on the waist of his disreputable cotton trousers and stared down at me. His eyes appeared larger than Guy's because the lashes were darker. I noticed his shirt had a hole in it and the breast pocket was torn off. He looked much more relaxed than he had on the evening of Ambrose's birthday party.

'Here we are.' Prim brought in the glass and poured the wine. 'Let's drink to the return of the native.'

'Friendship — old and new.' Vere raised his glass to each of us in turn. 'And to the discovery of congenial tastes.'

Prim looked sharply at me and then at Vere. 'What are you doing here, Vere? Did you want to see Freddie?'

'I was looking for Dusty. But it concerns Freddie, too. I'm a harbinger of ill omen, I'm afraid. You probably don't know, Prim, but Guy has been extraordinarily generous. He's given me *carte blanche* to run the estate. I've been going into the accounts and several things have struck me as needing immediate action. The mill has been making a substantial loss for years. It's got to be shut down. I've just told Dusty.'

'How's he taken it?' asked Prim.

'Surprisingly well. Apparently he realised it was on the cards. I've promised him as much thatching work as he wants for the next twelve months. We've several cottages on the estate in need of repair. Then he'll retire on a good pension. It hadn't occurred to him that we'd give him one and that's sweetened the pill no end.'

'What's going to happen to the mill?'

'Nothing for the time being. Dusty'll stay on in the house as long as he wants to, in return for keeping the machinery in good order. I've yet to decide. But it means you'll be out of a job.' He smiled at me apologetically.

'So it does. I'm both glad and sorry. It is terribly hard, dull work, but it was a living of sorts. I've got my dependants to think of.'

'Oh, what a clot I am!' said Prim. 'I'd clean forgotten. I've got the perfect job for you. The hospital board have decided to commission a portrait of their longest-serving member. I recommended you so enthusiastically that the motion was proposed and carried in the twinkling of an eye.'

'But you've never seen my work.'

'I know. You'll be sure to put two eyes in the proper place, won't you? No cubism or surrealist nonsense. We don't want Lady Frisk to look more like Quasimodo than she already does.'

'Lady Frisk! Oh dear! What will she have to say about it? I'm afraid she doesn't like me at all.'

'Her monstrous vanity is so engorged by the proposal that she only said that she felt she would be fulfilling a very necessary duty in keeping you out of the way of giving the wrong sort of encouragement to young men.'

'Well! Of all the — oh, you're teasing me! Aren't you? Anyway, it's very good of you to go to so much trouble on my behalf, Prim. I *am* grateful.'

'You haven't changed a bit.' Vere looked at Prim fondly. 'I think you ought to be Prime Minister. You'd soon have everything running efficiently and people toeing the line.' I saw Prim's expression change. 'That's what I remember best about you. Whenever something had to be organised — cricket matches, tea-parties, horticultural shows — you were the brains behind it. The rest of us were disgracefully lazy and arrogant, I'm ashamed to recall. Oh, good Lord, yes, that talent contest in the village hall — do you remember? — when the pianist began the accompaniment an octave too high and the soprano was screaming out the high notes?' Vere laughed at the memory. 'You swept on to the stage and gave the audience a tremendous ticking off for giggling. You can't have been more than eighteen at the time but even the rough element sank down in their seats in terror. Ha! Ha! Ha! I'd completely forgotten all that.'

'I'm glad it amuses you.' Prim's voice was deceptively mild.

'And there was Patience the Performing Pig!'

'Prudence,' said Prim. 'The pig was called Prudence.'

'When it tried to eat the ventriloquist's dummy — ' Vere was laughing so much now that his sunburned skin was turning ruddy ' — you got it off the stage by feeding it the juggler's apples and oranges! He was furious but you saved the show. You ought to have been a general. You're marvellous, Prim, really!'

'So you keep saying.'

Vere stopped laughing and perceived that something was wrong. 'Mm — well, I mustn't delay your lunch.' Prim looked stony. 'I think I'll get along — thank you for the wine — good to see you again, Prim — we must make time to catch up — I'd like to hear all your news.'

He looked at me, bewilderment in every feature. The thought came to me that despite his youthful misdemeanours this was a decent man, without guile or stratagem. Prim composed her mouth into the sort of smile adopted by a parliamentary candidate on the hustings who has failed to be elected by a handful of votes.

'I'll put out the knives and forks,' I said, grabbing some from the dresser drawer and rushing into the sitting room. When I returned a minute later, Prim's eyes were filled with tears and Vere had gone.

29

'Bicket! Bicket!' cried Titch, holding up her arms.

I took her on my knee. Frankie came and leaned against me. 'Hello, darling,' I put my arm round her and kissed her. 'What have you been doing? There's mud on your nose.'

'We've been makin' a surprise. In the velvet-dear.' This was Frankie's name for the belvedere overlooking the river. 'Come and see!'

'We will, as soon as we've finished our coffee. Who's that?' The window seat, where Prim and I were sitting, was bathed in light so the other end of the sitting room was shadowy. A girl stood just inside the front door, her hands behind her back, her head hanging so that she glowered at us from beneath dark brows.

'Is that Ruth?' said Prim. 'Come and stand where we can see you.'

It was her first visit to the cottage. She moved forward slowly, scowling with shyness. Her hair was nearly black, parted in the middle and tied untidily in two bunches with rubber bands. Her skin was olive and her general appearance decidedly Latin so I guessed she must be half-sister to the two younger girls. She wore a dress of lilac satin with a long tiered skirt edged with a band of lace, now bedraggled with mud and hanging down in loops.

' ''Tis her best dress.' Frankie had a piercing whisper, quite as loud as anyone else's normal voice. Ruth frowned more than ever and half turned to go.

'It's very pretty,' I said quickly. 'How kind of you to come and see us.'

Ruth lowered her gaze to the carpet and said nothing.

'Come and sit over here,' said Prim. 'I remember you

355

from Sunday school. You painted a very nice picture of Noah's ark.'

Ruth looked consideringly at Prim then came to sit on the edge of the window seat cushion, leaving a good three feet between herself and us.

'Have you been cryin'?' Frankie asked Prim. Very little escaped her penetrating gaze. 'You've got cascara on your cheek.'

'I've got a bit of a cold,' Prim said untruthfully, rubbing her eye and making matters worse.

After Vere had gone Prim had not actually cried but her eyes had watered to the detriment of her makeup. 'It was the surprise of seeing him,' she had explained. 'I wasn't prepared and I hate myself for being so cold and sarcastic. We won't say another word about it.' Obedient to her bidding, I did not mention Vere's name but several times during lunch she had sighed and said, 'I *am* a fool.'

'Not at all,' I had assured her, my response becoming a little automatic by the fourth or fifth occasion.

'I hate Sunday school.' Frankie picked her nose absentmindedly. 'I don't like singin' hymns. It's *borin'*. And lambs' legs are too hard to draw. Mrs Winnacott smells.'

'Nonsense!' said Prim. 'Don't pick your nose, dear. Your fingernails are black. You'll give yourself a nasty germ. And *certainly* don't eat it.' I had to hide a smile as Prim fussed with her handkerchief over an unrepentant Frankie.

'She does, too! She smells of the stuff what they put down the toilets at school. Disinfect-it.'

'Well, that's a nice clean smell.'

'It's got the bad smell in it,' Frankie insisted. 'When Mrs Winnacott leans over me I think of poo.'

'How unfortunate for her.' Prim abandoned her disciplinary role and laughed. 'Do you like Sunday school, Ruth?'

Ruth nodded. 'I liked ringin' the little bells.' She spoke very quietly. I noticed that after Prim's remark about Frankie's fingernails, Ruth had put her hands beneath her voluminous skirt and kept them hidden. 'Mum got ill and I couldn't go no more.'

'*Any* more. But she's better now, isn't she? You could come tomorrow.'

Ruth shrugged. I noticed she had a nervous tic, which made her nose twitch every few seconds. It was evident that she was under some strain.

'I *hate* them stupid bells,' said Frankie. 'They give me a headache. La! La! La!' she sang, very loudly, in my ear. Ruth's presence seemed to affect Frankie's behaviour adversely, probably because she felt she was no longer the centre of attention.

'Let's go for a walk,' I suggested. 'I'll carry Titch.' The baby was lying with her head in the crook of my arm sucking her thumb, her lids drooping.

'Yes, let's go to the velvet-dear!' Frankie jumped up. 'I'll lead the way. Shall we blindfold you?' She held up Prim's handkerchief.

'I don't think I could get down the path without tumbling head over heels into the river if I couldn't see. I'll shut my eyes when we get to the door.'

'Follow me, follow me!' shouted Frankie, which made Titch wake up and cry.

'Hello? Can I come in?' It was Edward. 'I did knock but you didn't hear me. Where are we supposed to follow you to, young lady?' He smiled kindly down at Frankie.

'It's my ex-perdition and I haven't asked any *men*.' Frankie's face was at its sharpest.

'That's very rude, Frankie,' said Prim. 'You should apologise to Dr Gilchrist.'

'That's all right.' Edward bent down so that he was level with Frankie. 'Whenever little girls come to my surgery I tell them to stick out their tongues. Let's have a look at yours.' Frankie stuck hers out. 'Oh, good! That's very rude. Come on, further, further. Very good! Now do this.' He stuck his thumbs in his ears and waggled his fingers, and Frankie began to giggle. Titch gave a fruity chuckle, the first time I had heard her laugh. Only Ruth did not smile.

'Come on, you fool.' Prim got up and pulled on her coat.

'Just a minute.' He pulled out a handkerchief and dabbed at her cheek. 'Either a smut or makeup.' He put a large red hand on her shoulder and looked tenderly down at her face. 'You're looking a bit peaky. Steady on, old thing.'

'You might as well say 'Whoa, Dobbin.'' Prim looked sulky but then her good sense got the better of her ill-humour and she laughed. 'Don't take any notice of me. I'm an idiot.'

'I can think of lots of things I'd like to call you but idiot isn't one of them.'

Edward's face spoke so eloquently of his love that I looked away, feeling that I was intruding on something intensely private.

'Come on!' cried Frankie impatiently.

The sky was yellow beneath massing violet clouds that promised rain. For the moment the sun held sway and the garden was ringing with birdsong. Frankie ran on ahead, singing 'How much is that *doggie* in the window? The one with the *wagg*-er-ly tail' at the top of her voice. Ruth walked at the tail of the procession. I closed my eyes at the door of the summer-house and was drawn inside by a sticky hand. When I opened them I was able to give a genuine and spontaneous cry of surprise. The walls were covered with flowers, mostly orange tulips and crimson peony heads with stalks of blue and white iris and between them were whole branches of leaves. The effect was striking and very jolly, though some of the petals were beginning to drop.

'My darlings, where did you get these lovely flowers? And what have you stuck them on with?' When I looked closer I saw that they had used copious amounts of glue, which had made long drips down the wall.

'I only picked wild 'uns growin' outside people's hedges.' Frankie looked a little guilty. 'I didn't go into any gardens. Roof made the cakes.'

The cloth was red velvet decorated with more flowers and leaves. The table had been laid with leaf plates on which were sausages, black and pink in stripes, and small cakes with currants in, rather grey. In the centre of the table was a green jelly, dissolving a little at the edges.

'It's magnificent!' I gave Frankie a kiss. She flung her arms round my neck, beside herself with excitement. 'How good of you to do this for me! What dear things you are!' I kissed Ruth who was stiff and unresponsive.

Frankie was hopping up and down with glee. 'The cloth is Mum's party dress cut up.' Prim and I exchanged glances. 'We made the cups outa clay from the river. We've brung our own kettle for tea and some tea-bags. We haven't got no milk but there's sugar. I'll go and start the fire.'

'Might a mere man be permitted to help?' asked Edward humbly.

'Come on, then.'

Frankie rushed outside. Probably there had been few times in her life when she was able to initiate events. While the kettle was boiling Prim, Ruth and I sat at the table.

'What lovely cakes, Ruth.' I said, shifting the position of the baby, who was very nearly asleep, in my arms. 'Do you like cooking?'

Ruth shrugged. 'It said to add an egg on the packet but there weren't none. Mum weren't well enough to go for the dole yesterday.'

I did not like to ask Ruth if her mother had been

drinking again. 'Do you think you could persuade your mother to let us talk to her? We could arrange for someone else to collect the money when she isn't well.'

'I dunno.'

'But, Ruth dear, how are you all going to eat?' persisted Prim. 'You can't go on like this, never knowing where the next meal's coming from. The baby will get sick if she doesn't have plenty of good, fresh food.'

Ruth looked profoundly unhappy and tired, her skin almost mauve under her eyes. I wanted to put my arms around her but I knew she would not like it.

'You buggers!' Wills came in, muddied to his armpits. 'You orter've told me. I'm bloody starvin'! I nearly caught a trout. It were a big one. I'm goin' to make a net and then it won't get away.'

'Hello, Wills.'

Wills ignored me but hovered over the table, one scratched black hand stretched forth.

'Don't you dare to touch anything, William Roker.' Prim's voice was stern and Wills drew back. 'The girls have worked hard to make this lovely surprise and you're not going to spoil it.'

When the kettle boiled we began tea straight away, though Prim and I had finished lunch barely an hour before. The clay cups started to dissolve when they were filled with hot tea. It tasted like thick, gravelly mud but we did our best to get some of it down. The sausages were raw in the middle. I performed my usual sleight-of-hand and put mine in my pocket but Edward threw back his head and dropped his in whole, chewing it with ostentatious noises of satisfaction. A twig had somehow become set into my portion of jelly.

'This is muck!' Wills opened his mouth to let the contents fall on to his plate and wiped it with the back of his hand.

'Now, young man.' Edward frowned at him. 'Speaking for myself I don't know when I last had such an exciting culinary treat and never one in such good company.' He smiled at us all and ruffled Frankie's hair. There was something so comfortable and cheering about his unstinting kindness and the honesty that gleamed in his soft blue eyes beneath the wildly curling fringe that I wondered that Prim could resist him. But, of course, sexual attraction has nothing to do with volition. Uncharacteristically heedless of example Prim had her elbow on the table and was cupping her chin in her hand, looking at him. He caught her eye and a dash of melancholy crept into his.

Prim stood up. 'Let's get some exercise.'

The woods were in their full glory. Now the canopy was green and luscious and reverberant with birdsong. Wood pigeons called seductively to each other and tumbled about among the branches. I stopped briefly to listen to the staccato drilling of an invisible woodpecker. Blades of light, sparkling with motes, flashed through gaps in the fluttering vault. Bluebells, their vivid stain shimmering just above the earth like a ghostly vapour, sweetened the breeze with their scent and mingled with the pungent smell of garlic that we crushed underfoot.

Chloë, Balthazar and Frankie ran in front, the latter stopping to pick bluebells until she had a fat bunch of stalks clasped in her dirty hand.

'We shouldn't let her pick them, really,' said Prim.

'She's so happy. Don't let's spoil things.' I panted. Titch grew heavier with every step.

'Let me have her.' Edward took the baby from my arms. She opened unseeing eyes for one second but fell asleep when he began to stroke her hair.

'Pooh!' said Wills. 'This place stinks! I wish I had a gun. I'd shoot those fucking birds.'

It was clear that Wills and Nature were not *en rapport*. 'Isn't it beautiful?' I said to Ruth. 'Look at those squirrels chasing each other.'

Ruth gave her usual shrug. But when we came to a

crab-apple in full blossom, dripping white petals like falling snow, she looked at it with an expression of something like delight.

'I'm leavin' a trail like in Hansel and Gretel,' cried Frankie, tearing up bits of leaf and throwing them on the ground behind her.

'Stupid! You'll never be able to find 'em again,' jeered Wills. 'It has to be something white like crumbs.'

'No one could ever find little tiny breadcrumbs again either,' said Frankie, 'so stupid yourself, you fat pig!'

'Children!' Prim was impatient. 'Either be quiet and behave or go home now. Let's try to enjoy this beautiful place without quarrelling.'

Frankie was silenced by this but I heard Wills stomping along behind me muttering, 'Stoo-*pid*, stoo-*pid*', with every step. He certainly was a trying child.

'Listen!' Frankie stopped so abruptly that I bumped into her. 'What's that funny noise?'

A sort of whoo-hoo-hoo, followed by an ah-h-h-hing ending in a shriek made the birds start into flight and the squirrels dash for cover.

''Tis the old witch comin' to put you in her oven 'cause you've bin eatin' her house!' sneered Wills.

Frankie put her hand in mine.

Wills was nearer the fact than he knew. We rounded a bend in the path to see Bar leaping nimbly into the air, uttering strange cries and flinging her hands above her head like a swimmer going down for the last time. Her hair was a delectable shade of butter yellow and she wore a skirt of patchwork squares in brilliant colours with a striped jersey. I thought what a good thing it was that she was fully clothed as we had Edward with us but then I remembered that Edward would hardly be a stranger to the naked female form. But Wills, one hoped, would have been taken aback.

'Be careful of my circle,' Bar called, when she saw us.

'I'm celebrating the summer solstice. It's the sexual union of the Sun God with the Goddess of Summer. Come and join me!'

'I don't think we ought — ' Prim began, but Wills and Frankie were already advancing towards the two heaps of burning sticks round which Bar was dancing.

'I'll cut a door for you to come in.'

I was amused by Frankie's look of awe as she stepped carefully through the space within Bar's sketched outline. 'Is it a door? Where is it? I can't see it.'

'It's a magic door of blue fire. You can't see it yet because you haven't been initiated but I can.'

'I'm coming in,' said Wills, unexpectedly, stepping with high strides across the invisible threshold.

Ruth hung back. 'Come on,' I said. 'It's good magic. It won't hurt you.'

Bar clapped her hands. 'Now, concentrate everyone. We're going to walk deosil — that's clockwise — round the cauldron of wine.' Bar pointed to a pottery bowl filled with purple liquid between the two bonfires.

It was like being a child at school again, in a music-and-movement class. I was tempted to swing my arms about, 'finding a space'.

'Put the baby down in the circle. The Goddess will see that she comes to no harm.' Surprisingly Titch made no complaint but lay on her back, sucking her thumb and staring up at the waving branches. Chloë and Balthazar saw something that begged to be chased and ran off. We did as we were told, the grown-ups feeling foolish, if my sentiments were anything to go by. 'Now we'll sing to the Goddess and the God. 'Here is the cup of joy given us by the Goddess.' Three times.'

We struck up obediently with wavering voices as Bar's tune ranged from piercingly high notes plunging dramatically to the deepest chest tones. Some of us were muddling the highs and lows. It became difficult, almost painful, to suppress the desire to giggle.

'*Singing*, Wills, not shouting,' said Prim. 'They can hear you in Tarchester.'

'Very good. Now we'll alternate that line with another. '*The God is setting sail for the Isle of Rebirth.*' And we'll speed up a bit if you've got the hang of it. Let's try skipping. We're asking the Sun God to rid the earth of all destructive forces, war and greed and cruelty, things like that. Concentrate on the prayer in your hearts as you dance and sing.'

It was such an evidently worthy prayer that I really tried to throw myself into it but skipping is something best done by children. Prim's generously sized breasts had declared independence.

'Excellent! Now, really let go!' panted Bar. 'Much faster! Lift your voices to the sky. Lovely big jumps. Twirl — around — think of industrial pollution — and pray for it to be — banished — throw out your arms — to embrace the — the sun and the — moon. Nuclear stockpiling — must go!'

There was so much to think about that I became confused. I hopped and skipped and leaped and sang and as I twirled I saw Edward's mouth wide open in his scarlet face, bellowing something about cups of rebirth and sailing for the Goddess as he kicked up his legs and waved his hands over his head as though bringing in a plane to land. Frankie was spinning round and round and getting dizzy and bumping into the rest of us and Wills was imitating a train, his arms working like pistons. Having been stiff with inhibition to begin with, we were now incited by each other's invention to further heights of self-expression. Even Ruth began to smile as she ran round on tiptoe, waving her arms like a giant lilac butterfly.

'Glorious!' Bar came to a standstill after several minutes. 'Can't you feel — the — kinetic energy being — released? Stop, now — everyone, gather round the cauldron and — we'll drink to — the Goddess.'

We stood panting round the bowl — sorry, cauldron. Frankie was so dizzy she had to lie down. Titch lay still, sucking her thumb and smiling. A feeling of exhilaration coursed through me, like being drunk on the very best champagne.

'Serotonin,' said Edward. 'Physical exertion — including exercising the lungs by singing — changes the chemical soup in your brain. Quite a tonic, isn't it? We should do it more often.'

'I must say I enjoyed that.' Prim looked beautiful, her complexion glowing, her eyes brilliant.

Bar took a sip from the cauldron and intoned, with an accent of reverence, 'I drink to fulfilment.'

She handed it to me. Something bobbed against my lips as I drank. I hoped it was fruit. Frankie tried it, made a face and clutched her stomach.

'Eugh! It stinks.' Wills spat out his mouthful, by mistake on Prim's skirt and she was briefly cross.

Edward drank solemnly. 'I drink to fulfilment,' he announced, in hollow, vibrating tones like John Gielgud.

'Now we'll sit cross-legged and complete the ceremony.' We knelt obediently on the mossy floor of the wood. 'Think about what pleases you, what fulfils you at the moment. Is it listening to music? Gardening? Painting? Curing a patient? Being out of doors? Making love?'

'Certainly not,' said Prim, with a frown in Wills's direction.

'It is your fate, as it is the destiny of the Sun God, to be changed irrevocably by fulfilment. Visualise this change, think about what you must do to bring it about. Offer up your deepest desires to the Goddess and she will grant them, though not necessarily all at once or in a way that you will immediately recognise.'

This had a familiar, exculpatory ring. But I was not in the mood to be cynical. I couldn't think what my deepest desire was. It was a question requiring advance

365

notice. In the end I offered up a vague confection of desiderata that included whatever everybody else had wished for plus the hope that Alex and Zara would be wildly happy. This last was entirely selfish, of course.

'Now consecrate your wands — any stick will do — by waving them in the flames and we'll invoke a blessing on the land. Peace and plenty! By the waxing and waning of the sun, may all oppression be put to flight!'

'Mumble — mumble — put to flight!' we echoed. A disaster was narrowly averted as Wills held his stick too long in the fire and nearly set light to Frankie's hair but on the whole the collective emotion was one of triumph as we brought the ceremony to its conclusion. We all felt inexplicably and immeasurably better for it. Except Wills.

'Is that it?' he complained, aggrieved. 'I thought you said there was goin' to be sex wiv the God and Goddess! I wunt've joined in if I'd knowed it were just silly dancin' and wavin' sticks.'

He got up and sloped off by himself, a figure of disappointment.

'Thank you, Bar.' Edward got up and offered a hand to Prim and me, sitting on either side of him. 'I can't remember when I've enjoyed myself so much. As a celebration it beats Christmas with my aunts, a frozen turkey and half a bottle of sweet martini into a cocked hat. I feel thoroughly invigorated. I wish I could stay but I've got evening surgery at half past five and my receptionist had her appendix out this morning, poor girl. The temp is on holiday and I shall have to run the show on my own. No doubt chaos will ensue.'

'I'll help you,' said Prim unexpectedly. 'I can at least answer the telephone and send the patients in to see you in the right order.'

'Prim! Would you do that? I hardly like to ask it of you.'

'You haven't. I've offered my services and I'll be happy to do it.'

Edward hid his smile of satisfaction by bending down to pick up Titch and kissing the top of the baby's head. 'Come on, then. We'd better go and start sorting medical records. Goodbye, young ladies. Goodbye, Freddie, Bar.'

I don't think anyone but me saw Edward give a little skip in the air and raise his hand in a salute to the sky as they left the clearing. I was in no doubt as to what his deepest desire might be.

'I quite like that man,' said Frankie, in a tone of grudging concession.

'I'll walk back to Drop Cottage with you,' said Bar. 'I'm in the mood for company. Wait a minute and I'll fetch some of the fennel and watercress cake I made this morning.'

Frankie made a face after Bar had gone skipping off to her house. 'Have we gotta eat it? It doesn't sound very nice.'

'I think it sounds rather original and delicious,' I said. Frankie looked at me, her brow corrugated. I took pity on her. 'I've got some sponge finger biscuits you can have. And chocolate spread.'

Frankie put her hand in mine. 'I do love you,' she said, with affecting simplicity.

When Bar came back with several brown paper bags filled with mysterious articles of food we took Titch's hands between us and went along very slowly so that she should have some practice in walking. She tended to hang forward all the time and drag her toes so progress was slow but I was concerned that everyone, including me, treated her like a badly wrapped parcel to be carried about and dumped down, so that as a result she was rather passive and lethargic. We set Frankie and Ruth the task of collecting kindling so they could run about and keep warm for the sun had gone behind the clouds. Soon there was a pattering on the leaves as rain began.

'Isn't it a beautiful sound?' Bar stopped to listen. 'And the smell of the earth!' Several drips of rain fell on her uplifted forehead and ran down the length of her pretty turned-up nose.

Soon it was crashing down and splashing up round our legs in a cloudburst. Chloë broke ranks and bolted for home. In a very short while we were all wet to the skin. Progress was necessarily slow because of carrying Titch.

'I like this rain,' said Frankie. 'It's part of our adventure.'

'Good girl,' said Bar. 'Let's sing. It'll keep us warm.'

So we tramped through puddles and mud and sodden undergrowth bawling a song that Bar remembered from her childhood over and over again at the tops of our voices. Ruth sang as loudly as anyone.

'Whether the weather be cold, whether the
  weather be hot,
We'll weather the weather whatever the weather,
  whether we like it or not!'

★ ★ ★

'It was ever such a lovely day,' sighed Frankie, when I took the children home after tea. 'Fancy Miss Watkins bein' able to do magic! My deepest desire is not to have to sit next to Sharon Loveluck at school. I wished she'd turn into a warty toad. I'm looking forward to Monday.'

'She doesn't do the kind of magic that hurts people.' Frankie looked disappointed. 'Think how happy we all were today. That's a kind of magic, isn't it?'

'I don't count that.' Frankie was decided. 'What did you wish for, Roof?'

But Ruth refused to say.

30

Cupid struck seven as I walked in. Bar had gone home to prepare the next day's lessons. I built up the fire, poured myself a glass of wine — sycamore sap, which tasted much better than you would expect — and fell into a mood of abstraction. Macavity was on my knee and Chloë lay at my feet. Not long ago I would have felt lonely and adrift but now, though I had no money, no real home of my own and my career was in suspension, I was as happy as I had ever been.

I did not really believe in witchcraft. I thought that Nature herself had cast some kind of spell over me. It was an education of sorts. I would not have gone so far as to call it liberation for I think that is probably always illusory. The human condition is in itself a sort of imprisonment, the particularities of body and temperament — what makes us different — are fetters and one can only hope to swap them for ones less chafing. But I liked what was happening to me. I liked these moments of real solitude when I seemed to lose recognisable traits, to be hardly myself.

I wondered if Guy would come. I hoped not. One of the things that had become clear to me in those moments of reflection, kneeling by the fire in the wood, was that the affair must stop. He was amusing and attractive but I was very far from loving him. Or even liking him, now I thought about it. I could forgive his lying to me about trivial things like train timetables, but there was something about his cold-blooded deception of Vere that I found profoundly shocking. I dreaded the inevitable row but I felt quite certain that I never wanted to make love with him again. I did not entertain for one minute the idea that we might be friends.

I wondered how best to tell him. I was turning over in my mind phrases that were, I hoped, kind yet incisive, when Chloë lifted her head and then ran, barking, to the front door. I heard a tentative knocking. Macavity gave a mew of protest as I moved him off my knee. The door opened easily these days since Dusty had repaired the hinges. It was too dark to make out the features of my visitor.

'Miss Swann? I'm ever so sorry to bother you but I was hoping we could have a little talk.'

The voice was female, youthful and attractively softened by the regional accent. It had something of a shiver in it. She came in out of the darkness, a small, slim girl with hunched shoulders, arms hugging her chest, spindly legs wobbling in absurdly high heels. A lock of fair hair fell over one eye that she pushed away ineffectually as she looked round the room, and from time to time quickly at me. I could see she was very nervous.

'Come and sit down.' I pointed to the chair by the fire. 'You look cold.'

'I'm ruddy freezing. I never thought it'd be such a long way to come. And I fell down a hill into the dirt.' She turned round to show me that her coat was plastered with mud. 'I thought I'd broke both me legs at first.'

'Take your coat off and we'll dry it by the fire.'

I saw that she was remarkably pretty, in her late teens perhaps. Her features were good with large eyes, the lids smudged with blue eye-shadow, her mouth slicked with orange lipstick. Her hair was curly and blonde with an inch of dark roots showing and her clothes were of the kind described in the high street as glamorous, a cheap imitation fur collar on a gaudy coat and shoes of scuffed patent leather, painfully pointed. Beneath the coat a short black dress revealed a childish flat-chested figure.

'You'll think it's a cheek me coming here but I'm that

upset . . . ' She put a hand with bitten fingernails up to her mouth.

'Well, why are you here?' I asked, smiling.

'I heard from Auntie Rhoda how he was seeing you a lot and that, and I got scared. Auntie Rhoda don't know — no one knows and I'm that bothered. I know I shouldn't've let him — ' She looked desperately about her and began to chew her thumbnail.

Despite the clumsy attempts to appear sophisticated there was an innocent wholesomeness about her that was charming. By now I felt I had some inkling of why she had come to see me. I tried to put her at her ease. 'My name's Freddie. What's yours?'

'It's Corinne. Isn't Freddie a boy's name?'

'It's short for Elfrida.'

'That's nice. Very posh.'

She continued to such her fingers and gaze at me with saucer eyes. We didn't seem to be getting anywhere. 'Would you like a glass of wine?' I asked.

'No, thanks. I don't like it. I always have a Babycham at the pub. It's nice and sweet. I reely like it but Guy says it's muck.'

'So you've come to talk to me about Guy?'

Corinne looked miserable. 'I thought you'd be different. I reely did or I wouldn't've come. Auntie didn't tell me you was posh. I thought if you lived in a little cottage you might be someone I could reely talk to. I could make you see what a spot I'm in. But . . . ' her mouth trembled '. . . I've been and made *such* a fool of meself!'

She burst into tears, hiding her face in her hands, her preposterous shoes pointing inwards like sharks engaging in battle. I found a clean paper handkerchief in the pocket of my jeans and went over to sit on the arm of her chair.

'Cheer up now, there's good girl. You *can* talk to me. Please don't cry. He isn't worth it.'

Corinne looked up at me with wet eyes. 'Don't you love him, then? Oh, you're just saying that! Course he's going to marry you and his dad'll think it's all right. I know his folk wouldn't like me. Auntie says they're ever so swell and have dinner with candles every night.' This vision of aristocratic life made her sob. I put my arm round her shoulders and waited. 'Guy said his dad don't matter nothink but I've read a lot of them books about people being cut out of wills and that.'

'You mean he's asked you to marry him?' I was amazed that even Guy would be so unprincipled.

'See me ring.' Even in the depths of her despair a note of triumph came into Corinne's voice as she showed me her hand decorated with something that I could see even by gaslight was a crude imitation of rubies and diamonds. This cruel deception made me feel terribly angry.

'Now, Corinne, I'm going to make you a cup of tea and I want you to stop crying. Come and help me in the kitchen. Do you like sponge fingers?'

The distraction of setting out the cups on the tray and putting biscuits on a plate restored Corinne a little.

'It's ever so nice here, isn't it? I mean, funny old things but they're reely sweet. Look at this old stove. Well, I never!'

We took our tea back to the fire and by the time Corinne had drunk hers and eaten all the biscuits, she had stopped crying.

'I do want you to believe that I'd already decided to stop seeing Guy,' I said. 'It's completely over, I promise you.'

Corinne sighed. 'You've been ever so kind and I know it was sauce to come. But the thing is — supposing you can't help yourself? I couldn't, though I said to meself over and over again no good would come of it. He says I make him so happy — I mean, a girl like me with a job on the check-out at Burden's! The first time I saw him he was horse-riding and I thought he looked just like King Arthur. We did him at school and there was a lovely picture of him with golden hair and that. I couldn't believe it when he stopped and spoke to me. I was staying with Auntie and I was ever so bored, having to weed her old garden, and he looked over the hedge — '

'Who is your aunt?' I interrupted.

'Auntie Rhoda. Mrs Creech that runs the post office. I stay with her sometimes when me dad goes away. Mum pushed off years ago. Auntie Rhoda gave me a right telling-off for talking to Guy. Mr Gildry, *she* calls him. She said I wasn't to go flirting with the likes of him. He was bad as bad could be and he'd only get me into trouble.' Corinne sniffed. 'I didn't make eyes at him, whatever she says. I had to tell him what the time was as he'd spoken politely. And then I told him who I was and where I lived because he asked me in such a gentleman-like way.'

'Where do you live?'

'Bexford. Forty-four Platt's Place. It's a terraced house, not very nice though I try to keep it tidy. Dad works nights so I'm always there on me own.'

I could imagine Guy's glee at this artless pouring forth of information. So he had been running us in tandem.

'Oh dear, Corinne. Of course, he's a very attractive man, but quite the wrong sort of person to fall in love with. He's utterly selfish and a liar. And probably incapable of being faithful to one woman.'

'That's what Auntie said. She said I were lucky I hadn't had nothing to do with Mr Gildry 'cause he'd got another woman in tow already though he'd only just broken with the girl in London he was engaged to. There isn't anything Auntie don't know about what people get up to. Except she didn't know I *had* been seeing him. I wanted to cry like anythink but I said,

'Ooh, do tell me, isn't he naughty?' so she told me about you, how you'd only just moved down here and lived in a broken-down cottage and worked up the mill but give yourself airs as though you was a duke's daughter. Oh, don't mind *her*.' I must have looked indignant for Corinne broke off her narrative to reassure me. 'She never has anythink good to say about anybody. I said I didn't know there was any old cottages without people living in them and she said, 'Oh, yes, there's one in the middle of the wood down by the river.' I got a crippled boy to show me. I had to give him fifty p.' Corinne looked about her with a considering air. 'I don't know that I'd call it broken-down exackerly. More like quaint.'

'Thank you. Doesn't the fact that he's been seeing me much of the time he's been going out with you put you off him just a little bit?'

'I know it ought to, but it just makes me sad. I'll never meet another man like him, so handsome and clever and funny. When he teases me he can have me in stitches. You know, I like that almost best about him. It's ever so cosy laughing with someone, ent it? You feel you reely know them.'

'But you don't know Guy. Nor do I. He only wants to get his own way and he doesn't care a bit about either of us.' Corinne looked unconvinced. It was disheartening to see so much unhappiness ahead. 'It isn't any of my business but if you stopped seeing him for a while you'd get a bit of distance on the thing and then probably you'd realise that he isn't worth loving.'

'It's too late for that now.' Corinne looked frightened. 'I'm expecting.'

'Oh no!' The dismay in my voice made Chloë sit up and look at me enquiringly. 'You poor child!'

'Oh well, worse things happen at sea, so they tell us.' Corinne tried to smile jauntily but her face screwed into an expression of pain and she broke down again. 'I'm sorry,' she wept, 'but there isn't anyone to help me. You're the only person I've told. Me dad'll kill me. He'll kick me out, most like, and Auntie Rhoda'll give me a thrashing. She's got a reely nasty temper.'

'Are you quite sure? That you're pregnant, I mean.'

Corinne nodded into the handkerchief. 'I went to the doctor's because I didn't feel well. I was as sick as anythink every morning. And me monthly visitor stopped. I never thought it could be a baby. I hadn't never let anyone go all the way before. Guy said it would be all right.'

'Have you told him?'

'I meant to tell him but I were afraid. He were so sweet and lovey-dovey. I don't want him to be angry with me.'

'How old are you, Corinne?'

'I'll be seventeen next month.'

I felt so angry that if Guy had walked in I could easily have hit him with the poker. It was as well, perhaps, that he didn't. More usefully, I had to find some way to help Corinne. 'Are you staying with your aunt?'

'I said I were going for a walk. I better be going back or she'll think I'm up to somethink. She's got a nasty suspicious mind.'

What a pity, I thought, it hadn't been suspicious enough. But common sense told me that short of locking Corinne up it would have been impossible to keep her from Guy's bed. He was a candle-flame to moths and I was fortunate to have escaped a singeing.

'I'll walk back with you. It must be quite dark now.'

'Ooh, would you? I didn't like that little plank bridge. I felt ever so wobbly. The country's reely spooky, ent it?'

With the aid of the torch we negotiated the difficult places. Corinne continually lost her balance, turned her ankles, tripped on stones, and had to be hauled out of ditches. The light was on in Mrs Creech's sitting room and the curtains left open. Mrs Creech sat entranced before the television screen as some imaginary drama was played out, unaware of the real emergency in her niece's life. As we watched she dug into a box of chocolates and popped one into her mouth.

'The mean bitch!' said Corinne 'I bought her those chocolates and she said she was going to put them away for a special occasion.'

'Come and see me tomorrow and we'll talk about what's the best thing to do.' I helped her out of the coat I had lent her.

Corinne's voice came through the darkness with a throb of emotion. 'You've been ever so kind. I'm reely sorry to spoil things with you and him.'

It was obvious she didn't believe that I had already decided to end the affair. Chloë and I walked back slowly. The rain had stopped and the air was redolent of wet earth and leaves. I was looking forward to some of Bar's fennel cake and the next chapter of *Wessex Tales* by Thomas Hardy. I was enjoying the correspondence between fiction and reality. Just as I was approaching the plank bridge I heard a voice calling my name.

'Freddie? Freddie! Where are you, sweet of sweets, duck of ducks?' It was Guy.

As the beam of a torch swung round in my direction I drew back behind a tree. I didn't want to see him. Not only was it necessary to explain that whatever there had been between us — in view of what I now knew about those visits to Bexford it could hardly be called a love affair — was over but I needed time to think about how to tackle him on the subject of Corinne. The first four notes of Beethoven's Fifth Symphony sounded sweetly in my ear.

'Lemmy?' The bush next to my tree rustled energetically. 'You gave me a fright,' I whispered.

'Are you hiding from him? Is he dangerous?'

'No, it isn't that. Just that I'm tired and I don't want to talk to him.'

'He gave Lemmy a ten shilling note. It's beautiful. Lemmy uses it to keep his place in books.'

'Ssh!'

Lemmy and I crouched in silence for another minute or two until I heard Guy come swiftly along the path. His footsteps sounded loud on the plank bridge, then he went rapidly out of earshot. I stepped out from behind the tree. 'All clear.'

Lemmy rose from the bush. His body looked bluish white in the darkness. He turned his face up to the sky and the soft sheen of starlight picked out the bones of his brow and cheeks. I wondered where I had seen a face like it quite recently. 'Go home. Lemmy will guard you. Lemmy will whistle if he comes back.'

He had gone, bounding like a hare from shadow to shadow, his bare buttocks silvered by the moon as it sailed from behind the clouds.

★ ★ ★

A letter from Viola was lying on the table. I threw a log on the fire and settle down to read.

Dearest Freddie, Florence beautiful, work satisfactory, weather perfect, paintings translunary. Giles sends love. Now, about you. Pitiless of Fate that you should ring when Alex was there. I said I didn't know where you were. I could tell he didn't believe me. His eyes got sort of narrow and threatening and he started to breathe very hard. I was really frightened. He kept questioning me and I went on denying I knew any-thing and all the time he looked blacker and blacker. Then he glared at poor Mouser in a way that made me extremely nervous. He's next-door's cat but he's sort of adopted me because I give him nicer things to eat. He's really beautiful, ginger with dark chestnut markings and a very fat round face. If Alex had tried to torture him I'm afraid I would have told him at once where you were. It's lucky no one has ever tried to recruit me for the KGB, isn't it? Even the threat of cutting a worm in half would make me confess all. Fortunately for Mouser and me, Giles came back early and he and Alex had a whisky together and talked about the new exhibition at the Tate. After Alex had gone, I told Giles what I suspected Alex was about to do. Giles didn't take me seriously at all. In fact he laughed so much I got quite cross, which is rare for me. Then he apologised and was perfectly sweet except that every time he looked at me I could see he was apoplectic with trying to suppress laughter. Should I be marrying a man who sees me as a figure of fun? Anyway we left to come here the next day and so far I haven't seen anyone who looks as though they might be following me. But, Freddie, I think you did absolutely the right thing not marrying Alex. One minute he was being charming and urbane and the next he seemed to have blood-shot eyes and long pointed canines. Then when Giles came in he was back in a flash to being chummy. Do you think he's the tiniest bit mad? After all it's all over London that he's going to marry Zara Drax-Eedes. Actually, I rest my case as Zara is the antithesis of you and hair-raisingly tough and only someone seriously deranged would risk looking lovingly into her eyes for fear of being turned to stone. Giles says we're already late for lunch so will finish here. So glad you like the cottage, of course it's yours for as long as you like. As soon as we get back to England I'll come and see you. Fondest love, Viola

Was Alex mad or simply determined to have his own way, I wondered, as I watched the sparks from the burning logs zigzag their way up the huge chimney. My own behaviour was as irrational as anyone's. I had skulked in the chilly darkness, cowering behind a tree rather than face Guy, and not many weeks before I had lurked by the dustbins in an alleyway, hiding from Alex. Were these the actions of a sane person?

And, much more significantly, had I not fled from everyone and everything I knew rather than face the consequences of my actions? At the time I had been preoccupied by the idea of hurting Alex. That guilt had been exorcised, more or less, by seeing him with Zara. I rejoiced that his heart was not broken. But what disturbed me now was that I saw clearly that I was a habitual escapee. I might make excuses to myself that I needed time for reflection but the blunt truth was that I would do anything to avoid confrontation. I had no confidence in my ability to withstand entreaty. I lacked the courage of my own convictions. I was afraid of other people's anger.

I got up and walked about the room for a while, summoning arguments to soften the severity of this judgement on myself but I had to admit it. I was a coward. I tried to remember occasions when I had stood up for myself and given no quarter. After leaving art school I had taken my own path to independence and resisted the experimental epicureanism of the crowd. But this had been in reaction to Fay's dominance rather than because I saw the inherent wisdom of such a course. It seemed to me now as though my entire life, from the age of eight, had been dictated by her — in the early days by helpless acquiescence to her will and in adulthood by a violent rejection of her influence. I realised with an increase of shame that I was still enslaved, not by Fay herself but by my hatred of her. And what was she, after all, but a shallow, snobbish, silly woman? I had given her powers she did not, could not, possess.

I looked still more closely at my own behaviour and the realisations came thick and fast. I hated Fay because

I blamed her for my mother's death and my father's desertion. But she had been responsible for neither. They had made their own unhappiness. As I thought of my parents and their failure to guard me and how much, despite this, I still loved them, tears ran down my cheeks. It is truly said that we cannot begin to grow up until we have forgiven our parents.

I went upstairs and took my suitcase from the wardrobe. From the pocket inside the lid I drew out Evangeline's leg. It was minus most of its stuffing now and the charred end had worn away to fragile strands of hessian. Even the shoe was rubbed thin from years of caressing and kissing. I took it downstairs and put it on the fire. It glowed brightly as it burned, crumpled to black cinders then fell to ashes.

31

I left my job at the mill feeling regret and relief, the latter emotion predominating. I loved the old building and I enjoyed the blessing of long, dreamless sleep that is the reward for physical labour, but I was glad to part company with the rats. Also I was itching to begin painting. Dusty was philosophical about the impending alteration in his way of life. 'New maister, new bondage,' he said several times, with a shake of his head, but I thought there was a gleam in his eye.

George was exultant. 'I hate the mill. I don't never want to hear the wheels a-grinding again. I only wishes we could leave the house an' all and go and live in Tarchester. I hate the village and all the folk in it. Well,' he modified this blanket appraisal, 'I don't hate you and Miss Yardley. And Miss Watkins ent so bad — though madder'n a pig up a tree. Is it true she runs around the woods wi' no clothes on?'

'You shouldn't listen to gossip. Surely you don't hate Mr Gilderoy? He pays for your coaching, after all.'

'No. I suppose I don't, though he do give you the feeling he'd make a fool of you if he could.' George's brow darkened and he clenched his fist. 'But I don't let him.'

I had another go at Dusty about taking George to see Edward. He was intransigent. 'We was told when he were born there weren't nothing the doctors could do. I reckon God sent 'un as a punishment for his mother's sin.'

'Oh, what rubbish! Anyway, if God were so unjust He deserves to be outwitted. Dr Gilchrist wants George to see a specialist in London.'

Dusty looked as aghast as if I'd suggested sending

George to the moon. 'Ye's outa yer senses, girl, if ye think I can afford to send the boy all that way. Why jus' the fares 'ould be more'n three months' wages I don't doubt.'

'Oh, Dusty, it's not the time to be thinking of money!'

'That's easy said by them as ha' got plenty. And I should have to go wi' the boy, stands to reason.' Dusty drew his mealy brows together. 'I'm all the kin he's got, though some seems to think they've got a perrogertive over the lad.'

'If I can raise the money from somewhere, will you take him?'

'It needs thinking about.' Dusty looked cunning. 'I'm not sure as I can allow meself to be an object o' charity. A man's got his pride. What canna be cured must be endured.'

'You're just a silly obstinate old man!' I couldn't repress my anger. 'It isn't *you* who's doing the enduring.'

'Ye can call me names but he's my grandson and I've got the rights to him. I've been wondering now about letting him go to that fine grammar school Miss Yardley's always on about. Happen it'll teach him to be ashamed of his granfer. His mother had schooling and what did it do for un? Led her into sinful ways till she drownded herself and broke her old faither's heart.' I realised that Dusty was warming to the theme of himself as victim. I stifled my annoyance and ate my sandwich in silence, apart from Dusty gobbling sauerkraut. He was already on the third tin.

★   ★   ★

I would have asked Guy to make Dusty see reason about George but for the fact that Guy was no longer speaking to me. Corinne had come to Drop Cottage as instructed that Sunday afternoon. I had tried to

382

persuade her that she must tell Guy about the baby but she was much too afraid of his anger.

'What do you imagine will happen when he notices that you're expecting a baby? You'll *have* to tell him sooner or later.' Corinne said she'd rather it was later. She really was a pretty girl and very sweet but extraordinarily dim. It was obviously not a situation that would improve with keeping and as it happened Fate played into my hands, for the next minute Guy himself came strolling into the cottage, just as Corinne was mopping up another burst of tears.

'What the hell — ?' Guy looked furiously at me and then at her. 'What are *you* doing here?'

Poor Corinne. She looked terrified and I didn't blame her for his eyes had lost their usual light of mockery and he looked quite murderous. She clutched my arm and mewed like a kitten. I decided to give Guy a chance to redeem himself. 'I'll put the kettle on and you two can have a talk. Let go, Corinne.' She was holding tightly to my jersey. 'There's nothing to be frightened of. He won't bite.' I hoped this was true. He had bared his teeth in a smile that was savage.

'I know this looks bad, Freddie.' Guy tried to detain me. 'I don't know what the little minx has been saying but you shouldn't believe a word of it. She's got some sort of crush on me and you know how it is.'

I walked away into the kitchen and spent a long time making tea. Though I had closed the door I could hear raised voices. When I heard a howl of misery from Corinne it required all the resolve of which I was capable not to rush in and defend her. I occupied myself by making cheese and tomato sandwiches for the children's tea later on. What does not kill you makes you stronger, I reminded myself. I think it was Nietzsche who said that, and by and large I had found it to be true. Corinne was learning valuable lessons about human nature but I felt wretched on her behalf. When the voices ceased I emerged from the kitchen.

'Where is she?' I put down the tray.

Guy looked up from the book he was flipping through. 'She's gone. What about coming on the river with me? It's a perfect day for a row. Among other things.' He smiled at me, his eyes appealing.

'But what have you arranged with her? What are you going to do about the baby?'

Guy's smile snapped off. 'God, I was a fool to have anything to do with her. That little tart's been fornicating with the entire male population of Bexford for all I know. It's none of my business. Nor, my dear Freddie, is it yours.'

'She's hardly more than a child. She has no one to look after her but that hateful Mrs Creech. She says you're the only man she's slept with.'

'She's a liar.'

'Oh, Guy! That from you!'

'All right. Don't let's quarrel about it.' He came over and put his arms round me. 'I don't care very much either way. I don't admit that the child's mine but I'll pay for an abortion, if that'll make you happy.'

I pulled away. 'It won't. I want you to look after her, be kind to her, find out what *she* wants to do about the baby. Why can't you be honest about something for once in your life? It isn't just the baby, it's the fact that you think everything's a game, that you can manipulate people to get what you want. You don't care about the truth.'

'You, I suppose, have a direct line to the fount of moral rectitude.'

'I think we have to believe there *is* a code we ought to live by.'

Guy stood with his hands in his pockets, his handsome face subdued in thought. 'You're right,' he said at last. 'Absolutely right. It's time I faced up to my responsibilities. I've been lazy and selfish. If you'll help me I'll try to do better.' He looked at me, his face solemn, his demeanour dejected. He took hold of my hands. 'I need you, Freddie, if I'm to reform. Give me another chance.' He allowed a boyish, repentant smile to play about his lips. It was tremendously attractive.

'You must think I'm a complete fool.'

Guy let go of my hands. 'Christ! She might have the brain of a mongoose but at least Corinne didn't bore on about ethics and principles.' He threw back his head and laughed. 'Of course, she wouldn't have a clue what they were. She was a lovely little fuck, very keen, desperate to please. I think I'll take her back.'

'Leave her alone! You've done enough harm.'

Guy raised his hand but when I didn't flinch he dropped it to his side and walked away. He slammed the front door. A chunk of plaster dropped on to the tray.

I sat down and nibbled absent-mindedly at a jam ring, though I don't like them very much. My hand was steady and outwardly I was calm. I had not believed that Guy would hit me. He was not the passionate type who forgets himself in rage. I had resisted him and ended our liaison, and I didn't regret it at all. I wondered why I didn't feel more triumphant. Strange how hurtful it was to be accused of sanctimony.

I remembered what he had once said about the fashionable code of liberalism. In the sixties, when the youth of Europe had discovered that the old rules and restrictions were nothing more than bluff, we had embraced the teaching of any old crackpot in robes, provided it sounded exotic enough. Our new gods were anarchy, spontaneity, experiment and tolerance. It had come to seem unattractively censorious to take up any kind of ethical position. I was as subject to *Zeitgeist* as anyone. A timid knock at the door was a welcome distraction.

'I hope I'm not the person from Porlock?' Swithin came in, manoeuvring around the furniture with his

385

peculiar loose-limbed stride, like a long-legged bird stepping through marshes. 'You look pensive. I don't want to frighten away the muse.'

'I'm very glad to see you. Have some tea. I was wondering exactly what was meant by the command 'Judge not lest ye be judged.''

Swithin's eyes, behind the thick-lensed spectacles, lit up at the prospect of a little theological argument. 'Perhaps more accurately it should have been translated 'Condemn not lest ye be condemned.' It can't mean judgement in the sense of deciding whether something is right or wrong. Personally I've always thought one ought to be willing to submit to judgement, even to welcome it. One hopes for mercy, naturally, but I don't see the value in washing around in a sea of moral neutrality.'

'Milk? And sugar?'

'Both, please. Oh, I say! Jam rings!'

I offered the plate. 'Have you got over your cold?'

'My flu, you mean? Yes, but I'm being careful. Early bedtimes and a nightcap of Bovril. Beryl's moved into the spare bedroom so I can have the window closed at night. It's wonderful to wake up without a sore chest. She's knitting me a bed-jacket.'

'Really?' I could not quite keep the surprise out of my voice at the idea of Beryl performing such an act of kindness.

'She's a good woman, you know. Devoted to duty. That doesn't always make for comfort, of course. When she saw how much better my chest was after sleeping with the window closed she apologised with real grace. Every stitch of that bed-jacket is crafted with guilt. The Dean believed that it was unhealthy to have one's bedroom windows shut, *ergo* Beryl believes it. She's not accustomed to waver in her ideas.'

'How different we are. I'm practically incapable of

386

making up my mind. There always seems to be another point of view.'

'"The native hue of resolution sicklied over with the pale cast of thought", eh? The Bard always has the sentiment exactly. But I think it's a good sign. It means you're not afraid to let doubt creep in. Often, people's opinions are bulwarks against the waves. They daren't acknowledge that existence is chaos.'

'Is it?'

'I fear it may be.' We looked solemnly at one another, encircled by the gloom of uncertainty, what Browning called 'the grand Perhaps'. 'It does me good to be able to say it. Perversely, as soon as I admit my doubts something inside leaps up to affirm my faith. I feel for a brief glorious moment a resurgence of the conviction I had as a young priest. You're very kind to listen to me without being shocked. I can't discuss it with my parishioners. Naturally they look to me to give the lead. The Bishop is bored by such things. He thinks I just ought to get on with it and not bother him.'

'What does Beryl say?'

'She can't stomach the smallest possibility that the Almighty might not be up there, totting up the scores. Beryl, you see, is hoping for a miracle.' I offered him another jam ring and waited for him to go on. Swithin looked at me reflectively as he bit into the red circle. 'She's always wanted a child. The desire has been the driving force of her life. When we were first married it was a joyful expectation. I was certainly taken aback by her . . . enthusiasm in the, er, bedroom. You don't mind my mentioning such things?' I shook my head. 'I don't know what I expected. We were both completely inexperienced. I was vain enough to mistake it for affection. But as time went on and no child came the joy went out of it, rather. But we plugged away.' He goggled a little at the memory and folded his lower lip over his upper set of teeth. Poor Swithin. My mind wandered involuntarily to picture that dreary bedroom and laborious sexual acts.

'I hadn't thought of her as someone disappointed. That's very sad.'

'It has made her uncordial, I'm afraid. Her despair is a sort of crucible in which she distils peace and comfort, friendship and cheerfulness until they become sour duty.' Swithin sighed. 'But compassion is close to — one might say inseparable from — love. I believe it's what many married couples come to feel for each other in old age. A protective, sorrowful, cherishing kind of love. I've seen Beryl's frantic hope crushed month by month, year by year and it has made me love her the more.'

'But surely — isn't Beryl — I *had* thought she was — perhaps her age?'

'Oh, she's fifty-two. That's why I say she's hoping for a miracle.' Swithin gave a sad little laugh. 'If there were any efficacy in prayer she ought by now to be the mother of triplets.'

'Oh, Swithin, I'm so sorry. Poor Beryl!'

'As you say.' He looked glumly at the empty plate that had held the jam rings. Then his expression brightened. 'I say, isn't that — no, it can't be! Do you know, for a moment I thought it was Macavity?'

He stared at the cat as he strolled downstairs and made for the table, his long whiskers magnificent, his fat white paws immaculate from a good wash, his eyes bright after a lengthy snooze. Sunlight fell on the glossy black fur encompassing his well-upholstered frame.

'I'm afraid it is. I do feel guilty, Swithin. I ought to have let you know he was here. The truth is, I've loved having him and I dreaded you taking him back.' This was part of the truth anyway. I did not like to accuse Beryl of starving him.

'Well, hello, old boy!' Swithin made clicking noises with his fingers. Macavity gave him a cool look and turned his gaze on me, winking his golden eyes hypnotically.

'Oh, all right. Just a little.'

I poured some milk into a saucer. A rolling purr emanated from Macavity's broad chest and his gleaming ears twitched as he drank.

'I'd quite forgotten what a handsome creature you are.' Swithin looked at him consideringly. 'Haven't you put on a little weight?'

★　★　★

A week later I was up early, packing a bag with paints and brushes, my head full of ideas, my stomach a little queasy, which had nothing to do with Bar's pickled broom buds of which I had eaten a great quantity the night before to disguise from her that the children were refusing to touch them. I was in that state of anticipated creativity that is a combination of burning ambition and a fearful reluctance to make a start.

There had been some difficulty in deciding where Lady Frisk should sit for her portrait. My cottage did not admit enough light, Lady Frisk's house was not on a bus route and at too great a distance for me to walk. Prim had offered her own house but Lady Frisk had objected on the grounds that she had once been bitten by a spaniel. Prim had confessed to feelings of relief and I didn't blame her. The other members of the hospital committee had apparently made feeble excuses — friends coming to stay, extensive building works, invalid relatives requiring absolute quiet — until in the end Lady Frisk herself suggested Gilderoy Hall. She was certain Ambrose could have no objection to such a proposal, the whole enterprise taking up so little room and painting being a silent occupation. What Ambrose really thought about it I was not privileged to know and a room was put at our disposal. Lady Frisk said she

389

could manage between ten o'clock and two o'clock for the next three weeks, excluding Saturdays and Sundays. She thought that ought to be enough for even the most dilatory painter.

I was a little alarmed at the prospect of being in Guy's domain now that we were no longer on speaking terms but the house was large enough for us to avoid seeing each other and I fell in meekly with Lady Frisk's suggestion that I should come and go by the back door, as this would be less disruptive for the family. I was amused to see that she herself arrived at the front door in her Rolls Royce, which she instructed her driver to park at the foot of the steps. Being at the top of a steep hill, the turning circle was narrow and the inhabitants of the house were obliged to park on precipitous slopes or in the stableyard that was half-way down the hill.

The morning room had been chosen for us for the good reason that it got plenty of light during the hours of our occupancy. It had evidently not been used for years and its furnishings, once pretty, were now tired-looking and dusty.

'Well!' Lady Frisk swiped at a bumble bee that had the nerve to fly near her in a desperate attempt to find a way out. 'This is poky, I must say. One would have thought the drawing room — perhaps they were worried about paint getting on the furniture. You must be very careful, Frederica, about drips. I hope I am not expected to sit on this.' She tapped with her stick on the seat of the sofa. A puff of dust made her cough. 'It's very bad for my chest. I shall speak to the maid.' She looked vaguely about, saw the bell-pull and gave it a jerk. It came away in her hand. 'Absolutely rotten! I might have injured myself. Ambrose cannot know the state of things. Men are so helpless without a woman. I wonder he did not come to the door to welcome me but probably his gout is too bad. He complained of an acute attack when I telephoned him to propose Gilderoy Hall as our meeting-place. I told him I should bring some veal jelly when I came. There is nothing like it for gout. My cook used to make it for Sir Oswald. He swore it did him more good than anything. That and complete solitude. I told Ambrose I would do what I could to avoid disturbing the household more than absolutely necessary. I shall require only a light lunch, nothing fatty and certainly no cheese or eggs and nothing more than a piece of plain Madeira cake with my coffee at eleven. I am not one who indulges herself, whatever others may do.' She looked at me severely.

I concentrated on positioning my easel so that the largest window, which faced east, was directly behind me. Prim had been angelic, driving me all the way to Salisbury to buy the necessary materials for the venture as I had brought only paints, brushes and a sketchbook with me from London. She had cooked supper for the children while I stretched, folded and hammered nails into the canvas before priming it. She had taken it up to Gilderoy Hall the night before as it was too large to carry. I set it up to my satisfaction and let out the poor bumble bee that Lady Frisk was attempting to poke out of the air with the ferrule of her stick.

'What is the name of the housekeeper? I forget.'

'Miss Glim.'

Lady Frisk opened the door and called loudly. 'Glim! Glim! I want you! How badly run this house is! Glim! At once, if you please!'

I heard her voice grow fainter as she pursued Miss Glim through the hall and out of earshot. I was in the process of squeezing delicious worms of white, black and charcoal on to my palette for blocking in the head when I heard a quick step outside the door. I composed myself to meet Guy with insouciance but it was Vere.

'Hello. I didn't know you were here.' He frowned. He was looking much better, less tired and his hair had grown to an attractive length. 'What on earth's going on? Who's that woman screaming the house down?'

'It's Lady Frisk. I'm going to paint her portrait for the hospital board. I'm awfully sorry to inflict us on you. It was her idea.'

'I'd forgotten you painted. Is this room all right for you?' He looked around. 'It seems rather neglected.'

'It's perfect. Wonderful light. Just give me a hand with this wing chair, will you? It's rather rickety but the most lovely faded plum colour.'

'It looks early to me, possibly Queen Anne. I ought to get it repaired. But there's so much else to be done. I've got to make the land pay before I can get round to details.'

'How's it going?'

Vere pulled down the corners of his mouth. 'Too soon to say, really. But at least I can stop money being chucked away with both hands. If we did nothing at all but allowed Nature to take her course we'd be better off. We've been running the traditional mix of fifty cows and four or five hundred sheep on the Spokebender hills. I'm going to sell the livestock and let the land. Immediately we'll be making a profit, albeit a small one, for the first time in ten years. The woods have been left to run wild but I don't want to take them out. It would ruin the beauty of the place. I've already got a couple of nature conservancy groups interested. We can get grants, you see, and by coppicing the woods on a ten-year cycle enough light'll be let in to encourage plant growth of the kind that caterpillars feed on. Several rare types of butterfly are in decline in this area, particularly the pearl-bordered fritillary and the wood white.' Vere's face was lit by enthusiasm. I was astonished that such a masculine man should be interested in such things as butterflies. 'I shall support the conservation project with market gardening. The soil in the valley's perfect, moisture retentive and rich. I thought I'd try unusual crops for the London restaurant market — scorzonera, seakale, Swiss chard, cardoons, asparagus, that sort of thing. Did you know there were more than two hundred varieties of potato? And higher up I'm going to plant fruit trees — unusual varieties of apples, pears and cherries.'

'I'm amazed. How did you think of all this?'

'Oh, I met a Frenchman in Rio a few months ago. He's going to open a restaurant in London. Apparently there's going to be a food revolution in England. I've already spoken to him since I've been back and we've sketched out a plan. I hope he's right. Anyway, it requires a minimal investment of capital.'

I felt very happy to think of my beautiful valley — well, it was hardly mine as I didn't own so much as an inch — but the Gilderoys' beautiful valley teeming with wildlife and succulent vegetables. 'What a good thing you came home.'

I noticed a ruddiness begin to suffuse Vere's face beneath the tan. 'I'm afraid that isn't the general view.'

'Is it you, Miss, that's been hollering fit to wake the dead?'

Miss Glim's face was redder than Vere's, with rage.

'Oh, no, I'm afraid Lady Frisk — '

'There you are, Glim!' Lady Frisk came in. 'My throat is quite sore from calling you. You had better not dust in here until after today's session. I fear for my asthma. But you can tidy those magazines,' she pointed with her stick to an untidy heap of papers on the desk, 'and see that the bell is mended, if you please. I am not accustomed to have to comb the house for servants. I shall require a glass of water immediately. Refreshments at eleven. Mr Gilderoy may not have remembered — the sherry medium-dry, the cake Madeira. One slice only. A light regimen is what I always adhere to. Oh, and there is the veal jelly for Mr Gilderoy.' Lady Frisk pointed to a carrier-bag on the table. 'You must put it at once at the top of the

393

refrigerator. It must be kept free from ice crystals but sufficiently cold to prevent it from melting. Now, don't stand about. Run along with you!'

Miss Glim was scarlet and white in patches. She showed no sign of running but picked up the jelly with slow deliberation. 'Will I do all this before I make the Madeira cake or after? Perhaps Madam would like to draw up a list of my tasks for the morning.'

'Well, if you really can't manage to organise yourself I suppose I . . . ' Lady Frisk paused and peered suspiciously at Miss Glim. 'If I thought that there was impertinence in that remark, Glim, I should be very much annoyed.' Miss Glim tossed her head and walked with dignity from the room. 'I'm afraid the war has a great deal to answer for,' said Lady Frisk elliptically, her expression brooding as she took off her tweed cape and a trilby hat of the same stuff, ornamented with pheasant tail feathers. 'Now, Vere, I've been meaning to speak to you about the hospital board.' She turned to where he had been standing but Vere had gone. 'Well! Really!'

'Do let's make a start, Lady Frisk, while the light's good.' I indicated the wing chair.

'It's got a very steep rake. I've no doubt it will ruin my back. But one must be ready to put oneself out for others. You will find, Frederica, as you get older, that life is not all fun and frolic.'

'I expect it isn't,' I said, moving the easel fractionally so it was to the right of the line between the chair and the far window. When I was certain the distances were right I marked the floor with masking tape where the legs of the easel and the chair rested. I went over to push back a shutter that had been left a little open. The west elevation of the house had been built right on the edge of a cliff-like drop and there was a view of twenty or thirty miles of Dorset fields and woods below. As I stared at the collage of hazy greens and browns and blues, I saw a golden globe fly up and out from the window adjacent to mine. As it spun across my vision its shape stretched and elided before it began to hurtle to earth. It was the veal jelly.

32

The portrait proceeded with unusual speed. The weeks of scarcely thinking about painting seemed to have done nothing but good. I found it easier than usual to keep my mind in a state of receptive emptiness — what Keats famously called 'negative capability . . . when a man is capable of being in uncertainties, mysteries, doubts, without any irritable reaching after fact and reason'. Keats held this mental process to be essential to the process of creation. I don't think anyone has come up with a better definition since.

Initially Lady Frisk's face appeared to be almost a caricature. Her high-bridged nose, set between drooping cheeks that had lost their muscle tone, and her slightly beaky upper lip gave her the look of an autocratic tortoise. Age had given her a rich variety of skin tones, pinks, purples, yellows and reds. The expression in her eyes was imperious and unforgiving. It suggested that the world had so far fallen very far short of what she had a right to expect. But, of course, there had to be much more than that if only I could tease it out.

She began the first session in haughty silence with her face set in an attitude of patrician disdain. I wanted her to talk, to reveal herself to me. I asked her about Charlotte. She could not resist the opportunity to give me some much needed instruction and soon forgot about looking superior.

'I have not seen the dear girl for almost three months. Her work is very demanding, naturally. She is hoping for a fellowship in the autumn. I find it quite wonderful that such a pretty girl can be so devoted to long hours of study. Those among us who imagine that a woman's sole purpose is to attract men are destined to find out their mistake when age has reduced their charms to powder and paint!' Her eyes were fierce. 'I flatter myself that I have always set an example of industry. Sir Oswald always said that it was remarkable how I differed from other women he had known in my absolute disregard for feminine frivolity.'

Lady Frisk expatiated on Charlotte's beauty, piety and propriety until I could have kicked the poor girl to the bottom of the hill with the veal jelly. With very little encouragement Lady Frisk went on to narrate the delights of her own girlhood and examples of her sagacity, industry and general superiority were so numerous that she talked without pausing for two hours even through mouthfuls of a very good Madeira cake.

By the end of the first week there was a recognisable face on the canvas. 'You have made my nose a little too long but otherwise you have done quite well,' pronounced its subject. 'I was a first-rate artist myself when young. My water-colours were praised by everyone. No doubt I could have had a fine career but naturally Sir Oswald would not have wanted his wife to be a painter. He did not like women who put themselves forward. You will find that few men do, Frederica. A little modesty is the mark of a gentlewoman.'

★　★　★

'Honestly the woman is a bag of wind,' I complained to Prim, over supper on Friday evening. 'Her only idea of conversation is to brag about her own cleverness and talents or else to laud Charlotte to the skies. What a mistake mothers make when they praise their children. Quite unfairly, it makes them objects of loathing.'

'As far as I know, all Lady Frisk has ever done is to make other people annoyed. She never contributes a

397

thing to the hospital, either money or services. She likes to tell everyone else what to do. And usually she's got it all wrong. Never mind, think of the yummy money. Three hundred pounds. You could almost retire on it.' Prim dug deeply into the remains of the rice pudding. 'This is so bad for my figure but irresistible. I must say your style of cooking has changed. It used to be two lettuce leaves artistically arranged beneath an anchovy fillet and half a tomato. Not that I'm criticising. Both are highly satisfactory in their different ways.'

'It's because of the children. Rice pudding is one of the few things Titch will eat. Tomorrow's Saturday, isn't it? I'm going to see if I can talk to Mrs Roker. I think she's drinking again. Frankie says she hasn't been for her social security money for two weeks.'

'Would you like me to come with you?'

'Yes, please. We'll ask Bar to come and pave the way. That's a very unusual hat.' I was referring to the khaki cap with a large peak she had worn throughout supper. What I really meant was 'why are you wearing it?' It went only too well with the corduroy knee breeches but it could not be said that it suited her *belle-laide* features.

'My father was a captain in the Home Guard. I thought it gave me a little extra authority for ordering people about.'

'Honestly, Prim, what Guy says isn't worth thinking about.'

'Have you stopped thinking about him?'

'Entirely. Well, practically. Certainly I'm not in the least unhappy about him.'

'Do you see much of him when you're up at the Hall?'

'Haven't set eyes on him once. He's avoiding me. He knows I wanted to talk to him about Corinne.'

'He really is much more of a shit even than I thought. What's going to happen to that poor little thing?'

'Well, I was getting so anxious about her that this morning I talked to Vere.'

In fact, I had been waiting for the opportunity to get him alone for several days and when Lady Frisk went to the lavatory I had seized my chance. We saw Vere every morning as he always came to ask if we had everything we needed and to make excuses for the non-appearance of Ambrose. As soon as we were alone I told Vere I needed to talk to him in confidence as soon as possible. Naturally he looked hunted and on the defensive as any man would, but he said he would come and find me the moment Lady Frisk was driven away.

She had been tiresomely slow about going, seeming to sense intrigue in the air. First we had had our usual argument about the length of her nose. At the end of each session I painted out the tip according to her instructions, sometimes so much so that it was in danger of becoming a snout, and first thing next day I painted it in again, hoping she wouldn't notice. There always is, of course, a lack of agreement about the way we see ourselves and the way others see us. It is one of the difficult things about the job. The only trouble was that because I don't like scraping off there was a considerable accretion of paint over the nose area. I should have to claim an intentional three-dimensional effect if we went on this way for much longer.

I became anxious that Vere would give up and go away without seeing me so I said that I absolutely must go. I helped Lady Frisk into her cape and feathered trilby and departed as though for the back door while she made her way to the front. Unfortunately in the hall Lady Frisk encountered Vere who had been prowling there, waiting for her to leave. I slipped into the shadow of the archway beneath the stairs that led to the cellars and Wewelsburg manqué.

'Ah, Vere! *There* you are,' said Lady Frisk in the way she had that suggested she had been kept waiting ages

399

for a purposed rendezvous. 'Please tell Glim a little more salt in the consommé. How is your father? I trust the jelly did him some good.' There was a looking-glass on the wall opposite my hiding place and in it I could see the crown of Lady Frisk's hat and, above it, Vere's face. He looked puzzled but he said nothing. I had noticed before that he was not good at making conversation. He only talked about things that interested him. I thought this trait admirable and regretted I was not strong-minded enough to practise it myself.

'I mentioned you in my letter to Charlotte last week.' Lady Frisk's feathers were bobbing up and down as she spoke. 'I have tried to correct any unfavourable impression she may have formed of your previous mode of living by telling her how swiftly you have taken over the reins and relieved your poor father of care. It is only what one would have expected but these days one can take *nothing* for granted.' Lady Frisk's shoulders heaved expansively. Vere remained silent. He had adopted the polite half-smile he wore when he wasn't listening. 'When Charlotte comes home I shall ask you to dinner. You will be very taken with her, I fancy.' Vere continued to smile. 'Alliances between families who thoroughly know one another are always to be preferred, don't you think?' Goodness, Lady Frisk was practically proposing on Charlotte's behalf! 'Do you remember how you used to let her sit on your big black horse when she was a little girl? I have never forgotten the charming picture you made together, she so fair and you very tall and dark. You were quite taken with her even then,' Lady Frisk gave an artificial laugh on a descending scale, 'though she was scarcely twelve years old and you were already at the varsity. But men must have time to sow their wild oats.' Her voice became arch. 'And you've had plenty.'

'Plenty of what?' Vere looked bewildered.

'Wild oats, my dear Vere.' She laughed indulgently. 'I don't doubt you thoroughly understand the ways of the world and are quite ready to settle down. *You* will not be ensnared by the wiles of those women who are desperate to entrap a man of social standing and property. The modern girl is blatant in throwing herself at a man's head. Naked bosoms, indecently short skirts and *far* too much lipstick. Smoking, drinking, making eyes — I am thankful my own dear Charlotte knows what is becoming.'

'Becoming what?' Vere frowned, then caught sight of me in the mirror, standing in the recess of the arch. I put my finger to my lips and widened my eyes in a pantomime of secrecy. 'Who is making eyes?'

'I was not thinking of any one girl in particular,' Lady Frisk said mendaciously, 'but now you mention it I *have* noticed that Miss Swann does everything she can to attract your attention whenever you are talking to me in the morning room.' In fact, I rarely said a word. It was entertainment enough to see Lady Frisk's carefully aimed shafts flying wide of the mark because of Vere's inattention. 'And *this* after hanging on your brother's arm at your father's birthday celebration for everyone to see. Perhaps it would be kinder to say nothing of the way she positively *flaunted* herself before that young German boy. Poor thing, I hear she is quite penniless. No one knows who her parents are. One should be charitable. I have no criticism to make of her work and I must confess I quite enjoy our little chats. But with regard to men it seems the poor girl is insatiable. I have been told, but of course it may be just a rumour, that she has left a perfectly respectable husband in order to follow her lover who lives somewhere about here. Quite shocking, isn't it?'

'Dreadful! And I hear that there are several infants in the case, heartlessly abandoned.' Vere was concentrating now, smiling down into Lady Frisk's face with an expression of keen enjoyment.

'No! Worse than I thought! And yet I cannot find anything particular in her appearance. So very pale and that hideous red hair. I'm sure you don't admire it.'

'Certainly not! An absolute fright of a girl!' Vere was grinning now.

'Oh, cruel! I dare say some will find her taking enough if they can overlook that tendency to freckle redheads always have. But young men are merciless!' Lady Frisk was purring. 'Her features are not so bad. Had she Charlotte's hair — the most exquisite gold — one might see something in her. Of course, a pleasant manner and a talent for daubing is quite insufficient to tempt *you*, my dear Vere.'

'I should as soon think of admiring a Gorgon!'

'Yes, well, I suppose so.' It was clear that Lady Frisk was unfamiliar with classical mythology. 'Now I must hurry away. I have several women to interview. My cook is leaving. The working classes have an inbred resistance to work. One does one's best but they are incapable of learning by example. Goodbye, dear boy. I shall give your love to Charlotte when next I write.'

★ ★ ★

'Now, do stop laughing and listen,' I said, after Lady Frisk had been driven off. 'I thought any minute she was going to see that you were teasing her.'

'I meant every word.'

'You realise the news that I've left several suckling babes to the care of a grief-stricken husband will be all round the county in a flash?'

'Do you mind?'

'As it happens, I don't. It'll be a pleasant change for them to be able to disapprove of me instead of you.'

'That's exactly what I thought.'

'But let's be serious for a minute.' I started to pack

away my paint and wash my brushes. 'I must talk to you.'

'I hope you aren't going to lecture me.' Vere perched on the edge of the desk. 'For a moment you looked just like Eva Frisk. A smaller nose, of course.'

'Well, it might sound as though I'm lecturing you and I can only apologise. But it really is important.' I began to explain about Corinne.

The smile left his face at once. 'Why are you telling me this?'

'Because Guy refuses to talk to me. He's angry because — oh, never mind why. The point is, that poor girl needs help. I thought, I don't know, that you might be willing to take some responsibility for Guy's child — as he's doing something about yours.' I laughed, embarrassed. 'You know, a fair trade.' I had intended to approach the subject in a light-hearted way but the minute the words were out, I thought they sounded accusing. I saw that Vere was annoyed. I had made a muff of it.

'What are you talking about?'

'Oh dear, I'm sorry. I know it isn't my business but I can't let that poor child — '

Vere interrupted me. 'What do you mean, Guy's doing something about mine?'

'Guy told me that George is your son. It wasn't his fault. I noticed the family resemblance. He made me promise not to tell anyone. Prim's arranged for George to have private coaching. He's very bright — he could win a scholarship. Of course no one ever thought that you might come home. We bullied Guy into paying for it, *in loco parentis.*'

'Very good of him.' Vere's tone was caustic. He looked down and began to fiddle with some pens that lay on the desk. I felt that I was pleading Corinne's case very badly.

'Oh, please, don't be angry! I know I must seem

horribly interfering. But Corinne's only sixteen! She isn't old enough to look after herself and there's no one else to help her.'

'I'm not angry.' Still he didn't look at me.

'I suppose it was tactless of me to mention George. I'm sorry. Of course we all do silly things when we're young. How trite that sounds!'

'Yes.'

I wondered if he was still listening. For some time he rotated a stick of red sealing wax between his fingers. I examined the musculature of his cheek. There was a hollow above the jaw-bone just as there was above Guy's. But Vere's face was squarer and there were deep lines from the corners of his eyes, no doubt from screwing them up against a brilliant foreign light. A large black bird flapped against the window making us both jump. It scrabbled ineffectually for a hold on the glazing bars then flew off. Vere put down the sealing wax and smiled at me briefly, coldly. 'I'll talk to Guy. Perhaps you should give me her address. Don't worry. I'll do what I can.'

I wrote it down for him. 'I'd better go.'

'I'll see you out.'

'You needn't bother.'

But Vere accompanied me to the front door.

'Goodbye.' I smiled at him. 'I'll be here at ten o'clock on Monday. I'm so sorry. It does seem a huge imposition.'

'Yes. Certainly. Goodbye.' He did not return my smile.

When I reached the point where the drive curved and fell precipitously away I looked back. He was still standing in the open doorway. I raised my hand but when he made no response I dropped it, feeling a fool.

33

'I don't see that you made such a bad job of it,' said Prim. 'It isn't easy to tell tales of a brother's villainy, after all.'

'It's pity when we were getting on so well. A few days ago, when he was telling me about his plans for the estate, he was friendly and enthusiastic.'

'I haven't heard anything about them.'

I told her about the nature conservation plans and the butterflies, the fruit trees and the market gardening.

Prim was dismayed. 'I must say I'd hoped that Vere had learned some sense in the last twelve years. But it seems he's the same old dreamer. Butterflies and seakale! I wonder how much scorzonera is eaten *per capita per annum* in the whole of Great Britain. Probably about ten pounds worth at a generous estimate. How on earth does he think he's going to keep a house the size of Gilderoy Hall going on exotic vegetables! It won't even pay the coal bill.'

'I hadn't thought of that. Of course, you're right. Oh dear! What a pity! He talked about it as though it was the realisation of a long-held ambition.' I felt disappointed on Vere's behalf and regretful of the inevitable disillusionment that must follow. 'How boring money is!'

'Boring in itself but I'm not sure having to earn it isn't a very good thing. If I hadn't been left a comfortable income I'd probably have a decent job by now and self-esteem to match.' Prim stirred her cup of coffee slowly, staring into its swirling depths. 'Do you know, Freddie, I've been a bloody idiot. I'm thirty-four and I've absolutely nothing to show for it. I spent my adolescence hopelessly in love with someone who didn't love me and my twenties mourning that love.' She looked at me and her face reddened slightly beneath the peak of her cap. 'It was Vere I was in love with.'

I managed, I hope, a passable imitation of astonishment. 'I think I can see exactly why,' was all I said.

Prim lit a cigar, threw the match end into the air and kicked it with the toe of her shoe. 'Sorry. Untidy habit, that.' She got up to retrieve it. 'I realise now I didn't want to get over him. I almost delighted in the cruelty of Fate. Just as looking after my parents saved me from having to go out into the world and make my own way, I could go on loving Vere and not let someone get close to me. I didn't have to measure up and perhaps be found wanting.' She looked up at me and laughed a little awkwardly. 'That's the trouble with death, isn't it? You can construct any fantasy you like without fear of contradiction.'

I thought at once of my darling mother and how I had been unable to bring myself to see her as she was, fallible and human, because I had thought this would be in conflict, somehow, with the love I felt for her. The badge on Prim's cap glittered in a straying beam of light. She fixed her eyes on me and went on talking: 'Sorry to burden you with the secrets of my bosom. I wanted to say it all to someone because now I understand what I've been doing I don't want to slip back into the old, bad ways.'

'I don't feel burdened. Privileged, rather.'

'I feel closer to you than anyone.' Prim's voice was gruff. 'Now I'm getting sloppy. One can go too far the other way.'

'Not with me you can't. Tell me what's brought all this self-analysis about.'

'Meeting Vere again, of course. It took about thirty seconds to dawn on me that there was never the least chance that he might fall in love with me. And the moment I realised that, I found I wasn't in love with him.'

'Was he different from how you'd remembered him?'

'No. To look at he's hardly changed at all. All the boyishness has gone, naturally — a bigger physique and a sharper bone structure, firmer mouth, that sort of thing. I still think he's Dorset's answer to Cary Grant. And he's the same old Vere in character. But I've changed. I'm no longer a romantic schoolgirl. Now I can see what Vere is and I know I can't offer him any of the things that he wants from a woman. He's as romantic and quixotic as he ever was. He needs some dreamy-eyed, unconventional beauty, ready to catch fire with him. I know myself better now. I could never be that. I'm much too earthbound and pragmatic. He wants subtlety, mystery, ambiguity, passion. I want rock-solid certainty, achievement, progress, security. One of the things that makes you love other people is that they reflect a good idea of yourself. You like the person you are when you're with them. Vere makes me feel hulking and clumsy and slightly ridiculous. We could never skip hand in hand to Paradise.' Hooray for Edward, I thought, watching the smoke from her cigar streaming in the draught. 'So goodbye, old love.' Prim blew a perfect smoke ring into the air and we watched it dissolve into a wisp.

Hello, new love, I said, but only to myself.

★ ★ ★

The next day Prim, Bar and I went to visit Mrs Roker. It was the most perfect May afternoon. Rooks cawed from tree-tops and tiny blue butterflies competed with bees for the nectar from pink campion and yellow archangels. Bar ran about gathering wild chervil and alexanders. She was looking extremely fetching in a kind of cheongsam, made from flowered brocade that

407

might once, I suspected, have been a pair of curtains. It was not the ideal garment for capering about in woods. After a while she rolled her skirt up to her thighs, exposing dimpled knees and extremely dirty bare feet. Prim was in her usual breeches but had exchanged her jersey for an old check shirt. I was wearing my regrettable jeans, not very clean and too big for me, but not quite so roomy as when I had bought them. Finishing up the children's food meant that I was putting on weight.

We were an odd-looking group, and had Vere been the sort of man who noticed these things he would have been struck by this when we met him in the lane. Chloë, who was running beside him, hurled herself on me and barked until all the birds launched themselves into the air in panic. It was excessive, considering that she had spent the night with me at the cottage, but I understood that her faithful canine heart was torn in two.

'What are you doing?' asked Prim.

He had an open book and a notepad in his hand. 'I'm doing a survey of types of tree for the nature conservation grant. They'll come and do one themselves but I want to whet their appetites. I've found several oaks that seem to be hybrids — not quite pedunculate, nor quite sessile.'

'I bet they've crossed with those two Turkey oaks down near the river,' said Bar.

He looked at her for the first time. 'Are you an expert on trees?'

'I know a bit about them,' she replied, with becoming modesty. She certainly looked very pretty with her tumbled bleached hair and her pink cheeks and arms full of white umbels and fresh green leaves. As I knelt to make a fuss of Chloë I was thinking of Prim's description of the sort of girl Vere might love and it occurred to me that Bar was all these things. Certainly she was unconventional. He continued to stare at her in a way that betokened more than usual interest.

'You two don't know each other.' Prim took charge. 'This is Vere Gilderoy. Barbara Watkins.'

'I can tell you where there's a wild service tree,' said Bar. I saw the charming dimple come and go in her cheek.

'Could you show me?'

We walked down the lane in pairs, Prim and me in front, Bar talking non-stop to Vere, Chloë running between us. We did a slight detour to admire the precious tree, which stood in a small clearing, covered in 'blooth' and girded about with white bryony, a hymn to natural beauty.

'Isn't that pretty?' said Prim.

'It's a sign from the Goddess,' said Bar. 'A blessing on our journey. She approves it.'

Vere looked surprised when Bar, her skirts still folded up so that we could see her knickers, began to skip — deosil, naturally — round the tree, chanting, ''O Goddess, who is generous to bless, Grant the crop the blossom begs, Endow us all with fruitfulness, Fill their pods with seeds, our wombs with eggs.''

'Yes, well, I think we'll get on,' said Prim.

It was only a short distance to the path that led down to the Rokers' house. We left Vere examining a group of wych elms.

'Hello, Mrs Roker. It's Miss Watkins,' called Bar, as we approached.

I could hear Titch crying. Ruth came to the door. 'Hello.' She looked at us all with dull eyes. 'Mum ent well.'

'Can we come in, dear?' asked Prim.

'It ent very tidy.' Ruth gave her characteristic shrug. 'I had to get up to Mum a lot in the night. I've been asleep since.'

To say that it was untidy was an understatement.

Clothes and crockery were all over the floor. Titch lay in her cot, weeping, her bedclothes trailing down through the bars. Frankie and Wills were sitting on a broken-down sofa kicking each other in a desultory manner. Frankie ran to throw her arms around me.

'He's such stinky pig! I wish Wills'd drop down a big hole like Joseph and never be let out.'

'Now, children.' Prim frowned, 'you're making too much noise. We've come to see how your mother is. Be good and quiet now.'

I went to pick up Titch. Her face was blotched with tears and there was dried vomit on her chin. She clung tightly to my hair and sobbed into my neck. Prim and Bar followed Ruth into the back room. I walked about the room with Titch, trying to soothe her, while Frankie hung on to my arm. Wills was pulling the stuffing out of the sofa and throwing it into the air.

'Wills, you're making a terrible mess.'

'I'm makin' snow. And it ent *your* house.'

Bar came out. She looked at me with eyes that communicated alarm. 'Could you go and telephone Edward and ask him to come at once? Keep quiet, children. Mummy isn't at all well.'

'I wanna come,' said Frankie.

'All right. We'd better take Titch. Wills, do you want to come with us?'

Wills bent his elbow and hit the fold with his other hand while raising his middle finger.

Frankie and I walked fast, taking it in turns to carry Titch.

'I thought Mum were gettin' better. She don't scream out any more. Yesterday she didn't say nothin' at all. Ent that a good thing?'

'I don't know, darling. We must wait and see what the doctor says.'

'Can we have a picnic today? You said we could when it got summer. Ent this summer?'

'Well, nearly, I suppose. We'd better wait and see.'

'Mum don't like picnics. She says she always gets crumbs down her tits. What's the matter?'

'Nothing. Give me the baby for a bit.'

'I saw you frownin'. Is it 'tits' you don't like? Miss Maybee at school told Janice Wilkins to write a hundred lines when she said it. What're they called, then?'

'Perhaps breasts would sound better.'

Frankie walked along beside me, thinking for a moment, then she said, 'I just saw a nest of baby blue-breasts in that tree.' She looked up at me grinning.

'You're teasing me.' I smiled back at her, but all the time I was praying that nothing would happen to acquaint Frankie with grief at an unduly early age.

We reached the telephone box. I made Frankie sit on the verge outside with Titch.

'Freddie!' said Edward, when he heard my voice. 'To what do I owe this unashush — unaccushtomed pleasure? Here we go gathering mushroomsh in May, mushroomsh in May, mushroomsh in May,' he sang.

'Oh, God, Edward, you're drunk!'

'Merely a little tiddly, my darling. It'sh my afternoon off and who'sh to shay I can't get a little intocculated — inpixilated — shmashed?'

'Edward, Mrs Roker's very ill. You know, the Nissen hut down by the river. Is there another doctor on duty?'

'Yesh. It'sh Potter Peter'sh turn. I mean Peter Potter. He'sh gone to help Mrs Shimpkins. Her twinsh have come early.' I heard a hiccup. 'What'sh wrong with her? Mishish Roker, I mean.'

'I don't know. Prim and Bar are with her. Bar looked scared. Edward, I think she may be seriously ill. Frankie said she didn't speak at all yesterday.'

There was a moment's silence. 'I'm coming.' Edward's voice sounded different. 'Have shomeone wait in the lane to show me the way down.'

411

'But, Edward,' I began, 'you can't possibly drive in that state — ' There was a buzzing from the receiver.

★ ★ ★

As we approached the path that led down to the Nissen hut, Vere stepped out from a group of trees, pencil in hand. 'Hello, again. I've just found a group of what I think are bird's nest orchids. Very rare.' He looked at my face. 'What's up?'

'Could you possibly wait here for Dr Gilchrist and show him where the hut is? Frankie's mother isn't very well.'

'I'm sorry to hear that.' He smiled at Frankie. 'Off you go. I shan't desert my post.'

Inside the hut Ruth was putting nappies through a mangle. She looked tired to death. There was no sign of Bar or Prim and the door to the bedroom remained closed. 'I'll do that for you,' I said, pushing her gently on to the sofa. 'Has Titch had anything to eat?'

'She had some bread and that custard what you give us yesterday.' 'Have you eaten anything?'

'I forgot.'

While the children quarrelled over a packet of biscuits, I mangled and hung the nappies on the rack to dry.

'Let's play a game,' I suggested. 'I love my love with an A because he is angelic.'

'I love him with a B because he is boo-tiful,' said Frankie promptly. We had played several versions of this game before and this was her favourite. 'Who's goin' next?'

'I can't think of anythin',' said Ruth. She was eating a custard cream with her eyes half closed.

'I hate my love with a C because she's a cunt,' said Wills.

'Oh, Wills, don't be such a show-off.' Anxiety made

412

me cross. 'It's babyish to use rude words to shock people.'

'Don't you call me a baby!' Wills shook his fist in my face and Titch began to yell deafeningly. I felt perspiration break out all over me.

'If you hit her I'll cut off your willy,' screamed Frankie.

Before I could do anything Wills had punched Frankie on the nose. Blood began to trickle down her face.

'That'll do.' Vere crossed the room in two strides, took hold of Wills by his collar and yanked him to his feet. 'It's cowardly to hit someone smaller and weaker than you are.'

Edward came in behind him. I almost didn't recognise him with wet hair plastered flat to his head.

'Hello, you lot. Where's the patient?' He disappeared into the bedroom.

'I'm not a coward!' Wills tried to get away from Vere's hold on him. 'You're chokin' me.'

'Only really hopelessly pathetic men hit girls. Now, apologise.'

'Shan't!'

'Shall I make you?'

'You can't hit me. I'm smaller 'n you. You just said!'

'Of course I don't hit silly little boys.' Vere turned Wills round and with a rapid movement had thrown him to the ground. Titch stopped in mid-scream to watch. 'Now, that's proper fighting. It's called jujitsu. Get up.' Wills did, snivelling and knuckling his eyes. Vere promptly threw him down again, so hard that the breath was knocked out of his body. 'Get up.'

'Shan't.' Wills shrank away from him.

'Up.' Vere pulled him up and threw him down again. Wills lay as though stunned. 'Now you know what it feels like when somebody attacks you and you can't defend yourself. It isn't a good feeling, is it? Are you

413

going to say you're sorry?'

'Sorry,' Wills muttered at last, on a sob.

'All right. If you give me your word not to hit a girl ever again in your whole life I'll teach you how to fight properly.' He pulled Wills to his feet.

'Wills never does what he says,' interrupted Frankie, tears mingling with blood on her face. Wills clenched his fists but then looked at Vere and dropped them.

'Well? Are you a liar as well as a coward?'

'No.' Wills lowered his head. His dirty hair hung almost to his chin. He rubbed his running nose with a filthy hand covered in scratches and cuts.

'Let's hope not. I'm prepared to give you the benefit of the doubt. Shake hands like a man.' Wills looked up at Vere in astonishment. Then, seeing that Vere was serious, he put his grubby paw into Vere's large brown hand. 'All right. Go and check that Dr Gilchrist's car isn't holding anyone up. Cut along, now.'

Wills cut, without more ado.

'Astonishing.' I said. 'Baden-Powell would have been deeply affected.'

Vere ran his fingers through his hair and tucked his shirt tail into his trousers. 'Boys are simple creatures. As, indeed, are men. Tribal rules apply. Like to borrow my handkerchief, young lady?' He offered his to Frankie.

'You going ter show Wills how to knock everyone down?' Frankie spurned the handkerchief and glared at him. 'We shan't never have no peace!'

'I'll show you, too,' said Vere. 'You could easily throw him if you knew how.'

'Really?' Frankie looked at Vere a little more kindly.

'I love my love with a D because he is dangerous,' I said.

'What's this fluff all over the floor?' Vere stared about him. 'Has the sofa exploded?'

Bar came out while we were laughing. She looked

very upset. 'Could someone go and ring for an ambulance?'

'I'll go,' said Vere, and went.

'Are they taking Mum away?' Ruth sounded frightened.

Frankie took hold of my hand. Bar put her arm round Ruth's shoulder and looked at me with a grave face. 'Let's take the children home with us.'

★ ★ ★

We had a good tea at Drop Cottage of bacon and eggs and crumpets and jam and afterwards we played Racing Demon. The children, even Ruth, appeared to forget about everything but the enjoyment of the game. Prim came in half-way through. I could see from her face that she was wretched. As soon as the game was over I volunteered to make hot chocolate and asked Prim to help me.

'All right, tell me.' I shut the kitchen door behind me.

'Oh, God! I feel so responsible! Poor Mrs Roker. Edward won't say but I know he thinks it's cancer. Her right breast is just one huge hard mass and there's another lump just below her rib-cage. She's drifting in and out of a coma. Oh, Freddie, if only we'd done something earlier!'

'You mean, it's nothing to do with drinking?'

'I don't know. Edward's gone with her to the hospital. It took them ages to get the stretcher up to the lane. She's a big woman and where the path's so steep she started to slide off. I never felt so useless. I tried to tell her we'd take care of everything but I don't know if she understood. Freddie, what *are* we going to do about the children?'

34

'If this is motherhood,' cried Prim, a week later, throwing herself down on my sofa and pressing her hands to the sides of her head, 'I want none of it. I demand sterilisation.' She was looking quite unlike her usual self. Her complexion was dull and there were bags under her eyes.

'Yes, but I suppose that's the point.' I was draping nappies and knickers over the clothes horse to air before the fire. 'It isn't motherhood. I do love these children — too much, probably, for my own good — but it must be different when they're literally your own flesh and blood. You must feel much more confident for one thing. We know we've got to try to be detached. And the fact that they've just lost their mother has thrown all conventional ideas of nurturing to the winds.'

After three days in Tarchester General Hospital Mrs Roker had died. On arrival she had sunk into a deep sleep and had not opened her eyes again. Edward had explained to us that as well as cancer of the breast she had developed a secondary tumour in the liver and there was nothing that anyone could have done for her. The brief period of abstinence from drinking had given her a temporary remission but her condition had been terminal for many months, long before I had met the children. Even had the cancer been discovered sooner nothing could have been done to save her. If I had contacted the authorities the Roker domestic arrangements would have been deemed unfit for dying in and she would have been sent to hospital. Unwittingly we had given the children a few extra weeks at home with their mother and she with them. He was reassuring about the pain of those last days. In his experience people with tumours of the liver simply got weaker until overtaken by unconsciousness. I very much wanted to believe this.

'Well, I can't say I have any difficulty in staying detached from Wills.' Prim groaned at the thought of him. 'In fact, if it weren't for Edward and Bar I might be languishing in jail at this moment waiting to be brought to trial for homicide. Only I reckon I ought to get off with manslaughter due to provocation. This morning I decided that Ruth and I would clean the silver — she likes doing that sort of thing — otherwise I might not have noticed for ages that the coasters and candlesticks had gone from the dining room and Wills with them. I zoomed out to the car to find the little blighter had siphoned out all the petrol. Luckily Edward found him in the bus shelter with my worldly goods intact, very fed up because none of the shopkeepers in Tarchester would touch them. He'd sold the petrol and my new four-gallon can to the gypsies, though. For tenpence! The boy isn't even a competent thief.'

'Oh dear! I do feel you've got the worst of the bargain.'

Prim was looking after Ruth and Wills while I took care of Frankie and Titch. This had been grudgingly agreed by the social services to be the best temporary solution as the children had no traceable relatives. They were to be away from school for two weeks to give them time to adjust to their bereavement. During the hours I spent painting up at the Hall, Prim and her daily looked after all four. Luckily Mrs Hopper had brought up six children with a mixture of clouts and rough kindness so she was not daunted by Wills. At night Frankie shared my bed and Titch slept in a borrowed cot next to us. Sometimes she cried to come into bed and we spent hot, wakeful nights crowded together with me in the middle because Frankie tended to lash out and kick in her sleep.

'Not at all,' said Prim. 'At least I've got hot running water and baths and a washing-machine. And Ruth is really a child of surprising depths. My heart absolutely goes out to her when I see her trying not to cry. She's such a brave little thing. I can hear her weeping at night but when I go in she pretends to be asleep. I suppose she needs to be allowed to let it all out in private. But I feel at a loss as to how to comfort her.'

'I don't suppose there's very much more you can do.' I remembered the time, years ago, when there had been no consolation in anything. It had seemed impossible, then, that I would ever become used to the frightening idea of being in the world with no centre but my own small, insignificant self.

'During the day she follows me around and asks to do housework. Perhaps she feels by putting external things in order she's holding her mind together, too. I'm a bit like that myself. She *is* starting to tell me things about her childhood. The time her mother made her a birthday cake with seven candles instead of nine because she'd forgotten how old Ruth was. Fortunately Ruth thought that was funny. From bits she's let out it seems to have been a rotten childhood but she isn't in the least angry. She really loved her mother although she used to get violent and hit the children when she was drunk. It's flesh and blood, as you say.'

'I think it's rather worrying that Frankie and Titch don't seem to want their mother at all now. Frankie cried a lot at first but actually she seems to miss Ruth more.'

'Yes, but she was already emotionally attached to you. That must have helped enormously.'

I sighed, thinking of my two little charges asleep upstairs. It was an attachment I returned but it alarmed me for the future. 'Where's Wills now? Were you terribly angry with him?'

'How could I be? The poor little sod's just lost his

mother. One look at his face, when Edward brought him back — sort of hopeless and helpless — took all the anger out of me. Anyway Edward said he'd had a serious talk with him. He's marvellous with children, much better than I am. You'll never guess what Edward did then.' Prim laughed as though the memory were a pleasant one. 'He went back into Tarchester and bought a colour television set. I mean, really, it must be giving the boy all the wrong signals, rewarding dishonesty and so forth. But if you'd seen Wills's face! He's been glued to it ever since. I've left him with his supper on a tray in front of it.'

'I think it was just the right thing to do. Wills needs to be made to feel that people care about him, that he's important. Good for Edward.'

'If it weren't for Edward I think the social services might well have snatched the children from our tender care. That ghastly Brenda Bickerstaffe goes quite gooey when she talks to him. It's something to do with him being a doctor, I suppose. Though when you think how many famous wife murderers and serial killers were doctors I wonder why she feels so reassured.' Prim and the social worker did not like one another. 'She's coming again tomorrow, isn't she? I'd better go and tidy up the place in case she condemns it as unsanitary. She's quite bloody twisted enough. I've left Bar baby-sitting. She's been a brick. But somehow the house always looks as though a hurricane has passed through it after she's gone.'

Bar had indeed been the most marvellous help, taking the children for walks and playing inventive games with them. Being a teacher she had all sorts of worthwhile educational projects up her sleeve. They were making a wall-hanging of people of different nationalities from scraps of fabric, with wool for hair and buttons for eyes. Prim had been quite annoyed to find a yellow silk cushion had been cut up for the Japanese and all the buttons removed from her best coat. Bar was very much like another child in some ways. I wondered if she had seen Vere again.

'Talking of Vere; why don't you get him to help with Wills?'

'We weren't, were we?' Prim looked puzzled.

'Oh no, sorry. I'm so tired, I'm getting confused. But I think he could sort Wills out pretty quickly. He's got a good line in the style of Sanders of the River, Davy Crockett, King of the Wild Frontier, sort of stuff. How to kill a grizzly with a catapult and a bag of peas, and make its skin into a pair of snow shoes and a hot-water bottle cover, that kind of thing.'

'Vere? You amaze me! He must have changed very much indeed! Of course, we've rather been avoiding each other since that first awful meeting. Are you sure? I always imagine him with a book of poetry in his hand gazing at the stars.'

'Then I think he probably has changed.'

★   ★   ★

I saw Vere the next morning when I went up to Gilderoy Hall. I was conscious that Lady Frisk and I were a perfect nuisance to everyone in the household. Lady Frisk's incessant demands for dietary fads must have made Miss Glim's life, already hard, completely exhausting. We had seen nothing of Guy or Ambrose and it must have been tiresome for them to have to lie low every time Lady Frisk swept up to the front door. I was careful to keep out of everyone's way, never venturing beyond the morning room and coming and going by the back door.

Vere continued to visit us each morning, standing patiently while Lady Frisk, who was now treating him almost as a member of her own family, gave him errands to run and made arch references to what she seemed to believe was a consuming interest in the doings of Charlotte. He pretended not to notice. Half the time I think he genuinely didn't. I derived a great deal of amusement from these conversations although I never took part in them. I imagined Vere must be longing to escape. But this particular morning he was waiting for me in the morning room.

'Just a minute, Freddie. I want to talk to you. Let's go in here.'

The library was lit by three diagonal shafts of light from the three east windows that brightened the faded colours of the rugs and turned the brass grilles of the bookcases to gold.

'This is such a beautiful room,' I said, looking at the lovely seventeenth-century walnut secretaire that stood open, bursting with papers. A mug containing dregs of coffee had made a ring on the leather. A pair of shoes, rather muddy, lay on the floor beside it.

'I've always liked it myself. I'm afraid it's got into a mess. Three men living together and Miss Glim with more than enough to do — it's getting pretty uncivilised. Although Guy isn't here much now.' He looked at me as if uncertain as to how much he might say. 'We had a bit of a row about the girl. He said it wasn't his. So I went to see her.'

'That was kind of you.'

'She's just a child, as you say. I don't think she's capable of making it up and sustaining the lie. I was inclined to believe her.'

'Good.' I felt relieved.

'I had to tell her that there was no chance that Guy would marry her. I thought it better that she should be under no illusion. Poor little thing, she cried a lot but I don't really think she'd been holding out much hope. Then she said she didn't want the baby. Apparently her aunt has strong views on unmarried mothers and Corinne lives in fear of her. I said I'd make her an

421

allowance until the baby was twenty-one so she could be independent but she was adamant that she couldn't live alone with a child.' It was clear to me that single parent families cannot be supported by sporadic sales of recherché vegetable crops but I approved his generosity. 'I've sent her to see Edward Gilchrist. He seems a sympathetic sort of fellow. It's a mess but at least we can see that she gets the best treatment. She seemed to me a decent little thing. I offered her money to be going on with but she said she didn't need any. She had a job and wasn't short of anything. I had to bully her into accepting fifty pounds. It was a very broken-down sort of place she was living in. Most girls would have taken the money like a shot.'

'What a poor opinion you have of us. Perhaps it's true. She's so sweet and pretty. A magnet for unscrupulous men, I'm afraid.'

'Ah! I see the poor opinion is reciprocated.'

'It's a great pity that we each have to find everything out for ourselves. Why can't we learn from the experience of others?'

'Some people don't even learn from their own. I hope Guy's latest flirt is out of her gym tunic, at least.'

I understood that he was trying to tell me gently that Guy had a new girlfriend. I went off to begin painting, delighted to find I didn't mind at all. Lady Frisk was late which was unusual. I did a useful bit of background while I waited. The sky was marvellous to paint. Of course, it changed almost every minute of every hour of every day but I enjoyed experimenting with impasto, building up thick layers of paint. That morning the sky was a singing blue, a perfect foil to the plum-coloured chair.

When Lady Frisk arrived I saw at once that something had happened to disturb her. Her shoulders drooped, her hands fumbled as she unclasped her cape. Her face looked haggard as though she had not slept.

Her eyes were puffy, her mouth pursed up as though she was making an effort at self-control. Even the pheasant feathers were less jaunty as though her hat were in moult. She sat in silence for ten minutes while I worked, exploring the new lines and planes of her face revealed by the change in her mood.

'How old are you?' she said suddenly.

'Twenty-eight.'

'Charlotte is twenty-four. Do you consider that is a sufficient age to know what you are doing?'

I paused. This was a new, reflective Lady Frisk. I could not remember that she had ever asked a question before.

'That must depend on the person, I suppose. I'm not sure one ever knows what one's doing — if by that you mean making decisions conducive to one's future happiness.'

'Yes. That is what I mean.' Even her voice had a new, doubtful timbre.

'I think perhaps decisions are more a product of temperament than of reason. I mean, put simply, a violent person will seek a situation in which he can be violent and a timid person a situation that appears unthreatening. Most people fall into things haphazardly rather than work out what they ought to be doing. But I suppose by twenty-four Charlotte's beginning to be able to identify her own ideas and desires. Before then I think one is too influenced by other people. That doesn't mean, though, that one isn't still going to make horrible mistakes.' I added with feeling.

'That is what I say!' Lady Frisk said, with a slight recovery of energy. 'I told her she was much too young to know what she was about and that I should take every step possible to save her from this awful — *awful* prospect!' Lady Frisk's eyes grew round with horror.

'What did she say to that?' I asked after a pause, wondering what she was talking about.

'She told me she knew exactly what she was doing and there was absolutely nothing, short of having her certified, that I could do to prevent her. By law she was an adult. I can hardly believe that our politicians have been so crass as to let this come about. I telephoned my solicitor as soon as she had gone and he says this is right. I am unable to prevent my daughter taking this terrible step to the ruination of all my hopes and happiness.'

'Won't you tell me what this is about?'

Lady Frisk looked at me sharply. 'Can I trust you not to divulge a word of it?' She rushed on before I could answer 'Charlotte came to see me last night, quite without warning. She arrived in the most vulgar motor car I have ever seen — some American thing with huge wings and chromium bumpers — however, that is beside the point. At the wheel was a man of a vulgarity to match — a suit that looked as though it had come from a theatrical wardrobe, rings on his fingers and in his ears.' Lady Frisk pressed her hands to her chest and closed her eyes as though to shut out the spectacle 'He was a — Negro!' She almost whispered the last word as though it were too frightful to be uttered in a respectable house. 'I do not think I can be accused of prejudice but when I saw this — this animal take my own girl's hand to help her out of that abominable vehicle I was nauseated beyond belief.' Lady Frisk searched her bag for a handkerchief and pressed it to her lips. 'Apparently his name is Elmer Golightly — Elmer! What sort of name is *that*? As I stood there, *faint* with the shock, he took my hand in his great black paw and shook it for all the world as though we were social equals! Charlotte ushered the man in and left me to follow as though it were not even my own house. He had the *effrontery* to compliment me on having 'a nice place'!'

I refrained from smiling for I saw that the experience

had shaken Lady Frisk to the roots of her being. 'What was he like?'

'Like? I hardly know. Charlotte says he is a nuclear chemist, whatever that may be. It sounds unpleasant and dangerous. I always said no good would come of Charlotte's insistence on studying science. I begged her to take up something cultured, like history of art. That girl has been nothing but a worry to me from the day she was born. Inconsiderate, disobedient and head-strong, with an appetite for the positively depraved.'

This was certainly a change. I preferred the new profligate Charlotte. 'Perhaps they're just friends.'

'She told me in the boldest way — I can hardly bring myself to repeat it — that they are 'completely stuck on each other' and intend to get married next year. Married! He sat there grinning at me with all his teeth and I thought I must be in the middle of the most appalling nightmare. Better she were dead!' Lady Frisk began to moan.

'Now, you're not thinking clearly, Lady Frisk. He may be a very good man. He must be clever.' I also did not know what a nuclear chemist was.

'Apparently Elmer is 'up for a chair'. I have no idea what she is talking about.'

'It means he may become a professor.'

'A professor! I cannot believe it. Of course, Cambridge is not Oxford, but one would have thought they had *some* standards.'

'Surely if he is kind and loves Charlotte — '

'Tush! Twaddle! Sentimental *nonsense*! He will make her pregnant and then be on the next banana boat back to Jamaica or wherever he comes from. I shall be left with a coffee-coloured grandchild. Our lives will be ruined. Thank God Sir Oswald is not here to see this!' Large tears rolled down her wrinkled cheeks.

'Oh dear. Try to be calm. You must understand that to my generation race isn't so important. I'm sure there are plenty of mixed marriages that are happy.' I reminded myself that Charlotte's happiness was not the consideration here but rather Lady Frisk's idea of what was *comme il faut*. 'And perhaps it won't come off. A lot can happen in a year.'

'Yes, yes! You're right. The young are volatile. And no doubt *Elmer*,' she put heavy emphasis on the hated name, 'has the morals of a tomcat. They have voracious sexual appetites, I believe.' I could not see why she found this idea comforting. 'I shall write at once to the chancellor of the university and ask him to use his influence. She must come home for the vacation and we shall see what Vere can do. Poor boy! I'm afraid he will be very shocked!'

I was glad that her thoughts had taken a happier turn. For the next hour she told me of all the people she would draw into her scheme to persuade Charlotte of the disastrous consequences of the relationship. It was obvious that any discretion on my part would be quite unnecessary as Lady Frisk proposed to mobilise half England. By the time the session was over she was flushed with hope and militancy.

'I shall slip away. I do not think I can face poor dear Vere just at the moment. But I am confident that between us we shall make that silly deluded girl see sense.' I was pleased to detect a softening towards Charlotte. 'Tell Glim not quite so much oil in the salad dressing. She is not a bad cook but one must be vigilant with them or they begin to be extravagant. This room has not been dusted again.' Her eye fell on a pile of pamphlets that had been carelessly stacked on the desk. 'Such untidiness. This must be the next issue of the Alpine Society's newsletter. Perhaps I had better take them as I am honorary secretary. Ambrose will have to think of resigning from the presidency if his ill-health goes on.' Her eye fell on the top sheet. 'What is this?' She put on her spectacles and began to read aloud.

' "The Fascists of England. To all members of FOE and its affiliated societies, BIFF, the British Institute of Fighting Fascists, and BUMS, the British Union of Militant Socialists. The time is rapidly approaching when we will be able to advance our cause openly. Nazism is on the march in Germany once more — " ' Lady Frisk looked at me, her face a study of bewilderment. 'Tell me I am dreaming! Is this a joke? 'In Holland and Belgium small but powerful groups have formed to promote the ideals of National Socialism. Non-white immigration is the chief problem to be tackled. We must halt this erosion of our genetic inheritance — ' Frederica, what does this mean? Surely this is a swastika?' She held up the sheet of paper that had almost more swastikas than full stops.

'I'm afraid Ambrose is a Nazi.' I didn't know why I was being apologetic. Perhaps it had something to do with the pitiful expression on Lady Frisk's face as she reeled beneath a second blow.

'You mean, Ambrose is a — traitor?' She looked around her wildly. 'I cannot believe it! Why, he and Sir Oswald used to play billiards in the officers' mess! There has been a terrible mistake!'

35

'Do you know, I feel desperately sorry for her.' I was standing in the kitchen at Yardley House, ironing the girls' clothes. Bar was baby-sitting for me at Drop Cottage. Prim was mending a pair of Wills's trousers. 'We practically had to stretcher her out to the car. Of course, she's an ignorant bigoted snob but there are millions like her. She's merely the product of her generation.'

'I know my parents would have been horrified if I'd come home with a black man.' Prim bit off a thread. 'Though they were decent, kindly people they simply weren't used to different races. I don't suppose there were any in Dorset until the sixties. As for fascism, my father would have fallen into a fit at the very idea that Ambrose Gilderoy was a Nazi, however tame a version. There's the doorbell.' She made a face. 'Brenda Bickerstaffe. Please, God, don't let me say anything I'm going to regret.'

Brenda was a plump woman with a round face and short, nibbled hair. She always wore a pale blue mackintosh, whatever the weather, of which she buttoned every button and buckled the belt, threading the end through two loops. It took her a long time to get in and out of it. She refused Prim's offer to hang it up, folding it across her knee instead and crouching over it proprietorially. She took a large notebook out of her bag, put on her spectacles and removed the cap of her biro. She glanced at her watch and wrote the date and time at the head of the page. This she did slowly and carefully with an expressionless face, avoiding all eye contact, as though we were wild animals who might spring on her at any moment.

'Now, ladies. How are the children behaving?'

'What about a drink, Brenda? You must be tired. I know I am.' Prim was trying the us-girls-all-in-it-together approach.

'No, thank you. I never touch alcohol.'

'What a lot you're missing. A good bottle of wine is one of the chief pleasures in life.'

Brenda looked at Prim searchingly for several seconds then began to write laboriously in a round childish hand in her notebook.

'Tell me about William,' she said, when she had finished.

'Oh, Wills has improved greatly since the arrival of the television set. I can hardly prise him away from it.'

'How many hours a day is he watching TV?' Brenda's magnified eyes took on an additional solemnity. The hand holding the pen twitched.

'Oh — well, I'm not sure.' Prim saw the trap. 'He particularly likes nature programmes.'

Brenda looked disbelieving.

'What about his general behaviour?'

'Oh, not too bad. You know what boys are.' Prim laughed. 'Up to all sorts of pranks.'

Brenda sucked her lips together and wrote something. Then she looked up. 'I have a report here from the police. Apparently a young boy took some items of value into a jeweller's in Tarchester and tried to sell them. The jeweller, suspecting them to be stolen, attempted to detain him while he telephoned the police but the boy ran off. A customer in the shop, who lives in Pudwell, was able to identify him as William Roker. Is that what you call a prank?' Her expression became minatory. 'Or did you not know that the boy was absent from home, wandering the streets unsupervised?'

'Certainly I knew.'

'It didn't occur to you that this was a serious matter

and that you should have contacted a child welfare officer at once?'

'No, not really. They were my things and I got them back, and Dr Gilchrist gave him a good talking-to.'

By leaning back in my chair and twisting my head slightly I could see what Brenda was writing in her notebook. 'Demonstrates ambivalent and overindulgent attitude to juv. behaviour. Unsuitable levity v. moral questions — esp. stealing.' Above it she had written. 'Possible alcohol problem?'

'And how is Ruth getting along now?'

'She seems well adjusted, considering everything. She likes to help me with the housework.'

Brenda was on to it like a kestrel pouncing on a shrew. 'How many hours a day does Ruth spend doing household chores?'

'Goodness knows!' There was a snap to Prim's voice. 'I don't walk about with a stop-watch in my hand, timing the children's activities.'

Brenda wrote carefully. 'Shows resentment of authority.'

'I think Prim's doing a marvellous job with those children,' I said.

Brenda looked at me disapprovingly and moved her chair round so I could no longer read what she was writing. 'Now, the good news is that we have found a local family who will foster all four together.' She looked at us over the top of her spectacles and spoke in a calming voice. 'We're *very* grateful to you two ladies for stepping into the breach but we all knew this was to be a temporary solution until a more satisfactory arrangement could be made. We don't want you to feel for one moment that any little criticisms there might be of your domestic arrangements,' she gave me a tweak of a smile, 'have anything to do with the decision to remove the children from your care as soon as possible.'

'You needn't sound as though you're the Lord High Executioner,' Prim was irritated into indiscretion. 'We don't have any ideas of trying to kidnap the children and hold them by force. Speaking for myself, a little peace and quiet wouldn't be at all a bad thing.'

Brenda wrote something — I couldn't see what — and ended it with what appeared to be an exclamation mark.

'In that case, Miss Yardley, if that is how you feel, we must do all we can to expedite matters. I'd like to see the children now.'

Wills came in, scowling. 'They've just got to the best bit where a man with a machine-gun has just stood up in this bloody great cake and killed all the gangsters dead, like this — ' He sprayed us with imaginary bullets. 'The two men what are dressed up as women are runnin' away from the chief gangster because they saw him shootin' all the men in a massacre in a garage and — '

Brenda held up a pudgy hand, disgust written on her face. 'We shall have to have a rule about no television after seven o'clock if this is the sort of thing you are going to watch!'

'Actually, I think it's a comedy called *Some Like It* — ' I began.

'This is my house and *I* make the rules!' said Prim, at the same time.

'I'm gonna watch what I bleedin' well like!' chimed in Wills.

'It isn't clever to swear.' Brenda gave him her most repressive look. 'You are a naughty little boy! You must apologise at once to these ladies!'

'That's unfair! What about this afternoon when she dropped the coal bucket on her foot.' Wills pointed an accusing finger at Prim, his voice an injured whine, his eyes cunning. 'She said fuckety-fuck. That's worse!'

Brenda's already pasty face grew lard-coloured. She

431

began to write extensively in her notebook. I caught Prim's eye and we started to laugh. Brenda closed her eyes for a moment, drew a deep breath and wrote on.

★   ★   ★

'No, no, no!' Frankie sobbed, clutching my arm. 'I hate her! I won't go!'

'But, darling, she wants to give you a nice home and make you happy. You'll all be together.'

'I don't wanna live with Wills anyway. I like bein' here with you.'

'And I love having you. There's no reason why you can't come and visit me.'

'Every day?'

'Perhaps not every day at first. It will be better if you try to get to know Mr and Mrs Winnacott, and you can't do that if you're always with me.'

'I wanna stay here.' Frankie's lip trembled, and she looked at me beseechingly with swimming eyes.

It was hard to pretend to be enthusiastic about the proposal that the children should go and live with Swithin and Beryl. It was obvious that Brenda Bickerstaffe considered it a solution made in heaven. She had a whole-hearted respect for orthodoxy and to her mind a clergyman's wife was automatically sanctified and a pillar of domestic virtue. Prim and I had tried to tell her that the Rectory was unsuitable for the most docile child, let alone the wayward Rokers, but her response to our objections was to remain silent and scribble in her notebook like one possessed. Her feelings of hostility were not helped by Balthazar deciding that the blue mackintosh was the perfect thing for his basket and attaching himself firmly to the hem with his teeth. Finally Prim had to prise his jaws apart.

★   ★   ★

We walked together, Prim, Bar and I and the four children, up to the Rectory. Where the two paths, deosil and widdershins, crossed Chloë and Balthazar left us and went bounding off together up to the Hall.

'Off to consort with the devil,' said Prim, 'while we continue on our virtuous way like Christian going to meet Obstinate and Pliable. How appropriate! I suppose Ambrose Gilderoy would make a good Apollyon.'

'I've never understood what people don't like about him,' said Bar. 'I've only met him a few times when Guy used to take me up to the Hall for tea, but I thought he was a dear old thing.'

Prim began to laugh. 'The other day Mrs Creech told Mrs Hopper, who was standing in front of me in the queue, that she'd heard from someone intimate with the family that Ambrose is a transvestite. Mrs Hopper asked her what a transvestite was and Mrs Creech said it was a man who got forbidden thrills out of dressing up in women's clothes. 'Vests, do you mean?' asked Mrs Hopper. I nearly got a hernia trying to keep a straight face. I could see Mrs Hopper was mightily perplexed by the notion that a man might be excited by something long and woollen, labelled Chilprufe.'

'When the school took us to the pantomime we saw a man dressed up as Aladdin's mum. Was he a vest-tight?' said Frankie, who had not appeared to be listening.

'Aladdin was a stoopid girl. It was crap,' said Wills, with feeling.

By the time we had enlightened Frankie and ticked off Wills we were at the gate of the Rectory. Swithin was standing on the doorstep, evidently waiting for us. 'They're here, Beryl!' we heard him shout. She appeared beside him. A transformed Beryl. Gone was the grey bun and in its place a neat brown bob. She wore a dark red dress, obviously new. She came forward to meet us.

'Hello, my dears.' She was smiling. I could see she

433

was nervous. 'Do come in.'

We stood in the hall. I was struck by a difference here, too. It was brightened by a vase of orange tulips on the hall-stand and a rug of ethnic origin. Prim introduced the children. Beryl and Swithin grinned like a toothpaste advertisement but Titch buried her face in my neck and the three elder children were too busy looking at their surroundings to notice. Wills was mining a nostril and I saw Prim tap his arm.

'What do you think?' asked Beryl. 'Do you like the house?'

'No,' said Frankie.

'Have you gotta colour telly?' asked Wills.

' 'Tis a bit dark.' Ruth was staring at the ebonised furniture and the varnished oak staircase.

'Well, yes.' Beryl looked too. 'You're right. It *is* dark. How clever of you to see at once what's wrong. We'll paint it. What colour do you think?'

'Pink!' shouted Frankie.

'I think white would be nice,' said Ruth, after a moment's thought.

'Yes. White. Swithin, ring Pillbeam today and tell him to paint the hall straight away.'

'I want it pink!' Frankie thrust out her lower lip.

Beryl smiled kindly at her. 'Would you like to have your bedroom pink? You've got the room at the head of the stairs and Ruth's is next door so you won't feel lonely.'

'I got me own bedroom? Just me?'

'Yes. It needs new curtains. I thought you'd like to help me choose them.'

'I might,' admitted Frankie grudgingly.

'Have you gotta colour telly?' persisted Wills.

'Oh dear, no. Swithin, we must get one at once. Perhaps you could run into Tarchester — '

'Don't bother,' said Prim. 'You can have the one Dr Gilchrist gave me. He meant it for the children, really.'

'You've got your own little sitting room,' continued Beryl. 'The television can go in there. It used to be Swithin's study but he doesn't mind giving it up. It's by far the warmest room.' Swithin drew breath to say something but Beryl rushed on. 'What about lunch now? Let's go and wash our hands. I've got sausages and baked beans and trifle. Do you like that?'

'I want chips and I don't like washin'.' Wills had got on to the other nostril.

'Chips? Certainly. You shall have them for supper. Swithin's very strict about washing, though. And he doesn't like boys to pick their noses. He thinks that's a dirty habit.' Wills transferred his belligerent gaze to Swithin, who blenched before it.

'We'll leave you to settle in.' I thought they would get on better without an audience. 'Will you take Titch, Beryl? She can walk perfectly well but she likes to be carried when she's tired. She ought to have a nap after lunch.'

Beryl held out her arms. I put Titch into them. She made a bleating noise as if she was going to cry.

'Don't cry, my little darling.' Beryl held the child to her bosom and gently stroked her cheek. 'Auntie Beryl loves you so much. Don't cry, my precious little lamb.' And Titch didn't. Beryl looked at Swithin, her face scarlet with emotion. Slowly, large tears rolled down her cheeks.

' 'O thou of little faith, wherefore didst thou doubt?'' I heard Swithin mutter as he took out his handkerchief and wiped his own eyes.

'I want ice cream, Coca-cola and a air-gun,' stated Wills, seeing that conditions were favourable for the granting of requests.

36

'Well, I really think you have quite a little talent, Frederica.' Lady Frisk inspected the portrait, nearly finished now. 'You have caught a certain . . . shall we say, gravity?, that I flatter myself is noticeable in my deportment. Others may well describe it as dignity. It is not for me to say.' Lady Frisk had recovered all her former self-consequence. I looked at the canvas, which had become as familiar as my own face in the mirror. The arrogant assertive stare of the eyes was contradicted by a mouth that was vulnerable almost to the point of fear but I did not expect anyone else, least of all the subject, to detect it. I thought it the best work I had ever done. I had been able to keep myself out of it, as it were, to let the brush and the hand move with a new freedom and confidence, to allow the subject to dictate. 'Yes,' mused Lady Frisk, 'there is a stateliness but there is also poetry. Sir Oswald always said I had a rare sensibility. He called me Medea, sometimes in fun. She was a Greek goddess, you know.'

I thought this mean of Sir Oswald, however provoked. 'I'm very glad you like it.'

'Just the nose, my dear, *still* a trifle too pronounced. I shall recommend you to my friends with the proviso that they must watch for this. I am attending the wedding a week next Friday of the son of a dear friend of mine. Lord Percival Bierce is marrying,' she lowered her voice as though a crowd of gossip columnists might be clustered round the keyhole, 'his mother's companion. Rather a *mésalliance*, you will think. But his mother, the duchess, is delighted. Lord Percival has been very wild and the young lady — not so young in fact, mid-thirties — will be a stabilising influence. The duchess is devoted to Veronica — that is the bride's name. I can see nothing special about her myself, quite mousy and definitely middle class, but then, the poor dear duchess had the most awful time with the duke and is troubled by nervous complaints, and the couple will continue to live with her at the castle. I shall suggest to the duchess that she employ you for a portrait of the bride.'

'Thank you.'

'Of course, it will be dull for you after this,' she waved at the painting, 'but you must expect to run a little after your daily bread, you know.'

⋆ ⋆ ⋆

'So tomorrow's your last day,' said Vere. 'You've made a splendid job of it.' We had met by chance in the hall. Lady Frisk had already departed in state. 'You know, I'm always surprised by how perceptive women are. You've found a frailty in that terrifying woman that's touching. I'll take your word for it that it's there but I can't begin to see it. But it's more subtle than a single expression. It's what Joshua Reynolds called 'the peculiar colourings of the mind'.'

'You flatter me.'

'I'm telling you what I think. I'm no good at compliments. I'd have made a rotten courtier.'

'You've been a model of diplomacy these last two weeks.'

'My father will be able to come out of hiding now.'

'So his gout isn't really that bad?'

'We agreed it would be better if I acted as host. He was annoyed by the way she commandeered the house. It's important he avoids agitation. The next stroke could kill him.'

'He's fortunate to have you to look after him.'

Vere looked gloomy. 'I feel I owe him a lot,' was all he

437

said, but I knew at once that he was thinking about running away with his father's mistress.

'How are things going?' I asked, to change the subject.

'The nature conservation people are definitely coming up with a grant. I've found a patch of lizard orchids down in the valley. Actually, they're not very pretty but they are rare. We'll start making hay next week in the bottom fields and then we can plough them in a month or so and start the market gardening. I've got two more restaurants interested, one in London and one in Dartmouth.'

'Oh, good. You know, Vere,' I grew hesitant, 'I wonder if it's going to be quite . . . enough. Of course, it's none of my business, but do you think these schemes, worthwhile as they are, will generate enough income to support the estate?' I felt myself growing warm at my own cheek. 'I mean, have you thought of fuel bills, rates, repairs and insurance? Besides,' I rushed on, feeling I'd better make a job of it, 'three people to feed and clothe. Four with Miss Glim. It would have to be a very big grant, wouldn't it, to cover all that? Don't be angry. It's just that I'd hate you to be disappointed. I know how easy it is to be carried away by the beauty of something and *wanting* it to be the right thing so much that one refuses to listen to the depressing voice of reason.'

'Yes.' Vere was gazing down at me with an expression I could not interpret. 'It is easy.' I could tell, though, that he was looking through me and thinking of something else. 'Isn't it odd how you can almost entirely forget something that happened to you — never think of it for years — and then suddenly it comes back to you with a vengeance and pursues you and obsesses you all over again.'

I remembered how, when I left Alex, images of my mother's death had surfaced to twine themselves with visions of his stricken face, as vivid and disturbing as twenty years ago. The association, of course, was guilt.

'I suppose that might be because something of the original circumstance has recurred,' I said.

'That must be it. Yes. Damn it all to hell!'

'Her ladyship's left orders for a crab soufflé for her lunch tomorrow.' Miss Glim had come up behind me, a piece of paper in her hand. 'She told me on no account to give her eggs. How am I to make a soufflé without eggs?' She ignored Vere.

'I'd just go ahead and make it the usual way,' I said. 'She won't know.'

'She says the crab must be fresh not tinned,' persisted Miss Glim. 'The fishmonger's not due to call till Tuesday.'

'Use tinned. I'm sure she won't notice the difference. I'm so sorry we've practically turned your house upside down.' I turned back to Vere but he had gone.

★ ★ ★

I allowed three days to pass before going to the Rectory to see the children. Frankie flew out of the gate to meet me, flinging her arms round me and pushing her head hard into my rib-cage. Her hair had been cut short and it made her face looked rounder and prettier. She was dressed in a navy jersey and a tartan pleated skirt and looked altogether different, thoroughly clean and wholesome, but perversely I missed the old untidy Frankie.

'I thought you wasn't comin'. I was plannin' to run away.'

'I'm glad you didn't. Mr and Mrs Winnacott would have been very unhappy.'

'She likes Ruth and Titch best.'

'You have to give it time, Frankie. Getting to know people happens slowly.'

'I wanna be with you.'

439

'Oh, darling! I'm not married, I haven't got anywhere sensible to live, or any money.'

'You could marry Dr Gilchrist. He's nice.'

'Yes, very. But he doesn't want to marry me.'

'I'll find someone for you to marry. A rich man.'

'Until then, sweetheart, let's make the best of things. I'm longing to see your bedroom.'

Swithin answered the bell. He looked grey. 'It's a revelation,' he said, when I enquired after his health. He led me to the kitchen, stooping like an old man.

Beryl appeared similarly distrait, hair untidy, cardigan buttoned on the wrong buttons, but I could see she was happy. Ruth was standing at the kitchen table, mixing something in a bowl. She said, 'Hello,' and gave me her usual tight little smile, then carried on beating with frowning determination. Titch, who was sitting at a little table clashing two wooden animals together, held out her arms and cried, 'Bicket.' I picked her up. She smelt of baby powder. Her face was clean, her hair brushed into shining curls. Her pink dress was appliquéd with gambolling rabbits, the tights stretched over her nappy were immaculately white. Black patent shoes were fastened to her fat little feet.

'What a pretty girl!' I kissed her. 'Show me your toys, Titchy-Witch.'

Titch gave me a cow. 'Moo moo!' She banged a horse across her little table, which was pale blue and painted with ducks to match the chair. A wooden farm was set up by the fender of the kitchen stove.

'It's a good thing you've come now,' said Beryl, her voice filled with pride and pleasure. 'Helen's going to have her nap soon. Perhaps you'd like to see the nursery?'

'Helen? Oh, yes.' I had forgotten that this was Titch's real name. 'Thank you. I should, very much.'

'Come and see my room first.' Frankie tugged at my skirt. 'Auntie Beryl's makin' me curtains. They've got cats on. There's a black 'un like Macavity!'

Beryl looked at us sharply.

'What are you making, Ruth?' I said quickly.

'Fairy cakes. I'm goin' to ice them and put hundreds and thousands on, see?' She showed me the packet. Her dark hair was gleaming and fastened back in a single plait, which suited her. She was wearing new clothes, too.

I went upstairs with Frankie. Her room was sunny with a marvellous view down the valley, brilliant with the heads of trees in every shade of green. 'This is lovely.' I looked at the bedclothes patterned with beribboned teddy bears. A lamp modelled like a toadstool house stood on the bedside table next to a book about Little Grey Rabbit. As a child I would have much preferred this sort of thing to the chilling elegance of the *lit à la polonaise* and the Victorian samplers.

'Look at me coat.' Frankie opened the wardrobe door to reveal a navy duffel coat with a red lining. 'It's new. Everything's new. Auntie Beryl and Uncle Swithin took us to Tarchester and we went to a big shop and she got us all these things. Then we went to the hairdresser's and the bookshop and we had tea at the Tudor Caff.'

'That must have been fun.'

'It would have been but Wills cheeked the waitress and Auntie Beryl said she was sorry and how we was orphans and hadn't learned how to behave yet. That made Ruth cry. So then I felt sad and cried and Titch started to scream. Wills ran out and Uncle Swithin couldn't find him for ages.'

'Oh dear.'

'When we got home Uncle Swithin tried to tell Wills off and Wills kicked him so he was sent to bed early. He climbed out the winder and fell and cut his head so Dr Gilchrist came and put in a stitch and Wills cried like anything. I cried, too, because I felt sorry for him.

441

Uncle Swithin said something about trials and tribe relations. I suppose he means us.'

* * *

'It could be worse,' I said to Bar and Prim that evening, as we gathered in Bar's exotic kitchen for supper. 'Actually I take my hat off to them both. Swithin is terribly kind and endlessly forgiving and Beryl is prompted by real feelings of love. You honestly wouldn't know her as the same woman. When I saw Titch's nursery I was amazed. You can hardly get in at the door for mobiles, musical boxes and toys. The cot's kitted out in *broderie anglaise* and there are towels with 'Baby' written across the corner. It's sad in a way that Titch is soon going to grow out of it all.'

'How can they afford it?' asked Prim, taking a tentative spoonful of horseradish soup. 'Pheow!' She flapped her hand in front of her mouth. 'Delicious, Bar dear, but fiery.' We were eating to the strains of *Götterdämmerung* on Bar's record player, which seemed a suitable accompaniment.

'I'm experimenting with it,' said Bar. 'Next time I'll put in more potato.'

'That's what I wondered. How they could afford it, I mean.' I swallowed a mouthful of soup. My eyes watered and I felt as though every tastebud I possessed had been instantly cauterised. 'Beryl came up with Titch to put her to bed. I know I was the one most against the Winnacotts having the children but I have to admit it was a touching sight, watching Beryl kiss her and talk to her in a soft, cooing voice while tucking her in with a toy elephant. Titch seemed mesmerised by the whole performance. She went off to sleep without a murmur. I complimented Beryl on the arrangements and she said it was a joy and a privilege to have them.'

'Even Wills?' Prim said, rather chokingly because of the soup.

'I asked her how he was getting on. She said he just needs affection coupled with a firm hand. Wills doesn't respect her and Swithin is too soft with him. I was amazed that Beryl was capable of talking in such a rational way. It shows how prejudiced I've been. I suggested she asked Vere to help and she said he'd already been to see them and is going to take Wills out on the river and teach him how to sail.'

'That *is* kind.' Bar's face was very pink indeed, and a tear caught in her dimple sparkled in the candlelight. 'He's my idea of Siegfried, so tall and good-looking yet reserved and introspective. Most men are so dull, only caring about cars and football. I can imagine Vere battling with giant snakes and fighting through fire and all that. How glorious to be his Brunhilde.'

'I seem to remember it turns out rather badly.' Prim found a handkerchief in her bag and mopped her streaming eyes. 'I don't think you'd like having to throw yourself on to his funeral pyre.'

'Beryl told me that Vere had given her what she called 'a most generous donation' for clothes and toys for the children. Of course it was good of him but I couldn't help thinking there goes the profit on the purslane. I tried to warn him about being too optimistic but he wasn't listening. As usual.'

Prim snorted through her nose like a horse. 'Sorry. It's the soup. I'll have a go at him myself if I get the chance. Though I'm going to be rather busy from now on. Edward's receptionist, Miss Brissel, has resigned in high dudgeon because I reorganised the filing while she was having her appendix out. Though I do say it myself, my system is much easier to use. Edward's asked me to be the practice manager. He's going to open a dispensary as well as a baby clinic. It's all rather exciting.'

'Prim! Well done!' Bar made a flag-waving motion with her hand as she sneezed several times in quick succession. 'You'll be so good at it! I hated Miss Brissel. If you were swollen with buboes, vomiting blood and had a crossbow bolt sticking out of your ear she'd ask you if it was an emergency.'

'I'm envious.' I leaned back, taking long, slow, cooling breaths as Bar took away my soup plate. 'Now I've finished painting Lady Frisk I've got to look for more work. I don't feel I can go back to London just yet. Not until the children are happily settled anyway.'

'You mustn't even think of going. We'd miss you far too much.' Bar put a slab of something dark-grey, like school socks, in front of me. 'It's Jew's Ear pâté. Don't worry.' She laughed, seeing our faces. 'It's a kind of mushroom. Tuck in, girls, there's plenty more.'

★   ★   ★

Going back to London was the last thing I wanted to do. Prim had put the cheque from the hospital committee into her own account so she could give me cash when I needed it. I ate simply and didn't need new clothes. I walked everywhere or was driven by Prim. I had books all around me and my dependants had been drastically reduced to a cat and half a dog. I felt almost affluent.

I bought some paint and began to decorate the inside of the cottage, matching as closely as I could the original colours. I borrowed Prim's sewing-machine and re-covered the sofa and chair in an old-fashioned chintz sprigged with lily-of-the-valley that Prim had found in the attic at Yardley House. Dusty finished mending the thatch and, on Vere's instructions, repaired the windows and patches of crumbling brickwork. I sowed more vegetables, cleared away the weeds between the bridge and the front door and planted along the edges of the path with old-fashioned shrub roses with evocative names like 'Souvenir de la Malmaison' and 'Cuisse de Nymphe'. The nice old man who owned the nursery between Pudwell and Tarchester gave me an apple tree and a gooseberry bush. I knew I wouldn't be living at Drop Cottage by the time they bore fruit but I was glad to think that someone in the future would have the pleasure of them. I replaced the ivy and brambles round the front door with a pale apricot-coloured rose called 'Phyllis Bide.'

Beneath the window that looked out over the valley I planted sweet-scented annuals, like mignonette and heliotrope. I discovered, head down in the earth, a small bronze bust of Napoleon. I concluded that it had fallen out of the window. I took it indoors, washed it and put it on the bookshelves.

Lemmy was a great help to me in these enterprises. He was wiry and strong and he liked digging. He also had a sharp eye and showed me many plants that had survived from the original garden that in my ignorance I had thought were weeds. We cleared around their roots and cut away the branches that shaded them and quickly they put out strong shoots and buds. What I had thought was a bundle of old sticks was a rose arbour which Lemmy rebuilt for me. He could weave branches with a wonderful dexterity and knew how to make the best use of the natural twists and curves of the wood, binding them together with willow withies. I had given him a hammer and some nails but he threw them down with disdain.

When I showed him the belvedere he threw back his head and crowed with delight. Over a period of days he stripped it to the bare frame and rebuilt it, only stopping to eat when I made him.

I watched him weaving a section of wall like a giant basket. 'Lemmy, you must have done a great deal of this kind of work before.'

'Lemmy made his house. That is how he learned.'

'Where is it?' He pointed to the hill on the other side of the river. 'Will you show it to me?'

Lemmy worked on in silence so I assumed he had either not heard or not understood. I set up my easel on the path near the back door and began to sketch the cat-slide roof. I had decided to make an anthology of paintings of the cottage, the garden and the river. I had already begun a scrapbook with fragments of fabric and drawings of the interior and I was pressing flowers from the garden to put between the pages. In years to come, when I was surrounded by buildings, pavements, traffic and the hum and buzz of people creating news and art, I would be able to turn the pages and return in spirit to the place where I had been so happy.

Naturally I had daydreams of staying in Pudwell for a long time. No doubt Viola would have agreed to rent the cottage to me almost indefinitely. But how was I to make a living? Once Alex became officially engaged to Zara Drax-Eedes I thought it would be reasonable to ask him for my share of the house we had bought together in Melbury Street. I had some furniture in store and a few thousand in our joint bank account. Carefully invested, the money might keep me in bread and butter. Drawing the cottage and the garden had given me exciting ideas about landscape but I was not sanguine about the financial rewards. Even Constable had had a hard time of it. I was bound to go on painting portraits for a while longer and to get commissions I had to spend time with those people who could afford them.

'Lemmy will show you his house. Because of your hair.' Lemmy had crept up behind me. 'The sun has made it like a torch, a flambeau, a comet's tail.' He touched it and made a chattering motion with his teeth as though he longed to bite it. 'Come on, then.'

Lemmy had no idea of doing things except at the

446

moment they occurred to him. I would have liked to put away my easel in case of rain but he was already loping away down the path. I had to run to keep up with him. By the time we reached the river I was panting. Lemmy sprang like a goat from boulder to boulder across the water. I stood wobbling on the nearest one, which was slippery with moss. He saw me hesitating and came back, taking my hand in his. His palm was as hard as horn. I slithered across, rather frightened and resolved to come back the long way.

The path Lemmy took up through the hanging woods was the most direct route. After a few yards it became steep and I had to clutch at tree roots to stop myself sliding backwards on the dry, stony earth. It was worse where we came to a rill trickling almost vertically down a gully. Here the ground was muddy, crumbling and precarious. Lemmy's bare feet above my head were leaving me behind. 'Wait for me!' I yelled, but he continued to climb. I struggled on, grabbing at brambles and nettles until my hands were numbed by scratches and stings. When the climb became sheer and a stone loosened by Lemmy bounced on my head I decided to turn back. I was horrified when I looked down and saw how far we had already come. The river was obscured by trees. I looked up. A shelf of land jutted out a few feet above my head. I could only climb it by defying gravity and hanging almost upside down. I felt a paroxysm of absolute terror. My weight began to dislodge the root I was clinging to and the rock under my right toe moved. My vision blurred, my head swam.

'Help!' I cried, in a voice that was not my own, a squeal of fear. A bee flew into my face and crawled about on my forehead. I could not save myself. I had no choice but to go down with the root and the rock. I closed my eyes and prepared to die. I addressed God apologetically, asking him to overlook all my mistakes and to see that Uncle Sid, Frankie and Macavity were all right without me. I hoped it would be quick.

I heard a bark above me and felt a hand grip mine. A voice said, 'Steady, now.' I wanted to explain that it was out of my power to be steady or otherwise but fear had deprived me of speech. My past life was flashing before my eyes but there was not enough of it. I was too young to die — I felt a pain in my arms and the next minute I was flying through space. I landed hard on my back with the taste of earth in my mouth. My nose throbbed. Hot winds were laving my brow and my chin was wet. Chloë was licking my face.

37

'You're all right, now. You're quite safe.'

I tried to focus my eyes but the world was still spinning. I coughed and licked my lips, which tasted of blood. I became aware that it wasn't Lemmy crouching beside me but Vere. He looked cross. 'What on earth were you doing? You might have killed yourself!' He dabbed at my face with something white. 'You've grazed your nose. Sorry. I had to drag you up. There was no time to do it gracefully. What an idiotic thing to do!'

'I didn't know we were going to scale the Matterhorn,' I panted. I put my arms round Chloë's shaggy neck to stop her licking me and lifted my head. We were on the top of the cliff. The relief was physical, a hot prickling sensation over my entire body from my ears to my toes. I sat up.

'You might have fallen and killed yourself,' Vere said again. 'There's a perfectly good footpath. What possessed you to try to climb an almost vertical hill?'

My nose began to stream with blood. 'Could I borrow your handkerchief again?' There was a definite quiver in my voice.

'Oh, now, look!' Vere sounded alarmed. 'Steady.' He put his arm round me. 'All right, I won't scold you any more.' He patted my shoulder as though I were a shying horse. It was oddly comforting.

'I was following Lemmy and when I thought about turning back it was too late. I'd forgotten how scared I am of heights. Sorry to be so pathetic.'

'I don't think it's pathetic to be afraid. It's all about imagination, isn't it? I've been frightened more times than I could count. Are you strong enough to stand?'

I was slightly dizzy but otherwise all right. I did some

controlled breathing and, apart from the throbbing of my nose, I felt restored. 'Better now. It was lucky for me you were here.' I did a little more breathing when I thought of what might have happened.

'Why not come with me and see the ruins of the Abbey? I've been putting it off since I came home. I know it'll be depressing. It would be good to have company.'

We walked through the thinning trees towards Spokebender Abbey to the accompaniment of grasshoppers, the broken stammer of a cuckoo and a string of repeated notes that I thought might be a thrush. An elder was in full flower, its cream corymbs gleaming. The sun made little darting zigzags on the swirls of bark. 'How beautiful it is!' I said. My nose had stopped bleeding. It was good to be alive.

'Look! Scarlet pimpernels.' Vere pointed to a cluster of tiny red flowers growing at the edge of the woods. 'I've seen hills of rhododendrons in the Himalayas, fields of gentians in the Alps, acres of lilies in Africa. Yet this little flower, to me, is just as beautiful. There's Lemmy.'

He was running towards us, his arms held out at the elbows, cantering sideways, crab-like.

'Don't tell him off,' I said quickly.

'I wasn't going to. It wouldn't do any good anyway. I don't suppose it occurred to him that you can't do what he does. Hello, Lemmy. Have you found any dyer's greenweed yet?'

'Yes. Lemmy will show you. And spiny restharrow. Rare.' He glanced obliquely at me. 'Blood. Cut nose.'

'It's nothing to worry about.' It stung quite a bit but I didn't want cobwebs and plantain leaves and a handkerchief knotted round my nose. 'What about your house?'

'Come and see it.' He capered about in a fair imitation of Laurence Olivier as Richard III.

Vere put his hand on Lemmy's arm. 'Stand up, there's a good chap. Shoulders back, arms relaxed.'

Lemmy did as he was told and swung his arms in a stiff imitation of Vere's walk. Had he been clothed you would hardly have known that there was anything different about him. Except perhaps for his blank, black eyes that never looked into yours.

The ruins of Spokebender Abbey were dismal. We went in through the front door, a massive piece of oak that had resisted the depredations of weather and vandals. Inside crimson damask and hand-blocked papers hung in tatters from the walls, scored and patched with black. Some rooms had fireplaces, the grates containing charred wood and the remains of ashes. In others they had been torn out, leaving splintered sockets. The ceiling was down in the drawing room, its magnificent sixteenth-century bosses smashed on the rotting boards. Lemmy stayed with us. I suppose, because the sky was only too evident above our heads, it did not count as being indoors.

'When I was here last this was panelled and painted,' said Vere, as we walked through the refectory, now scarred, naked plaster. 'Wonderful frescos. And the floor was black and white marble. It was falling into ruin even then but the downstairs rooms were salvageable.' He ran his fingers over the fine chasing of a brass lock. 'I used to dream of saving it. It's too far gone now.' He groaned as he surveyed the ravages where the architrave and pediment had been hacked from the door. 'This should never have been allowed to happen. It's unforgivable. I ought to have come home sooner.'

'Come home,' said Lemmy.

'All right. Let's get out of here.'

We crossed the library, which had an ash tree growing in the middle of it, through french windows that had battered themselves almost to matchwood in countless storms, down steps covered in weeds and moss.

451

'Look at all these different kinds of lichen.' Vere squatted down to examine a bright orange circle. 'Did you know it takes a century to make a patch ten centimetres in diameter? There are more than a hundred different species.'

Lemmy was disappearing through a hole in a yew hedge that had grown tall and ragged at the end of what must once have been lawn. We followed him, pausing briefly to examine the orangery. The iron framework was intact but every single pane was shattered. The tender palms and exotic shrubs were twisted brown skeletons. Beyond the yew hedge was a jungle.

'This was the arboretum,' said Vere. 'At least this can be saved. We can take out the suckers and undergrowth. Look at all those pines, half-strangled by self-sown sycamores and elders. I wonder what kind they are?'

'Macedonian Pine.' Lemmy had come back to find us. '*Pinus peuce*. Rare, south-west Balkans. Bud cylindrical, abruptly pointed, leaves in fives, bundles densely set.'

'You're as good as a book,' said Vere. 'You're a great help to me.'

Something almost like pleasure ran fleetingly over Lemmy's inexpressive face.

'I suppose it wouldn't cost very much,' I reflected. 'But you'd need a winch for some of the bigger saplings. And there'd be labour expenses.'

In the darkest, densest part of the arboretum, amid a group of unpleasantly prickly hollies, there was a ladder of sticks bound with withies. I followed Lemmy up and put my head through a hole at the top.

'This is lovely! Like being in a giant nest!' It was a tree house made from woven branches. There was even a roof over half of it. Admittedly there were slivers of blue sky in the gaps and one side was quite open. Beneath the covered section was a platform of thicker branches making a kind of bed, piled with cushions and knitted blankets in bright patterns. I recognised Bar's handiwork. Beside the bed there were heaps of books, neatly arranged beneath a blue tarpaulin. I pulled myself up on to the platform.

'I could live here quite happily,' I said, as Vere followed me up. 'Listen to it creaking like a ship. Look, a wall of wild roses!' I pointed to a briar rose that had twined itself through boughs into the sun.

'You're obviously a hopeless romantic. Imagine it in November drizzle.'

Vere examined an arrangement of animal bones and another of eggs. I was touched to see that a trusting bird had built her nest in the branches above Lemmy's bed. He seemed to have forgotten about us, sitting cross-legged on the heap of blankets, methodically turning the pages of a book. When we said goodbye he did not answer or look at us.

All the way back, along the overgrown drive that took us down to the valley floor and across the river by an ancient pack-horse bridge, Vere was silent. He strolled along, hands in pockets, relaxed, abstracted. I was happy to admire the beauty of the landscape and to imagine how once our path must have been thronged with traffic as monks, pedlars, lepers and pilgrims toiled up and down the hills from the Abbey to Tarchester. Chloë was delighted to have both her charges in view and walked beside me carrying a horribly dribbly stick, which she refused to let me throw for her. With such undemanding companions I was able to let my mind wander freely.

It would be sensible to get a job before the end of the month. I would buy more paints and canvas with the hospital-board money. The Tudor Café in Tarchester displayed amateur paintings for sale. I would do some studies of the Abbey ruins and try to sell them. But I needed a regular income. Some straightforward labouring work would do, preferably out of doors to take advantage of the marvellous weather.

'We're starting hay-making on Tuesday.' Vere's voice broke in on my thoughts. 'Like to lend a hand? Two pounds an hour, lunch and tea provided.'

'You know, you could make your fortune as a mind-reader.'

'Does that mean you will? Good.' He turned to look at me. 'For such a delicate-looking creature you've plenty of grit.' I felt flattered. My spirits rose absurdly high. Vere continued to look at me. I began to feel self-conscious. 'Come back to the Hall,' he said, with something almost like tenderness in his voice, 'and I'll find you some TCP. I think your nose is beginning to swell.'

'Thank you. Perhaps I'd better.' We walked on, again in silence. My spirits had drooped as swiftly as they had risen. I imagined my nose to be huge and red. I wondered if he was suppressing a desire to laugh.

'Supposing I repair the orangery? For Lemmy to live in.'

Of course he hadn't been thinking of me at all. 'What a wonderful idea! Oh, but wouldn't it be terribly expensive?'

He smiled. 'What a girl you are for commerce.'

'Remember, income twenty pounds, expenditure nineteen pounds, nineteen shillings and sixpence, result happiness.'

Vere laughed. 'Quite right, Mrs Micawber. We might only do a section of it. Enough to give him proper shelter. I'll see if he'll agree to come into one of the greenhouses up at the Hall before I spend so much as a ha'penny on it, I promise.'

As we approached the front door of Gilderoy Hall we saw two large suitcases on the steps. Guy appeared a moment later.

'Hello, Vere. Freddie.' The look he gave me was cool. I was not forgiven. 'Or rather goodbye. I'm going to

Ireland for a bit. Perhaps several weeks.'

'It's rather sudden, isn't it?' It was obvious that Vere was annoyed. 'What about getting in the hay?'

'Oh, you've got Deacon to help. And there's Dusty. Put a bit of pressure on Plumrose. He's behind with his rent.'

'He'll be even less likely to turn a profit on his own land if he has to help me with mine. Deacon can't drive a tractor with that torn ligament, as you well know, and Dusty's too old to learn. Can't this trip be postponed until later in the year when we're not so busy? There's the stock sale in three weeks. I'll need help with that.'

'Freddie'll give you a hand.' Guy glanced at me again and frowned. 'What have you done to your nose? Have you and Vere been fighting?' He smiled unpleasantly. 'I've had a pressing invitation to stay at Castle Fitzpatrick. It would be rude to refuse.'

'You don't mean Castle Fitzpatrick in Tullireen?' I said, amazed.

'You know it?'

'I've known Oonagh Fitzpatrick for years. We were at art school together.'

'It's Moira I'm going to see.' Guy laughed, rather smugly.

I remembered Moira, Oonagh's youngest sister, the best-looking of the Fitzpatrick girls and the wildest, which was saying something. During my hideous sojourn at Castle Fitzpatrick Moira had displayed a regrettable fondness for pranks. On the first day of the shoot she had taken the keys from all the bathrooms and lavatories and thrown them into the moat. As there were twenty guests and only three lavatories and bathrooms between us, they were heavily oversubscribed and forty-eight hours of highly embarrassing encounters, between dowagers with drawstring spongebags and retired generals with moustache nets, were

455

undergone before the locksmith in Ballinadare could supply new keys.

The forty-watt bulbs high in the rafters of the great hall had been too feeble to illuminate the gravel that Moira had mixed with the pre-prandial nuts. Several of us jarred our teeth painfully, and first thing in the morning Lord Portree had to be driven to Galway to have his plate repaired. Fortunately, her amusing jape of bursting into the drawing room wearing a balaclava, a jacket stencilled with the letters IRA and carrying one of her father's shotguns backfired. Lieutenant-Colonel 'Blinkers' Bracegirdle, who had survived campaigns in unpleasantly sweaty jungles and arid plains as well as rain-lashed trenches, decided he was not going to have his lights put out by a mad Irishman. He crept up behind her and whacked her over the head with a bronze of Wellington astride Copenhagen. Several bottles of heart pills had to be sent for and everyone was jittery for the rest of the evening but Moira had to have stitches in her head and was, to everyone's relief, *hors de combat* for several days.

'I'm sure you'll have a marvellous time,' I said, hardly able to hide my amusement.

'Thank you. I intend to.'

'That was more generous than he deserved,' said Vere, as we watched Guy drive off in the Lancia, the only remotely comfortable vehicle on the estate.

A note of sympathy in his voice made me suspicious. 'If you think I'm even remotely jealous, you're very much mistaken.'

'I'm glad to hear it.'

'What did Guy tell you?'

Vere looked uncomfortable and muttered, 'Oh, well, naturally, finding out about Corinne, you were bound to be upset.'

'That's not true.' I spoke calmly but I was angry. 'I'd already decided to break it off with Guy before I knew anything about her because — because he's a liar. I'm sorry to say that of your brother.'

'All right. I believe you.'

I struggled with annoyance. 'I suppose he told you I was broken-hearted out of revenge. Well,' I shrugged, 'it's only my vanity that's wounded. What does it matter, after all?'

Vere stared at me and opened his mouth as if to say something but evidently thought better of it. We went into the hall. I looked again at the portrait of Vere's mother. It must have given Ambrose some satisfaction to hang the paintings of the two lovers face to face, now that death had parted them for ever. Colonel le Maistre's black eyes were amused, intensely alive, not blank at all — 'Oh!' I cried. 'How stupid of me not to see it before! Of course! Lemmy!'

'What?' Vere looked at me as though I had gone mad.

'Look at it! The ears, the width of the cheekbones, those arched brows, above all the dark eyes set so wide apart. I knew there was something familiar the moment I saw him in the garden at Drop Cottage. Lemmy. Le Maistre. It's been staring me in the face, literally!'

I heard laughter behind me. Ambrose was working his way towards us, bent over his sticks, his face convulsed with enjoyment. 'Clever girl!' He put his hand on my arm and held it tight. 'It's taken more than twenty years for someone to make the connection. How unobservant people are. Except for you, my dear.' Ambrose gave me a look that chilled. 'Well, Vere, how do you like your half-brother — the half-wit?' Vere did not answer. 'Asset to the family, isn't he? An ornament to the drawing room.' Ambrose bared his teeth in silent laughter. 'Your mother generously allowed me to think that she was carrying *my* child. Harry had been moping at his club in London, grieving for his house, gambling away his last few thousand. I always thought her more acquisitive than concupiscent. It did not occur to me that she

457

might still be seeing him, now he was a homeless spendthrift.

'As soon as the child was born I realised my mistake. Miserable creature that it was, it had Harry's face. It was not expected to live and no one wished it to. Your mother disliked it on sight. Harry never saw it. A month after it was born, your mother took her furs, her maid and the family diamonds and left me the brat sired by her paramour. Kind of her, don't you think? Ha! Ha!' Ambrose threw back his head and laughed as though genuinely enjoying the joke.

'Father, if you could hear how bitter you sound, bitter and — frankly, I think your mind has been poisoned by unhappiness.' Vere voice was level but I saw that he suffered.

I felt I ought to leave them to quarrel alone but Ambrose had a tight grip on my arm. His expression became malevolent. 'What do I care for your opinions? You think you can come back here to pick over the bones of the property and revile me into the bargain? If there's been unhappiness, haven't you helped to make it by staying away for twelve years without a word? And didn't you leave with the woman to whom I had given my heart?'

Ambrose leaned on my arm so heavily that he would have fallen if I had pulled away. A look of sadness came into Vere's eyes. 'I deserve that reproach, I know.'

Ambrose gave a shout of laughter. 'You always were a soft, sentimental fool. I gave her nothing — neither my heart nor my purse. She was a slut like all the others. She meant nothing to me.'

'I don't know if that's true,' Vere spoke slowly, 'but I'd like to think it was. It doesn't excuse my behaviour. It seems to me that everyone in this family is vitiated beyond belief and it sickens and saddens me. It's time we started to behave like sane people with some notion of responsibility to others.'

458

'Hypocrite! Sanctimonious humbug!'

'Oh, let me go!' I tried to free myself. 'I can't stay and listen to this!'

'Ha! You don't like to hear me call him names.' Ambrose's face was twisted with cunning as he stared at me. 'Perhaps you see yourself as Mrs Gilderoy of Gilderoy Hall, eh? That *would* be a mistake. Let me tell you that this man,' he pointed a stick at Vere, 'has nothing. Not a penny to his name. Tomorrow I'm going to get that fool Windebank up here. I shall change my will and leave everything to Guy. Vere will be a beggar.'

'I think you've said enough.' Vere's face was pale with anger. 'Freddie, I'm sorry you've had to put up with our appalling manners. I'll walk home with you.'

Ambrose let go of my arm. 'You'll give my regards to the village idiot, if you see him?' He panted a little with excited spite. I went to the door. The sunlight was brilliant after the darkness of the hall. 'Your brother, I mean. Blood's thicker than water, they say, don't they?'

'Yes.' Vere said slowly and, I thought not without satisfaction. 'And it's true. I shall do everything I can to persuade Guy to return Spokebender Abbey to Lemmy, to be held in trust. We got our hands on the property by a disgraceful trick. I've always been ashamed of that. While I believed the le Maistre line had died out, nothing could be done. But now — '

I was standing on the top step when I heard Ambrose scream. 'You stupid — fool.' His sticks clattered to the ground. 'I — won't — let — ' I turned to see his face suffused with blood as he crumpled and fell.

I ran back into the house and down the hall passage to telephone for an ambulance. My eyes were dazzled. Vere was a dark green shape of spinning specks, kneeling by his father. The receiver felt like ice against my cheek. I said, 'I think it's a stroke.'

The operator said. 'Don't worry, me duck. I'll get them out to you right away.'

459

I knelt beside Vere, who had one hand beneath his father's head to protect it from the cold hard flags. 'It was my fault,' I whispered. 'I shouldn't have said anything about Lemmy.'

Ambrose's face was uncharacteristically peaceful. Bubbles of saliva gathered in the corners of his slack mouth and he began to snore.

'No.' Vere pushed back a strand of hair that had fallen over Ambrose's flushed forehead. 'I was angry. I wanted to hurt him. If he dies, I shall go away. It was a mistake to come back. This time I've killed him.'

'But, Vere, the estate will need you more than ever! Guy doesn't care about it. You must have realised that by now.'

'Oh, yes.' Vere smiled coldly. 'But he can sell it and live on the proceeds.'

I said no more about it because, of course, it was none of my business. But as we knelt in silence by the slumbering, wheezing body I imagined Guy squandering the purchase price and ending up a bankrupt, disillusioned roué and Vere wandering the world, rootless and sick for home and, though I had no reason to suppose that my petition deserved any consideration, I sent up a prayer that Ambrose might live.

38

Hay-making began on a day of unclouded skies. Clover, moon daisies and thistles grew plentifully in grass long enough to tickle my arms. The fields were bordered to the west by the river purling serenely over its gravel bed, a different creature from the roaring beast it became further down by the cottage. The hum of insects was drowned by the approach of an ancient tractor driven by Vere. I hadn't seen him since the day of Ambrose's collapse.

He gave me a brief, preoccupied smile and jumped down, leaving the engine to idle. Chloë, who had spent the night at the cottage with me, abandoned a rabbit hole and dashed over to hurl herself at him. Deacon and Dusty clambered down from the trailer with a pantomime of effort due respectively to the torn ligament and age. Dusty gave me a nod. Deacon ran his eyes over me appreciatively, winking and limping extravagantly, like Long John Silver played by Robert Newton, whom he closely resembled. Fortunately the scab had fallen from my nose that morning and I no longer looked ridiculous. The trailer was taken off and the mowing machine hitched to the back. Conversation was impossible because of the noise of the tractor.

Vere started to cut the first swathe and we followed behind with pitchforks. We tossed up the long strands of grass, clouds of pollen drifting down upon our heads and bare arms. The delicious smell of the hay was as powerful as a narcotic. Rabbits bounded away, frightened by the roar and clatter of machinery. At first Chloë chased them but their abundance created *ennui*. We were accompanied in our slow progress by marbled butterflies, emerald grasshoppers and, less attractively,

461

flies. After an hour of repeatedly stooping and lifting, I began to feel giddy with heat. I thought of all the people, long dead, who had done this same work. Two thousand years ago we could have been tribesmen of the Durotriges working for our Roman masters or, six centuries later, men of Wessex, cropping common land or, only a hundred years ago, Bathsheba Everdene's farm-hands in *Far from the Madding Crowd*.

I recited the poem 'Tarantella' under my breath. 'The tedding and the spreading of the straw for the bedding, And the fleas that tease in the high Pyrenees, The wine that tasted of the tar.' I realised I was getting the lines muddled but the important thing with physical work was to find a rhythm and stick to it so you needn't think about what you were doing. My hands were blistering but I was no longer the urban *ingénue*, victim of every change of circumstance and freak of weather. As well as the broad-brimmed hat I had borrowed from Prim to protect my complexion, I had brought a roll of sticking plaster and scissors. The palms of both hands were covered with it by the time we took our first break.

Vere had the tractor bonnet open and was fiddling with something deep within so Dusty, Deacon and I sat in the shade against the bole of a giant oak and drank lemonade. Chloë rested her head on my feet, too lazy to snap at flies when they settled on her back. The men rolled cigarettes and made hard work of spitting out the shreds. The pungent smoke hung in the air like blue threads. Dusty offered his pouch to me with an interrogative grunt but I declined.

'What have you done to your leg, Mr Deacon?' I felt bound to enquire after he had spent several minutes flexing and rubbing it and groaning.

'I were castratin' this calf, see, only it didna want its love-life put a stop to.' I had forgotten what a grim conversationalist Deacon was. He grinned, exposing nicotine-stained fangs like chips of wood. 'So it leaped in the air and I wen' after it and twisted me leg round like so.' Deacon gave a graphic description of the wrenching of muscles and what followed, to which I stopped my ears. Instead I admired the rippling hills, the rocky summits and the soft grasses, all cast into violent extremes of light and shade by the pulverising sun.

Before I had run out of uplifting thoughts Vere signalled that the break was over. We worked on, stoop, lift, stoop, lift. I lost any sense of time and purpose. The sweat rolled down my face and I wiped it away with my forearm. You could no longer see the sun. The sky had become a white, incandescent shell. I saw in the corner of my vision a black shape moving slowly against the beating glare. I shaded my eyes. It was Miss Glim. She had parked the Land Rover at the gate and was walking along the boundary of the field, carrying a basket. Vere stopped the tractor and went to take it from her. She strode quickly away, not looking around her, ignoring the beauty of the landscape. I was sorry for her, lonely without the man she loved.

'At this rate you won't be able to bend your fingers by tea-time,' said Vere, when he saw my hands, fat with vivid pink plasters. 'Are they very painful?'

'Not at all.' This was a lie because they stung as all blisters do. But I resolved not to complain for the other two were grumbling like drones about heads, hands, backs and legs. I sat down in the shadows that struck as cold as running water.

'Aha. Wench's hands are good for nobbut light work.' Dusty spat near my packet of sandwiches. He displayed his calloused, horny paws with quite unjustified pride, I thought.

My ears buzzed in the silence for Vere had turned off the tractor ignition. Now we heard the calling of birds and chafing of crickets.

'A lapwing.' Vere pointed to a black-and-white crested

bird, stalking about the stubble. 'They're getting rare. Too much intensive farming. We shall rue the day — or our descendants will. What's been allowed to happen in this country in the last ten years is nothing short of criminal. Historians will look back and wonder why we did nothing to stop the rape and ruin of the land.'

Dusty and Deacon munched Scotch eggs and cold sausages, their eyes dull, their thoughts elsewhere. I stared at flecks of light on the toe of my shoe and tried to get my brain to work.

'How is your father?'

'Much the same. In a coma.'

'I'm so sorry.'

'His doctors say he isn't in pain. They think it's unlikely he'll recover his senses. But he might live for months, even years. There's nothing they can do for him. He's being moved to a nursing-home in Bournemouth next week, which specialises in the care of comatose patients.'

'You aren't still thinking of leaving?'

'No. I rang Guy in Ireland to tell him what happened. He said he couldn't see why he should cut short an enjoyable holiday to sit and look mawkish beside an unconscious body.' Vere laughed suddenly. 'One thing you can say for Guy, he's not a hypocrite. I told him I was thinking of going away and he said he'd be extremely put out by any change in the present arrangements and not to be a fool.' I wondered then about the size of the allowance Vere made Guy that he should be content to give up his inheritance so blithely. Vere's tone became mocking. 'I thought he was right, actually. I'm too old to go storming off into the blue again. There's a flavour of melodrama about doing it twice that offends me.'

'Besides that, it would break Chloë's heart.'

Chloë lifted her head, hearing her name and looked longingly at the cheese. I borrowed a lethal-looking knife from Deacon to cut off a piece for her. She ate it quickly and went back to sleep. Vere was staring at his half-eaten sandwich, obviously miles away. He would have been very difficult to paint for if he was not talking he at once withdrew into reflection and it was impossible to read his mood. His eyebrows, like Guy's, were set high above the eye. Because they were darker than Guy's they were more dramatic. Now that his hair had grown thick and long enough to touch his collar the similarity of their bone structure was striking. But Vere's face was more strongly constructed, a broader jaw, a longer, straighter nose.

''A cat may look at a king, said Alice.'' He turned to me so swiftly that I had no time to look away.

'Do you like the Alice books? Strange how few people really do. Having them forced on them as children, I suppose.' I was annoyed with myself for having been caught staring. 'He's the only writer my uncle ever reads. 'He thought he saw a buffalo upon the chimney-piece, he looked again and found it was his sister's husband's niece.' Uncle Sid can recite Lewis Carroll for hours. He maintains it's all the philosophy a man needs.'

''He thought he saw a banker's clerk descending from a bus, He looked again and found it was a hippopotamus.' What were you thinking about?'

'I was just wondering — how are you getting on with Miss Glim?'

'If I try to make my own bed or wash up a cup she immediately does it again herself. She insists on ironing my socks even though they've all got holes. I have dinner in solitary state in the dining room under her unfriendly eye. She makes me think of the fabulous cockatrice, half snake, half bird, that could kill with a look. I expect every mouthful to be my last.'

He looked amused. I wondered if Vere was lonely in that large house. What had happened to the woman

465

with whom he had run away all those years ago? 'Poor Miss Glim. She has that passionate sort of temperament that fastens on one person to love exclusively. Can't you be firm with her?'

'When I suggested we might shut up some of the rooms to save her work she made a noise like a tyre bursting and spent the day spring-cleaning the house from top to bottom, even the attics. She's supposed to have afternoons to herself but she was beating rugs in the stableyard when I came back from exercising Guy's horse. Supper was five courses in the dining room with the best silver. I don't dare to propose any more economies of labour for fear of further martyrdom. I don't understand women. I'm just an ordinary, clumsy, brutish male who takes a wag of the tail to mean pleasure and a growl to mean hostility. Women speak a completely different language and it baffles me. I suppose it's because I've had so little to do with them.'

'Oh, no.' I spoke with certainty. 'It isn't that. The bafflement is universal. And it works both ways. Probably the state of being in love requires incomprehension. We can make it up as we go along. The truth is simply not romantic.'

Vere rotated his wrist to examine a brilliantly coloured beetle that was crawling slowly down his arm. His face was in shadow but his eyes were lit by the reflection from his pale blue shirt. Very gently he touched the iridescent wing case with his finger. 'And yet I've always hoped it might be possible to know someone through and through, and to be able to be entirely oneself — ' A loud snore from Dusty interrupted him. Vere stood up. 'We'd better get on.'

Grumbling, the men resumed their work. The sun grilled the earth until it shimmered. I could no longer focus my eyes. My scalp beneath my hat was damp with sweat but mindful of freckles I kept it on. Suddenly the trance I had fallen into was shattered by a bellow of pain. Deacon was lying on the ground, his face screwed up in agony.

''Tis this bloody leg,' he groaned as I ran up to him. 'It give way on me and I fell on me knife. It do come open sometimes. Ah-ho-o-w!'

By now Vere had seen us and cut the engine. Blood was dyeing Deacon's trouser leg crimson. His face was grey. Vere took the knife from Deacon's pocket and ripped the fabric, exposing the flesh. I felt rather sick when I saw the blood pumping from the wound. He tore off a strip of cloth and made it into a pad to press over the wound. 'Here you are, Deacon. Hold it on as firmly as you can. You might have hit an artery. We'll have to get you to hospital. Freddie, can you keep that leg as high as possible?'

Deacon was a tall man and enormously fat. Vere took his shoulders and we pulled and struggled and panted until finally we managed to roll him unceremoniously into the trailer. Vere reversed the tractor and hitched it up. 'I'll take him to the post office and telephone for an ambulance from there. I may be an hour or so.'

I ran to open the gate. One man down and we had only just started. I went back to join Dusty who was still stooping and tossing, oblivious of the world.

★ ★ ★

'I'll come and help on Wednesday,' said Prim, when I told her that evening what had happened. Vere had returned to the hayfield, having seen Deacon into the ambulance with Mrs Deacon who was inclined to be cross as it was wash-day. Deacon had been uncharacteristically silent beneath a rain of scolding. 'It's my day off from the surgery. It sounds enchantingly bucolic. I've always wanted to be Tess of the d'Urbervilles. Except for the last few pages, of course.'

'I'll come tomorrow afternoon as soon as I've finished

tidying up the art room,' said Bar. 'It's half-term. The weather's going to break soon. You've only got two more days of fine weather before the storms begin. On Friday there's going to be terrific thunder and a deluge of rain.'

'How do you know?' I imagined the casting of runes, or at least a piece of damp seaweed.

'I heard the long-range weather forecast.'

We were in the garden at Yardley House. The herbaceous borders were blooming in carefully graded colours, from cool white and blue delphiniums at the ends to hot red oriental poppies in the middle. Prim said they had been planted in accordance with the dictates of Gertrude Jekyll and were the equivalent of hard labour in the *gulag* to maintain. On the surface of the lily-pond floated pale yellow water-lilies, like delicate porcelain teacups. A massive teak table, silver with weathering, stood on a raised dais beneath a rose arbour, making a pretty rustic setting for the supper of galantine of chicken and gooseberry tart that Prim had made for us. A bowl of dark velvety roses, cut in the cool of the evening, stood between the dishes, shedding a delicious scent that was balm to my tired senses and aching body.

'It'll be such a shame if the hay gets spoilt,' I said. 'It's the only income Vere will have for ages.'

'He's a very interesting man,' said Bar, absent-mindedly plaiting her hair round the rail on the back of my chair. 'Besides being so good-looking. I think he's really quite mysterious. Other men want to make an impression and they aren't at all interested in what you've got to say. But Vere listens as though he really wants to know. He asked me all sorts of things about being a witch. Whether witches are necessarily archetypally strange — outsiders to be revered as wise women or persecuted as dangerous. What was the difference between a witch and a pagan. He knows so much about so many interesting things. In India, apparently, the first day of spring is celebrated by worshipping the god of love — the equivalent to the witches' Eostar. They have feasts in which everything is yellow. Yellow food, flowers, tablecloths, decorations and so on, and they all wear yellow clothes. Apparently Hindus are obliged by their religion to consume the five products of the cow, whom they look upon as the Universal Mother, every day. Milk, curd, butter, urine and dung. Imagine!'

'I'd rather not.' Prim looked at her forkful of chicken and trembling golden aspic with a frown.

'Where did you meet him?' I asked.

'In the woods, last week. It was just before midnight. Full moon is the high tide of psychic power and a very good time for casting spells. I thought I'd invoke a new love. I'm getting awfully fed up with being on my own. Only it was rather cloudy. I tried hard not to be frightened because I knew that the trees were protecting me but it was horribly dark and shadowy. I'd just anointed my silver bell with rose oil and I was tinkling away, listening to it reverberating in the astral realms, when a huge black shape rose up from a clump of bushes and I screamed like anything.'

'Didn't it occur to you that this might be the new love responding with admirable promptness to the psychic call?' asked Prim.

'I have to admit it didn't. I thought it was the Horned One and I must say it was a relief when it turned out to be Vere. Luckily I hadn't taken my clothes off yet as it was a bit chilly. Of course I absolutely long to see the Lord of the Night, as we sometimes call him, but not on my own and when I'm unprepared. He's half goat, half man but nothing like a satyr. He's only interested in joyful sex and the inner quest for wisdom.'

'Not much like other men, then,' Prim commented.

'Vere was badger-watching. He'd been there since sunset and had already seen the cubs playing. The

469

mother badger had brought back the remains of a wasps' nest, which is their favourite food. He told me lots of other things about otters, which are related to badgers, and he wants to encourage them to return to the riverbank. Then I explained what I was doing and we had a good talk about magic rituals.'

'Did you finish casting the spell?' I asked.

'I asked Vere if he'd like to join me in a trance but he said he was afraid he wasn't sufficiently sensitive to spiritual auras to be of any assistance. I'm sure he's wrong but, anyway, after he'd gone Lemmy came wandering along and he played the reed pipe, which I'm awfully bad at doing, and we got undressed and danced until we were as hot as anything and if ever a spell was well cast that one was. I think Vere has a great deal of purity of intent and in my next trance I'm going to ask for the expansion of his psychic awareness.'

'Oughtn't you to warn him first?' asked Prim. 'It could come as a nasty shock if he's not expecting it.'

Bar looked at Prim with a doubtful expression as though she suspected she was being teased, but luckily we were interrupted by the arrival of the children who had let themselves in by the orchard gate. Frankie almost knocked me off my chair in her enthusiasm. She smelt strongly of soap. I kissed her tenderly and stroked her like a cat, which she always loved. Ruth stood by and passively allowed her cheek to be kissed. She was looking much better, with brighter eyes and a clearer skin. She wore a smocked blue-and-white striped cotton dress that suited her quaint, prim manner. I saw the beginning of something like beauty in her dark looks.

'Wills!' I was surprised to see him, having imagined that the television set would always be a superior attraction.

'Wotcher.' Wills sauntered past me, hands in the pockets of his new grey flannel trousers. I found out afterwards that Swithin had given him a pound to come and see us.

While Prim served the gooseberry tart Frankie sat on my knee with her arms round my neck. Ruth drew her chair up neatly to the table, hands in her lap, waiting to be told to start. Wills flung himself down and sprawled across the table, knocking over a glass with his elbow.

It had been a minor triumph to get Beryl to agree that the children might come to see us. She had frowned at Prim's offer to give them supper and it was apparent that she was fiercely jealous of their nurture so I suggested that they might come afterwards for a short period between supper and bedtime. I knew better than to attempt to see Titch at such a late hour, though I missed her very much. Very properly, she would be tucked up in a nest of baby-pink cot blankets, her head supported by a pillow embroidered with chicks or ducks.

'How are you getting on with Mr and Mrs Winnacott?' Bar asked.

'It's all right,' said Ruth. 'I helped Auntie Beryl to top and tail gooseberries for jam this afternoon.'

Frankie pushed back against me. 'I saw this film on the telly where there was a horse called Black Beauty and it had ever such a sad life and it made me cry and I hated it. Auntie Beryl said it was a car-sick story and she'd read it to us at bed-time. I shan't listen if she does.'

'Classic, I think she must have meant. It means its good and important.'

'But people were so nasty to the poor horse and it fell over and its knees got broke.' Frankie's eyes filled with tears at the memory.

'It was crap,' contributed Wills.

'How's Titch?'

'Auntie Beryl says we've to call her Helen.' Frankie

471

made a face. 'She's *my* sister and I've known her much, *much* longer.'

'Auntie Beryl says the teachers won't like her being called Titch when she goes to school,' said Ruth. 'We've gotta get her used to it.'

I saw that Ruth was prepared to conform to life at the Rectory and I was heartily glad of it.

'What are you doing, Wills?' Prim spoke sharply. Having finished the tart he was leaning back in his chair zipping and unzipping the fly of his trousers. 'That's highly inelegant.'

'He hasn't had a pair before with a zip that works,' said Frankie. 'Mum used to get us second-hand clothes and it was always the zip what had gone.'

I saw that Ruth had turned white at the mention of her mother. I remembered the feeling so well. The dread of her being spoken of, the racing of the heart, the terror that one might cry.

'Guess what I did today?' I said, hoping to distract her.

'You met a loverly man and you're going to marry him,' said Frankie at once.

'You give him a blow-job,' suggested Wills, grinning horribly.

'Don't be so silly, Wills.' Bar was matter-of-fact. 'You don't even know what that means.'

'Course I do.'

'Rubbish!' I was surprised that Bar, who with her pink-and-white skin and dimples looked hardly older than Ruth, could be firm when the occasion called for it.

'I went hay-making.'

'Can I come?' asked Frankie at once. 'I want to make hay.'

'If Mrs Winnacott says you can.'

Frankie screwed up her face hideously and tears filled her eyes. 'I shall come anyway. She hasn't *bought* me. I belong to meself.'

472

I was in two minds about whether or not to discourage this assertion of independence. Edward arrived at that moment. Observant man that he was, he saw Frankie's distress and said, in a stage whisper, 'Why is Miss Watkins fastened to Freddie's chair?' We all looked at Bar, who had got her hair into a terrible tangle. 'Perhaps she's a sacrifice to the gods like Andromeda, who was a princess nearly as beautiful as Miss Frankie Roker. The sea-nymphs were jealous of her good looks so she was chained to a rock and a great monster with black wings and five heads, who lived in the depths of the sea, was sent to eat her up.'

Frankie giggled, her sorrow forgotten. 'What happened to her?'

The gate opened again to admit Vere. I saw Bar turn the colour of a rose. She snatched the scissors that Prim had used to cut the roses and snipped off the tangled locks of hair.

'I've come to beg assistance with the hay.' Vere's eyes fastened on Bar who was now scarlet with embarrassment but, despite having one side of her hair much shorter than the other, still managed to look charming, if eccentric. Then he looked at me. 'Mrs Deacon has just telephoned me from the cottage hospital. Dusty has food poisoning. It seems he's been eating strange things out of ancient tins. He's in the bed next to Deacon.'

'Oh, no! Poor, silly old man. We've all warned him about that.' Prim was exasperated. 'Oh dear, and there's George with no one to look after him. He'd better come and stay with me.'

'It's all right.' Vere prodded with his toe a patch of moss in Prim's otherwise immaculate turf. 'I've taken him up to the Hall. I've left him having supper under the less than tender eye of Miss Glim. Fortunately he's accustomed to being on the receiving end of unreasonable bad temper.'

'That's very decent of you, if I may say so.' Edward,

who had uncorked a bottle of wine he had brought with him, raised his glass in Vere's direction.

'Not at all. There's more than enough room. Besides,' Vere squinted up at the sky to watch a phalanx of swans flying over the garden with a clamour of beating wings, 'who else should take responsibility for George? After all, I am the boy's father.'

39

Vere and George were probing the insides of the tractor, deep in talk of fuel pumps and carburettors, when I reached the hayfield the next day. Vere gave me a fleeting smile. George ignored me, his brows knotted in thought, his handsome face liberally smeared with oil as he fiddled with nuts and bolts.

No one had been able to think of anything to say when, the evening before, Vere had so unexpectedly declared his responsibility for George's existence. Even Frankie had been silenced. I had experienced a sense of relief, as though a burden had been lifted, for which I could not properly account.

'Good for you!' Prim had said gruffly, at last.

Edward had shaken Vere's hand heartily then looked confused, as though wondering if this was, indeed, a case for congratulation.

'I do think it's romantic,' said Bar dreamily, after Vere had gone. 'What can it be like for George to be whisked out of obscurity and find himself the son and heir of Gilderoy Hall? It's like a fairy-tale.'

'It's fuckin' unfair.' Wills looked sulky, the thrill of the working zip altogether eclipsed by the discovery of George's silver spoon.

'Language!' said Prim at once, to which Wills responded by pointing a grubby finger at her. She had the grace to look abashed.

'Freddie!' Frankie was running across the field, followed by Ruth. Wills came along more slowly. He had his hands in his pockets, lips pursed in a whistle. George looked up as Wills came to peer into the works.

'I bet you, for all you think you're so clever, you can't

make that thing go,' said Wills at last, chucking down the gauntlet.

'I can, too, better'n you,' said George, snatching it up. 'You couldn't mend a busted bicycle!'

'Maybe I couldn't,' conceded Wills. 'But I could ride it, which is more'n you could, Cripple.'

The two boys rolled around in the stubble, creating a cloud of dust. Wills was bigger and stronger but George had more science and fought with ferocity. Ruth and Frankie screamed, and I turned away, unable to watch.

Vere waited for a minute or so before pulling them apart. 'All right, that'll do, you two. You've had a scrap and that's got to last you for the day. Anyone who starts a fight from now on gets sent straight home. No wages. Understand?' George and Wills, with a swelling eye apiece, nodded. 'Shake hands. Go on!' The boys did so, perfunctorily, and for the time being honour was satisfied.

I gave the children a pitchfork each and tried to get them to work to a rhythm. Ruth got the idea at once and applied herself diligently. Frankie wanted to talk while we worked and often stopped to emphasise the point of what she was saying. Wills was bored after twenty yards and ran about, trying to balance the pitchfork on his head, until I got really cross and shouted at him. George plugged away steadily, determined to prove himself. But we were unable to keep up with the tractor.

'You'll have to go home, Wills.' I was already hot and bothered by tiny flies that boiled in swirling columns above each of our heads. 'You nearly ran Frankie through, then. For goodness' sake! Put the wretched thing down!'

Vere came over to inspect our progress. 'Like to drive the tractor?' he asked Wills.

'You bet!'

I thought it was extremely rash of Vere to put

England's answer to the Reign of Terror in charge of a powerful, killing machine but, in fact, the minute he was behind the wheel Wills behaved in an exemplary manner. He drove slowly and carefully round the field, his tongue sticking out of the corner of his mouth as he concentrated on keeping the line straight. When he was satisfied that Wills was competent Vere joined us spreading the hay. We got on much faster.

'That was clever of you,' I said to Vere when we stopped for lunch. 'Though what Brenda Bickerstaffe would say if she saw him, I shudder to think.'

'Guy and I used to drive tractors at that age. It's simple enough. Wills is bored. He needs taking in hand.'

'What luck that you have disciplinary skills Dr Arnold of Rugby would have envied.'

Vere smiled. 'Nothing like a misspent youth for teaching you the peculiar workings of a boy's mind and heart.'

'I'm so glad you've taken George under your wing. I'm sure you won't regret it.'

'I don't think I will. He's very bright. And very unhappy.'

Something in Vere's voice brought a lump to my throat and I bent to the task of unpacking Miss Glim's well-provisioned basket.

That afternoon we were joined by Bar. She looked very pretty in a bright flowery dress, her head protected by a scarf edged with dangling coins. She had chosen it to keep insects away, on the same principle as corks in Australia, but the flies, perhaps attracted by the dazzling, winking surfaces, singled her out for special attention. Frankie's shoulders and nose began to blister, despite frequent applications of cream, so I sent her to sit in the shade with Chloë with the directive to make up stories to entertain us during the tea-break. The reel of sticking plaster ran out but we worked hard and finished the field. There was one more to cut and then we could begin baling.

'Though the monster had five heads it swallowed Princess Anne Drum-thingy down whole wiv only one of 'em,' said Frankie, her expression far away. 'She were an enchanted princess so she could hold her breath under water. She tickled the monster's throat an' he coughed her up, along with two ships and a lighthouse. She went walkin' along the bottom of the sea on a road made of pearls and she met a mermaid who was eatin' a seaweed-flavoured ice cream.'

There was much more in this vein, which I enjoyed listening to, lying on my back, staring up at the undersides of the leaves as they shivered in the hot air. Wills sat next to Vere, eating fruit-cake, his restlessness and discontent sated for the moment by the esoteric pleasures of machinery.

'It's nice here,' said Ruth.

It was. A lark trilled exquisite liquid notes in the mid-distance. The hills on the far side were rich with glittering blues and purples above the soft greyish-green of the shorn valley bed.

'Can I ask you summat?' I overheard Wills say in a low voice to Vere.

'Go ahead.' Vere spoke in kind, avuncular tones.

'What's a blow-job?'

George gave a guffaw of consummate scorn.

★　★　★

The following morning we had an unexpected addition to the workforce. Standing on the back of the tractor behind Vere, blond head reflecting the sun's rays like a mirror, tiny shorts exposing muscular legs the colour of a good piece of furniture, was Werner.

'My dearest Miss Freddie!' He sprang to the ground and applied his lips passionately to my knuckles. 'The time parted has seemed a hundred years.'

478

'What are you doing here, Werner? I thought you were about to be married.'

'*Ach, wirklich*! So I am. But I could not stop myself from the delight of coming one more time to England where I feel so homelike. But vat do I find? Herr Gilderoy is badly sick. I am so sorrowful.'

'Bar, this is Werner von Wunsiedel.'

'Ho, ho, *ho*!' cried Werner, looking at Bar. Having found the gypsy ensemble of the previous day rather cumbersome, she was wearing shorts almost as short as his own. Her hair, quite as fair as Werner's, was trimmed in jig-jags to accommodate the missing section. She looked like a provocative elf. He clicked his heels, noiselessly as he was wearing canvas shoes, and bowed over her hand. 'This is happiness, Miss — ' he tittered, ' — Bar. You know vat this means in German, *ja*? It means vithout any clothes. *Ach, wie herrlich*! Forgive, please, the freedom!'

We set to work. Werner was a miracle of physical fitness. His lithe body had the grace of a ballet dancer as he tossed the grass high into the air and soon Bar was inspired to execute *arabesques* and *entrechats* in an elegant *pas de deux*. With such an energetic workforce we were easily able to keep up with Wills, and by lunchtime the field was done.

'This is the English *Träumerei* — vat do you say? Reverie?' Werner made rapid work of Miss Glim's pork pie. 'This is Constable, Turner, Samuel Palmer.'

'Why, I was thinking just the same!' said Bar. 'That it was like a nineteenth-century landscape, I mean. Are you interested in painting?' Werner assumed a lofty intellectual expression and stared down the neck of Bar's T-shirt as she bent forward to dip her hard-boiled egg into the salt. 'Actually,' she went on, 'apart from the tractor it could be any time since the beginning of agriculture. Not a fence or wire or pylon in sight. But still essentially English. The softness of the colours. It's hard to imagine what French painters like Pissarro and Monet would have made of this.'

Soon they were deep in discussion of the merits of the Impressionists. Werner's rather fleshy nostrils flared every time Bar's dimples appeared and when she gathered her hair into a top-knot to cool her neck, an action that lifted her bust into shapely prominence, he swallowed his boiled egg nearly whole and had to be slapped on the back. I saw that Vere was amused.

After lunch Vere spent some time sniffing the fescues and rolling them between his fingers, debating whether or not they were dry enough for baling. The forecast of storms ahead was the decisive factor in favour of making a beginning. The baler was as ancient as the mower and much more temperamental. It made a belching, bronchial noise, and threatened to die on every third or fourth cough, something like *ca-chong, ca-chong ca-a-a-ah-chong*! The bales were held together by orange twine which tended to tie itself into great loopy knots during the stopping and starting process. Wills drove the tractor that towed it while we raked the hay into lines for it to devour. Brick-shaped parcels dropped from the back of the baler with mutinous irregularity.

George came into his own with that wretched machine. He discovered, even faster than Vere, its numerous caprices and was infinitely patient and adept at sorting out the mechanism that fed the string. Vere called him his chief engineer and I saw him ruffle the boy's hair when he thought no one was looking.

Strands of cloud were knitting across the face of the sun now and it was much pleasanter to work. I tossed away my hat and it spun like a discus into the hedge. I never did retrieve it. We sang all the rustic songs we could think of like 'Green Grow The Rushes, Oh' and 'A North Country Maid' and 'Kitty of Coleraine' and then we went on to harvest festival hymns.

> '*Up, my neighbour! Now the corn*
> *Ripens at the harvest morn*
> *Let it to our sickle yield*
> *And pile with sheaves the golden field . . .* '

we sang at the tops of our voices. Frankie had a voice like a klaxon and an imprecise idea of pitch, but as I watched her face bright with enjoyment, her thin hair flopping and her sharp little elbows jerking in time with the song, I was so moved by her resilience to misfortune that I couldn't sing at all for a while.

I paused in my raking to watch George put the baler right for the eighth or ninth time. Vere stood over him, his face very brown by contrast with his pale yellow shirt, the sleeves of which were cut off above the elbow, the edges left raw. His jeans were rent above one knee. I had never known a man so indifferent to appearance. Despite this dishevelment, there was something tough and dependable about Vere. Werner's blond athleticism seemed to lack substance by comparison.

So I thought, leaning on my rake, dreamily following the shadows of the racing clouds as they fled over the slashed stalks and marvelling at the grace of a pair of swifts as they sketched huge arcs in the speckling sky. The baler began to *ca-chong* again and we went back to work with renewed energy, conscious of the waning of the day.

★ ★ ★

I was the first to arrive at the field the next morning. Chloë sped off at once to check that the ancient burrows had not miraculously bred inhabitants overnight. I heard the tractor engine. Vere was alone. 'Where are the others?' I asked, when he turned off the engine.

'George is showing Werner the way to the post office

so he can telephone the mother dragon to ask for an extension of leave. Since meeting Barbara his enthusiasm for Pudwell has been fanned to combustion point.'

'Are you finding him a terrible nuisance?'

'No, not really. I've forbidden him to mention, on pain of immediate expulsion, anything to do with politics of any colour. He's tremendously keen to be helpful and spends his spare time sawing logs in the stableyard. That's when he's not swinging Indian clubs and gulping in all the oxygen for miles around. Apparently the girl he's marrying has put him on a strict exercise regime. She sounds appalling. He's worried about being able to consummate the marriage. I find myself feeling rather sympathetic.'

'Any news of Dusty and Deacon?'

'I called at the cottage hospital last night. Deacon's wound has become infected and Dusty has been moved to the isolation ward with suspected botulism.'

'No! How terrible!'

'It's very rare. Probably Matron's wishful thinking. She's hoping for a variation on septic toes and influenza. He'd be taken to a proper hospital if there was any real danger of it.'

'Why is Werner telephoning from the post office?'

'The telephone at the Hall's been cut off.'

'Oh dear! Can I — would you be offended if I offered to lend you the money?'

'Thank you, that's very kind but it isn't necessary. I simply didn't think of it, that's all. Ow. Bugger! Sorry.' Vere, who had been delving the insides of the baler, sucked a gash on his thumb.

'Let me look.'

'It's only a surface cut. Quiet now. Good girl.' This was addressed to Chloë, who had returned disappointed from her quest and, sensing excitement, began now to bark.

482

'It looks quite deep to me. You'd better have something on it.' I got out a new roll of Elastoplast. 'We don't want you ending up in the cottage hospital as well.'

'What a *fidus Achates* you are, to be sure. Provident, prudent and economical. Artistic, domesticated, good with children and animals. Prompt with bandages. Are there any limits to your talents?'

'Keep still and don't be absurd.' I took his hand to extend the thumb and assess the length of plaster needed. 'A good inch, I think. Now, where are my scissors?' I groped in the pocket of my jeans then glanced up as the swifts swooped, screaming, over our heads. Vere was looking down at me, his expression amused. I frowned reprovingly. The sky was reflected in miniature in his eyes, which were a dark hazel, ringed with black. As I looked into them a strange paralysis affected my limbs. The scent of the hay seemed to cloy my brain and make me giddy. The heat of the sun was mysteriously intensified until it throbbed in time with a pulse in my throat. The golden-green bowl in which we stood rose up to cradle us in its embrace and the great weight of the sky pressed down upon me. My breathing was restricted and my heart beat with difficulty.

'Freddie!' I felt his hand close over mine.

'Freddie! Freddie!' Ruth and Wills were climbing the gate. Frankie was already over and running towards me.

'Holla!' Werner was skipping briskly across the field. George limped in his wake.

I saw Bar, Prim and Balthazar strolling down the lane towards us. The day's work was about to begin.

40

'Come in, everyone.' Vere ushered us into the hall. Rivulets of water were running down our faces and we were wet to the skin. The storm had broken just as we finished baling. We had gathered the bales and stacked them under tarpaulins in pelting rain while lightning cracked over our heads. But the hay was safely gathered in and we continued to sing as Vere drove us back to the house.

'It was a lovely storm.' Frankie's eyes were dark against her white skin that was purpling with cold. 'Is it really God movin' His furniture about?'

'Course not, you daft thing! Girls are crap,' jeered Wills.

'What is it, then?'

'It's clouds gettin' wet and blowin' up.'

'You mutt!' George smiled with infinite superiority. 'It's a discharge of electricity.'

Wills raised his fist.

'All right, that'll do, you two,' said Vere. It had become something of a catchphrase. 'Werner, I need help to back the trailer into the stableyard. Then we'd better get the cows in. They've a genius for herding under the tallest tree. Freddie, see if you can find Miss Glim and ask her to run some hot baths. I hope you'll all stay for supper. I'll be back in a hour.'

I did not have far to look. I was attempting to peel off my sodden jersey when I saw Miss Glim coming down the stairs, carrying two suitcases. She made a wry face as she surveyed us. Probably we were not an attractive sight, red-nosed, shuddering with cold, our hair plastered flat to our heads. I noticed that she was wearing a coat and hat.

'Are you going away, Miss Glim?' I asked, fatuously in the circumstances.

'I'm going to Ireland to take care of Mr Guy. He telephoned this afternoon to ask me to come. 'Cissy', he said, 'all is not as I would have it in this land of bogs, bungalows and leprechauns. Your deft hand is needed to make things light and lovely.' That's Mr Guy for you. Such a way with words.' She looked at me triumphantly out of slightly mad eyes. 'You thought you'd trap him, didn't you, with your town ways and airs and graces? But it isn't you he wants. *I'm* the one what makes him comfortable and that's what men like — everything orderly about them, not flirting and sheep's eyes.' I stared at her, not knowing what to say. I couldn't bring myself to spoil her moment of triumph by telling her about Moira Fitzpatrick. There was a blast from a car horn. 'That'll be Will Dewy. I can't stand about talking. I'm to catch the overnight ferry. First class.'

Dumbly we watched her walk to the front door and pass through it without a backward glance.

'Well!' said Prim. 'It was amazing cheek but you have to feel sorry for the poor thing.'

'You'd feel even sorrier if you'd ever been to Castle Fitzpatrick,' I said, with feeling.

'Do you think Guy sleeps with her?' asked Bar.

'He certainly allowed me to think so.'

'Why does he do that?' asked Frankie. We had forgotten that the children were listening.

'She means they have sex with each other, booby!' said Wills.

Frankie giggled. 'Isn't she much too old?'

'Nah, stoo-pid.' Wills was scathing. 'Men don't care about that. They'll screw anythin' what's got a — '

Prim's hand was over his mouth before he could finish. 'William! Where *do* you pick up all this gutter talk?'

'It's what me mum used ter say.'

485

Prim was silenced by this.

I was amused but did my best to hide it. 'How is Vere to manage without a housekeeper? And what about supper?'

'Oh, we can rustle something up between us, surely.' Prim wiped a drip from her chin. 'Just let me recover some feeling in my feet.'

'What on earth can it cost to travel first class all the way to Tullireen?' I wondered gloomily.

★ ★ ★

An hour later we were warm, clean and dry, though somewhat strangely garmented. I wore a jersey and a pair of jeans belonging to Guy. Prim was too large to fit into his things and Vere's clothes were too disreputable to consider. She had the choice of walking home in the storm or borrowing the Land Rover which, being old, was a brute to drive and positively dangerous to take down the hill. In the end, not without many misgivings, she borrowed a dress and cardigan from Miss Glim's wardrobe.

The Roker children, Frankie protesting vehemently, had gone home. A few days before, Vere had unblocked the gate in the wall between the Hall and the church so it was now only a short walk to the Rectory. George was dispatched to the library with cocoa and toast. I looked in a few minutes later to see him lying with his feet up on the sofa, deep in a book, looking thoroughly at home. Prim, Bar and I went to the kitchen, prepared to be inventive, but found a large pan of soup, two ducks already stuffed and trussed and a large trifle in the larder. We could hardly believe our good fortune. It seemed a great deal of food for two men, however large and hungry.

The mystery was solved half an hour later. On my way to the dining room to seek Armagnac for the sauce,

486

I paused by the hall table. Next to the telephone was a note, evidently written by Miss Glim. 'Lady Frisk called to say that as you have not answered her letter she is assuming it will be agreeable if she and Miss Charlotte come this evening at 7.30. She has rung several times but your telephone has been out of order. She says this has been extremely inconvenient. I told Lady Frisk several times this was not my fault as I do not attend to the paying of the bills.'

I broke the news to Vere as he came in with Werner.

'What? Oh, God! I'd completely forgotten. She sent me a note yesterday. I meant to telephone and put her off. Damn and blast! I suppose she expects to be asked to stay to dinner. What does that wretched woman mean by coming here unasked and bringing that girl with her?'

'She means Charlotte to be the next Mrs Gilderoy.'

Vere looked at me in amazement. 'You're not serious?'

'Oh, Vere! Do you ever listen to anything anyone says to you? Lady Frisk has talked about virtually nothing else for weeks. How can you be so blind to what's under your nose?'

'You're under my nose.' He smiled. 'I can see quite clearly that you want to save me from my own ineptitude and I'm very touched.'

'There you are, Vere.' Prim came into the hall. 'Need we bother with proper table-laying as there are only five of us?'

'Seven.' I waved the note at Prim. She read it, dismay creasing the space between her brows.

'This means table-laying à *toute outrance*.'

'Oh, rubbish!' said Vere. 'What do we care about Lady Frisk?'

'Men know nothing.' Prim made for the dining room. I had to agree.

We found knives, forks, spoons, plates, salt,

pepper-pots and napkins. While Bar, Prim and I peeled potatoes, chopped shallots and shelled peas, Vere and Werner brought bottles of wine up from the cellars, polished glasses and lit fires to counteract the gloom of rain slashing at the windows and thunder rumbling round the hill.

A tooting from the drive, imitating the opening bars of Beethoven's Fifth, announced the arrival of our visitors. Through the open door I glimpsed a sleek, shining car in a strong shade of yellow.

'Such weather! I am *soaked* through!' boomed a well-known voice. Lady Frisk stepped into the hall. She was wearing a voluminous waterproof cape sprinkled with a few dots of rain. She flung it off in Vere's direction and threw her headscarf after it. 'Luckily the rain held off for much of the wedding. Lord Percival Bierce, you know. The crowned heads of Europe. So many old friends. The duchess was affectingly pleased to see me. Charlotte! I am catching pneumonia while you dither.'

Actually the hall was warm, for we had piled the grate high with logs and the panelling glowed chestnut brown with reflected light.

'Oh, how beautiful it looks!' said Charlotte, following her mother in.

I liked her at once for saying that. She offered her hand to Vere.

'Lovely to see you again. It must be ages since we met.' Then she blushed, no doubt recalling that there was an element of disgrace attached to Vere's departure and long absence. She looked younger than her twenty-four years, with fair curls brushed back from a smooth high brow and large innocent eyes in a face that was pretty rather than beautiful. She wore jeans and a denim jacket and no makeup. 'I hope you don't mind. I've brought a friend of mine. This is Elmer Golightly.'

Elmer was even taller than Vere. He had long, curly

hair standing out in a fan-shape round his high forehead and a thin angular body, clothed in a tight suit of midnight blue velvet. At his neck was a jabot of lace fastened with a huge Cairngorm brooch. He included us all in his smile, which was dazzling. 'Hi, man.' He clutched Vere's hand with carat-laden fingers and shook it energetically. 'Wow, this is some pad!'

Lady Frisk looked pained.

'Thank you.' If he was surprised, Vere hid it admirably. 'Let me introduce you.'

'Oh, my!' Elmer's protuberant eyes were dancing as he waved at us. 'You got a harem here. Hi, chicks, mighty nice to meet yah!'

Lady Frisk closed her eyes.

Vere ushered us into the drawing room.

'Yep!' said Elmer. 'You aristos know how to live. That's a cool painting, man.' He pointed to the Watteau. '*La Gamme d'Amour*. The gamut of love.'

'It's only a copy,' said Vere.

'Sure, man. I seen it in the National Gallery. I may be blacker than your hat but I ain't wholly ignorant.' Elmer laughed, showing shining teeth. Next to him we all appeared muted and lacklustre.

Werner brought in a tray of glasses and a bottle of wine and further introductions were made.

Lady Frisk greeted Werner with cold eyes. 'And how is your mother, the Baroness? She will be sorry to hear of Ambrose's illness. Your little . . . society will be quite broken up by it.' After that she said not another word to Werner for the rest of the evening.

'Do tell me what a nuclear chemist does?' I said to Elmer, in the awkward pause that had fallen.

'Man, my work is the sun.' Elmer leaned back in his chair and held out his arms as though embracing it. 'Right deep inside it there are nuclear reactions happening all the time and they're my business, baby.' I saw an expression of disgust on Lady Frisk's face.

'Charlotte and me, we're trying to find out whether the sun has changed its original composition. You ever heard of cosmic abundances?'

I had to shake my head. My perception of the universe was generally confined to metaphors of a metaphysical kind and I had to make a real effort of will to imagine a solar system in which masses of hydrogen and helium, throbbing with ions and electrons, blundered insensibly about the heavens. Elmer gave me an energetic résumé, no doubt in layman's terms of which I understood about a tenth. I had to cut short the lecture to go with Prim and attend to dinner. Bar was talking to Werner and did not notice our departure.

'I rather like Elmer.' I stirred the apple sauce, while Prim basted the ducks and potatoes. 'Will two ducks go round eight?'

'They're quite large ones. Let's do some bacon rolls as well, to make sure. I wonder what he sees in Charlotte. Quite sweet but not particularly exciting. Probably because she's been dominated all her life by her mother.'

A flare of lightning lit the kitchen for a split second and left reversed images on my vision. A growl of thunder made Chloë quiver and move closer to my feet. Balthazar had adopted a position under the sink and was defending his post against all-comers with savage snarls. 'The attraction must partly be due to two great scientific brains getting together. This is her moment of rebellion and she's certainly showing some style.'

'I wish I'd rebelled.' Prim paused, holding a spoonful of duck fat, to consider it. She looked delightfully old-fashioned in Miss Glim's cotton frock, which was green with white polka dots. Also, she was without that ridiculous cap. I suppose I was particularly struck because it was the first time I had seen her in anything feminine. 'I was twenty by the time flower power came along. I already felt too old to trip up a mountain in

Nepal with a sitar. Besides, I've never liked chaos. I always want to put some kind of order into things. A commune in Wales with dreaming junkies and full ashtrays would have driven me to distraction. I was born out of my time.'

'Rebellion's a luxury really. Plenty of people from art school dropped out and became hippies. Those communes weren't self-sufficient because that takes really hard work. Love and peace don't generate cash. There was always someone with money who supported all the others. It was a dream that became a lie like a lot of the sixties doctrine — exploiting ancient laws of hospitality in India, and that sort of thing.'

Prim sighed. 'I'm afraid it didn't have much impact in South Dorset. In Bournemouth the boys grew their hair over their ears and the girls wore Indian bedspreads made into smocks but the ideology passed us by. Did you notice the length of Elmer's fingernails? And purple, pearlised nail polish! Mine never grow like that.' Prim looked regretfully at her hands with their short square nails and ragged cuticles. 'I rather suspect Elmer's foppery is his little joke on the world. He's obviously sending up all the stereotypes. I like that.'

'Who're you talking about?' Edward walked into the kitchen. The shoulders of his coat were dark with rain. 'Should I be jealous?'

'Oh, bugger! You made me spill hot fat on my hand. What are *you* doing here?'

'I couldn't get near the front door because of the Land Rover and that extraordinary yellow monster. So I had to park in the yard and walk up. Vere telephoned ten minutes ago and asked me to dinner — apologised for the short notice but said he needed another man. Why are you doing the cooking? What's happened to Cissy Glim?' Edward came over and dropped a kiss on Prim's brow. Balthazar gave a growl but it was half-hearted. 'You're looking very lovely this evening.'

She was helpless to resist as she was wearing oven gloves and holding a pan of broiling birds. 'Ass!' she said. 'No! Don't touch it!' as Edward attempted to take the ducks from her. 'It's white hot, you fathead! We nearly had those nimble surgeon's fingers ruined.'

'Miss Glim's gone to Ireland to look after Guy,' I was stirring bits of lettuce into the peas and shallots. I wondered if Vere, myopic though he was when it came to women, had seen Edward's love for Prim and was intending to further his chances.

'Talking of surgeons,' Edward bent down to stroke Chloë who was so depressed by the storm that she had only given one brief hollow bark on his arrival, 'this afternoon I made an appointment for George to see a specialist in London. Vere wants it done privately so that we can get it through quickly before George's scholarship.'

Prim frowned down at the glistening domed breasts of the birds. 'Well, he may have made a great many mistakes but he's certainly making amends. And that's all one can ask, isn't it? I mean who hasn't got it badly wrong at some time?'

'Who, indeed?' I said. 'But won't it be very expensive?'

Prim looked a little sad. 'When Vere decides to take someone on, he'll give them his very last ha'penny. Meanness was never one of his faults.'

'I suspect Vere means more to you than I quite like.' Edward smiled but there was a return of the old anxiety in his eyes as he looked at Prim.

'Oh, rubbish!' Edward's expression did not change. 'Don't look like that, you ridiculous man. All right. I had a crush on Vere when we were young. He thought I was a jolly playmate and that was all. I saw myself as a tragic heroine and I nursed my injuries.'

Edward had turned pink. Drops of rain trembled on his springy curls. He traced with his finger the whorls of a knot in the wood of the table. 'I see. And when he came back?'

'I realised at once that we were completely unsuited. The fantasy fizzled out. I could never be his *beau idéal* and he could never be mine. I shall always be fond of him because he's a part of my youth.'

I saw that Edward still did not look happy. 'I'll go and tell them dinner's ready, shall I?' I said.

The telephone rang as I walked through the hall. I picked it up. 'Hello?'

'Who's that?'

'Hello, Guy. It's Freddie.'

'Well.' There was a pause. 'You don't waste time, do you?'

'How's Moira?'

'She's a tiresome little brat. She needs to be soundly whipped. Only I can't be bothered to do it.' I smiled at the unmistakable pique in Guy's voice. 'But I've done with her. Isobel is much more to my taste. A woman of experience.'

Lady Isobel Fitzpatrick, the girls' mother, was nothing if not experienced. I remembered her as a frightening creature, all flashing eyes and floating hair, who went through lovers like a fox through a hen-house. 'I hope you're enjoying yourself,' I said, with complete sincerity.

'Is Vere there?'

'Yes, but talking to guests. Shall I ask him to telephone you?'

'Just tell him to send me a hundred pounds, would you? I could do with something other than the paving stone that passes for a pillow in these parts. And Lord Fitzpatrick's idea of claret is something one might write sermons in.'

'I know you'll say it's none of my business but has it crossed your mind that Vere needs every penny he's got to try to keep the estate going? I don't suppose the hay we've just finished baling will sell for much more than the amount you want to blow on soft pillows and fine claret. He's only just been able to scrape enough together to pay the telephone bill.'

I heard laughter at the other end of the telephone.

'Well, well. So you're boiling his eggs and folding his socks for love. That's really sweet. Perhaps you *are* as pure in heart as you like to make out. My dear Freddie, Vere could buy up the Fitzpatricks and the Gilderoys ten times over and still have enough left over to buy a whacking great yacht. I've tried to persuade him to do it — I really fancy a jaunt round the Med with Isobel. But he always was a bit of a Puritan.'

'What are you talking about?'

'Vere's as rich as Dives. He sold up for a fortune in South America.'

'I don't believe you.'

'Ask him. Vere never lies, you know. He's got a sickly, invalidish conscience like yours. Only he won't thank you for it. He only told me because I asked him.' Guy laughed again. 'All the time my father was scheming to pay Vere out by leaving the estate away from him, Vere could have bought one bigger and better any time he chose. Good joke, isn't it?'

'Hilarious.'

Guy rang off as soon as he had my promise to petition Vere for the money. I put the receiver back on its rest and walked slowly to the drawing room to summon them to dinner. Vere was piling logs on the fire. He turned to look at me. Something in my expression changed his smile into a look of enquiry.

The dining room was pleasantly warm. Chloë insisted on lying on my feet, heating them to a slow, rolling boil. I had put candles on the table and some dark pink roses into a vase with branches of philadelphus. The room looked lovely and the food, thanks to Miss Glim, was delicious. We took it in turns to serve and clear plates.

But there were tensions. Lady Frisk ignored overtures from Elmer and Werner and was inclined to be scratchy with the rest of us. Bar and Werner, who were sitting next to each other, had an impassioned argument about the significance of the Holy Grail that was unintelligible to those unfamiliar with the canons of witchcraft and Teutonic myth. Edward made efforts to be cheerful but when he was not talking his face fell into gloom. Vere had brought up from the cellar several bottles of a very good Burgundy which Edward was drinking steadily. Already he seemed rather drunk.

Elmer could not understand that we found it difficult to think in the language that was argot to him. 'See, man,' — he never said 'men' but as his eyes ran round the table every time he paused to gather his thoughts, I assumed he was addressing us as a crowd — 'we don't *know* that interior nuclear reactions are taking place. It's an inference.' His wandering gaze fixed on my face. He stared at me with wide excited eyes. I felt as though I were a child again, holding the parcel as the music stopped, dreading to be asked to do a forfeit. I tried to look intelligent.

'I find it a provocative idea,' Vere came to my rescue, 'that we are, as far as we know, the only creatures capable of exploring and evaluating the universe. Could that be the purpose of man's existence? To interpret the nature of the cosmos?'

Predictably, everyone had different answers to that ancient conundrum. Lady Frisk talked everyone else down. She had no doubt that the universe was masterminded by the God of the Authorised Version of the Bible, not only Christian and Protestant but also English and upper-class. She dilated with great authority on eternity. Her thesis could be reduced to the single idea that heaven was much like earth but without the annoying, impertinent ways of the lower classes who were transformed by death into persons of taste and breeding.

'Well, Mama', said Charlotte, with deceptive mildness, 'where do you think heaven actually is? Georgian silver and satinwood card tables suspended at cloud level? These days rudely invaded by jumbo jets?'

'Voltaire said, rather neatly, that if God created us in his own image we have more than reciprocated,' said Vere.

I looked at his frayed shirt and cheap wrist-watch with its battered leather strap and wondered if Guy might be telling the truth. If so I had made a complete idiot of myself, admonishing Vere for extravagance and offering to lend him money. He had never said he was hard up. I had simply assumed it. But he might have told me. My idea of him underwent a change. Still a dreamer, a romantic and an idealist, but not, after all, improvident and rash. It was the second time he had made me look a fool by keeping his own counsel. He was reticent to a fault. He happened to catch my eye. I frowned.

Elmer held up one immensely long finger. 'Diderot talks of wandering in a vast forest at night with only a faint light to guide him. A stranger appears and says, 'My friend, you should blow out your candle in order to find the way more clearly.' This stranger is a theologian.'

'I do not consider this a suitable subject for the dinner table.' Lady Frisk looked offended.

'But, Mama, *you* introduced the subject of religion.' said Charlotte. That girl rose in my estimation every minute.

'I was not questioning the existence of my Maker, Charlotte. That even *I* would not presume to do. Education has a great deal to answer for. It gives consequence to those not trained from their earliest moments to bear its obligations.' She looked sternly across the table at Elmer, pressing her chin so far into her chest that it was engulfed by the folds of her neck.

Elmer laughed very gently and very long. Which was as good a reply as any.

'I think everything's an illusion, including heaven and hell, and we aren't really here at all,' said Bar. 'We're just psychic energy floating and dreaming in the realm of Ether. We are trees, we are the moon, we are snails, we are even mud. As we die we shall be made one with the Goddess of all love.'

'Nonsense!' said Lady Frisk, with great firmness.

Werner said nothing, but sat chewing slowly and staring at Bar with a soppy smile on his face.

'I'll tell you what I think.' Edward held up his glass and spilt some wine on the table. 'I think it'sh all a crying shame. I believe in hell, all right. I'm in it.' He wrinkled his face as though he was going to cry. 'It'sh all torment and shorrow and demonsh and pish-forksh.'

'Edward!' Prim looked shocked. 'You're hopelessly drunk.'

'And what if I am?' Edward's head was weaving about as he tried to pin his gaze on Prim's face. 'The girl I love better'n all the world won't have me because she thinks I'm weak. I'd be stronger'n a lion if she'd only love me. I'd have a reashon not to drink then. I'd be in heaven if she'd let me lie in her arms. Ash it is I may ash well go to the devil.' He pointed a waving finger across the table at her. 'I'll tell you shomething for free, Miss Yardley. I am weak. I freely admit it. But you're weak, too. You're sho shcared of life you'd rather drive a poor fellow down to hell than rishk yourself with a little human loving. I want to look after you and show you that you needn't be afraid because you're the loveliesht, darlingesht, adorablesht — thing.' He seemed to have lost the thread rather. A tear glistened on his cheek. With an effort he dragged himself to his feet. 'Ladiesh and gentlemen, raishe your glashes in a toasht! I give you Lushifer, the Prinsh of Darknesh!'

There was an almighty crack of thunder and all the lights went out. Chloë tried to get on to my knee.

'Now you've done it,' said Bar.

41

'Edward, give me a hand, will you? We need more candles.' Vere took hold of his arm and practically dragged him out of the dining room. They were gone some time.

Lit only by the firelight and candles, the shadowy room seemed to shrink in size and the mood became intimate. Bar and Werner were talking in low voices, their blond heads close together. I saw Elmer put his hand on Charlotte's shoulder. Lady Frisk began to talk hurriedly as though to distract Prim and me.

'On the whole my portrait has been very favourably received, Frederica. Though people have been quick to see that the *nose* is not quite as it should be. Ernest Ringrose said he thought it was too short! He's a very stupid man. His grandfather married a tailor's daughter. There are always unfortunate consequences when people forget their obligations. Henrietta Bartlemy-Parr married the local vet and their first child was a congenital idiot. Thank you, I will have another glass.' I filled it for her, wondering if she was also a little tipsy. Her voice was more than usually loud and emphatic. 'Sir Oswald used to say there wasn't a cellar in the *county* that could compare with Gilderoy Hall. Poor dear Vere, having so *soon* to take his father's place. I think he will succeed very well, however. Unlike his father Vere knows the value of *breeding*. I have been pleasantly surprised in our little talks to find his views on the subject accord so *exactly* with my own. He would make a *splen*did Lord Lieutenant. The current one is bow-legged. *No* one could find fault with Vere's handsome face and deportment. There cannot be a girl in the county who will not set her cap at him.'

Her arrows were flying wide of the mark. Elmer was sitting back in his chair, grinning at Lady Frisk, while Charlotte gazed raptly up into his face, not listening to a word her mother said. I looked at Prim who was sitting on his other side. She was staring at the remains of her trifle, her eyes filled with tears.

'What is the matter, Miss Yardley?' With consummate tactlessness Lady Frisk drew everyone's attention to Prim's distress. 'I hope you are not refining on that unfortunate display by our general practitioner? I intend to speak to the hospital board about it. The professional classes are *not* what they were.' She added, in a tone intended to mollify, 'You cannot hold yourself responsible. Dr Gilchrist was re*volt*ingly drunk.'

'On the contrary. I *am* responsible.' Prim's expression became quite fierce.

'I saw a joanna in the lounge.' Elmer stood up. 'What do you say to a jam, chicks?'

'Good idea!' I picked up the candlestick nearest me.

'Does anyone have *any* idea what that man is talking about?' grumbled Lady Frisk, as she followed me into the drawing room.

The storm had travelled round the circle of hills and was directly overhead once more. Rain beat against the windows and every few seconds the valley was dramatically lit by lightning. I drew the curtains and put more logs on the fire. Elmer put the other candlestick on the piano, sat down at the keyboard and flexed his fingers.

'What'll I play, Miss Charlotte, ma'am?' he asked, in accents of the Deep South.

'Play 'My Melancholy Baby'.' Charlotte squeezed herself on to the piano stool beside him and put her arm round his neck.

'Yes'm'.'

Elmer began to play at a rollicking rate. ''Come to me my melancholy baby,'' he sang. ''Snuggle up and

500

don't be blue. All your fears are foolish fancy, maybe, You know, dear, that I'm in love with you.'' Prim had gone to make coffee. Lady Frisk sat very upright beside me on the sofa, her expression suggesting that she was undergoing a severe form of torture. Bar and Werner got up to dance.

'What can I play for you, Lady Mother?' called Elmer, having brought Melancholy Baby to a triumphant conclusion.

'I fear you will be unfamiliar with what *I* consider to be music.' Lady Frisk's tone was lofty. 'From our nursery days my mother brought us up to revere the great composers, Mozart, Bach, Beethoven . . . ' She waved her hand. I suspected she couldn't think of any more.

Elmer began to play a Mozart sonata. Lady Frisk looked mortified. She tried to mask it with disdain but eventually muscle fatigue took over. Her face relaxed, her eyes closed, she sank back and began to breathe slowly and deeply. As Elmer played the last notes I heard a little snore.

Prim came in with the tray of coffee cups. We were careful not to chink the spoons against the saucers. Elmer struck up quietly with 'You've Got Me Crying Again'. Bar and Werner wrapped themselves more tightly round each other and circled the drawing room languorously.

'I humbly beg your pardon.' Edward had loomed up out of the darkness. His hair was flat to his head which made his ears stick out but he was sober, more or less. He looked down at Prim with troubled eyes. 'I'm the biggest fool that ever was born.'

'It's me that's the fool.' Prim held out her hand. Edward took it hesitantly. 'Can we skip the apologies on both sides? I hate saying I'm sorry. You'd better know that about me.' She stood up. 'It's years since I did any dancing.' Edward's expression was disbelieving. 'Well? I think you deserve much better but if you're fool enough still to want me — here I am.'

Edward, his smile transfixed like a man who has had a glimpse of Paradise, took her in his arms and they moved slowly away. Lady Frisk gave a little snort but continued to slumber. I felt a hand on my shoulder.

'Are you going to tell me what I've done?' Vere's face, as he leaned over the sofa, was theatrically lit only on the left half.

'What are you talking about?'

'You've been giving me looks all evening as though I'd made a fur coat out of the family pony.'

'Don't be absurd.' I couldn't help laughing.

'Since everyone else is behaving as though we're in a Costa Rican dive why don't you come and dance with me? It takes a power-cut and almost total darkness to make the English lose their inhibitions.'

I wondered what he had seen in the last twelve years that made his countrymen seem repressed. It reminded me that he was almost a stranger. I knew practically nothing about him.

'Well?'

'Well what?'

We were at the farthest point from the piano and could talk quite easily. He danced very correctly, his right hand on my shoulder blades, a decorous nine inches of space between us.

'What have I done? Strangled a kitten? Kicked an old lady downstairs?'

'You aren't poor at all!'

He laughed. 'What an unusual girl you are! Most women would be delighted to discover that the man whose arms they're in is solvent. You've been talking to Guy.'

'He wants you to send him a hundred pounds.'

'I see.'

'Why didn't you tell me?'

'I can't think of any way to inform someone that you have money in the bank without sounding distinctly vulgar.'

'"Tears in my heart. Oh, how my soul cries for you,'' sang Elmer.

'Perhaps not. But you carry secretiveness to extremes. Laconic is hardly the word. Mute would be more like it.'

'You're probably right.'

'"Once there were moonbeams that used to dance around my heart. You brought the storm clouds, the lightning flashed and the thunder crashed.''

There was an explosion of thunder. 'The storm's getting worse. Poor Chloë.'

'Am I forgiven?'

'It hardly seems the occasion for the bearing of grudges.'

The nine inches became two.

'"Am I your love or not? Please make it clear. Why don't you tell me what I long to hear?''

'Would you call this jazz or swing?' The darkness was not quite enough to divest me of my own inhibitions. I was aware that something was happening to my breathing over which I had no control. 'These are torch songs, aren't they? Billie Holiday. Tragic life. I've always loved Ella Fitzgerald.'

'"I'm just a fool to love you so, what is your answer, yes or no?''

'Do you consider Bessie Smith to be the greatest classic blues singer?' I felt myself on the edge of an abyss.

Vere said nothing. The two inches became less than one. I let go and dropped in. I felt his heart beating hard as it was pressed to mine. My bones seemed to be dissolving and — the lights were blazing. We sprang apart.

'Oh, what a shame,' cried Bar. She spoke for us all.

'The electricity board isn't usually so efficient.'

Though there were only a few table lamps burning, the precipitate shift into the light gave them an extra brilliance. Lady Frisk, who was lying with her head back, her mouth wide open and Chloë's muzzle pillowed on her knee, gave a grunt and opened her eyes.

'A very nice little piece.' Lady Frisk's feet sought her shoes, which had fallen off. 'Of course, an amateur performance does not do Mozart justice.' She stood up, her eyes watering as she fought back yawns. 'A delightful evening, Vere. So good of you to have us *à l'improviste*. I fancy you will have given Charlotte plenty to think about.'

'It's time you hit the sack, Lady Mother.' Elmer got up from the piano stool. 'You look pooped.'

Lady Frisk bridled. 'I do wish you would not call me by that ridiculous name! And I am not in the least tired.'

I heard her say to Vere, as everyone went into the hall, 'A little wildness is natural in a young girl. She will soon have it out of her system. I can't thank you enough for putting up with that frightful creature.'

'I'll take you home if you'll wait a minute,' Vere said to me, as he picked up Lady Frisk's cape and scarf. 'I must make sure George has gone to bed.'

'Oh, we'll take Freddie,' said Prim. 'Edward's going to drop me off. Come on, Bar.'

'I shall valk home vith Bar,' said Werner firmly. 'Ve shall enjoy a moonlight stroll.'

'But it's pouring with rain,' Prim objected.

'In that case I borrow the Land Rover if Vere does not mind.'

'Go ahead.' Vere looked amused.

We exchanged mutual thanks for cooking, hospitality and entertainment. Elmer set off first down the hill with Charlotte and Lady Frisk. Edward, Prim and I followed behind with Balthazar, who had recovered his *sangfroid*.

He smelt strongly of duck. Chloë had taken one look at the weather and crept back to the fire. Behind us came the Land Rover, its brakes squealing, one headlight broken.

'Such a lovely evening,' sighed Prim. 'You can drop me first, Edward. It'll save you having to double back.'

'I'm dropping Freddie first.' Edward spoke with resolution and Prim said not another word.

As I climbed into bed beside Macavity half an hour later I wondered if I was the only person in Pudwell feeling wretchedly alone.

★ ★ ★

It was late when I awoke. The storm had cleared and the sky was an unclouded blue. The scent of jasmine drifted in through the open window and a blackbird sang cheerfully. My dreams had been troubled and extraordinary but the minute I opened my eyes they broke into hazy fragments. The bedclothes were in disorder and I felt exhausted, as though I had been making hay all night.

I dressed and went downstairs as Cupid struck ten. I turned on the tap to fill the kettle but nothing came out. I gave it a shaking. A flake of rust fell into the sink. I wondered what to do. In the general way of things I would have consulted Prim. On this particular morning I was reluctant to disturb her. Directory Enquiries would be able to give me the number of the water board. I took an apple to eat on my way along the path. There was a joyful bark as I emerged from the hedge into the lane.

'Hello, darling girl.' I knelt to put my arms round Chloë's neck.

'Good morning.'

I looked up. It was Vere.

'Hello.' I dropped my apple core discreetly. I couldn't

remember if I had brushed my hair. 'I was just going to ring the water board. There's nothing coming out of the tap.'

'They won't be able to help you. The supply comes from a spring. It's a very primitive system. I expect the storm has washed stones over the entrance to the pipe. It used to happen occasionally.'

'Oh dear. I've absolutely no idea where the spring is.'

'It'll be overgrown by now but I think I'll be able to find it. There's an oak nearby with a peculiarly twisted trunk. It was struck by lightning years ago.'

'How lucky that you know that. Were you a friend of Viola's godmother?'

'I may have met her. I can't remember. But — I expect you're going to be cross — I knew I'd have to tell you one day. This cottage doesn't belong to Viola's godmother.'

'What?'

'This isn't Viola's godmother's cottage,' he repeated, smiling.

'But — oh, you're teasing, of course it is.' I stared at him, wondering what on earth he was talking about. 'Viola wrote to me — she told me all about it.' I looked around wildly, then thrust aside a branch to show him the figure attached to what remained of the gate. 'There you are! Number nine, Plashy Lane!'

Vere pushed it round until it stood on its head and said, 'Six. The nail must have fallen out of the top.'

I was silenced by this. It was impossible. I refused even to consider such a crazy idea. But — it couldn't be, could it, that all this time I had been living in the wrong house? All my feelings, my deep affection for it, the happiness I had found there, rebelled against the notion. I looked more closely. By daylight the nail hole was visible.

'But — but — where — whose?'

'I'm afraid it's mine.' Probably my mouth fell open at

this point. I was dumbfounded. 'It's part of the estate. I moved out of the Hall when I was eighteen. Father and I were rowing all the time. I came to live here.'

'But . . . ' I put a hand to my forehead, my brain whirling. 'Just a minute. Who was Anna?'

'Anna was my father's mistress. You must have heard that we — she used to come here. My father behaved very badly to her. She'd come and tell me about the dreadful way he treated her and cry. I fell in love with her. We became lovers.'

ANNA THOU LADY KILLEST ME. I remembered the words scratched on the window. But that meant — I felt something like a shiver run over me. Vere had written that. It was Vere's copy of Rossetti beside the bed. It was his table I sat at, his sofa I rested on beside *his* fire, his books I read, his music I listened to, his garden I tended, *his* possessions I cleaned and polished and restored and loved. It was his bed I slept in, wearing Anna's nightdress. As, presumably, she had done.

'You ought to stand with your mouth open more often,' said Vere. 'You look very sweet.'

Sweet! What he meant was ridiculous. 'Why?' I said, when I could command my voice sufficiently. 'Why didn't you *tell* me?'

'Now you're looking angry.'

'How could you let me make such an *idiot* of myself?' I had invited him to visit whenever he wanted. That was when I had thought he was Lemmy. I had told him about my affinity with the owner of the cottage — I closed my eyes and tried to remember what I had actually said.

'Even when you're angry you look beautiful.'

'Oh.' The abyss began to threaten once more. 'But I don't — why didn't you — couldn't you have calmly and quietly put me straight?'

'Look at it from my point of view. I'd been dreaming of the cottage for twelve years. The place where I'd once experienced heaven and hell. When I got to Pudwell I came straight here before going up to the house. I didn't even know if the cottage was still standing. I thought my father might have had it demolished, as he'd threatened. Imagine my feelings when finally I dared to set foot in the place only to find the loveliest girl I'd ever seen in residence.' My anger evaporated a little. 'It was the last thing I'd expected. I was intrigued by the situation. And not a little amused.' I frowned. 'And, later on, I saw how much you loved it. It would have been a shame to spoil things, wouldn't it? What did it matter, after all? I'd planned to live at the Hall, to try and make a go of things with my father. That was one of the reasons for coming back. And I liked the idea of you living here.'

'But why didn't anyone else tell me?' I was still desperately confused. 'Guy or Prim?'

'Guy knew you'd made a mistake. But he had his own reasons for wanting you to stay.'

'Oh. Yes. Of course.'

'And Prim probably thought you'd rented Drop Cottage from the estate. My father has let several from time to time. Bar's cottage, for example.'

'I see.' I had assumed, without giving the matter any conscious thought, that Bar owned Hintock Cottage. 'But Prim and I talked about Anna . . . ' I paused, trying to remember the conversation. Prim must have thought that because I knew Anna's name I was familiar with some of the Gilderoy history. I saw now how we had continued at cross-purposes. There remained the unanswered question.

'What did happen — to Anna?'

'My father found out about us. Anna used to come down from the Hall every morning, early, while my father was still asleep. He never got up before ten. I begged her to leave him and let me take care of her but she always had some excuse — the time wasn't right or she couldn't face a row. One morning my father followed her to the cottage. There was an appalling scene. He'd always had rages but I'd never seen him so angry as he was then.' Vere started to laugh. 'It was farcical. I'd just got out of bed. I was stark naked. At the time, though, it wasn't funny. It seemed as though the world was coming to an end. He punched Anna and split her lip. Then he picked up a bronze of Napoleon and tried to hit me with it, so I took it off him and chucked it out of the window. Of course, I was younger and stronger and I could easily have thrashed him, but I was so angry I didn't dare lay a finger on him. Anna just stood and screamed with blood running down her face. My father started to shake and then he fell down. It was a stroke. After we'd got him to hospital we decided to go away. Does that sound callous? Anna's face was a mess. I loved her.'

'It doesn't sound callous to me.'

'Well, anyway, we were going to be together — the world well lost for love. I was absurdly happy and wretchedly guilty at the same time. Neither of us had any money. So I sold everything I could — my car, my horse, my watch — for whatever I could get, that same day. I couldn't sell the cottage, luckily. I'd probably have been mad enough to do even that. I was infatuated. It seemed worth chucking my family and everything I'd ever known to try to make her happy.' He laughed again. 'At twenty-three I was idealistic and naïve. She was forty-five and very experienced. Three weeks after we got to Paris she left me for a banker she'd met while I was trying to find work. She left me a note saying goodbye. But she took all the money. She didn't leave me enough to buy myself a cup of coffee. I'd burnt my boats here. I had no choice but to continue with my self-imposed exile.'

Vere continued to smile in self-mockery but I thought of a young man alone in a foreign country, heartlessly betrayed and cruelly disappointed and I felt like weeping.

'Don't look like that.' He took my hand. 'It was a long time ago. Until I came back I hadn't thought about it for years.'

'Do you know what happened to her?'

'I spent three months working as a waiter, keeping myself together, just about. Despite everything I was hoping she'd come back to me. I had fantasies about forgiving her. It was going to be *Manon Lescaut* all over again. I was a romantic idiot. I was scraping plates into a newspaper in the restaurant kitchen when I saw the report of the accident. She and the banker had been killed in a car crash. They'd gone through the barrier of the Corniche on their way to Monte Carlo. That was the end of it. I sent a letter to my father, telling him she was dead and apologising for having hurt him. The next week I started work as a stoker on a ship going to India.'

He was still holding my hand. No amount of conversation could save me now from tumbling into the abyss.

'Freddie.'

'Yes.'

'Because of what happened, I suppose I haven't allowed myself to care very deeply about anyone. I thought it was better that way, but I never imagined anything like this — '

A car appeared at the top of the lane and swept down dangerously fast towards us. It stopped with a screech of tyres and the window on the driver's side purred downwards.

'I say! This wouldn't be Plashy Lane, by any chance?' The young man, whose complexion was pale green, blinked a little when he saw Vere's furious face.

'Freddie! Darling! I thought I'd never find you!' A delicate, manicured hand fluttered at the open window. I bent to look in. It was Viola.

42

'Poor Aunt Netta!' said Viola, as we stared over the gate of nine Plashy Lane. 'It looks terribly depressing!'

The dilapidated bungalow was hidden from the road by an overgrown privet hedge which was why I had never noticed it. It had been built some time between the wars and modernised during the sixties when cedar shingling was *de rigueur*. Crazy paving, sprouting grass, led up to a fake Georgian door with a fan-light cut into its panels. Plate glass windows, one smashed, were cast into gloom by eaves of green concrete pantiles. The name of the house, displayed on a section of log, was Cosy Nook.

'I expect it will sell for more than Drop Cottage,' said Vere. 'It's got electricity, for one thing.' Unsightly strands of wires looped across a plantation of pampas grass. 'And plumbing.' Plastic drainpipes criss-crossed the shingling. 'And it's much more accessible.' A rusting bedstead had been chucked over the hedge on to the lawn.

I was wondering what would have happened if that nail had not fallen from the gatepost. One hour at Cosy Nook would have been enough to end my retreat. It might well have driven me out to seek the nearest tree from which to hang myself. I felt a frisson of something like terror with the realisation that such seemingly insignificant things can dictate the course of one's life.

'You can't stay there, that's certain.' I put my hand through Viola's arm as we strolled back down the lane. 'It's lovely to see you, you dear thing. But why didn't you tell me you were coming?'

'Didn't you get my telegram? The minute I realised Veronica and Percy's wedding was practically on your

511

doorstep it seemed too good an opportunity to miss.'

Light dawned. 'You've been to Lord Percival Bierce's wedding.' It went some way to explain why at eleven o'clock in the morning in surroundings of unrelieved ruralism Viola was wearing a yellow silk coat and, on her dark curls, a very fetching pillbox hat decorated with a spotted veil and dyed yellow feathers. She looked stunning but a trifle overdressed.

'I've known Percy all my life. The duchess is my godmother. And Veronica and I were lodgers in the same house until I moved in with Giles. It was me that got her the job looking after the Duchess. Percy used to be a dreadful old goat but when Veronica refused to go to bed with him he fell a-worshipping. She's so transparently good, no one could help loving her once they've seen that. I'm so proud of myself for playing Cupid successfully. It isn't often I do anything right.'

It could not be denied that Viola was a little accident-prone. 'How long can you stay?'

'Only till tomorrow. I've got an important lecture on Monday on Gainsborough. I'm mad about his painting but it's a pity I can't think of him without thinking of Alex. Giles said I imagined the whole thing about him having me followed but I'm certain I didn't — ' She broke off and looked at Vere. 'Oh, well, anyway, what does it matter?'

'You can stay with me at Drop Cottage — that is, I suppose I ought to ask permission.' I glanced at Vere. He was looking thoughtful.

'What? Oh, you know perfectly well it's yours for as long you wish. But we must do something about the spring.'

In the excitement of seeing Viola I had forgotten the problem with the water supply. Together Vere and I shepherded Viola down the path to the cottage, holding back brambles that might tear her clothes and half carrying her over the mud. 'I'm sorry to be such a

512

nuisance,' Viola took off her high-heeled snakeskin shoes when we came to a particularly boggy part, 'only everything I'm wearing belongs to my aunt. She's so generous about lending me her beautiful clothes. The least I can do is to return them in one piece. Oh, Lord!' We had come to the steep drop, a slide of mud after the storm.

'It's lucky you haven't any luggage,' I said, when Vere had deposited Viola on firm ground, having carried her down on his back.

'Well, darling, of course I brought a suitcase with things to change into after the wedding. But I met this sweet old man on the station who asked me if I'd buy him a cup of tea as he hadn't any money so of course I did and when I came back from the cafeteria I discovered he wasn't sweet after all. He'd scooted off with my case that I'd left with him to look after. Luckily it only had jeans and a jersey and my nightdress in it. And comfortable shoes. I most regret those. These are killingly tight.'

'You two go on to the cottage,' said Vere. 'I'll see if I can find the spring.'

'Golly, they make them strong and handsome round here!' Viola said, as soon as he was out of earshot. 'I hope I didn't do the wrong thing, talking about Alex. It suddenly occurred to me that Vere might be the reason you're looking like a sort of beautiful cat. Sleek and dreaming. You've lost that fragile waif look I always admired so much. But I like this new, shapely, glowing Freddie better.' She hugged me again, enfolding me in a delicious nimbus of Diorissimo. 'You *are* happy. I can see it.'

'Yes.' I could tell Viola wanted to know more about Vere but there was really nothing to report that would not sound wholly unsubstantial. 'Here we are.' I surveyed with pride the exterior of Drop Cottage, trying to see it with fresh eyes.

Viola's response was entirely satisfactory. No detail was lost on her. She insisted on walking all round it, admired the porch, windows, cat-slide roof, and all my improvements to the garden. Even the privy was praised.

'Ah!' she cried, when we went inside. 'This is perfection! Look at these curtains! And the clock!' Cupid obligingly struck the half hour. 'And those darling sheep by that Cooper man! Oh, a pussy-cat!' She put her hat carefully on the cushion of the window-seat, sat down beside it and took Macavity on her knee. He remained tightly curled like a Chelsea bun but I heard purring. Viola looked up at me, her grey eyes solemn. 'Freddie, you'll never be able to leave. London has seen the last of you. Well, I'll try not to be selfish about it. This is so absolutely right for you.'

'I do love it here. I love the absence of striving, the idea of 'getting on' in the world — what Hardy calls 'eclipsing things which nip the bloom of bonhomie'. But I don't think I can spend the rest of my life odd-jobbing on the farm and taking in strays. I've got to be realistic. This is a dream and I don't want to wake up. But sooner or later something will jolt me out of it and I'd better be prepared.'

Viola opened her mouth to say something then obviously thought better of it. She looked around with a smile of satisfaction. 'I do think it's funny you've been living all this time in the wrong house. I'd have known at once this wasn't Aunt Netta's cottage. I only met her once — she was fearfully grumpy because my father smoked his pipe indoors and didn't have any Horlicks. Netta was his sister. She could never have chosen these things. She had as much romance about her as a sack of sand. She wasn't officially my godmother but she was so offended not to be asked that Jenkins and I made her an honorary one.'

'Jenkins?' I was becoming confused.

'Jenkins is my father. And my aunt's gardener. He and my mother had a brief affair and I was the result. He's the dearest man in the world. My aunt brought me up as my mother wasn't interested in children. But the whole thing is the deepest, darkest secret. You're the only other person I've told, apart from Giles, of course.'

'Of course I shan't tell a soul. I feel very honoured to be so trusted. But wasn't your aunt angry with Jenkins? It seems extraordinary that he's gone on working for her all these years.'

'My aunt's only conventional on the surface. She and Jenkins are devoted to each other in their way. She wanted me to know my father. She's very good, you know.' She bent to kiss the tips of Macavity's ears. 'To think how worried we've been and all this time you were shut up in measureless content — not that you're at all like Lady Macbeth, of course. It's what I'm reading at the moment. *Macbeth*, I mean. Awfully good isn't it?'

I realised how much I had missed Viola — her charming face, her enthusiasm and her erratic style of conversation. I was delighted to find there was something of the old life that was precious to me. 'Awfully. How was the wedding?'

'Veronica looked so lovely I could have cried. Well, actually I did, copiously. Even Percy looked quite civilised, shaven and wearing proper shoes. He's always fancied himself as a Bohemian, writing poetry about sex and painting pictures of bottoms. Veronica's managed to make a silk purse out of him, defying all the laws of nature. There were lots of people I knew but mostly ones I wished I didn't. We drank quarts of champagne and rattled round the gloomy old castle and had a fairly jolly time. Only the trouble is — I don't *really* enjoy myself if Giles isn't there. He's working very hard, preparing a series of lectures. And I know it isn't the sort of thing he enjoys. Most of the guests were utterly feathered-brained, if not mad. I like to pretend I'm a free spirit but the truth is, love is a tyrant. Without him the light is dim and the hearth cold. Pathetic, isn't it?'

'I don't think so. So who was the pale young man who brought you here?'

'That's Ferdy Fenwick. He's got a bad hangover, that's why he looks like a mouldy cheese. I met him at the reception. He seemed perfectly harmless, though he talked like a character out of Dornford Yates. When he offered me a lift I thought my luck was in but he turned out to be the most terrible lecher. Every time he got spoony he closed his eyes and his Adam's apple bobbed up and down and we took a gash out of the nearest tree. My throat's raw from screaming.'

'Let me get you a drink. Oh dear, of course, we've no water.'

Chloë ran in, panting and muddy, and laid a paw on Viola's knee.

'Please don't scold her,' Viola begged. 'She only wanted to be friendly. I'll try and sponge it off — only there isn't any water. How one takes things for granted.'

'I found the spring.' Vere had followed Chloë. 'I'm afraid it's blocked further down the pipe, beyond arm's reach. It's rusting away. The whole thing needs digging up and replacing. I'll get someone on to it on Monday.' I tried to look at him as Viola must see him, with the eyes of a stranger. The small scale of the cottage made him look even taller. There was a leaf in his hair. His fraying shirt was open at the neck, missing a couple of buttons. It was a strong face but it was reserved. When raillery sharpened his eyes he looked like Guy, but generally his expression was aloof, unreadable. I had looked at his face so often, wondering what he was thinking, that I felt sure I could paint it from memory with complete accuracy. He gave me that look of enquiry I knew so well. 'You'd both better come and stay at the Hall.'

I packed my suitcase and put the perishable contents

of the larder into carrier-bags. Viola changed into a shirt and skirt and a pair of sandals I had found for her while Vere closed the windows and looked for a basket in which to carry Macavity. I felt a vague sense of dislocation during these preparations to leave. Of course I would be back, I said to myself, just as soon as the pipe from the spring was repaired. The poignancy of the moment was dispelled by a frantic search for Viola's hat. It wasn't until I lifted Macavity up to put him in the basket that we discovered it. His avoirdupois had flattened it.

'It's not as though it could have been comfortable,' I said reproachfully.

'He's a duck and a lamb.' Viola was staunch in Macavity's defence. 'We can steam it into shape — when we've some water, that is.'

I left the others to go ahead with Macavity, who was howling piteously from inside the basket, while I made a detour to the post office.

'Mrs Hopper tells me you've a visitor.' Mrs Creech wrapped a loaf very slowly and with unnecessary care in order to detain me. 'She saw the car come through the village and stop outside yours. A young lady, very smartly dressed. Will she be staying long?'

'Only tonight.' As it was such a lovely day and I was so pleased to see Viola I decided to be generous and give her some harmless snippets to relate. 'We're going to stay up at the Hall. Our water supply's dried up.' I remembered that Viola was a hearty eater. 'I'll have four pork chops, a packet of prunes and half a pint of cream as well, please.'

'Butcher brought those fresh this morning. Killed a pig yesterday. That'll be George and Mr Vere and you two young ladies, then? I hear from Will Dewy that Cissy Glim's gone running after Mr Guy. The idea of it, giving herself airs! She'd only have doings with the Tarchester shops but when it came to *other* things she weren't too proud to get it locally. *Very* locally, if what they say is true.' Mrs Creech's face was malevolent.

'I'll have a cabbage, please.' I was already regretting my impulse to be friendly.

'Cut this morning.' According to the testimony of the outside leaves this was certainly a lie but I was not in the mood to argue. 'Quite a bolt from the blue, wasn't it, Mr Vere's adopting George?' Mrs Creech kept her eyes on my face as she packed my purchases into a carrier-bag. 'I said to Mrs Hopper, 'Mrs Hopper', I said, 'I never thought I'd see the day when a member of that family was prepared to act like a Christian.' *Not* that it'll pay him. I hear he's going to have the boy's leg operated on. Mark my words, *that'll* never get right.' Mrs Creech nodded with satisfaction. 'Mrs Hopper, poor simple creature that she is, was all for believing that Mr Vere is the boy's father but I was able to put her right on *that* straight away. 'Alice Hopper', I said, 'are you getting senile that you've forgotten how it all happened? It were *Mr Guy* that were sweet on Lizzie.' I remember seeing 'em on the river together any number of times before she got in the family way.' She narrowed her eyes and looked at me severely. 'I don't know what it is about boats. Folk seem to think they're invisible when they're in 'em. 'If that's Mr Vere's bastard, Alice Hopper', I said, 'I'm Sophia Loren.' ' As I stared into Mrs Creech's sly little eyes, the colour of mud, I was convinced that in this, at least, she was right.

★ ★ ★

Lunch was taken in the dining room with the french windows wide open, giving us an unrestricted view of the valley. We finished Miss Glim's soup and made inroads on a truckle of Cheddar. George entertained us with riddles. We ought to have guessed 'What's more frightening the smaller it is?' The answer is a bridge.

'What is it that you want but when you have it you don't know you have it?'

There was a distinct philosophical bias to many of George's riddles so we tried things like happiness, wisdom, humility and riches, all of which might have done but George held out against our arguments.

'Sleep,' Viola was finally inspired to guess, and she was right.

'What can you keep after giving it to someone else?' asked Vere.

'That's easy.' George grinned. 'Your word.'

'And mind you do.'

'Yes, Dad.'

It was the first time I had heard this appellation.

'What shall we do this afternoon?' I wondered. 'I vote for something out of doors.'

'I've got to read poetry with Miss Yardley.' George pulled a face. 'Then Roker and me are goin' to catch fish.'

'I thought you two were sworn enemies,' I said.

'He wants to be friends with me now I live at the Hall. He's given me his penknife. Of course, it don't mean much. He'll just steal another. But I might as well.'

Vere laughed. 'Yes, I think you may as well. But I'm glad you're under no illusion.' He put out his hand to detain George as the latter stood up to leave the table. 'Say goodbye properly to everyone. And don't be late for supper.' He laid a hand affectionately on George's arm.

George turned obediently to me. 'Oh, I forgot. These are for you.' He rummaged in his pockets and placed three crumpled notes and a telegram in front of me. 'Goodbye, Freddie. Goodbye, Miss — I've forgotten. Cheerio, Dad. See yah.' He limped from the room.

The telegram was from Viola, announcing her imminent arrival. The first note was from Prim.

'Edward and I are going to Blandford to have lunch and buy a present for Bar's handfasting though I'm not sure what the etiquette is — perhaps a besom and a black kitten? I'm assuming we'll see you tonight but I can't resist telling you now that you were right. He *is* exceptional.'

'A promissory note for a million pounds?' suggested Vere, seeing a smile of satisfaction on my face.

'Something much better than that.' Two could play at being inscrutable.

Werner's note was longer.

Dear Miss Freddie, I have taken my courage in my two hands and telephoned Germany to say that I will not marry the princess. I think she does not love me so she will not be sad. It was only for money. I love Bar so much and we are like doves, flying about in the beautiful clouds, in the height of happiness. But not please to tell Bar of the princess. [This was underlined.] I will speak it myself when we know each other a little time longer. She is so pure and I fear she may not understand, mit freundlichen Grüssen, Werner.

The third note was from Bar.

Dearest Freddie, I'm so happy. I never imagined love could be like this. I feel completely fulfilled and in harmony with all created things. Please don't say anything to Werner about Guy. I feel furious with myself when I remember that I cried for weeks over him. Naturally when the time's right I'll tell Werner but I don't want to spoil things. He is so idealistic! You remember when we celebrated the summer solstice together in the woods? And then I cast a spell with Lemmy for a new love. Well, the Goddess has granted my heart's desire. Werner and I are two halves of the circle. I know he had something to do with Ambrose's dreadful fascists but he has explained it all and how he thought it was a kind of poetry to make life less mundane. He's so romantic! But now he knows about our beautiful good magic he wants to be initiated at once. We are combining it with our handfasting and we hope all our friends will come. That specially means you, dear Freddie, as Werner is very fond of you, too, and he doesn't know anyone else. Except Vere. It would be wonderful if you could persuade him to give us his blessing. So please come to the woods at eleven o'clock. Though I'm a hedge witch — that means I work alone — as this is such an important occasion I'm asking all the local witches, the more the merrier. We shall be heartbroken if you don't come. Blessings, Bar.

I put down the note and looked at Viola. 'Two witches I know are getting married in the woods tonight, at midnight. Would you like to come to the ceremony?'

Viola gave a scream. 'Try to keep me away! Just like *Macbeth!*'

'Possibly more like the rustics in the Forest of Arden. No eye of newt or tongue of toad. More cheerful than that.'

'Will we have to take our clothes off?' Despite the impression she frequently gave of charming naïvety, Viola had a surprising amount of *savoir faire*.

'I'm not going to. And I don't expect Vere will.'

'Oh, now, just a minute, you don't think I'm going to have any part of this?' Vere looked horrified. 'Has everyone gone quite mad in England?'

'Yes! And isn't it lovely?' Viola was laughing.

'Bar particularly wants you to come.' I held the note out towards him. 'I think she looks on you as a sort of father figure. And it's something you're so good at being.' Vere's expression became wary. 'You've only got to stand in a circle with the rest of us and look pleased.'

I thought I wouldn't mention the dancing and singing. I knew from experience that this was something best undertaken on the spur of the moment.

'I'm really sorry that Giles isn't here,' said Viola. 'Though I know he'd take Vere's side and be stuffy and self-conscious about it. What shall we do in the meantime?'

'Let's go on the river,' said Vere.

'You're right, Freddie.' Viola jumped up and began to clear away the plates. 'This is a dream and one doesn't want to wake up.'

Vere looked at me enquiringly.

★ ★ ★

The water oozed like molten glass, divided by the prow of the boat. Vere took the oars while Viola and I lounged on the cushions. Naturally I remembered what had occurred the last time I had been a passenger in this boat. Perhaps it was the relaxing heat of the day or the effects of the wine we had drunk at lunch but I felt very little disturbed by the memory. Guy had gone out of my life as painlessly as he had entered it. That is to say, there had been some anguish in the arrival and the departure but it had been nothing more than a stumbling. I had done with guilt. It was generally a self-indulgent emotion and too much of my life had been given over to it.

Mayflies skittered over the surface of the river and expanding circles showed where the fish had tried to dine on them. Now the banks were bright with rosebay willowherb and purple loosestrife. Brown speckled ducks dived among wild water-lilies of an intense shade of yellow. Each time Vere dipped and raised his oars he examined carefully the flora that came up on the blade.

'Water parsnip. Canary grass. Bur-reed,' he informed me at intervals. 'Ah! A golden-ringed dragonfly!' I had seen something black and yellow whiz by. 'I wish I'd brought my notebook.'

'This is quite, quite perfect!' Viola leaned back against the cushions and closed her eyes. 'You'll forgive me, darlings, if I snore. Rather a late night.'

Vere and I continued on our nature trail. 'Look, a dipper!' He pointed to a fat little bird with a snowy breast. 'I don't remember many of those.'

I looked up and saw George and Wills appear briefly near the summit of the hill. Then I remembered that Prim had gone to Blandford with Edward so George would not have been able to have his poetry lesson. It was entirely out of character for Prim to forget the duty she took so seriously. Love makes us unpredictable.

'George isn't your son.' I did not mean to say it. The words tripped out of my mouth.

'No. But I'd be grateful if you kept that to yourself.'

I glanced at Viola. She looked relaxed, her head back, eyes shut, her mouth a little open. A tiny feather floated in the current of her breath. Very slowly it rose as she breathed out, only to be drawn down again as she inhaled.

'I promise I won't tell a soul,' I said, in a low voice. 'No wonder you were angry with me when I threw it in your teeth. Only it wasn't meant to be an accusation.'

'I wasn't angry with *you*. But it was a shock. Once you'd pointed out the likeness, I realised he was Guy's son. I remembered then that he and the miller's daughter — I can't remember her name — were pretty thick together. Guy was twenty and she was something like sixteen. George must have been born soon after I left. I didn't mind being cast in the role of arch-seducer and villain. But it was the cold-blooded neglect, leaving the boy to struggle with no one but Dusty to look after him, the heartlessness of it. Well, he's my brother, no matter what.' Vere rowed on in silence for a while, looking out across the water.

'Will you tell George?'

'I don't know. Probably not. I think it might be better left this way. It doesn't matter really whether I'm his uncle or his father, does it? I suppose your unerring eye for lineaments gave the thing away. Luckily that's a rare accomplishment.'

I debated with myself. Vere would be unhappy if he knew the village gossip. I thought the charity of the intention justified the lie. 'Mm.'

'Have you always had that discerning eye or has it developed from practice?'

'A bit of both, probably.'

'I can't think what Pudwell has done to deserve such an exceptional resident.'

'Now you're teasing.'

'No.' Vere stopped rowing. 'You seem to me as different from the usual run of people as though you were another species. I never knew a woman before like you. Even now after all these weeks I have no idea what brought you to my cottage.' He smiled and shook his head at the same time. 'When I saw you standing in the garden I actually thought I might be hallucinating. I still don't know why you're here. What makes a beautiful, intelligent, cosmopolitan woman hide herself away with simple rustics like me?'

I looked again at Viola. She had slipped down in the seat a little, her limbs sprawling. The feather was rising and falling with rhythmical precision.

'I was running away.'

'From a man?'

'Yes. And, in a way, from myself.' The boat, caught in the current, began to turn in a circle as it drifted. 'I thought I loved him. When I found out that I didn't I got hopelessly confused. I needed to go away from everything I knew so I could try to understand what I was doing.'

Vere leaned on the oars, looking out over the water. A

reflection from its surface spun a coin of light across his face. 'Are you certain? That you really don't love him? Perhaps if you saw him again?'

'No. It wouldn't make any difference. Besides, he's already engaged to someone else. I feel immensely relieved. I hated to think of him being unhappy.'

Vere lifted an oar idly and watched a stream of diamonds trickle from the blade. 'What was it about *you* that you wanted to run away from?'

'It might have been that I was running to *find* myself. I know I'm not making sense. After my mother died — I was eight — I was frightened and intensely lonely. I tried to build a shelter for myself. Like those insects that stick bits of leaves and twigs and stones on themselves for protection.'

'Caddis-fly larvae.'

'Yes. I wanted to be safe so I concentrated on being what the world considers successful. Alex was a sort of culmination of that. He had all the virtues — he was clever, accomplished, good-looking, charming. He seemed to me so strong that I imagined I could creep from my case and he would keep me safe. But there was one thing he didn't have.' I fumbled in the pocket of my jeans. 'I carry this about with me as a reminder of what I nearly forgot.' I held out my hand to show him the little brass pixie. Vere looked mystified, as well he might. 'They're cheap tourists' trinkets, supposed to be lucky. My mother gave this to her brother during the war when he went to fight in France. They bought it together on their last holiday, before she married my father. It was a joke. My mother said that anything so ugly needed to be lucky. And that beauty is not everything. Sometimes it gets in the way of more important things. Uncle Sid always had it with him and he was the only one of his friends who came back. He sent it to me as a wedding present. He said he thought I'd know why it was important, though in itself it was worthless. He said that it was rich in what Saint Paul calls charity but Uncle Sid preferred to call it loving-kindness. He said that it wasn't clever or fashionable but it was still the most precious thing in the world. I tried to explain it to Alex. He called it sentimental rubbish. But I realised that loving-kindness was something Alex didn't have. The ugly, the vulnerable, the weak, the pitiable were annoying and dispensable. And that was what Uncle Sid had been trying to tell me. I knew it, really, but I didn't want to admit it. I hope I don't sound quite mad?'

'No. Not at all.' We were travelling rapidly downstream now, caught in a swift current. Vere leaned towards me and took the hand that held the pixie. 'I want desperately to believe that Alex means nothing to you now. Because I — '

'Look out!' yelled Viola.

Vere ducked as a low branch swept over his head. As he sprang forward to push me out of the way the boat rocked wildly. The pixie flew out of my hand and caught the sunlight for the last time before it sank beneath the water.

43

'Thank goodness you woke up when you did!' I paused in the middle of polishing a glass to look at Viola. We were washing up after supper while Vere and George fed and groomed Guy's horse. 'Vere might have been brained. I can't think why I didn't see it coming.'

'I've got a confession to make.' Viola looked apologetic. 'I wasn't asleep at all. Only when we got into the boat I saw the way Vere was looking at you while you were admiring the scenery and I realised I was *de trop*. I'd been wondering all day what was going on but you're such a hugger-mugger pair. And if ever a man looked with eyes of love, he did then. Short of throwing myself overboard and swimming for shore I was stuck with being an unwilling third party. So I thought I'd pretend to be asleep.'

I laughed. 'You were very convincing.'

'Was I?' Viola looked pleased. 'I felt guilty listening to what you were saying. It's impossible to stop your ears mentally. Anyway I knew all that about Alex so I thought it didn't really matter. But when Vere started to say that he — well, what he never *did* actually say — I felt terribly uncomfortable being an eavesdropper so I opened my eyes preparatory to the polite cough and then I saw we were drifting towards that branch. *You* didn't notice because you were thinking of other things.'

I put down the glass and sighed. All day I had felt sick with conflicting emotions. During supper the atmosphere had been exciting and auspicious one minute and unbearably tense the next. When I happened to catch his eye Vere looked either abstracted or perplexed. 'Oh dear. I wish — '

'What?' asked Viola when I paused.

'Oh, nothing.'

'Do you mind very much about the lucky pixie?'

'No. I hope I've learned that particular lesson. It was only a kind of superstition that made me carry it about and that's just another self-made burden, isn't it?'

'I'm jolly well going to take myself off before Vere comes back. He must be wishing me at Jericho. I never felt so superfluous in my life.'

I put my arms round her and hugged her. 'I'm loving having you here. Please don't feel that.'

Before Viola could answer Frankie came running in and flung herself at me. 'Freddie, you gotta make her let us come. I'm gonna run away else.' She looked up at me with beseeching eyes.

'What's happened?'

'Miss Watkins has asked us to come and see her get married to that Vunner. And Auntie Beryl says it's too late. But there ent school tomorrow and Mum always let us stay up.'

Ruth stood in the doorway. 'Please, Freddie, ask her. I want to wear my new dress.'

'And I wanna to see if they're really going to have sex in the circle.' Wills came slouching in, picked a peach from the dish of fruit and bit into it, then hurled it away in disgust. 'Plumrose says that's a 'ssential part of the ceremony.'

'Mr Plumrose to you, Wills. Put the peach in the rubbish bin if you don't want it. And what does he know about it?'

'He's a witch too.'

I had met Mr Plumrose occasionally about the village. Our intercourse was restricted to nods and waves as he was always astride his tractor. He was a scrawny, morose-looking man. Presumably his spells weren't working.

'Before I even think about it I want you to say hello to Viola.'

'Hello.' Frankie turned her eyes for a split second in Viola's direction and Ruth muttered something but Wills went over and shook her hand. I was pleased by this proof that civilising influences were at work but Viola told me later that he had winked at her and licked his lips in quite a frightening way for a ten-year-old.

'Tell you what, I'll promise to make myself responsible for you and see if that will carry any weight. But that means if there is anything . . . unsuitable, you must come home with me at once.'

'I don't wanna see people doin' that to each other anyway,' said Frankie.

'Nor do I,' I said, with perfect truth.

Luckily Swithin answered the telephone. I explained that it was going to be a re-enactment of an old country tradition, eccentric but harmless, and I would be careful to protect his charges from anything calculated to injure the juvenile mind.

'Don't worry, Freddie. I trust you with them completely. Quite honestly, I think Beryl could do with an evening off. She's devoted to them but it *is* tiring. I shall be firm with her. Just watch Wills if there's anything alcoholic about. He's drunk all my communion wine *and* the sherry I bought for pre-prandial drinks tomorrow.'

'It won't be that sort of party. Just singing and dancing.'

'Really? I can't think why Wills is so keen to go.'

I returned to the kitchen and began to put away the clean plates. 'You can come.' My ears rang with the shouts of triumph and excitement. 'But remember, I've promised you'll be home not much after midnight and if there's anything I think you shouldn't see it'll be sooner than that.' I didn't believe for a moment that Bar would have asked the children to come if she intended anything approaching the orgiastic.

'I love you very, very best of all.' Frankie kissed my

arm, which was the only part of me freely available.

There would have been no point in Viola taking herself off, as she had threatened to do, as Frankie stayed by my side for the rest of the evening. Viola and I played Monopoly with her while Wills and George watched television in Miss Glim's sitting room and Vere, who came in after we had begun the game, sat in the drawing room with us, reading Montaigne's essays. But most of the time, when I happened to glance in his direction, he was staring into space with that look of his, as though he were in Greenland or Peru.

Ruth came in at about half past ten, looking bashful and pretty in a dark red dress with a white Peter Pan collar.

'You look very elegant, Miss Roker.' Vere got up and bowed.

Ruth giggled. Then she said, with a timidity that ought to have melted the hardest heart, 'Please, are you comin' to Miss Watkins's weddin'? Wills won't take notice of nobody else. He always spoils things. And it ent fair on Frankie and me 'cause folk think we're all the same.'

Vere sat down again quickly. 'To please you, Miss Roker, I would do almost anything. But to expect me to stand naked in a wood at midnight, doubtless being called upon to make embarrassing professions I do not believe in, in the company of my neighbours similarly unattired, is asking too much. On this I am firm.'

★   ★   ★

'You needn't take off your clothes,' I said to Vere, as we walked down the hill later that evening. 'I'm certainly not going to.'

'Nor am I,' said Viola.

Even Wills declared his intention of remaining fully dressed. The moon was high and washed the landscape

530

with tones of alabaster, dove grey and amethyst, like a silver-point drawing. Though it lacked only an hour until midnight the air was still warm and scented with wild honeysuckle and meadowsweet.

'Listen.' Vere stopped. 'A nightjar. Hear that humming noise? It's supposed to sound like a spinning-wheel. No one these days knows what that sounds like. It's an odd-looking bird. It flies about with its huge beak wide open to catch moths.'

'I've seen them nestin' on the ground,' said George, who had decided at the last minute to accompany us. 'Nothin' but a scrape in the earth.'

'I'd stamp on 'em if I found 'em,' asserted Wills.

'That's because you're a fool.' George's tone was contemptuous. 'It's stupid to go around killin' things if you don't need to.'

'All right, you two, that'll do,' said Vere, after there had been an exchange of blows. 'You're making Chloë bark. The next person to make a row goes straight back home.'

We were all respectfully silent after that. Chloë ran around like a puppy, thrilled to have all her favourite people doing something sensible, for once. The wood seemed dark by contrast with the lane. Glow-worms made tiny transient gleams in the deep shadows between the trees. An owl glided silently above our heads. Frankie took hold of my hand.

We smelt smoke and saw the distant light of a bonfire. Then we heard voices. Prim and Edward were standing by the fire, looking self-conscious. They greeted us in accents of relief. Mrs Deacon, Mr Plumrose and a woman I assumed was Mrs Plumrose stood next to them. Mrs Hopper, Prim's daily help and Mrs Creech's crony, gave me a tentative smile. Five people unfamiliar to me stood in the shadows around the circle that had been marked by stones. Frankie began to giggle uncontrollably as they were all, except

Prim and Edward, skyclad. There is nothing at all funny or embarrassing about nudity, I told myself sternly. But giggling is infectious. I caught Prim's eye. Soon we newcomers were in agony with suppressed laughter. Viola had to go away and hide behind a tree. Vere was the only one of us whose expression was solemn, even fierce. Then I saw a spasm pass over his face and he had to join Viola behind the tree.

Bar appeared, looking lovely in a flowing white dress with something like a veil on her head — I couldn't quite see in the firelight. She was leading Werner, who was wearing some kind of robe, by the hand.

'Welcome, dear friends.' Bar was smiling and unselfconscious. Her evident pleasure in the occasion sobered us and we stood to attention. 'We shall begin by invoking the elements.' She threw something into the flames, which sprang up blue and green and immediately the air was redolent of incense. 'By air and fire and water and earth, In the names of the Triple Goddess of the circle of rebirth, We call you to witness by this roundelay, The solemn vows we take upon our wedding day.' We started to skip clockwise round the circle, repeating this refrain to a vague sort of tune. At least some of us were singing and skipping and some of us, like Vere, were walking round with our mouths firmly shut. Werner knelt in the middle of the circle while Bar tripped round him carrying a candle, a wand and a flower.

There was more of this with slight variations and I felt myself begin to relax and enter into the spirit of it. When the chalice filled with wine came round we sipped eagerly, the better to oil our throats. There was a little hitch to the ceremony as Wills insisted on draining the chalice each time it got to him. Mindful of my promise to Swithin I planned some sort of tactful intervention.

'That'll do,' said Vere quietly, the next time it was

Wills's turn to drink. He took the chalice and handed it on to Prim. Wills went away in a sulk and sat behind a bush. I could see the firelight shining on his bare knees.

'Now, join hands, everyone, and jump over the broomstick.' Bar laid this object near the centre of the circle. 'The higher you leap the better pleased the Goddess will be.' Breasts and other appendages bounced as naked forms hurled themselves enthusiastically into the air. Viola executed a graceful *grand jeté en tournant* while Frankie landed on the besom and fell over. 'Never mind.' Bar was serene as she touched each of our foreheads with something oily, which ran into my eye. 'This is the milk of the sacred mother.' It smelt like rancid butter. 'Now while I praise the Goddess I want you all to dance as fast as you can and think of the binding powers of married love — the sexual act is sacred. Imagine yourselves performing it with your beloved.'

Wills came back into the circle. We whirled round at speed. I wasn't really thinking of anything at all. I was enjoying the exhilaration of dancing and being thoroughly uninhibited.

'Now, everyone, down on your knees, close your eyes. We're going into a collective trance. Absolute silence, now. You must listen to my voice.'

At first there was a tremendous amount of puffing and blowing and sniffing. Bar waited until we were quiet. Then, when the only sounds were the hissing of the flames and the hoot of owls, and Frankie breathing rather adenoidally as she always did when she was concentrating, Bar spoke softly, in a monotone. 'As this knot is tied, so may the link be made and may the link be love. You are now going on a journey. Your body feels very cool for you are floating along a vast river towards Avalon, the Island of the Blessed Souls. You rest peacefully in a silver boat, drifting past banks of roses that shower their petals on your upturned face. The

Goddess caresses you as you pass. Feel her hands brushing your cheeks.' I almost imagined that I could but it must have been a moth. 'The roses are darkest crimson, womb-coloured, the colour of blood.' I heard Prim on my left, shift uneasily. 'Feel yourselves rise from the water and float up, up into the arms of the moon. You are going to dance with Herne the Hunter, one of the many forms of the Horned God, Lord of Life and Death. He is pure energy and therefore dangerous but you are in a blue sphere, which will protect you.'

I found I was no longer listening to Bar's voice but my thoughts were wandering dreamily in some ethereal region and if not actually dancing, I was certainly weaving about. It was very enjoyable, like being in that last state of consciousness before sleep overtakes one. I felt an extraordinary sense of well-being.

'The Horned God asks all the women here to make love with him.' I came to with a jolt. 'If you wish you may experience the dangerous bliss of sex with the great pagan God of Love.' This seemed rather hard on the men. What were they supposed to be doing, meanwhile? I was back in my own everyday self now, fully awake and alert. I felt the hardness of the earth beneath my knees. I opened my eyes and saw Wills picking his nose.

'Quiet, everyone.' Bar was anointing a silver bell with oil. She glanced over towards me and I closed my eyes guiltily. 'I am going to summon the Horned God himself. You may feel a terrifying wind rush over you but do not be afraid. The Goddess will protect you. It is his way of making love.' I peeped at Prim. She was looking severe. I wanted to giggle but I controlled myself and waited, head bowed. 'Hush! O Lord of Day and Night, Pan, Goatfoot, Father of Nature. Visit us with your mighty powers of life and make us fruitful. Hear us as we beg thee to appear unto us!'

There was the sound of a bell tinkling, repeated several times. We waited patiently. Distantly the silence was broken by the sound of snapping twigs. Footsteps were coming through the woods towards us. The undergrowth crackled as they approached swiftly. Tension mounted. 'Don't look!' cried Bar. She sounded frightened. 'Whatever you do, you mustn't look! You must not see his face!' Frankie clutched my arm. The footsteps were close behind me now. I screwed my eyes up tightly and felt something brush past me into the circle. The Horned God left a trail of — Chanel Pour Hommes.

'What on earth's going on here? Has everyone gone quite mad? — Freddie!'

I opened my eyes. It was Alex.

44

'That was a wedding?' Alex was sitting beside me in the back of the Rolls as Bax drove at a sedate pace up the hill. 'Has rustication turned your brain, Freddie?' He began to laugh. 'I don't know what I expected but certainly not that!'

He opened the window to let out the smoke of his cigar, still chuckling. My heart continued to race from the shock of seeing him. When I had opened my eyes to find him standing in the middle of the circle I had screamed. Naturally everyone else had opened their eyes and was very much surprised to see the Horned God wearing a suit and smoking a cigar. Alex had been the only one of us whose presence of mind did not desert him.

'I'm interrupting something, I can see. I've been wandering about these damned woods for what seems like hours. I was thankful to see evidence of civilisation. Or so I thought. Well, Freddie, are you going to introduce me?'

I stood up with difficulty. My heart was pounding, I felt sick and my thoughts were so disordered I could hardly speak.

'Oh, just a minute — ah — this is Alex Moncrieff, everyone.' I went round the circle of those whose names I knew. I was thankful for the protective camouflage of the firelight. I knew my face was flaming. Vere didn't look at me anyway. Alex kissed Viola on both cheeks. I thought it was to his credit that he shook hands with the vast naked bulk that was Mrs Deacon without turning a hair. 'But, Alex, I don't quite — this is so — What on earth are you doing here?'

'I came to see you, of course.'

'But — but — I thought you were in London,' I finished lamely.

'Well,' he spread his hands and looked down at himself, 'you can see I'm not.'

'But how — why — what are you doing in this wood?'

'I couldn't find your cottage. I knew it was somewhere in the middle of a benighted copse off that damned lane — a mile long and not a street-lamp in sight. Bax and I have been cruising up and down it all evening. Then I thought I'd get out and walk.' He looked at me, smiling. 'I could do with a drink.'

'Oh! Yes. Of course. But — oh dear, I'm not staying at the cottage any more.'

It was then that Vere said, still without looking at me, 'You'd better come and stay at the Hall.'

The ceremony was unquestionably over. I had kissed Bar and Werner and congratulated them in a voice that shook. I felt a sympathetic pressure from Bar's hand.

'We'll go now.' Prim was standing next to me, looking uncertain. She kissed me tenderly and whispered, 'Telephone if you need me,' before taking Edward's arm and marching him quickly away.

'Goodnight, Freddie,' he called back through the trees. The other wedding guests dispersed to various heaps of clothing and began to dress in silence.

'Well, Viola.' The tip of Alex's cigar glowed red as he inhaled. 'How are you? I've just bought a few drawings Giles might be interested in. He's keen on Lawrence, isn't he?' It was more than confusing to hear Alex making polite conversation as we stood by a bonfire in the middle of a wood at midnight. I wondered if I was going mad.

There had been some difficulty about the return to Gilderoy Hall. We emerged from the trees to see the parking lights of the Rolls glowing, not far off. 'You'll have to come with me, Freddie, to show me the way,' said Alex, not unreasonably.

'Oh! No!' I disliked intensely the idea of riding in the car while the others walked. 'You go ahead with Vere and I'll bring the children and Viola.'

'Don't be silly, Freddie,' said Vere. 'Go on. We won't be long.'

When he saw me Bax sprang out and held the door for me. 'Very good to see you again, madam,' he said, with touching warmth.

'Thank you, Bax. How — how are you? How is Mrs Bax's sciatica?' This had been a frequent topic of conversation between us in the past.

'Not too bad, madam, considering.'

We purred serenely along, Bax in darkness in the front. Alex had switched on the interior light and I felt that he was examining me. I peered into the darkness and waved at the dim shape of Frankie, who turned her face towards me as she walked with the others along the lane. Chloë ran ahead of us for a little way. 'Don't worry, madam, I shan't run him over,' said Bax.

'What's this place like that we're going to?' Alex was as calm as though we were on a touring holiday. 'Any chance of something to eat?'

'Oh, yes. I'll scramble you some eggs, if that will do. The cook left yesterday.'

'You're obviously pretty much at home there. Free run of the kitchen.' I knew it was a question though there was no upward inflection.

'Well, I've been helping on the farm. I'm pretty much a hired hand.' I tried to laugh but the effort was almost beyond me.

'I see. That accounts for the clothes. Mm. This is what I call a hill.' We were at an angle of forty-five degrees now. The Rolls made nothing of it, hardly changing its engine note until we drew to a standstill before the portico of the Hall and Bax turned off the ignition. 'I take it there's somewhere for Bax to sleep? It

538

looks quite a big place.'

'Oh, yes. There are plenty of bedrooms. I'll find some sheets.' Again I felt Alex scrutinising my face.

He ground his cigar butt on the gravel and we went inside.

'Perhaps we ought to wait here for the others,' I suggested.

'All right.' Alex looked at the portraits of Vere's mother and Colonel Harry. 'What's the name of the fellow that owns this place? Something Gilderoy?'

'Vere Gilderoy.'

'Doesn't mean anything to me.'

'He's been abroad until recently.'

'Married?'

'No.'

He continued to study the portrait of Georgiana Gilderoy. 'Not a good mouth,' he said, at last.

'Alex,' I began, 'I'm so sorry, so very sorry that I ran away. If I hurt you I didn't want to — '

'Hurt me?' He swung round to face me. His eyes were very dark against the paleness of his skin. I had not remembered what a striking face it was. 'You damned near killed me. I didn't know I was capable of feeling such pain. Perhaps it's unmanly to complain,' he shrugged, 'but you ought to know the effects of your behaviour, don't you think?'

'Yes. I — ' I felt tears rising. 'I'm sorry from the bottom of my heart.' The cliché was wholly insufficient to express my penitence.

Alex looked at me for a long time before he said, 'You've changed. You've put on weight. And your skin's almost tawny. It suits you.'

'Thank you.' I saw with a stab of compunction that Alex was thinner. The suspicion of the double chin had gone.

Chloë pushed open the front door with her nose and ran up to me in a frenzy of relief to find me there. Alex was looking out towards the drive. I saw Viola, George and Vere walking up the steps.

'Well, it's good to see you again, anyway.' For the first time Alex put his hand on my arm and then quickly, before I knew what he intended, he kissed my mouth, not hard but with a light, easy familiarity. Viola's eyes, when she walked in, were wide with alarm. I guessed that she had seen him kiss me. I supposed that Vere must also have done so.

'Bed, George. 'Night,' Vere smiled at George, who looked white with tiredness and went upstairs without a word. Vere turned to Alex. 'I'll get you a drink. What will you have?'

'Whisky, no water, no ice. It's very good of you to put me up.' They went off together into the drawing room.

Viola and I rushed to the kitchen like children let out of school.

'Oh, my God!' she cried. 'What is he doing here?'

'I don't know.' I groaned. 'Perhaps he just wanted to see that I was all right. Exceptionally kind of him in the circumstances. Don't you think?'

Viola lifted her eyebrows. 'Remember that lesson you learned so painfully? It doesn't sound like Alex to me. When I remember how he looked at Mouser . . . ' She looked indignant when I began to laugh.

'This is absurd,' I said. 'We've just let the whole fanciful business of this evening go to our heads. All that magic and mystery and unleashed powers of darkness. There's *nothing* to be worried about. We're all grown-up civilised people.'

'None the less, I'm going to take Macavity to bed with me tonight to make sure,' Viola said darkly. She stopped and thought for a moment. 'How on earth did Alex know where to find you?'

★ ★ ★

'Ferdy Fenwick is a friend of mine,' Alex said later, in answer to her question.

We were sitting in the drawing room and Alex had a tray of bacon and eggs on his knee. It was a scene of intimacy and comfort. The fire was burning well, Viola and I had a glass of champagne and Vere was drinking whisky. Macavity was on Viola's knee and Chloë lay at my feet, perhaps because I had the chair nearest the fire. Viola looked at me. I knew quite well that Alex would not countenance as his friend a man so evidently lacking in major attractions. Ferdy had been gauche and dull-witted. Unless he was a good actor. Either way I knew, without being told, that Ferdy had been in the pay of Alex. Viola telegraphed abject apology with her eyes.

'Your father sends his love.' Alex looked at me and smiled.

'Really? I thought he was very angry with me.' I could not keep the eagerness out of my voice.

'No. I explained how things were. It's Fay, as you well know, who's the problem. Your father loves you very much. As we all do.'

'I'd better go and do some paperwork in the library.' Vere stood up suddenly. 'Goodnight. I hope you'll all be comfortable.' He nodded in the direction of the chimney-piece and went out. Chloë padded after him.

'Er, I think I'll go to bed.' Viola yawned convincingly. She edged towards the door, Macavity in her arms. 'Goodnight. Sleep well.'

Alex put aside the tray and went to stand before the fire. 'Bloody cold, these country places always are, even at the height of summer. It's the damp, I suppose. Come here.' When I didn't move he said, more softly, 'You're not frightened of me, are you?'

'Certainly not. Don't be ridiculous.'

'Well, then. Aren't we old friends? I don't think you realise how much you hurt me. Of course, that's in the past and I forgive you entirely.'

'You do?'

'Really, Freddie! We're not living in the pages of a melodrama. Let's just agree to call it a day, shall we?'

'Oh yes! You can't think how relieved I feel! I bitterly regret making you — unhappy.'

'I know that. No one knows you as well as I do. Or probably ever will.'

'I hear you're going to marry Zara Drax-Eedes.'

'Ah, yes. Of course, you saw us together in the restaurant.' Alex laughed, a little mournfully. 'Tell me, what did I ever do that made you so — pitiless? I loved you, Freddie, better than — I could ever imagine caring for anyone else.'

'It wasn't anything you did, really. It's just that I found I wanted something — different. I don't think I could make you understand.'

'Try.'

'Well, it all sounds rather feeble when I attempt to put it into words. Loving-kindness — by which I mean compassion, tenderness, sympathy — none of these words is quite right.'

Alex raised his eyebrows. He looked sceptical. I really couldn't blame him. He put his hands in his pockets and then drew one hand out. 'I almost forgot. I brought this for you. A goodbye present.'

'That was kind of you,' I was feeling more and more penitent. 'I feel I hardly deserve — '

'Come and see what it is.'

He held his hand out towards me. I went to the fireplace and took it from him. It was an exquisite enamel snuff box, early nineteenth century, I guessed, the cover depicting a castle in a landscape.

'It's beautiful.' I opened it. The inside was decorated with a pair of tiny doves. I hesitated. It would be ungracious to refuse a parting keepsake. 'It's exactly what I like.'

'Oh, yes. I know what you like.' Alex put his hand on my face and turned it towards him.

I looked into his eyes, which were filled with regret — and something else. At that moment the clock struck two. 'Good heavens, is that the time?' I sprang away from him and almost ran to the door. 'I'm going to bed. I'm exhausted! You're in the third room on the right. Bax is next door, in your dressing room. I hope you'll be comfortable. Breakfast will probably be rather late.'

Alex neither moved nor spoke but looked at me, unsmiling. I walked swiftly past the library towards the stairs. A crack of light showed beneath the door, which was firmly closed. It seemed that on this occasion Vere was not going to come to my rescue.

The moment I entered my room I locked the door then went back and took away the key. I undressed as fast as I could and turned out the light. As I lay in bed, staring out at the moon through open curtains, I heard footsteps pause by the door. Someone turned the handle and shook it a few times. Then the footsteps went away.

To my surprise I slept deeply and dreamlessly, but the moment I woke I was gripped by an unpleasant sensation of something between irresolution and panic. I lay for several minutes, looking at the curtains of my bed, a half-tester hung with a chintz of blue roses and brambles on a white ground, faded but still elegant. The charm of the room, with its pretty furniture, soft blue carpet and the view of the valley, restored me to something like confidence. The terrors of the night faded in the light of another beautiful, cloudless day. I washed and dressed and went downstairs.

It was barely eight o'clock but Alex was up before me. He looked sleek and energetic in country clothes, well pressed and brushed, his shoes reflecting the sun that poured in through the kitchen window. Bax was frying sausages and tomatoes.

'I haven't seen Viola. She must still be asleep,' he replied, in answer to my question about the rest of the household. 'Vere asked me to tell you that he would be out all day and not to worry about dinner.' Alex looked pleased. I felt a contraction of my heart. After all, it seemed he did not care very much.

As Bax had already laid the table, made toast and coffee and put out butter and marmalade, I had nothing to do but sit down. I made a remark about the glorious weather, Alex said how much he liked the house. 'Needs money spending on it, though,' he added, looking at the cracks in the ceiling and the damp patch above the window. Bax waited on us in discreet silence, politely but firmly spurning my efforts to bring him into the conversation.

'Give my father my love if you see him before I do,' I said.

'I will. I'm having lunch with Fay next week, in fact.'

'Really?' I was surprised that he was bothering to keep up the friendship now that it was no longer useful.

'I don't dislike her. There's a spirit about her I find quite appealing. Not sexually, of course. You shouldn't hate her, you know. She's perfect for your father.'

'Really?' I said again, rather stupidly.

'He's weak and she's strong. They're complementary. She wants to rule, he wants to be ruled. That's how it works.'

'Does it?' I thought about it and decided he was probably right.

Bax, wearing Miss Glim's apron, was standing at the sink washing up. Alex put down his coffee cup. 'Come into the drawing room for a moment,' he said to me. 'I want to talk to you.'

George was in the drawing room, picking out Chopsticks on the piano. We went into the library. Though it was my favourite room at Gilderoy Hall, it gave me a feeling of desolation. Vere's riding boots were leaning up against the fireplace. His desk was the usual mess of papers. Several had drifted on to the floor. Others were stacked up, carelessly weighted by a paper-knife. I saw that the letter on top had been scrawled over in black ink. I looked more closely. My own name, 'Freddie' had been written twenty or thirty times. I felt my spirits rise.

'Freddie. Darling.' Alex walked up to me and put his arms round my waist.

I tried to disengage myself. 'This is goodbye, Alex. We needn't be demonstrative about it, need we?' I tried to laugh. 'I don't think Zara would be pleased if she could see you with your arms round another woman, however innocently.'

'Fuck Zara.' Alex's face was a little flushed and he was breathing faster.

'Alex! Don't make me think badly of you. I'd much rather remember the happiness we had.'

'We can be happy again. You need me. I know you, I know everything about you. I can give you happiness in a way no other man can.'

'I'm so sorry.' I was back against the wall. His arms were either side of me pinning me there. 'But you *don't* know me. I've changed. I'm not the old scared, doubting Freddie. I can decide for myself what I want.'

Alex laughed and took hold of my hair with one hand to pull my head back while undoing the buckle of my belt with the other. 'I don't think so.'

To my left was the secretaire. I grabbed the paper-knife. 'Take your hands off me or I'll stick this knife into your arm.'

For a second Alex hesitated and I ducked out of his reach. It was proof, if I needed any, that he did not know me, if he believed me capable of stabbing him. None the less I continued to hold the knife.

'This isn't about love.' I was almost calm. 'This is about your will. You want your own way at any cost and you can't bear it that I left you. It's about ego and pride and dominance, but none of these things have anything to do with love. You only want me back so you can show the world that I'm in your power again, that you haven't failed. You'd better take Zara and try to make her happy. That way, perhaps, she'll learn to love you. I never shall.'

'Freddie?' George had come in, perhaps hearing our raised voices. He saw that I was holding the paper-knife. 'Are you okay?'

I put it down on the nearest table. 'Yes. I'm fine.' I put my hand on his shoulder and we walked out of the room together.

★　★　★

I called Chloë and we started out down the hill. Alex and Bax had driven away five minutes before. I had waited in the drawing room with George until I heard the car turning on the gravel.

'Was he the Horned God after all?' asked George.

'No.' A slight breeze cooled my face. I had left a note for Viola, explaining that I was going for a walk and would be back in an hour.

'There isn't any such thing, is there?'

'I don't think so. No one has ever seen him that I know of. Except in imagination.'

'I'd never waste time imaginin' anything so daft.' George had regained his customary air of scorn. 'I'd like a car like that, though. It'll be the first thing I buy when I'm rich.'

Wills's grimy face appeared over the wall between the Rectory and the Hall. 'I'm startin' a camp down the river. Wanna come and see it?'

'I might as well.' George limped away. 'Back for lunch,' he shouted over his shoulder.

Chloë and I walked on alone. At the bottom of the

hill the lane stretched out, invitingly cool in the shade of trees. I heard a whistle, then a snatch of the trumpet fanfare from *Aida*.

'Lemmy,' I called softly, 'where are you?' The hedge rustled. Lemmy's face appeared in it, black eyes darting warily up and down the lane, tendrils of ivy garlanding his brow. 'What are you doing? Come for a walk with me.'

Lemmy shook his head. 'Lemmy's guarding a nest. Blackbirds. Look!' I bent down and saw, in the shelter of a tangle of twigs, a bird brooding in the shadows. 'The fledglings of the first hatch were eaten by that fat black cat.'

'Oh dear. I'm afraid that's my cat. At least . . . ' Macavity wasn't mine, really. None of this was mine.

'Fire.' Lemmy put an arm covered with red scratches through the hawthorn and touched a strand of my hair. 'Flame. Scorch, blister, burn.'

'There's nothing to be afraid of. It's only hair.'

'Hair.' Lemmy teeth chattered and his eyes gleamed. 'Go home.'

'What?'

'Go — home.' Lemmy put his finger to his lips and withdrew into the thorny darkness.

I decided to take his advice. Chloë pushed ahead of me along the lane, running eagerly as though she had some aim in view. The idea came to me, looming indistinct in the fog of my distracted mental processes, that she might be looking for her master. In a flash, as though the workings of his mind had been revealed to me by Very lights over no man's land, I knew where he was and why.

I pushed through the gap in the hedge and hurried down the path. I scrambled down the drop and dashed across the plank bridge. I pushed open the door of the cottage. The sitting room was tranquil, receptive, filled with the scent of dying lilies and heliotrope from a vase on the table. What was a single night of desertion after those twelve long years when it had fallen slowly into decay — unloved, neglected, forgotten, except by one man, lonely and far away? But there was no one there. Tears of disappointment stung my eyes.

I heard Chloë barking outside. For a moment I had believed, I had been certain, that he would be here, waiting for me. What had Viola said in her letter? That love is about letting the other person do what they want. I thought he had gone away to give me the freedom to decide for myself what I wanted. Chloë ran in and jumped up to lick me. I wiped away a tear that had fallen on her fur.

I heard footsteps behind me.

'Freddie.' I stood still and closed my eyes. I felt his arms steal round me. I leaned my head back against his chest as my limbs grew weak with love. 'Are you — do you — ? I didn't dare to hope.'

He turned me within the circle of his arms. I opened my eyes. He was smiling but that look of enquiry was urgent. I couldn't speak for love. He must have read the answer in my face for he bent his head and kissed me. 'If you hadn't come — if you'd gone away with him — if I'd never seen you again, never held you in my arms, never made love to you — ah, it would have been bad for me then.'

'If,' I said laconically.

We do hope that you have enjoyed reading
this large print book.

Did you know that all of our titles
are available for purchase?

We publish a wide range of high quality
large print books including:
Romances, Mysteries, Classics
General Fiction
Non Fiction and Westerns

Special interest titles available in
large print are:
The Little Oxford Dictionary
Music Book
Song Book
Hymn Book
Service Book

Also available from us courtesy of Oxford
University Press:
Young Readers' Dictionary
(large print edition)
Young Readers' Thesaurus
(large print edition)

For further information or a free
brochure, please contact us at:
Ulverscroft Large Print Books Ltd.,
The Green, Bradgate Road, Anstey,
Leicester, LE7 7FU, England.
Tel: (00 44) 0116 236 4325
Fax: (00 44) 0116 234 0205

Other titles in the
Charnwood Library Series:

LOVE ME OR LEAVE ME

Josephine Cox

Beautiful Eva Bereton has only three friends in the world: Patsy, who she looks upon as a sister; Bill, her adopted cousin, and her mother, to whom she is devoted. With Eva's father increasingly angry about life as a cripple, she and her mother support each other, keeping their spirits high despite the abuse. So when a tragic accident robs Eva of both parents, Patsy, a loveable Irish rogue, is the only one left to support her. Tragedy strikes yet again when Eva's uncle comes to reclaim the farm that Eva had always believed belonged to her parents. Together with Patsy, Eva has no choice but to start a new life far away . . .